The Vamp Squad Series

Strange Beginnings - 2015
The Death of Innocence - 2016
The Secrets of San Leyre – 201?

I0532555

The Death Of Innocence

Vamp Squad Series: Book 2

by Miriam Matthews

The Death of Innocence
Vamp Squad Series:Book 2

By Miriam Matthews

Published by Miriam Matthews
Edition 6.2016.v1HC

Published in digital format by Miriam Matthews, 6.2016.v1DIG and available at most digital providers.

This book is a work of fiction. Any reference to persons, living, dead or undead, or places, events or locales is purely for the purpose of enhancing the story. The main characters are productions of the author's imagination and used fictitiously.

ISBN: 978-0-9914555-6-0

Dedication

To all the Susannahs of the world who went to play and came away
changed forever…or simply never came back at all. My heart goes out
to you and your families.

To my husband, Timothy. Your love and support and hours of arguing
over words and semantics has made me a better writer.

To the ladies of the Alaska Romance Writers of
America, *thank you* is such a small word for the years
of support, critiquing, encouragement, brainstorming,
etc. I love you all!

Note to Readers

Foreign words have been phoneticized from the actual language text, if
the text is not written with the English alphabet.

TOP SECRET

Center for Disease Control (CDC)
Medical Alert (Report Date: 22 JULY 1954)

Vampticious Meticulosus Deliriotum n
(Also called VMD or Vampire Virus)

1) A contagious virus causing an individual-specific genetic mutation following a death-like comatose state. The VMD virus is transmitted through blood-to-blood transfer, the VMD T-cells retain the base genetic strain of the parent virus thus providing a genetic link to the parent and progeny virus and host.

2) A virus that causes death and then rebirth as a vampire – in European folklore; a dead person who rises from the grave to live off the blood of humans by biting the neck of an individual and sucking blood through extended fangs.

MISCELLANEOUS INFO: Infected individuals initially enter a coma which imitates a death-like state while VMD begins to mutate the genetic code and physical body. As the virus grows and multiplies, more mutations occur and initial mutations become enhanced. Continued introduction of the parent virus speeds the process while increasing specific side effects including; (1) bone and joint pain, (2) muscle growth and extreme cramping, (3) development of extended canine teeth as a feeding mechanism, (4) the need for additional amounts of plasma and blood products to sustain mutations and tissue repair, (5) enhanced metabolic recovery rates, (6) increased cerebral tissue functionality (up to 98% tissue usage), (7) heightened cell replacement, (8) low body temperature accommodating hyper-metabolic rates, (9) temporary psychosis including Obsessive Compulsive Disorder (OCD), Narcissistic Personality Disorder and/or Sexual Addiction, (10) VMD specific allergic reactions (sun, silver, some types of water, garlic, etc.)

PROGNOSIS: Genetic mutations of VMD are irreversible and continually adapt to accommodate the apparent survival instinct of the virus (unsubstantiated theory; Dr. Helga Anderson, US Services Institute of Genetic Study, Walter Reed National Military Medical Center, Bethesda, Special Projects Department). Mutated individuals seem to develop extraordinary abilities, however, individuals lack adequate melanin in the skin causing a severe allergy to ultraviolet radiation (sunlight). In reaction to this allergy, VMD initiates a sleep cycle in its host causing extreme exhaustion and weakness during daylight hours. A mutated individual's cell structure no longer contains the human genetic code; instead possessing deoxyribonucleic acid, or DNA with 3 chromosomes in a triple helix design.

**********CLASSIFIED: TOP SECRET **********

TOP SECRET

**********CLASSIFIED: TOP SECRET **********

Chapter 1

Time: A Merciless Enemy

Check it.
Watch it fly.
Feel it drift away.
See it drag on.
Recognize its passage in the eyes of your children.

Hate it.
Love it.
Need more of it.
Dream of stopping it.
But know the danger of time and place, off track.

Philliono Talligio, Colonel
CENSI, Paloma, Spain, 2001

Susannah was totally gianormously, megaseriously pissed at herself as she sat, dejected and miserable in the webbed seat of Chopper 2. Why was it that everything she touched, did, said, even thought, turned to total goat shit in a heartbeat? Susannah kicked the weapons pack that lay at her feet.

Damn it!

The Vamp Squad existed because of her. It was her father's way of keeping his "unique" daughter safe and protected. But WTF? Why was that same daughter and operative such a screw-up on this mission endangering her team members?

Susannah fought back the tears. Despite the effort, one somehow slipped through. She let her long blonde hair fall forward, covering the lapse in professionalism and the red traces on her cheek.

Another slip up. Emotions were unacceptable on a mission. An operative was supposed to be focused, ultra competent, an expert at the tasks assigned. She kicked the pack again and drew a cold stare from Colonel Maddox… Colonel Daddy.   The tears threatened with renewed fervor, creeping ever closer.

Why did her father treat her like a child, exposing every slip-up?

Every mistake? Each misstep? As if he were disciplining a three-year-old? He did not treat the other operatives like he did his daughter. She drew in a deep breath and held it, focusing on suppressing her misery.

Susannah knew the answer to her mental question. The others didn't mess up on a regular basis, or cause a team member to be injured. That was why.

What was wrong with her?

Why couldn't she get it right?

She'd been a vampire for almost five years now and the future stretched before her like an open wound that would never heal. It seemed like the harder she tried, the more she screwed up. Susannah hugged her arms to herself feeling like a lost soul adrift in the universe. The entire population of said universe scrutinizing her every move.

God she wanted to be a hundred!

But right this minute she wanted to be with Uncle Rob at the hospital where they'd left him in the care of military doctors and a surgical team. His condition was totally her fault and everyone in the squad knew it.

Worse yet, she knew everyone knew it.

Worser yet, if that was even possible, she knew it from the depths of her soul to the tips of her fangs.

And if she was human, it probably would have killed her with guilt. Those hateful tears surfaced despite her will to squelch them, and she hung her head to cover the emotional lapse.

The chopper descended to the landing zone near their covert headquarters at the Maine farm. It was time to face the music. Susannah wiped her tears away as a reassuring hand landed on her shoulder.

"Captain Devlin is a very strong human. He will be fine, daughter." Elizabetta spoke over the engines as they landed, emphasizing her verbal statement with a mental nudge. "And so will you."

Susannah felt a light kiss on her smeared cheek as the Coven Mistress stood to deplane. "Head up, young lady." A chuck beneath the chin did little to raise Susannah's spirits. She'd let everyone down, even the woman who'd become her surrogate mother.

Deep beneath Olney Farm the Vamp Squad stumbled down the sterile corridor and through the huge imposing steel doors. Susannah was aware of their silent closing only by the subtle shift of air pressure in the subterranean complex. She followed a few steps behind the group.

"Stow your gear in the armory and get your butts to the training room, ASAP!" Colonel Maddox stormed across the central lounge toward his quarters as he shouted the order. "No exceptions, and I do mean ASAP!" His angry words hung in the air long after he stomped down the hall toward the human quarters at one end of the facility.

Susannah could tell her father contained his anger through a thin veil of professionalism. It seemed to her it was always that way with him.

Susannah turned toward the vampire quarters. The huge complex beneath the ground was an amazing feat of subterranean construction. It sprawled like a giant octopus. The central lounge and mess were the main body of the beast with human quarters in one tentacle, the research lab and exercise gyms in another, the vampire quarters directly across the lounge from the human wing. The Operations Command Center was opposite the labs. Camouflaged by the barn above, the motor pool and armory were connected to the complex by a passageway large enough to drive a tank through with room to spare. The seemingly decrepit barn and cozy farmhouse above effectively disguised the enormous facility below.

"Merde, he is in a... how do you say? Smit?" Monique brushed red-brown dirt from her Kevlar vest.

"Snit, Monique, snit. And yes he is. Puh-leese! I need a bath and a manicure before I will feel even close to human. But daddy is daddy... and I'm just a fuck-up!" Susannah whispered to her coven sister. The humans would not hear but her vampire family couldn't miss the words despite the whisper.

"You are not human, or even close to human *and* your father's temper is on your shoulders, young lady. I suggest you do exactly what he says and as quickly as possible." Elizabetta, the Coven Mistress as well as leader of the Vamp Squad, commented as she and the rest of the Vamp Squad headed for the armory, dragging their weapons and packs.

A familiar humming rattle sounded throughout the installation signaling the departure of the two helicopters above ground. "There goes any hope of escape." Susannah's comment told more about how she really felt than her tear-stained face and hunched shoulders.

"Dev's in the hospital and you crack jokes? Not cool, Suze." Head hanging, Sergeant Miller stumbled after Elizabetta dragging a rucksack containing the left-over explosives and detonators. Yuri quietly took the sack and slug it over his shoulder, lending a strong hand to the human sergeant who struggled on the verge of exhaustion. They were all tired, but the fatigue showed more in the human contingent of their squad.

"You don't think I know that? I know it was my fault Captain Devlin got shot. I got it. I'm sorry. I know I screwed up." Susannah stood in the lounge watching her squad moving away. "I didn't do it on purpose. I tried to …" Her words trailed off.

No one was interested in hearing her excuses at that particular moment.

"Humans don't heal the way we do, Susannah. We need to protect them, not carelessly expose them to danger. You should have followed protocol." Natalia commented as she pushed by to catch up with the others, leaving the young operative alone in the lounge feeling the deep hurt in her soul, way more than miserable… if that was possible.

"Apparently I am the only one who ever makes mistakes in this group. Do you really think I let Captain Devlin get shot on purpose?" Ten heads swiveled and stared at the young blonde from within the dim hallway; five human and five vampire. No one spoke. "I made a mistake. I always seem to make mistakes. I'm a lousy operative!" Susannah flapped her arms in frustration.

"Susannah, we're all dirty, tired and worried about Captain Devlin. For the moment, let's just take care of business." Elizabetta's comment calmed the scene as she led the group toward the armory in silence, leaving a frustrated and tearful Susannah to follow.

The mission in Somalia had gone well until the final day. During the team's extraction, Captain Devlin and Susannah were late to the rendezvous point. Overrun by guerilla fighters before the entire human team could be hoisted into their hovering choppers, Devlin took three hits. Two were flesh wounds but one bullet pierced his left lung causing internal bleeding and collapsing the lung. Medics worked feverishly to save his life as they sped toward safety. Now, lying in a bed at Walter Reed Hospital in the capable hands of some of the best doctors in the world, his prognosis still remained unknown.

Within minutes a somber armorer checked and accepted their weapons and then hurried them on toward the training area. Practically everyone in the facility heard the news and the Colonel's loud command upon the Squad's return. All eyes watched his daughter with interest. Most of them had been witness to how hard the young woman worked to overcome her inexperience and adjust to life as a vampire. It was abundantly clear that in a very short period of time, in vampire life anyway, she had come a million miles. But everyone agreed she seemed to walk beneath a *Polly Anna Curse*. She tried hard to be as good as the other squad members, but most times with very different results. Most things Susannah touched turned to dog shit despite her best efforts and Elizabetta's steadfast tutelage.

"How long do you think he'll keep us?" Sergeant Jonathan Azuel, better known within the squad as Blue Boy, whispered to MorningStar as they headed for the gym. His blue eyes sparkled knowing full well every vampire within yards could hear his whisper.

"As long as it takes, Sergeant." The statuesque Native American vampire responded in her calm, even manner.

"As long as what takes?" Blue knew what she was referring to, but played along for effect.

"Teaching his daughter to be on time, of course." MorningStar let out a long breath, basically for effect since she did not usually breathe at all. It was as close as the serene vamp came to displaying frustration. She did however, smile when a huffing sound was heard from the trailing Susannah.

While MorningStar's comment was intended to be good-natured teasing, Blue's words generally had a sharp edge that was almost always aimed at Susannah. The youngest member of the squad knew it all too well. Susannah slogged along feeling the weight of her mistakes as if she carried ten tons of twisted metal and stone.

Reassembling in the training gym next to the complex's research laboratory, the vamps paired up with each other while the humans did the same. The team was ready. All except Susannah who stood in the entryway with her back against the doorjamb, without Devlin, her wounded partner. Half hoping someone in the squad would notice her misery and do something to make her feel better, she watched beneath lowered lashes, feeling lost and dejected.

Awaiting the appearance of the Colonel, Susannah agonized over the near miss in Somalia and placing her human team members in harms way. Without really watching, she instinctively knew where the team would stage themselves. They did this a million times before the mission. Blue Boy stood shoulder to shoulder with Maxwell next to the mission obstacle course, his arms casually crossed, a nasty twinkle in his eyes. She could feel his increasing hunger and exhaustion. From across the room Susannah could hear his stomach growl.

Fascinated with all paranormal things from the very beginning, Blue hacked into classified intel and found out about vampires as well as the special anti-terrorist squad Colonel Maddox was assembling.

He virtually jumped at the opportunity to join the special unit called the V-Force, without a second thought. Susannah wondered how he felt now in light of this last mission.

Next to Blue, Max's posture was much more telling. He leaned against a post, his head hanging, hands in his pockets. She could read exhaustion in his posture and feel the disgust even though he tried to hide it from her. Sgt. Maxwell Boreman was an Army Ranger before joining the Vamp Squad's V-Force. While looking for prospective recruits, Sergeant Miller came across Boreman's profile while researching paranormal events within the armed forces. Miller found Boreman in a psychiatric unit at Ft. Eustis, Virginia. His incarceration was due to the fact he reported being attacked by a vampire while on a sniper mission in Honduras. Joining the Vamp Squad literally saved his life and validated his sanity.

Bear and Tank lounged on the floor mats patiently waiting, tired to the bone but true soldiers in every sense of the word. The two always treated Susannah with respect and often helped her with difficult combat moves. She could feel Bear's warmth a mile away. The man was an industrial strength furnace and his nickname suited him well.

Tank was the brother she lost, along with her mother all those years ago. He nodded toward her with a wink. It felt good to have at least two allies on the human side of the squad.

Sergeant Miller lay sprawled behind Bear and Tank, his eyes closed. With no time to wash up, white circles showed where his night vision goggles kept most of the dirt out of his eyes. Susannah knew the Sergeant could care less about soldiering and military bearing.

His partner, Lt. Previn stood straight as a rod near the entry. Never has there existed two soldiers with more opposing bearing and character. Previn would have stood at attention had he been half dead and mortally wounded. He probably lay at attention when he slept, Susannah thought with a restrained grin.

She disliked Previn with a passion but shared a kind of "outsider" persona with the ever-ready-to-scam Miller. Miller was one of the original team she first saw when she "awoke" to her new existence. Thank God Elizabetta was waiting and ready to teach her a new way of life.

Natalia and Yuri leaned against the back wall, arms wrapped around each other's waists in a casual embrace. Prior to the emergency mission in Somalia, the two lovers were knee deep in wedding preparations. Those plans came to a screeching halt with the

Squad's hasty assignment. Now, with the wedding just two weeks away, it was clear to everyone Yuri and Natalia were meant for each other as a mated pair, a very rare thing in the world of vampires.

And that was the root of Susannah's little green monster. It hid at the back of her brain when it wasn't parading out front for everyone to see and hear. Every time she looked at the lovers, her emotions spun out of control, frustrated by what they seemed to have... and she did not. The little green monster squirmed in her mind as Susannah heard Elizabetta, across the gym perched on a stack of mats next to the gracefully posed MorningStar, discussing the up-coming nuptials in low voices.

Monique slouched seductively along the wall eyeing Bear's massive frame with interest, as usual. The French vampire lived for all things sexual and Bear exuded masculine mystic without even knowing it. Something about his six foot eight frame and XXXL shoulders that just screamed *come to me baby*. Love did not really exist for Frenchy, but desire and passion were ever present in her mind. Susannah had formed a close sisterly bond with Monique and the two shared their most intimate secrets with each other. The upcoming nuptials were simply a prelude to great sex, at least to Monique. More than that, Monique never tired of listening to Susannah vent her frustrations and always had a sympathetic shoulder to catch the bright red tears of her younger vampire sister. Of all the members of the Vamp Squad, Monique seemed to understand Susannah the most and provide the unconditional love that pushed Susannah to try just a little harder, move just a little faster, learn just that touch more. And when things went down the toilet, Monique was there with a hug, a bag of spiked synth-blood and some old corny video they could watch together and laugh their heads off.

Susannah shifted from one foot to another. Despite her incredible strength and enhanced senses, she was tired and heartsick. She'd known Capt. Devlin since her human childhood and was having trouble swallowing the bitter reality that she was truly responsible for his injuries. He was medevaced straight to Ramstein Air Base, before being transported to the Walter Reed National Military Medical Center. Devlin's condition was critical.

She flinched and took a deep breath preparing for the assault to come. From the sound of stomping footsteps in the hall, her father was on his way. She stood a little straighter and moved off to one side, out of the blast zone.

Miller struggled to a sitting position. "Tet-hut." The military contingent stood at attention. The vampires simply looked up but remained where they were.

"At ease." The Colonel motioned to his men. "Operation Sierra Storm was successful, but with casualties. That is unacceptable." The Colonel paced across the floor, his hands clasped behind his back.

Susannah pictured MacArthur addressing his men after an unsuccessful beach assault.

"We will re-run the last phase of this mission until it is flawless. Practice makes perfect and permanent. Take your places. On my mark and by the numbers. Count and mark by increments of...?" The glowering Colonel looked at his daughter who had taken up position in the corner behind him.

"Five," she answered just above a whisper.

"What?" Blue snickered and nudged his partner. He was the best of the V-Force humans at pushing her buttons.

"FIVE!" She spat at the smirking soldier.

"Five. Roger that. Every five seconds." The Colonel repeated for the human contingent. "Take your places."

Susannah felt the brunt of her father's punitive orders. The team was dog tired and he just had to press the point. *They* did everything correctly. Didn't he understand that there was no reason to punish the team? It was her fault and the punishment should be hers, and hers alone. He was making it harder for her by torturing the entire squad to punish her.

Or was that his goal, knowing the outcome?

The group assumed their positions on the obstacle course that was constructed to represent the building they used at the extraction point. Susannah was the last in place as she tried frantically to catch Elizabetta's eye, without success. The Coven Mistress was a mother to her and had been since her awakening as a starved, half-crazed animal in a cement cell. Right now Susannah desperately needed a little mommy intervention.

She had no watch.

She'd lost it in Somalia; hence the botched extraction.

She tried a mental nudge with no results. Elizabetta was focused on the team and the op.

Then it was too late.

"Mark." The Colonel shouted and the entire squad sprang into action moving like a well-oiled machine despite their exhaustion. Air currents drifted and swirled with their silent moves as Yuri and Natalia v-ported from the make-believe street to the fabricated roof with their simulated satellite fuel component while Monique and MorningStar flew recon above the simulated building. Bear and Tank perched on a small platform near the top of the gym symbolizing their position in the helicopter that would transport the first component. Susannah carted the second component with the missing Devlin imaginarily attached to the opposite side. A cable and carabineer dangled to the ground from the second imaginary helicopter with Max and Blue on a platform above.

Susannah strained to see the clock above the door of the gym watching for the exact second she was to attach the canister to the cable to be drawn up. Timing was crucial since both helicopters operated within a few inches of each other's rotors. The plan called for Devlin and the canister to be raised together.

She glanced at the clock one more time and reached for the carabineer. Her hand came away empty. She could hear Blue's quiet chuckle above her.

"VS5, report." A large vein protruded from the Colonel's forehead as he shouted at his daughter.

"What?" Susannah shouted back as she spun to see the cable several feet above her reach.

Colonel Maddox jumped down from the scaffolding. "Can you, or can you not, tell time? It's not a difficult task. Everyone here seems to be capable of it. What is your problem?" He was not losing his temper. He'd already lost it back in the hallway. "Oh, that's right! Mickey doesn't have a third hand does he?" Maddox loomed over his daughter screaming the insult as Elizabetta floated quickly and quietly to stand beside him. Her restraining hand landed solidly on his shoulder with vamp strength.

"It's not my fault. I had to watch the clock up there." Susannah stomped and pointed at the clock on the wall above the door. "I couldn't do both things at once!" She shouted back at her father in the same tone.

Elizabetta shot Susannah a stern look and sighed. Susannah was definitely the Colonel's daughter and the Coven Mistress was not willing to let this unfair punishment continue. Elizabetta securely cloaked her own thoughts on the matter and sighed again. To give Susannah her due, her father was not exactly acting like a professional soldier either. Neither Maddox was at their best at the moment. It was clear to everyone in the room. Elizabetta moved to intervene and ducked the Colonel's flapping arms.

"Why not? You can listen to your pod thing, watch TV and paint you toes neon orange at the same time. But you can't seem to hang a canister on a hook with both hands in a timely manner. I don't understand what your…"

Elizabetta made her move.

"Excuse me, Colonel?" The practice session was in danger of turning into a father-daughter knockdown-drag-out in front of the entire squad. When it came to Susannah, Elizabetta knew Maddox would not hold back.

She laid her hand on his shoulder. The Colonel drew in a deep breath to continue but the Coven Mistress increased the pressure of her hold to the point of pain. It was her intent to gain his attention quite rapidly.

It worked well.

He fell silent…with a wince…

"Susannah, where is your watch?" Elizabetta spoke in a calm modulated tone.

"I lost it in the desert. I was looking for it when Captain Devlin said we had to go. It was my Corum Trapeze that mom left me." Her attempt at a little pout was lost on her father.

Elizabetta was sure Colonel Maddox didn't know a designer, diamond-studded watch from a kitchen appliance.

"The turquoise one she loved." The young girl whispered, a tear forming near the corner of one eye.

Elizabetta could feel the Colonel gearing up for a real blow-out and increased the pressure of her hand once again, but refrained from breaking the human's fragile bones. It would not do to have two of the team in the hospital at the same time.

"You did not feel the need to let someone know before the exercise began?" Again, her voice was calm and steady.

"Elizabetta, I tried to get you to notice, but you were more concerned about the stupid wedding. All anyone wants to talk about is Natalia and Yuri and that damn wedding. Like it was the only thing that mattered. I…" Susannah's explanation trailed off knowing it fell on the deaf ears of the Coven Mistress.

Elizabetta was very much aware of Susannah's little jealous streak. They talked many times about Susannah's self control and romantic desires. In the long run, Elizabetta understood. Susannah should be a beautiful twenty-three year old experiencing life and love and anything else young people did in a world of excitement and possibility. Instead she was starting her life over as something very different from that, a vampire, under strict controls and rules that did not come close to squelching her blood lust and those developing desires that so outweighed anything a human could comprehend. Elizabetta understood Susannah's emotional turmoil but did not condone her surrogate daughter's disrespectful and often childish behavior. Like any girl growing up, Susannah would have to learn. Unlike any girl growing up, it was imperative for the young vampire to learn self control much faster since human lives were at stake.

"That is enough, young lady!" The Colonel's voice boomed, echoing through the gym increasing the sound by three fold.

The combination of guilt and anger threw Susannah over the edge and right into deadly territory. She could feel herself slipping, and on some level, she was aware that she should just shut her mouth. Unfortunately, her human teen immaturity rose to the surface and spilled right across the gym, engulfing her father in a wave of verbal self-righteousness.

"What are you going to do Daddy, send me to bed without dinner? Why can't anyone treat me like an adult? I'm just as much a part of this team as any one of you. In fact, more so, because without me, you all wouldn't even be here." She rounded on her father. "You would not have your precious squad of vampire operatives, and I would be dead and out of the way. Right?"

The tears began to flow. Streaks of red marred the beautiful young woman's perfect skin.

"No stupid little blonde girl to worry about. You'd prefer that, wouldn't you? Me out of the way, so you can be the lone hero in the family? So you don't have to do anything but be what you want to be. Some super soldier, charging around saving the world. Well, you couldn't save me, so you got Elizabetta to do it for you. And you're not even happy with that."

An emotional tsunami flooded Susannah's mind and heart. She let fly with the canister in her hand. It just missed Blue, who jumped down from the platform out of the way.

"Hey, careful with the tantrum. I break." He effectively dodged the metal container, but landed on his backside flipping the young vampire off with a flourish.

She had more than enough from Blue. Susannah closed the distance between them with vamp speed, grabbed Blue by the shirt and lifted him to his feet. Her fangs descended and she hissed, pulling his neck close.

"SUSANNAH!" Both Elizabetta and Monique screamed simultaneously.

Surprised and embarrassed at the extent of her loss of control, Susannah dropped Blue to the floor and fled from the room.

Sgt. Miller swung down from his position on the scaffolding, swiped a lazy salute and sauntered past a speechless Colonel. "Well, I guess that ends our little practice session. I don't know about you all, but I could use a hot bath, a good meal and a soft bed. Later folks."

One by one the team members made their excuses and departed leaving Elizabetta still holding the Colonel down by his shoulder... but with a little less strength in her grip.

Chapter 2

Children

They are our joy, and our life,
Our sorrow, and our strife.
They enrich us, and make us crazy,
Playing games, seeming lazy.
But in those moments of dark loneliness,
They're what make our onliness!

Sallini Fangouch, Philosohpher
Rights of Passage
Cyprus, Italy, 1472

"What am I going to do with her, Elizabetta?" Frank Maddox was close to despondent. His daughter just committed the ultimate, unforgivable sin in front of his men. With one of his men! The fragile alliance between humans and vampires required strict rules. Threatening a human with fangs bared was a total breach of protocol, as well as just plain bad manners.

More than four years as a vampire, and still his daughter could not control herself. "Not only does she have childish tantrums, she has childish vampiric tantrums. And for the humans who work with her, those are more dangerous than just embarrassing."

"Love her. Teach her all the things a father is supposed to teach. Be her Commander as well. But mostly try to understand." Elizabetta patted Frank on his sore shoulder. "Come. Sit." She took his hand and pulled him to the stack of mats she'd been seated on earlier. Hopping up on the stack with an uncharacteristic thump, she patted the mat next to her.

Frank followed and for a few minutes, they both sat in worried silence.

"Give her time, Frank. She has so much to learn, and so much more time than a human to do it in. For our kind, time moves much more slowly. Like our aging… we experience things and mature much more slowly as well. If you think about it, your daughter has come a very long way, even for one of our kind." She patted his thigh companionably. "She is dealing with so many conflicting things, you have no idea. You can't really comprehend the extent of what she is handling at all, you're male…and human. You were born that way and have remained so. Remember when I first came to help with her? She was little more than an animal, a starving monster in a cage." Elizabetta sighed and smiled, remembering the first time she met Maddox and the baby vampire that was his daughter. "Even as a human, growing up for a young man is much easier than for a young woman. Especially in this day and age. Then, at the height of her teen years, she became something beyond human. In a little more than a few short years, Susannah has had to come to terms with her new self, all of the horror stories that surround her species, accept a different kind of womanhood, become a highly trained operative for her government *and* accept her father as her boss. That's a lot to take on." Elizabetta looked at Frank to see if he was following her. "Now she carries the additional guilt of having contributed to the injury of a man she's cared about since her human childhood."

"But she is so emotional, so irresponsible. Christ, she lost her watch in the middle of a mission, screwed up and got a team member shot. I would have been court martialed for that." Maddox shook his head. "She needs a keeper, not a job as an operative."

"Yes, VS5 lost her watch. But don't confuse the issues. Captain Devlin was shot by a *terrorist* when the mission was overtaken by guerillas. Intel reported there were no unfriendlies in the area." Elizabetta sighed again. "Frank, of all the things your daughter needs, protection from humans, if you forgive the slight, is not one of them. She needs understanding, a firm hand…"

"By the way, I felt that firm hand, Elizabetta," interrupted Frank as he winced and rubbed his shoulder.

"… and time. I'm not asking you to make exceptions for her. What I am asking is that you treat her the same way you do the rest of the Squad. Admit it, Frank, you would never speak to Natalia or Monique as you did to Susannah." Elizabetta raised her left eyebrow punctuating the statement.

"Natalia or Monique would never act the way she did." Maddox countered.

"Possibly, but consider this, Natalia is almost five hundred years old and Monique is what? Over two hundred, right? MorningStar, well, she doesn't even know how old she is."

"I am surprised when MorningStar simply speaks, let alone envision her screaming at me in front of my men." Frank chuckled at his own comment.

"MorningStar is an enigma for sure. Even I don't understand the source of her power and talent, but she seems to be at peace with her world. And your daughter will be as well, given time." Elizabetta clasped her hands and hopped down to land gracefully on the hard wood floor.

"Will I live long enough to see it?" Frank's temper crawled in from the hallway and lodged in the pit of his stomach, growling loudly. He patted the offending gut, chuckled and hopped down taking Elizabetta's arm in his. "Dinner? Can I treat you to a quart of synth-blood, my all-knowing Coven Mistress?"

She stifled a yawn. "With pleasure, Colonel. Would you care to join me?" It was her turn to chuckle.

"I prefer my blood bovine in type. Surrounded by muscle. Medium rare." Maddox paused. "Thank God we found you, Elizabetta. I can't imagine handling Susannah on my own. I sometimes still have trouble thinking of vampires as real beings let alone seeing my daughter pop out a pair of fangs. I hate to admit it, but I have never been good with my daughter, and especially since her mother and brother died." A wave of sadness passed over his features and then was gone. "And now…well at least you can understand what she is going through. I want you to know how much I appreciate the way you are with her."

As they entered the lounge, Elizabetta caught a mental whiff of tears and a runny nose in the vamp quarters. She promised herself to check on Susannah as soon as she finished eating. The young vampire's anguish would keep everyone from resting if Susannah continued to cry through the day sleep they all desperately needed.

In her quarters, Susannah sat against the corner of her small suite viewing the destruction and noisily blowing her nose. She threw the last piece of tissue on the floor with the rest. New tears flowed at the sight of what she had done to her prize possessions.

Scattered across the floor was her collection of stuffed animals that usually sat in a neat row on a shelf above her bed. A t-shirt and fuzzy scarf hung from a crooked picture on the wall. The covers from her bed lay scattered in various lumps where they landed after a short flight. Her mother's vanity mirror lay on the floor, a crack splitting the reflective glass in two parts.

Susannah groaned and reached for the only remnant of her mother's life that was left to her. Why couldn't someone love her like her father loved her mother? She remembered how they'd been with each other, so tender and happy. That was before the accident, but still…

She picked up one half of the mirror and studied herself in the reflection. If her father couldn't love her, why couldn't she find someone like Natalia had? Yuri was so handsome, so strong and yet so gentle with his mate. Natalia returned his love with a passionate fire that ran through all of their minds, and bodies, at times. Natalia made Yuri a vampire yet he still loved her beyond reason. Technically she was his Dama, the female equivalent of a sire, but their connection went much deeper. It was apparent in everything they did and said. It seemed to Susannah, they even moved and thought the same thing at the same time.

Where was her sire? Why had she never met him? Known him? Why did her life as a vampire have so many mysteries? A quiet knock interrupted the reflective calm after her emotional storm.

"What?" Susannah snapped, not really in the mood for company.

"Little sister, are you alright?" Monique pushed the door open the few inches it would allow, given the amount of stuff littering the floor. She poked her head through the opening. "Merde!"

"You might as well come in since you're almost here anyway." Susannah tippy-toed through the mess and kicked enough out of the way to allow Monique entry.

"Well… this is not as bad as the last time, ma petite soeur." Susannah was beginning to understand all of Monique's French phrases of endearment. "Would you like a little help with this?" Monique opened her arms wide indicating the breadth and width of the mess with a questioning half grin.

"Sure, why not? Maybe I can get it straightened up before anyone else gets a laugh out of my temper." Susannah kicked her stuffed weasel across the floor onto the bed.

It landed on her pillow letting out a wheezing squeaky noise.

"Sorry Weaky." She flopped on the bed and hugged the toy to her chest as more red tears dribbled down her cheeks. "What's wrong with me, Monique?" She pulled the pillow over her face and sobbed. It came away dotted with brilliant red stains.

"Ah, ma petit chéri, there is nothing wrong with you. Before I was turned, I was a sweet young girl with nothing in my head but fantasies of handsome princes who would come and make me their princess. I did nothing all day but wander the gardens, embroider with my grand-mère and play childish games. But there comes a time when you must leave childhood behind. For me it happened on the darkest of days and I had no choice. My sire was ruthless and perverted and cared not for my emotions or family. He took me and hideousness became everything in my life. I survived by my wits alone. You at least have a choice in what you become now. You have Elizabetta and your coven and we love you. But you too, must grow up." Tenderly she pulled on the stuffed weasel's leg. "There are some things you must give up."

Susannah giggled through her tears. "But not Weaky. I'll never give up Weaky."

Monique hugged her little sister, squishing the weasel between them. "Oui. Never Weaky. But the temper? " Monique waved at the mess across the floor. "It should go. Oui?"

Weaky squeaked pathetically pressed between the two sets of well-endowed bosoms.

"Let us clean your room and nothing more shall be said of this."

Monique and Susannah set to straightening the mess. A crunch sounded from beneath a crumpled blanket.

"Oh my goodness!" Susannah pulled the blanket away to find shards of glass covering her high school cheerleading squad picture, a remnant of her lost life as a human. "Oh well, I'll never cheer again. At least not like that." She shook the frame over the wastebasket, plucked the picture from the frame and handed the surviving photo to Monique.

"This is cheering? Puh! How does it compare to destroying a Taliban stronghold, or saving new clear gadgets for the government?" Monique aimed her finger as if to shoot the picture.

"That's nuclear fuel gadgets for the government, and you have a point."

Susannah was coming out of her blue funk.

"Can you imagine my twentieth high school reunion? I'll probably still look like this and everyone else will have wrinkles, dyed hair and potbellies. Huh! Take that Marilee Sebastian, Miss Perfect Back Flip!" Susannah poked at the photo, then dumped it in the basket. "I guess you're right, Frenchy. Somehow making the cheerleading team doesn't seem all that important now. It used to be all I could think about." Susannah heaved a sigh and plopped on the floor scooping the broken glass onto a flat paper. "I used to practice hours on end trying to get the same perfect back flip Marilee had. Now I could flip seventeen times to her one. Actually much higher and faster, too. I guess it just goes to show you how things can change. Course I'll never be able to rub her face in it."

"And why, pray tell, would you want to rub her face in your flip?"

Monique obviously did not understand the meaning of the saying.

Susannah gave her sister a blank stare. "I don't really know any more. Things are just so mixed up in my head."

"Then give it not one more thought. We have much more important things to worry about." Monique bent to fold a shirt that landed on the small loveseat across the room.

"Like world peace?" Susannah jumped up and fanned her face like Sandra Bulloch in *Miss Congeniality*. Tantrum over, Susannah was back to teen cutie.

"Of course like world peace." Monique imitated her little sister, fanning with both hands. The girls hugged and dissolved into a fit of giggles. They watched the DVD together just before leaving for Somalia. Both loved Sandra Bullock's FBI character.

Susannah's cell phone burst forth with a Shakira song alerting her to an unknown incoming call. Monique's phone chimed from her belt.

Both women answered at the same time.

"Oui?"

"Yes?"

A recorded voice reported mechanically, "Captain Robert Devlin is out of surgery and resting comfortably. His doctors report that surgery was successful and his condition is expected to be upgraded to stable within hours. Next report at 15:30, 12, August. Questions can be addressed to Major Carmel Johnson at this number. Goodbye." The recorded call automatically hung up.

Susannah dropped her phone and hugged her sister fiercely, crunching Monique's phone to her head. "That's wonderful!" She squealed.

"Yes, but he is not out of the bushes yet." Monique cautioned.

"That's woods, and I know, but it's still wonderful news! I'm hungry." Susannah yawned. "And tired. Wanna grab a bag and hit the rack?"

Monique gave her sister a quizzical look.

"Food and sleep, Monique?" Susannah shook her head. Monique joined the Vamp Squad almost three years ago after being liberated by Miller's research and Colonel Maddox's unique military skill. Susannah and Monique became so close, the two women almost lived in each other's back pockets. However, Monique still misunderstood many of the little idiomatic sayings Susannah was so fond of using as a modern American teenager.

The intercom sounded in her room. "Ms. Maddox?"

She hit the red button by the door. "Yes?"

"The Colonel would like a word with you."

"On my way." She punched the button and turned to Monique. "Might as well eat without me. I'll be eating crow. I think this may be a long one."

Monique took her sister's shoulders in a fierce grip. "Promise me, little sister, you will talk back and listen." She pressed a finger to Susannah's lips.

Talking against Monique's finger, Susannah giggled. "That's *not* talk back and listen. And I will. I promise."

*****

Susannah perched on the edge of Captain Devlin's hospital bed holding the hand not connected to any IV lines or the heart monitor. "I feel so ashamed. I let you get hurt. It's my fault you are here, Uncle Rob. If I hadn't lost my watch and spent so much time looking for it, we…"

"Ah, sweetie," he squeezed her fingers with more strength than she thought him capable of, considering the amount of painkiller she could smell flowing through his veins. "Don't even think about it. I certainly didn't lose my watch and there is a reason I was assigned to be the senior specialist on the mission, not you. If anything, I am responsible for me being here."

"Yeah, but Daddy said…" Her father's long lecture included specific instruction to visit Uncle Rob to apologize for her ir-responsible behavior.

Like she needed to hear that.

"Sweetie, you don't understand your father at all. Let me clue you in. He acts the way he does out of fear, his own fear. You are all he has left of his emotions and his heart. When your mother and little Peter were killed, his world crashed for a while. Then it sort of congealed around you and solidified. It's not a good explanation, but that's what happened and that's why he has always been so protective and strict with you. So unbending, if you will." Again, he squeezed her slender fingers.

"But, Uncle Rob, he's just so mean all the time. He doesn't treat me like a person."

"Of course not, honey. He treats you like a precious possession he can't stand to lose. It would kill him. It almost did. You never saw him when he had to go identify your body. Why do you think he worked so hard and pulled in every favor he ever garnered to establish the Vamp Squad? Why do you think he snatched Miller out from under General Collin's gavel to do his searching for vampires? He couldn't let you go. He had to fix it, to make a place for you in the world that would be safe, no matter what you became."

Susannah squirmed under Devlin's long hard look.

"He wasn't always that way, hon, I remember the day he married your mom. I was just an enlisted grunt back then, and your dad was a new lieutenant. God she was beautiful, a lot like you now, except for the fangs and all.. Your father was bursting with pride and love. You could see it in his eyes. He could hardly stand up at the altar when she came floating down the aisle. They were tender around each other. Nothing like he is now. Then, when you were born... did you know he carried you on a pillow because he was so afraid he would break you?" Devlin chuckled, then winced as he coughed. "His entire life and soul were wrapped up in your wrinkled little carcass, pooping and crying on that hospital pillow. Your mom laughed at him a lot in those days and he didn't even care. We all laughed at him then. That was before we ended up just like him, wrapped around your tiny finger! His entire outfit became your babysitters and sworn protectors. Do you remember your first tank ride? It was your second birthday."

Susannah blushed. "I puked on the rocket launcher and everyone laughed. I don't remember, but Dad used to tell the story every birthday party until... Mom and Peter died. Then I didn't have birthday parties anymore."

"Yep, and that was a mistake, on his part. You deserved a better life but after the car accident, he just cocooned within himself. He's my best and oldest friend, and I couldn't help him. When he came out of it, he was hard and focused. Not much was left of the family man with the huge laugh and goofy smile. The rest of us just did what we could to replace what he lost, to give you some sort of family. Heck, Suze, you were only twelve when we lost your mom and Peter." Emotions played across the Captain's face.

"Damn, these stitches itch." He released her hand and lightly rubbed the thick bandage on his chest.

"Can I do anything?" Susannah asked. The interruption of their trip down memory lane gave them both a chance to calm the high tide of emotions that had suddenly flooded the room.

"Nah, sweetie. Well, how about some juice?" A container sat unopened on the opposite side of the bed, right next to the hand that was strapped to an IV board and connected to three clear tubes with a finger monitor. "Why is it the orderly brings sustenance and always puts it just out of reach?"

Laughing, Susannah retrieved the carton, pealed back the opening and popped a straw into the hole. "Army efficiency, of course." Handing it to Devlin, she sat back, perplexed.

"I just wish I knew more about myself, Uncle Rob, the vampire part. Dad doesn't talk about it and Elizabetta only knows what she read in my file when she agreed to leave Romania and come take care of me. Those days are so… blurry. Maybe if I knew where I came from, I would be better at figuring out where I am going. I don't know. There are just so many questions floating around in my head all the time."

Devlin sucked on the straw like a thirsty man straight out of the desert. A slurping noise signaled the end of the juice and Susannah took the empty carton, tossing it in the trash. "I can tell you that there wasn't much to know. By the time your father identified your body, ah, retrieved it, so to speak, and headed north, he was a complete mess. He was running on instinct. If it hadn't been for Ted's unique talents and quick thinking, you would have killed them both. As it was, when he figured out what was going on, and what you had become, it was too late." Devlin tried to change positions and gave up following another wince.

"I mean, think about it, Suze. He got told his only daughter was dead and to come identify her body. He gets there, and all the red flags go up when he tries to find out what happened. Not trusting local law enforcement and some dumpy coroner talking tales about an animal attack, he steals your body. Then you wake up with some unique orthodontia, all hungry and ready for a quick snack. That's a lot to assimilate for a concrete military man like Frank, let alone a father."

Susannah had to snicker at Devlin's description of the chain of events that led to her father's initial awareness of vampires. It must have been next to impossible to accept vampires as a fact, not a work of fiction portrayed in some horror movie. "What happened to all the records? There must have been a report about my death."

"Good question, my little operative. When Frank and Sgt. Miller started digging, the trail hit not one, but several brick walls. Big high brick walls. Apparently someone, or something in Florida has a great deal of power. While you were recuperating under the care of Elizabetta, your father took a little trip to Daytona Beach. He probably never told you about that, but he came back angry, frustrated and super-motivated to find a way to make a protected life for you. It quickly became apparent to his brilliant military mind that vampiric powers could be of value and, voila – the Vamp Squad. The past was so much water under the bridge." Devlin took a deep breath and closed his eyes for a moment.

Susannah knew she had overstayed her visit.

"I need to let you get some sleep, Uncle Rob. I didn't mean to bring all of this up right now. I just wanted you to know how sorry I am you got hurt and I accept my part of the responsibility." She stood to leave.

Devlin grasped her hand, restraining her from departing so quickly. "You are not responsible, hon. Get that through your pretty little head right now. We work as a team for a reason. I am glad you did not get hit along with me." His stern words made an impression.

She bent and kissed the man she called her *uncle by choice*. "I love you, Uncle Rob. If I'd been hit, it wouldn't have mattered. I'm immortal, remember." She smiled and kissed his forehead one more time.

"It still hurts, kiddo. I have that on good authority." He wagged a pointing finger at her in a fatherly fashion. "Speaking of good authority, how are wedding plans going for the engaged couple?"

Susannah straightened and made a face. "The big white wedding of the millennium? Oh fine. I'm just sick of it all. Yuri and Natalia can't keep their hands off of each other. Everyone is scurrying around smiling and joking about sex stuff. The farm looks like a freaking flower nursery and Elizabetta is floating around like the Dowager Duchess of Kent."

Her snort said it all.

At that description, Devlin laughed outright, grabbing the bandage on his chest. "I thought all women like that kind of thing. How come you're not all starry eyed and tied up in the preparations?"

"Because I am sick of being the odd one out. Elizabetta has my dad. They act like stodgy parents. Natalia has Yuri. Monique has any man she wants and MorningStar has her ghosts and crazy music. What do I have? Nothing! I don't even have a history that anyone knows of. It's just not fair, Uncle Rob." Susannah flounced back into the chair and crossed her legs with a huff.

"You are absolutely right, honey. It isn't fair. But then, not much in life is. Learning that is a big part of growing up. Seeing what you have in life is more important than focusing on what you don't have. You should be happy for your sister vampire and her mate. They are so in love it makes the farm sizzle." He chuckled again. Everyone, even most of the humans could feel the couple's love and passion at times.

"Sizzle is right. My nerves jangle every time they… you know." Susannah thrust her hips a couple times and Dev laughed with another wince. "There's a lot of things I should be, Uncle Rob. Unfortunately, I'm not, and everyone is fond of letting me know." Susannah frowned and huffed again.

"I understand, sweetie, but give it time. Don't be in a big hurry to be perfect. It's a hard standard to live up to." Devlin's voice trailed off and his eyes closed again. "When Ted gets back, you two should sit down and have a long talk. He might be able to fill you in on a few things. Answer some of the questions you have. He was in much better shape than your father for most of the trip back here."

Susanna sat for quite a while just watching as her uncle's face relaxed in sleep. She'd stayed too long but truly treasured his last few sentences. Uncle Rob was always the giver of pearls of wisdom. There was love in his features and she felt he really understood her. He didn't blame her for everything that went wrong. He knew she had faults yet accepted her anyway. She took a deep cleansing breath even though her lungs didn't need the oxygen.

"Sometimes I feel like a hollow shell, just nothing inside. Will there ever be someone for me?" She whispered, mostly to herself.

"Of course, sweetie. When you least expect it someone will come along and blow your socks off." Uncle Rob opened his eyes and winked at her, then seemed to doze off again.

She sat muddling through what little memories she had of her death and rebirth as a vampire.

What was her real history?

Why was everything about her becoming a vampire so mysterious?

Who was her sire?

If she ever found him, would he love her like Yuri loved Natalia? She closed her eyes and thought hard about that night in Daytona Beach. That night was fairly clear but what followed that night was still an empty mystery full of holes and unanswered questions.

Susannah let out a quiet sigh. Someone had to have those answers.

*****

March 18, Four Years Earlier, Daytona Beach, Florida...

From the shadows of the boathouse, a man stood, watching in the night. He loosened his black satin bow tie and casually undid the top buttons of his starched and ruffled shirt. Excitement surged through his body at the sight of such a luscious and provocative morsel. Something else, something foreign coursed through his body as well, but that would only make the prospective seduction even better.

Aware in some alcohol drenched part of her brain that a stranger watched her, Susannah slid her toes through the fine soft sand of the beach. It tickled the soles of her feet and spurred her on to dance under the stars. She giggled riotously, twirling and dancing with the twinkling light, filling her lungs with the tangy salt air. Rich and melodious jazz music drifted on the waves drawing her toward the bright patterns reflected on the surface of the water. Soft sea foam slid across her ankles and tickled her calves, calling her deeper as she downed the last of her fruity drink and tossed the little pink parasol into the beckoning waves. A slight frown creased her perfect, nineteen-year-old features.

How many little parasols had she done away with tonight?

Delicate porcelain skin glowed with a slight sheen of perspiration. Long blonde hair draped and curled sensuously around her face and bare shoulders caressing her skin like a lover's soft kisses. A petite girl on the verge of stunning womanhood, Susannah hiked her little cocktail dress up and jumped the lines of froth on the incoming waves, playing like a child. With each wild movement, the red spandex confection she wore inched lower on her ample bosom showing more of the cleavage that had probably impressed several high school football stars at her alma mater.

The man stood immobile, watching.

How many spring breaks had he participated in?

How many of these wild scenes had Kellan Burke the III been the sole observer of?

Over how many years?

He was a man who got what he wanted and it showed in his stance, his every manicured nail and the perfect cut of his evening attire. Kellan was a man who made his own rules, took what he desired, and gave no quarter. Especially in the bedroom, or, actually, wherever the mood struck him. A chuckle emanated from deep within his chest as he unlatched the top hook of his slacks. His erection was in full bloom and he slowly rubbed the extended protrusion through the silk of his slacks. An animalistic sound escaped his perfect smiling lips.

Still somewhat aware of her observer, Susannah frolicked with abandon, laughing at the top of her lungs. It had been a wonderful eight days and she had definitely taken advantage of her first spring break in Daytona Beach. Even though it caused a hellacious argument with her father, she'd argued for the right to be a regular college kid and won. Here, she was just like all the other girls at her college that came to participate in the wild rites of spring. Here she could forget the "steel cage" that held her captive at home during all of her long high school years. She was an adult now and on her own, sort of. Daddy still paid the bills so he had a say in what she did, but a say was so much more freedom than the complete control he exerted throughout most of her life. This was her adventure and she was going to enjoy it to the max!

No security details scrutinizing her every move. No military "rules of the roost." No more Colonel Daddy's disapproval at every turn. Just beautiful free Susannah doing whatever she wanted to do. She was living life on the edge, invincible... and very drunk.

Susannah missed a wave and plopped down on her fanny in the knee-deep water. Laughing uproariously, she tried to stand and failed, initiating another fit of drunken, uncontrollable laughter.

Through the giggles she felt strong arms lift her to her feet and she turned to face... an angel in a tuxedo! Her savior held her steady as she gazed adoringly into deep brown eyes set in a face that could have easily graced the cover of GQ Magazine. Susannah smiled coquettishly. Thinking through her provocative smile, she would have preferred to see him gracing the center pages of Playgirl Magazine, without the tux. Actually, without anything! Something in her middle fluttered as she caught the delicious scent of him letting her inebriated mind mull over the options.

"I think we should get you out of the water, young lady. You seem to have lost your sea legs." His voice thrilled Susannah to the core. She shivered with delight as his deep tones delicately stroked the most base center of her mind.

This could be fun.

Chalk up one more adventure to *Girls Gone Wild at Daytona Beach*.

"You're cold," he whispered seductively, his breath caressing her cheek. She shivered in his arms and giggled. Goose bumps covered her arms and chest making her taut nipples rub against the fabric of her dress. Like a geyser welling from deep within the earth, Susannah could feel the excitement build and threaten to erupt.

Kellan knew he had this one nailed. She was a bit of human putty in his hands. Sliding out of his jacket, he draped it around the girl's creamy shoulders. Picking her up easily, he waded to shore, angling towards the privacy of a nearby boathouse.

Susannah floated in his arms. He smelled luscious, all spice and expensive wine. His skin was smooth and tan, perfect for her lips. She could feel the iron hard muscles beneath his crisp white shirt and knew she was in good hands. Snuggling against his chest, she slipped a hand inside the unbuttoned shirt and felt his skin. It was cool with a light covering of smooth, silky blonde hair. She accidentally flicked a nipple and giggled at his sharp intake of breath. He almost stumbled as she grasped his breast and squeezed slightly, her hand conforming to his well-endowed peck. Again he drew in a deep breath. His arms tightened around her as her eager lips sought that little juncture at the base of his throat. Using her tongue she drew little circles there, aware of something not quite right, but unable to resist the growing heat in her core. His skin was luscious and cold in the heat of the night.

Kellan could smell her scent, her blood, and the moisture that had begun to flow freely with her excitement. She was ripe and ready for the taking. He was ready to take, actually, more than ready.

Using Crysillus Extract made sexual encounters literally, to die for. And once again, he'd indulged himself in the forbidden drug known in the seedier vampire circles as CE. In fact the word indulge was not the best descriptor of what he had done. More than just a little too much, he had surrendered to his addiction once again and submerged himself in the CE experience.

Now he wanted release.

No *needed* release.

In a big way.

He was holding the way in his arms and it was holding him back. He flexed and was not surprised by the sensuous sigh followed by a fit of giggles. Young, full lips caressed his neck as he struggled to stay upright. His strength was not failing him; it was the desire threatening to overwhelm that left him off kilter. They were not yet in a safe enough place to allow him his kind of seduction.

Susannah felt his cock jump and she wiggled in his arms. The game was to tease and tease and then, when she knew he would be crazy with lust, have her way with him. She wanted this stranger who held her so safely in his big strong arms. She could taste his aftershave on her lips, musky and a touch bitter. Slinging an arm around his neck, she let her head fall back offering him a perfect view of her breasts as the spandex stretched and inched lower. She moaned with ecstasy as her lover brought them to his lips and covered her sensitive flesh with little nips and kisses. She could feel the bodice of her strapless dress slip below her taut nipples as he took first one and then the other between his lips and sucked gently.

"Nnnn...a...ame. Your name." Susannah ground out between waves of sensual electricity. "What's... your.... name?" She felt the man pause and chided herself for breaking the mood. But there was no way she was going to seduce this guy without knowing a name to scream when she climaxed.

Kellan could wait no longer. He was in agony. "Kell." He murmured into her ear as he slid his tongue along her jaw line then towards the side of her neck. He smiled as more goose bumps rose making her nipples jut pebble hard. It did not matter that she knew his name. He would take it from her mind as he took her blood and her life.

"Sus...Susann...ah. Susannah." She could hardly talk. Between the alcohol and Kellan's ministrations, she was in heaven. Passion was the arsonist that ignited her mind and body as Kellan slowly released her, letting Susannah slither down his body until her toes reached the ground. Her arms locked around his neck and she stood on tiptoes drinking in the heat of his chocolate eyes. Good enough to eat, she thought, licking her lips, leaving a thin coating of moisture to reflect the glittering starlight, her own little enticing trick.

Good enough to eat, Kellan thought, forcing himself to control the hunger that rose like a tidal wave, threatening to demolish what little grip he maintained on his sanity. For a second his vision blurred with blood lust. *Hold on Kellan*, he told himself; *it will be better this way, so much better*.

He grasped Susannah by her hands and raised her body bringing her lips to his, devouring them as she hung, suspended in warm evening air.

Susannah felt herself lifted off the ground and hung for a second, allowing the ravage of her lips before her legs closed around Kellan. She took his lead and opened to his probing tongue. It licked and swirled sending delicious little impulses through her body. Captured, she captured back, locking her legs around Kellan's hips and rubbing down low across his groin. Her dress rode high over her hips with the motion eliciting Kellan's deep growling response. The only thing separating them was the simple draw of a zipper. Susannah tightened her hold, sliding up and down with a purposeful glide.

Kellan held Susannah fast with one hand, devouring her lips, stealing into her mind. The other hand worked the zipper of his slacks. He could contain himself no longer. He was so hard even the gentlest touch was a taunting pain. Kellan stumbled forward into the shadows of the boathouse, stepping out of his pants at the same time. His hard cock freed at last, he plunged himself into the woman who embraced him with her silky legs, tearing the tiny slip of panties that protected nothing. He heard her cry of ecstasy from a place in his mind that throbbed, hyper-excited with the forbidden CE. Again and again he buried himself in her, each thrust deeper than the last.

Susannah matched him stroke for stroke, escalating his lust with her cries. Dragging him back each time he pulled away, she felt the intensity of his passion as if it were her own. Finally, he released her hands and she sunk her nails into his shoulders, riding him for all she was worth. Without warning, it came, a flood of the most incredibly powerful sensations. Beginning low in her belly, it rose through her body, firing every nerve, exploding her senses, blinding her body.

Binding her mind.

"Kell!" Susannah screamed, tossing her head back in the throws of orgasm.

Kellan howled, their minds and bodies locked in a sexual bond held by preternatural strength. He came, ramming into her with one final incredibly deep thrust and let their combined climax take him.

Any control he thought he could maintain was gone. An explosion of animal lust fired his need for blood. The CE forced his vampire nature into overdrive. Total bloodlust enveloped his body fueled even more by the CE flowing through his veins. He could restrain himself no longer and, frankly had no desire to. Susannah's cleavage, so deliciously exposed, drew his eyes higher. Her slim, young neck, so welcoming, so deliciously... delicious.

The carotid artery pulsed just below the juncture of her jaw and ear, singing to Kellan of delectable promise. His mouth watered as he sank his fangs into the pounding pulse just below the sparkling crystal stud set in her dainty earlobe... and tore... and tore.

And tore again.

Chapter 3

Empty Awareness

It's so cold and dark within these walls.
Yet within my mind still, I walk the halls,
Of life's unjust end.
The rules I did bend.

A different kind of life, alone away from sight.
Abandon, isolated in death is my plight.
I no longer breath... the air is still.
I scream... the sound so shrill.

Monique Merchant, Vampire
The Journal of a Captive, 1889

Darkness.

Susannah always hated the darkness. Hysteria rose like bile in her throat, burning it's way to the surface of her mind.

Cold.

It was so cold. She could not move. Her limbs seemed to be frozen in time and space, yet her mind was free to roam. Her lips could not form the shape of a scream. Her vocal cords were stiff and dry. Her face could not reflect the mounting fear that tore at her lack of senses.

What was going on?

Was she dead?

Was she in hell?

Is this what death was like?

If she was dead, how could she be conscious of her existence? Susannah fought the mind numbing terror that smothered her. She gasped for breath with lungs seized by a steely paralysis.

Oh God, I can't breathe, the young woman screamed behind leaden eyelids that would not even flicker. *Help me! Someone, anyone! Please help me!*

"Sleep child," came a calm, gentle voice from somewhere, far off in the distance. "Sleep my wild little thing. Do not cry out so. You are safe in the dark. Wait for me. I will come."

Susannah did not want to sleep but the voice was so beautiful, so alluring, a voice she knew from... She was pulled deeper into oblivion, hunting for the source, compelled without a will of her own.

She complied.

A sweet desire settled so deep within her it enveloped her very being. Still she sought the voice, reaching into the blackness, grasping for a shred of… and then there was nothing.

Across town Kellan concentrated on smothering the waking consciousness of his little mistake. Susannah's mind virtually screamed in his head. If he could hear her, there was a possibility others of his coven could as well. If the Master found out Kellan sired a possible fledgling, his undead life would be worthless. Actually, less than worthless, he would be so much dust left behind by the cleansing fire of Master Metolius' punishment. He would be made an example and his destruction would be long and painful. Metolius would send his lieutenants to do the actual dirty work, but each member of the coven would hear and feel his agony. The Master ruled with iron discipline and demanded unwavering loyalty.

He'd broken the rules.

Again.

"Shit! Why did I do it?" Kellan sat on the edge of his bed, steel shutters blocking the direct sunlight outside. He should be deep in day sleep by now, but his little mistake awakened him with her cries.

How could she be awake?

How could she have turned?

Without blood?

His heart twisted in his chest. He groaned at the word play. His heart really did nothing in his chest, but it was the intent of the statement that counted.

He rose and paced.

As great as the sex was, Susannah should never have turned. It was totally his fault. Why did he leave her with her head and heart intact? On the beach where she could be found?

Fuck!

He'd indulged in the Crysillus Extract again.

That pretty pink CE.

It was so addicting. Every vampire knew of it and gave a wide berth to the drug that made you feel human sensation again. Using CE allowed a vampire to recapture, if but for a few hours, the days of walking in the sun and loving like a human being. But the bloodlust that followed was insatiable and dangerously unmanageable.

Susannah had been a convenient coincidence. Totally blitzed out of her mind, the pretty blonde was simply wandering in the wrong place at the right time, for him. Regretfully, it was his lack of judgment that put him in this situation, not hers. He hadn't needed to turn her. He thought he'd left her truly dead.

What was he thinking?

Damn that CE...

Therein lay the problem. He wasn't thinking. He was high. Incredibly, lusciously, lovingly high on life, human life. He felt himself harden at the memory. "Kellan, you're a dead man. Well, you're already a dead man, but now you're really a dead man. And just possibly a dead vampire too." Kellan paced the dark room talking to himself.

He was alone and safe for the moment. "A cover up is what I need. But... for right now I have to keep her quiet. Man, if she awakens again and starts screaming, Metolius' men will find her. Then they'll find me. Not good, man. Your ass is ash, Kell." In business he often talked his way through issues with himself. It clarified things and helped him resolve difficult problems. It was not working very well this time.

Kellan flopped backward onto the satin sheets, pinching the bridge of his nose as if he were experiencing the debilitating migraines he suffered as a human. Vampires didn't get headaches but they did get cock-aches. He lifted his head and stared at the tight erection produced by the simple memories of his encounter with the blonde wild-child. God, she was good.

His cock pulsed.

It protruded from his groin with a length he was quite proud of. In fact, among his coven, he was known for its size and the pleasure it could offer. "Down boy, you and I are in deep kimchi as it is."

He rolled onto his stomach and groaned as the satin sheets caressed his stiffness. "How hard can it be to find her? Undoubtedly she was in a morgue somewhere. What does it take to break into a morgue, steal a body and find a place to burn it?" The muffled words sounded incredulous. Even to him.

He felt no remorse at the idea of burning Susannah. She was just a play-toy and until she drank her first blood, she wasn't even a true vampire. She was nothing. What would it matter if she was destroyed? It was his ass he wanted to keep from burning.

*****

Across town a grieving father, one Colonel Frank Maddox, finished packing his bag and adjusted his navy blue sport coat. Tailored to cover the slight bulge beneath his left arm, the Colonel studied his reflection in the full-length mirror. Loose khaki slacks efficiently concealed the mini arsenal strapped to his ankles: a small back-up pistol on the left, his Ka-Bar D2 Extreme tactical knife on the right. Extra magazines hung unnoticeable, pressed into the small of his back, secured to his leather belt. Tugging slightly at the sleeves of his coat, his fingers felt the butterfly knife affixed to his right arm by its rapid release system.

He was comfortable.

Actually, content.

Proper accessorizing did that for a man of his caliber and his caliber was nine millimeter in a Beretta style.

The rented hearse and driver waited below double parked in front of the hotel.

It was time.

Maddox slung the bag over his shoulder and headed for his date with the coroner. There was only one thing to call what he planned to do; a crime.

Actually, a whole bunch of crimes.

As he took the stairs two at a time, Maddox counted up the laws he was about to break; forging official documents, theft of a body, tampering with police evidence, kidnapping a hearse driver, car theft, or rather hearse theft. The list went on and on. Maddox hit the first floor before he ran out of charges that could, and probably would be filed against him.

He'd been to the morgue, lived through identifying the remains of the only thing left in the world he loved. Now he was going to do the only thing a father could do; find his daughter's killer. He listened to the cockamamie story the coroner spun and knew it for what it was - bullshit… piles of it. His years of tactical training would come in handy if he could hold on to the anger.

Anger made him think.

Plan.

Calculate.

Act.

It made him mentally and physically hard. He needed to be hard as granite. He was about to risk his career and his life to find the truth, and the killer of his baby girl.

The driver introduced himself and opened the side door, stowing the Colonel's gear behind the passenger seat. "Kind of unusual, a live person riding with me. Nice to have company that can talk back." The young man was obviously nervous as he headed into the morning traffic trying to make the best of the situation. "Sorry about your daughter, Sir. But we'll get her home for you. I guess we'll be driving north? Grandview Maine, right? I brought a bag and some tunes. Grateful Dead. Just joking." The young man smiled at his remark pretending to concentrate on the road as the pregnant silence stretched on.

"On the right Mr. Vanderloss. Take the ramp. We'll park under the building near the security door to the morgue." Maddox indicated with a wave.

"Sure, and please, Sir, call me Ted. It's a long way to Maine." Ted made the turn and competently backed the hearse into the marked area for delivery trucks and couriers.

"Wait here." It was an order.

Ted had no desire to disobey.

His boss warned him that Colonel Maddox was a man on the edge. He also mentioned the open account and the fact that money was no object. A grieving father and an open account? Ted was sure he knew which the funeral home supervisor cared more about. That was a fairly easy bet, even for a simple driver on a road trip.

He watched as Maddox was buzzed into the facility, disappearing quickly behind the steel security door. The young man plugged in his tunes and settled back to wait. Releasing a body could take some time and it was only a little after eight o'clock in the morning. Then there would be placement in the casket, etc. It would be a bit of a wait before they hit the road. He closed his eyes and drifted with the country music.

By the end of the third set of tunes, Ted was jarred from his short nap as Maddox burst through the door with the sound of a minor explosion. Stunned, Ted watched as the Colonel took out both security cameras with two perfectly aimed shots, the gun in one hand, a body bag thrown over the opposite shoulder. Maddox easily jumped down from the loading dock, hit the ground at a dead run and headed straight for the parked hearse, wildly motioning with his gun to get the back door open.

Ted moved as if motivated by a crazy man with a loaded gun and a dead body.

Rapidly.

In a heartbeat he was out of the car and wrenching the cargo door open. The auto slide engaged rolling an empty coffin out on silent rails.

"Open it." Maddox huffed. "We're in a bit of a hurry, Ted." Maddox shifted his weight, set the gun on the top of the hearse and gently laid the bag and its contents into the coffin. Carefully, but efficiently arranging the crumpled plastic, he slammed the lid and locked it with a large ornate key. "Bit of a hurry, Ted."

His iPod dangling from his ears, Ted stood in stunned silence as *Burnin' Ring of Fire* played disturbingly on the device.

He grasped the young man's shoulder and shook him. "Ted, let's get on with it, son."

"Yes Sir!" Ted stammered as he pushed the button to retract the rails and closed the cargo door. The whole scene was some surreal take out of a grade B horror movie.

Dragged toward the passenger side, Ted was perfectly okay letting the madman do whatever he wanted. He felt a solid hand on his shoulder push him down into the seat. Maddox had a gun and resistance was dangerous. Ted was familiar with that kind of danger.

"I'll take the first leg, Ted. Buckle up. We're in a bit of a hurry. Remember?" Maddox half jumped, half slid across the hood and climbed into the driver's seat. "Ah, Ted… buckle up. That box is hooked down isn't it?"

"Yes Sir." Ted croaked fumbling with the clip and belt. With shaking hands it took several tries before an audible click signaled the belt locked. The vehicle had already exited the garage, tires spinning, as it slid into traffic at a high rate of speed. Ted gulped. "I guess you didn't get the paperwork, Sir?"

"Got that, did you? You're quick, son." Maddox's feral smile scared the hell out of the younger man. "Just sit tight Ted. No one got hurt and no one is gonna. I just need to get my daughter somewhere safe until I can get some answers. That piece of shit they call a coroner couldn't find his ass with both hands and a map. I need answers, Ted. I can't let go of this. No county doctor with a white lab coat is gonna bullshit me. Especially where my little girl is concerned."

"No, Sir." Ted mumbled quietly as he gripped the handle above his window.

Chapter 4

Bloodlines: A Sire's Own

Fight it. You will not win.
Hate it. The love begins.
Scorn your life, but soon you'll learn.
Deep inside the need will burn.

Embrace it. Take it to heart.
Your place in the coven, is just a start.
You will find the power in death's sweet embrace.
Accept the darkness, bestowed with grace.

A new beginning, strange though it may be.
It takes time, but soon you'll see.
We all find our place, here on earth.
Accept this gift of dark rebirth.

You are mine, a child of our way.
Come to me, always to stay,
Within my grasp, beneath my wings.
Never bothered by paltry things.

You break my rules, diminish my trust
The punishment is clear, one quick thrust.
Or burn in the light, the fire so bright
Come to me child, alone in the night.

Metolius Gallcius Proctor, Master Vampire
From; On Hunting, Writings of the Master, 1592

Kellan found what he needed in a lone apartment on the third floor of his building. Being out in daylight required fresh blood. He had simply knocked, been invited in, and helped himself. Two children in apartment three-ninety-eight lay cold and unconscious. The sitter and her sickly red-headed son sat watching some mindless cartoon on the television as if no monster had entered their abode, sucked the life from two toddlers and left without being noticed. They would remain where they were left, watching TV until the parents arrived for their children.

Then the trouble would start.

However, Kellan would be long gone and the sitter would have no knowledge of him or his visit. That was his coven's way. Not just the taking of blood from children. They took from anyone they wished. He belonged to a coven of true vampires, in the oldest sense of the word. They were naturist vampires – at the top of the food chain.

By eliminating the memory of a visit from his kind, the coven's security and anonymity remained protected. There were strict rules for the members. Heaven forbid a coven member break from Metolius' rules. The Master used his lieutenants to keep subordinates in line and placed little restraint on the enforcers, as far as their methodology and tactics were concerned. In fact, the more brutal the punishment, the better the lesson for the others in the coven.

Metolius Gallcius Proctor was a harsh taskmaster. Over two thousand years old, he ruled with an iron fist and never, NEVER, allowed his rules to be ignored or circumvented. A warrior in ancient times, he was turned on the battlefield as he lay dying of a mortal wound. His master did not live to see the end of the campaign. Ruthless to the end, Metolius Gallcius Proctor's personality never changed with the times. Few vampire masters like Metolius, stuck to the old ways of thinking and doing in the modern world. It was too messy. Metolius liked messy, employing his enforcers with endless amounts of work.

Kellan feared him with good reason.

A shiver ran up Kellan's back as he smeared V-screen across his face and hands. It was broad daylight and he would be out in the sun today. Protected by clothing made from special UV inhibiting fabric, covered with V-screen and feeling strong and virile, he headed for the basement and his Maserati Quattroporte Sport GT. At one hundred-nineteen thousand dollars, the car was his pride, joy, and safe haven when the sun was up. Metal-flake black, it also had smoked UV inhibiting windows, a built-in blood cooler always stocked for the occasional snack, a bar in the back seat and that special little compartment he had installed to accommodate at least three vials of CE. That was another infraction he would pay dearly for, if discovered. The Quattroporte was definitely a party machine stocked for a hot time in the old town. It was an extension of Kellan's personality. It was indulgence on wheels – a very expensive indulgence on very expensive wheels. Money was only one perk of his species and it bought him the celebrity and status to live comfortably within the coven.

The warm air of the dry basement inhibited his breathing for a few seconds before he remembered to cease the useless effort. The joys and jobs of a hundred-plus years allowed for a more than a comfortable standard of living. His penthouse was kept meticulously clean with filtered air and water. If he needed to maintain the rouse of human needs, he wanted it clear of human filth. Kellan punched the auto start mechanism on his key ring and thrilled at the purring sound of his foreign car's incredibly well engineered motor. It purred like a satisfied woman. The tuned rumble of the engine was a symbol of personal fulfillment. He liked satisfaction in all of its forms. Another button opened the doors with an alert tone and a soft click. Already the air conditioning unit had cooled the inside and cleansed the air. Slipping into the driver's side with practiced grace, Kellan luxuriated in the feel of fine Corinthian leather and sophisticated ergonomic engineering.

God, it was good to be wealthy, handsome, well endowed, and immortal!

Leaving the garage with a purposeful squeal of the tires, he headed for the Daytona Beach Coroner's Office and an appointment with an unresolved mistake.

A quick call to the Mango Bango club earlier confirmed his suspicion. Some guest found the girl's body and alerted the authorities before the staff could intervene. She was undoubtedly at the morgue by now. How long had it been since his beach party?

Three days?

More?

Minutes later Kellan stormed out of the Coroner's Office in a fit of anger tinged with fear. How could her body be missing? She should have been tucked snuggly into a cold vault awaiting the end of her pretty little life.

Fuck.

Complications.

He did not need complications.

He slid stiffly into his Quattroporte and punched the cell-set button. The car responded with a perfectly modulated female voice, "Would you like to make a call, Mr. Burke?"

"Yes. Call Jordan." He spit the words at the digital receptor with vehemence.

After a few quiet rings the phone was answered by a voice

message system, "No one is available to take your call. Please leave a message."

"Jordan, pick up. Pick up the fucking phone, you little shit." Kellan glanced at his watch. His son was probably sleeping like he should have been. "Fuck. This is your father. I'll be out tonight. Stay away from Proctor, and stay out of trouble." He punched the end button with a taut knuckle and banged his forehead on the steering wheel in frustration. "Ahhhhgh. Where the fuck are you, you sneaky little bitch?"

Kellan focused his mind, cast his senses and called softly to the girl who had turned into more trouble than a bite and a fuck on the beach should have been. What did he have to go through for a little fun and a quick snack these days? This was truly out of hand.

Little one, awake. Tell me where you are and I will come to you. We will be together forever, my lovely. Reach out to me, my sweet.

For several minutes he sat concentrating on his mental image of the lovely blonde girl he hardly remembered from his drug induced revelry. He tried to see her eyes and couldn't. What color were they? Then it came to him; the taste of her, the warmth of her blood.

Susannah stirred.

Kellan felt a moan and heard a light whimper.

Ah, good girl. Again, my love. Call to me and I will come. I will ease your hunger and warm you with my kiss. I will hold you close once again.

Kellan could feel her now as she began to wake. He could sense the confusion of her mind and the fear she broadcast. He revved the car and sped in the direction of her feel.

Chapter 5

For the Want

The want is oft not worth the having,
So said someone smarter than God.
The having is oft not worth the getting.
And so goes life for the living.
But what about the dead?

Maria St. James, Vampiric Philosopher
Spanish Morocco, 1872

Olney Farm, Maine, August, Present Day...

Susannah watched as Natalia and Yuri stood beneath the silvery moon in a secluded meadow behind the main house at Olney Farm. The late summer evening was heavy with humid scents that assailed her mind and taunted her desires. In a circle around the couple stood their coven and family, the members of their support team and Colonel Maddox. Natalia Vyrubova wore a long gown of cream brocade satin with seed pearls and sequins outlining delicate patterns across her bodice. Around her slender neck hung a diamond and pearl necklace set in white gold. Gobs of diamonds and pearls dangled from her earlobes twinkling in the moonlight. She looked like a Russian Tsarina covered in royal jewels about to be crowned. Susannah smiled at the thought of Natalia's sparkling jewelry. She remembered Yuri pocketing the set when their mission in Afghanistan uncovered a cache of untold millions stashed in a secret cavern belonging to a Taliban general. They probably were royal jewels from some once flourishing country that now lay in waste. Natalia's long, luxurious chestnut curls piled high on her head framed a face glowing with love. The entire scene made Susannah squirm with jealously and sexual tension. It was difficult for a 'young' vampire to be in such close proximity to an erotically charged event without an outlet for her almost uncontrollable needs. She clamped a tight hand on her emotions and pasted a happy smile on her lips. She would not ruin this event with her mouth or her actions. Natalia and Yuri deserved each other and the happiness they had found. This was one event she would not fuck up.

Captain Yuri Milassoviech stood gracefully, next to his beautiful bride, a chest full of ornate medals decorating the Russian formal army dress uniform. Although "officially dead" and no longer a part of the Russian Army, pride dictated the attire he wore when he married the woman who saved his life, gave him eternity as a vampire and made him part of the coven he had grown to love and cherish. Yuri's preternaturally handsome features clearly reflected his love for the woman whom he called his Dark Angel, the one about to become his wife.

"In the presence of your coven, you both have come, in the sight of the blessed moon, to declare your love and dedication to each other. Once each thousand years, the powers that take our human lives and make us what we are, give back a bond stronger than anything a human can endure. As a bonded pair, you Natalia, and you Yuri, have been given a gift, a connection that will span the years and bind you until the end of time." Elizabetta took a wreath of Moonflowers from Petra and placed it around the couple's clasped hands. The white and pink blooms were full and bright at the witching hour of the night. "As two have been joined in the power of one, your essence blends and merges, unified in thought and emotion, binding you unto eternity." Elizabetta raised the couple's flower-bound hands to the moon, ducking under to kiss first Natalia, then Yuri. Petra and Kraz came next, fully entitled as Natalia's human family, to hug and kiss the newlyweds.   They'd traveled to Maine just last week and were overjoyed at Natalia's happiness. Kraz, leaning on his cane, stood for his lifelong friend as Yuri's best man.

Susannah moved back into the shadows, watching as the forever-bound couple held their hands high and faced the coven. Each member slowly came forward to plant a confirming kiss on the couple's cheeks as they stood beneath an arch of flowers silhouetted against the star filled night sky.

Elizabetta caught sight of the young woman hiding beneath the huge branches of a thickly leafed, ancient oak tree. Frowning, she motioned Susannah forward.

Susannah hesitated, looking speculatively at her own tightly clasped hands, a single moonflower crushed between her taut white fingers.

Susannah, your sister and Yuri celebrate great joy this night. At least come forward to confirm their bond. Elizabetta glared with purpose at her errant surrogate daughter in the shadows.

Susannah felt the mind speak of her Coven Mistress with a great deal of guilt. She wanted to turn and run from the cozy scene, but chose to stay and join the celebration. Her reticence went unnoticed by everyone except the concerned and semi-disappointed mistress.

We will speak of this later, young lady. Elizabetta's words were offered in motherly warning, but did not bother the young vampire one bit. By the time her mistress came to lecture her about the latest transgression, she would be long gone.

After her visit with Uncle Rob, she had carefully developed a plan and everything was in order for the final piece; finding her own roots and hopefully bonding with her own sire. Susannah was determined to settle the question of her history and finally find what Natalia and Yuri had. If it meant using all the resources at her disposal to search the world for her sire, she would find the one who took her humanity and planted within her the virus that made her a vampire.

She was immortal.

She was powerful in her own right.

She had grown into her powers over the last couple years.

She would not be shamed by her own inabilities and lack of confidence any more. She would not be told what to do by her human father, like some small child. She was a grown woman before turning and now she was a grown vampire. A grown vampire with a mission and, thanks to her training, she had the covert skills to accomplish it.

It was time to find her *own* self and with it, her eternal love.

Strolling the grounds alone, away from the group, Susannah could hear the sounds of the party behind her. Not trusting her emotions, she could not bring herself to join the reverie. Her coven celebrated with the humans who had become part of the Vamp Squad family in the last few months after Afghanistan. They made Natalia and Yuri's bonding a truly unique celebration.

Her family celebrated.

She just hurt.

The mission to Afghanistan was a resounding success and its booty was still being tabulated by a secret group of government bean counters and property specialists. Looking beyond the tremendous wealth they uncovered in the caverns below Hafsa Tokkar, completing their first assignment as an undercover squad of vampire operatives was a stellar success. The obvious results proved their worth and secured their safety and protection in the human world with the American government. Their subsequent success in Somalia was just that much more gravy, despite the casualty who now sat in a wheelchair eating cake and hugging anyone who came near enough to be caught in his gregarious embrace. She would miss Uncle Rob but she had to find her life.

Well, not her life, but essentially the end of her life.

Susannah's father was now permanently assigned as the Joint Services Liaison to the group, with Elizabetta Zoeltel as their official representative and Coven Mistress. The existence of the team was kept top secret and under deep cover. Their subterranean home-base at Olney Farm, an old safe house, was being rapidly expanded. Now their support team officially included Doctor Helga Anderson, a researchist and top endocrinologist. Their little family was growing, as was their security and protection.

Music reached her ears. The party had shifted into high gear and she could hear her Uncle Rob's loud laughter as Petra swung his wheelchair in time to the beat. Susannah looked back toward the meadow. Lieutenant Previn leaned against a tree watching the dancers under the twinkling lights. He'd been assigned to the group a few months back and was, unfortunately, the eyes and ears of the military. The team ''liberated' Previn from Fort Leavenworth after he'd been convicted of murdering his sister. He allegedly cut off her head and burned her body. The Lieutenant was accused of the gruesome crime and immediately convicted by his own startling confession. During his short trial, he claimed that his sister was a vampire and he was saving her soul.

Of course, at the time, no one believed him. He went to prison full of righteous indignation and with a huge bag of garlic. When the military finally became aware of, and accepted the existence of vampires, his case was reviewed and Previn was offered a lucrative deal to join the Vamp Squad. From the standpoint of the Joint Chiefs, his hatred of vampires made him the perfect governmental watchdog. To the casual observer, his posture spoke volumes. To Susannah he was a man to avoid, in any posture.

In the center of it all, Milo spun Dr. Anderson around to the wild folk music Natalia chose from her native Russia. Sergeant Milo Miller was having the time of his unique life, about as unique as the group to which he'd been assigned. In a last ditch effort to extricate his military career from the toilet and save his own worthless hide, he had accepted a 'Top Secret' assignment without much specific background information. In debt to bookies, on the run from the local police in several small towns he was called before a general for dallying with his daughter. After that, Milo needed to disappear. It was an easy guess that he would be in favor of a deep cover assignment.

He was also one of the first humans Susannah met after her awakening. It was something she preferred not to dwell on. She also had a sneaking suspicion it was the root of his determination to avoid being alone with any of the vampires. His 'Klingeresque' talents were indispensable and he found a home with the Vamp Squad, no matter how ill at ease he found himself with its non-human operatives.

The newest member of the group was Milo's dance partner, Dr. Helga Anderson. Searching databases, historical accounts and leads throughout the world, the doctor's job was to compile as much information about vampires as possible. She and Elizabetta immediately became fast friends, often talking for hours and pouring over research materials. Amazingly, Dr. Helga also seemed able to correspond quite freely with the Librarian Frabriaci in Orsova, at the Vampire Council of Elders. As a human, it was the doctor's most unique resource and an honor she coveted. During her exhaustive research, Helga uncovered an original compilation of the work done within Nazi Germany on the uber-secret creation of elite vamp-soldiers during World War II. After painstaking translation, it provided the most in-depth knowledge on VMD yet... which she, of course, shared with the Council.

Her coven, her family, her home... the ties that bind wound tightly around her throat as she watched her vamp sister catch Natalia's bouquet.

Monique?

What kind of husband would the French vampire accept? Probably some hunk of a vampire with oodles of money, a villa on the Riviera, private jet and closet full of Armani suits. He'd definitely have to be a good dancer!

Susannah shook her head. No, Monique would never give up the freedom she so dearly cherished after the dungeons of San Leyre and 200 years of torture by the resident monks who held her there.

It was time to go, to get away and be on her own. Susannah glanced wistfully at the snug little farmhouse one last time before getting into her car. Monique would know where she was going and hopefully no one would miss her for a couple days. The entire farm would be cleaning up after the wedding and party.

Though it looked like home in the rearview mirror, Susannah knew good and well, that sweet little farmhouse concealed a world of self-doubts and painful memories. With the entry to their growing underground installation disguised, the little house looked to be a warm and friendly farm set in the middle of a meadow with an ancient barn leaning off to one side. The only discrepancy in the cute country setting was the well kept and often used gravel road. The two miles of smooth, well-packed gravel looked more in keeping with a military base or a government installation than a sleepy country farm. She was ready to leave it and the memories behind, at least for a while. Until she could find her sire and the answers she hoped awaited her, her brand new sports car would be her home.

Susannah shifted into third gear and slid around the last turn, bouncing up onto the pavement of Rural Route 4 in search of her own personally decided future. Her white fingers gripped the wheel with pent up emotion as the radial tires screeched on the asphalt. A suitcase and cooler slid across the leather seat behind her.

She would find the man who made her.

She would get the answers she needed to straighten out her life.

Then, she would find a way to make her sire fall in love with her.

Susannah was determined to have what Natalia and Yuri had. Staring resolutely into the dark, her car wound through the hills of Maine toward a beach in Florida and the painful memories of life… and death.

On Monique's bureau lay a sealed envelope containing a short note. It ended with one sentence; *Please don't tell Dad until you absolutely have to.*

Chapter 6

Addiction to Life

To live is the reason you persist,
Come, understand the pragmatist.
It is the way of all things vampire,
The craving, the need, the irresistible desire.

It's simple. It's easy.
And oh so sleazy.
Accept the caress,
Just say yes!

Metolius Gallcius Proctor, Master Vampire
From: The Essence of a Vampire, Writings of the Master, 1892

Jordan slouched in the office chair against the richly paneled wall, watching the discourse from beneath hooded eyelids. He liked the spaciousness of Metolius' office because he could maintain a healthy distance from the Master and his key players as they discussed the latest disciplinary action. Metolius took great joy in dispensing his own form of justice, if that was what it could be called. Jordan almost felt like a fly on the wall when he kept his lids low and remained still.

When he first arrived with his father, he thought the place a wonderland. But now the smell of aged orange oil and decaying vegetation lent the air a dominating odor that assaulted the senses, oppressing the olfactory nerves. After a short period of time, it oppressed the person.

Metolius' trap was beautifully baited and his father had no compunction about tossing his son right in. Before Jordan realized, he'd been wholly ensnared. Caught was still caught, no matter the grandiose nature of the prison. In Jordan's opinion the Proctor Estate was just that, a prison full of overly decorated rooms with ostentatious furniture instead of cold steel bars.

The estate's sumptuous Tudor-style mansion sat in a secluded tangle of ancient weeping willows and overgrown swamp vegetation. At times it seemed the leaves truly wept, adding their tears to the eternally damp and moldy ground. Metolius Proctor conducted his furtive business from behind the hand-carved walnut doors of his private office in a thirty-five room main house. The mansion had ten bedroom suites and another fifteen bathrooms. There were several dining rooms; a private theater, and a secure high-tech conference room that made the White House Command Center look obsolete. Metolius Proctor may have been over two thousand years old, but he kept up with the times as he watched the world change.

Jordan's own quarters, along with those of other young vampires in the coven, sat above a thirty-car garage protecting the master's collection of vintage vehicles. The estate's stables had long since given up housing equine flesh. The refurbished stalls now held a collection of pathetic humans. They served the coven's elite as a food source or for the hungry servants of a Master who might need an incentive or deserve a sweet tasting reward. Sprawled lavishly across almost a thousand feet of private waterfront on Tomoko Basin, the estate was home to twenty of the coven's high-ranking members as well as a staff of fifteen permanent human familiars.

For sure, it was not Jordan's home of choice. It was his personal prison and would certainly be a deadly prison should he step out of line. He was forced to move to the compound shortly after his father joined the coven and Proctor's huge pharmaceutical conglomerate. Jordan always suspected he was *collateral*, held to guarantee his father's loyalty and behavior. Shit – that had worked well… Not.

After a string of transgressions Metolius had Jordan's old man destroyed anyway. His father's final coup-de-grâce was due to a personal lack of self-control. He'd bit a young college gal in some torrid sexual stunt and left her for dead. Only she didn't die – she turned. Apparently good ol' dad shared more than sex. In Metolius' book that was the ultimate no-no. Only the Master added to the family. Too big a boo-boo to ignore, Metolius' First Lieutenant was sent to clean up the mess and punish the errant vampire. Even though Kellan Burke did not belong to Metolius' linage, the Master somehow made sure his disciplinary action was known. The death of Jordan's father was felt by everyone in the coven as Kellan burned to ashes in a parking lot somewhere up north. Not much of a loss, all things considered. If Jordan had more balls, he would have done it himself long ago.

If…

"Yes, Sir. Successfully dispatched, Master Metolius." Jordan watched the Master's Lieutenant stand at attention before a wide ornately carved Black Forest desk. Past the Lieutenant, Jordan watched the Master's stark white hands which lay at rest atop the vast expanse of oiled wood. Their color highlighted the contrast between the highly polished dark surface and the Master's pale, almost translucent skin. Still as death, nearly feminine in their repose, they hid horrendous deeds and camouflaged incredible power. Atop the desk as well, but to one side, lay the inert body of a young girl, her once beautiful figure clearly abused and harshly used.

"Well done, Drechell. You serve me with distinction." Metolius surveyed the vampiric thug with cold silver eyes. One more of his coven whom displeased him was gone and, in the Master's opinion, another lesson well taught. He would tolerate no defiance by his children. "I am pleased. You are free to feed from the larder without restriction for the rest of the week. However, have a care as to the trash you leave in your wake. We need no more petty human scrutiny. It is such a bore." Metolius absently waved the Lieutenant toward the door as he sunk his fangs into the femoral artery of the young naked woman who lay, sprawled across one half of his desk. Drechell glared at Jordan and stood his ground.

A small, weak moan drew Jordan's attention toward the mass of bloody blonde hair that covered the girl's face, hiding her youth in the throws of imminent death.

Fifteen?   Fourteen?   Twelve? The Master was taking them younger and younger these days. Jordan heard gossip, but now saw the truth with his own eyes. As the Master grew older, he required less blood to keep his strength and rejuvenate his youthful appearance, but his need was quite specific. Virgin blood was the most virile blood of the human race next to that of an infant. Since virgins were younger and younger, so was the Master's food source.

Jordan pondered the gossip. What did it matter if babies, virgins, or old women supplied blood? Humans were food and that was that. He snorted in disgust. As much as he disliked it, he knew no other way. What other way could there be in his coven?

"You disagree with my Lieutenant's reward, young Jordan? Perhaps I should double the days? Or perhaps you are unhappy at the errant soldier's punishment, considering your father's demise. Ah Jordan, you of all people should understand why I have rules and why I must punish those who flaunt their disobedience. Hum?"

Jordan knew Metolius was baiting him, dissecting his thoughts, playing mind games to search out loyalties.

"My old man was a pain in the ass. He was my human father and my sire, but beyond that, I could care less. Drechell makes a good bitch, running around taking care of your messy business. How about give the old Nipper a month of unrestricted hunting? Maybe he'll actually get a piece."

Jordan grinned at the Master's enforcer with derision. It was common knowledge around the coven that Drechell had only one fang and no balls. The brutal vampire was burned within an inch of his dead existence at one point during the Salem Witch hunts, and could only regenerate a portion of his original self. One side of the Lieutenant's face was quite scarred and he was blind in one eye. It made Drechell a great enforcer with the face and attitude to play the part to the hilt. So much for a vampire's perfect immortality.

"Jordan, Jordan, Jordan. Children these days, gentlemen. What shall we do with them? Jordan, go find me some better form of sustenance and take this garbage out to the swamp." Metolius waved a pale effeminate hand at the young man in dismissal.

Snapping to his feet, Jordan hefted the whimpering girl over his shoulder and left the Master's office as quickly as possible. Pissing off Drechell was one thing, but Jordan knew better than to irritate the Master in any way. Once, as a newly turned vampire, he cursed at the coven leader and refused to hunt. Repulsed by his own need and behavior, he tried to starve himself. Jordan's punishment was long and excruciating, and shared by his father, Kellan. It had not endeared the son to the father and it almost cost Jordan his existence.

Fortunately, Marisella, the Coven Mistress and Metolius' favorite, interceded to lessen Jordan's sentence and saved his life, a favor he would never forget. At almost ninety years old, he still had trouble concealing his frequent erections in her presence; something he knew would end his miserable life if Metolius ever noticed.

Behind the Master's mansion was the entrance to the swamp in Toscana Park, a great place to dispose of anything organic and digestible. Jordan dumped the girl's body in the water and tugged a rope suspended from a low hanging tree limb. A bell toned deep and resonant in the thick air. The local host of reptiles and swamp life was efficient at taking care of the coven's trash.

"For whom doeth the bell toll? It tolls for…Bengie…" Jordan turned his back a second before the enormous albino alligator surfaced. "Bon appetite, Bengie."

The sun had gone down at least an hour before and it was time to hit the streets for a snack. As a young vampire, he was allowed to hunt alone off the grounds of the coven's estate, but still required to live on the property. His quarters were near the stables where a bevy of young women and men were kept captive and happily addicted to one of the many drugs the Master's pharmaceutical corporation produced. Acquired from bars, homeless shelters, out of rehab programs and off the streets, the humans were kept as special rewards, but no one fed without permission. Most of the coven had their favorite haunts where the local establishment was paid handsomely to turn a blind eye to a little fang action. Taking from humans was approved as long as no one left a string of bodies behind without suitable explanation. Most members of the coven fed from willing human donors they groomed and kept in style.

Jordan longed for the kind of freedom his father had enjoyed. Another ten years and he would be eligible for limited privileges and the opportunity to serve as an employee in Metolius' mega corporate structure. The money he earned would be his own and he could live where he chose, but the coven rules remained in place and his allegiance to Metolius would be continually tested. It was the way of his coven.

Jordan snorted again. His snorts were becoming a habit he would need to learn to control a little better. At least he hadn't been asked to dispatch his own father. Not that he wouldn't have, if he'd been asked. His father turned him as a teen, a horrendous thing he never forgave the old man for. All because his father wanted a companion to 'hang" with through the centuries. Kellan bit his own son and gave him eternal life… as a monster.

Jordan frowned at the memory. What warped inhuman animal turns his own son into a beast just so he would have someone to complete some sordid family? Why would his father need Jordan to keep him company? Like some perverted form of Boy Scouts or Indian Guides? Father/Son Vampire Guides? Who would do that to their kid?

His father, that was who… or what.

Jordan knew, at some point soon he would be assigned a distasteful task to prove his dedication to the coven and his loyalty to Metolius. There was no escaping it. And there was no refusing the duty.

He lived within easy grasp in one of the many quarters on the estate. Entering his apartment, he immediately headed to the bathroom to wash the blood and stench from his hands and ditch his filthy clothes. Jordan never *settled* into the lifestyle of a naturist vampire and still hated dead bodies and drinking blood. It never got any better for him. He would have let himself die from starvation if he could have. However, every time he tried, the blood lust became uncontrollable and hideously painful. The burning hunger for human blood was a hundred times worse than any other kind of addiction. Both times he tried to resist the need for it, the pain and insanity drove him to hunt in dangerously stupid and risky ways.

The only one who really understood him was Marisella, the Coven Mistress, and she was unavailable most of the time. Not to mention way out of his league. At the mere thought of the Latin beauty, Jordan's body tightened. He ran cold water over his hands and splashed it on his face. *Control the trouser trout, or you'll end up with no balls like Drechell. Or worse, a pile of ash, like your old man.*

The cold water wasn't working.

His cock would not settle down. Jordan leaned down to the sink placing his face under the chilly water. Droplets splashed across the mirror and wall. He kept his face there as long as he could tolerate the cold that bore into his bones and brain. Still, his wandering mind and errant appendage would not cooperate.

Damn! She fired his blood and set his teen hormones to rage like no other woman.

Well, lately… there seemed to be another woman, a mysterious blonde that only appeared in his dreams. Marisella was as dark as the other was fair. A blonde was not his usual choice for sexual fantasies but her face and hair slipped into his dream world more than once in the past week waking him hard and needy.

Stripping, he left his grimy Dockers and stained polo shirt on the Moroccan tile floor, flipped on the shower and stepped behind the etched glass panel that separated the shower area from the rest of his spacious bathroom. He stood for several minutes beneath the tepid water, tracing the erotic patterns in the glass with a wet finger. No wonder he had trouble controlling his libido. His quarters belonged to Marisella before her elevation to First Female. She'd decorated the place herself.

As a human artist, she'd been talented, however, two centuries of study served to hone her skills to the point of exceptionality. She knew the human body in intimate ways no other creature could and created the glass extravaganza he now fingered. Feeling each subtle figure, caressing the bodies entangled in orgasmic bliss portrayed in relief on the warm glass, Jordan mentally insinuated himself into the scene. Almost the temperature of a human body, the figures were wet and slick as if they had come to life in heated passion. His useless heart spurred to life, sending rippling pulses through his body to surge and throb with his engorged manhood. He reached for body wash and pressed the plunger. His hand filled with silky soap smelling of roses and vanilla, smelling of Marisella.

Jordan closed his eyes. Without conscious thought he massaged the soap into his aching sex, circling his fingers in the blonde tangle of hair at the root of his erotic pain. His cock pounded and twitched, begging for more contact, a stronger touch. *God, she smelled good.*

Marisella was the only woman who had bothered to afford him even the slightest hint of human feeling. The woman stood up for him, maneuvering the Master into lessening his torture, helping him through his first healing. Of all things, she allowed him to feed from her when he was too weak to hunt for himself. Like a babe nursing for the first time, it was an extraordinarily nurturing gift that would never leave his thoughts. With time, the feeling grew into a more basic and needful sense. It possessed his mind with a passion and desire that took on a life of its own over the years.

The slightest touch of his own hand became an agonizing pleasure as soap slicked his strokes. He could feel her breath on his face; her hand on his nipple. Like the night he'd fed from her, a fire burned through his body teasing each nerve until it danced and fought for release. He pressed his forehead to the glass, touching a cheek to the female figure that lay in repose, frozen in perpetual gasping passion. His hand clenched tighter, feeling each pulse, each throbbing movement, feeling the power of desire flow through him on waves of ecstasy. He could taste the scent of Marisella in the air as he breathed deeply. Gasping with the rhythm of each stroke, Jordan lost himself in hot, erotic fantasies, weaving a scene of wild sexuality between Marisella's exquisite image and the many women he had used over the last decade. With each passing thought his need grew and burned, like an electrical overload between monstrous storm clouds.

On and on, the pressure built in his mind and body.

With one last animalistic growl, Jordan released his seed, covering the glass wall with creamy cum. His legs gave way and he slid to the wet floor of the shower.

Jordan lay there for a time, curled in a ball, pelted by the hot spray of the shower. In final surrender, he cried for the lost child who existed within, alone and unloved - for the innocent youth so cruelly betrayed by his own father.

Chapter 7

Lost

Such a precious existence lost to all,
A child whose innocence did fall,
From Grace, from God, from life itself,
To the depths of hell; the land of Satan's stealth.

If truth be told, the child did find,
A way of her own, the strength of her mind.
Lost or found, she's child no more,
But a thing of death that all abhor.

Father Paul Michael LaRue, Proctor
Monastery of San Leyre, France

It was close to dawn and the faint rays of the sunrise painted the sky blood red. Susannah was hungry and tired from driving through the night. She was close to the northern border of Georgia and still one state away from her destination. The interstate was empty and her little sports car sped along, free of the confines of traffic.

Soon she would need to find a place to stay. Although her car was equipped with UV filters that kept her safe from the rays of the sun, she felt the heavy draw of day sleep. A very young vampire, she knew she could only resist for a short time before her lids would close. It would be better if they closed when she was somewhere other than behind the wheel of a speeding sports car on an interstate highway.

The neon sign ahead flickered red and green; its glowing presence displayed a huge circle and a picture of a cabin.

It was better than nothing.

Susannah needed to stay low-key on her slim budget. She convinced Milo Miller to help with her research without revealing her plan, but leaving a clear electronic trail would only bring Daddy Dearest down on her head before she found what she was looking for. Ferreting away enough cash for her personal little mission had been more difficult than she planned. She would find her sire – there was no doubt in her mind, but her search would require careful attention to money if she didn't want to use a traceable credit card.

Guilt niggled at the back of her brain, but Susannah pushed it away. Monique would know by now where and what she was up to. This was Susannah's opportunity to figure out her life. She didn't want anyone interfering until she had the answers she sought. She trusted Monique to keep her confidence. However, she had not told Monique of the identity she planned to use to avoid detection as long as possible. Some things a girl just needed to keep close to her vest.

She steered the car off the main road and into the parking lot of the small strip mall with its zero star motel. It would have to do for the day and it was almost dawn.

Susannah settled into bed behind drawn curtains as the sun rose over the lush foliage that shaded the hotel and the whopping three cars in the crumbling asphalt parking lot. Within minutes the young woman slept deeply, a 'Do Not Disturb' sign hanging outside of her room.

Susannah dreamed, as she often did, of her sire. The handsome blonde man was looking for her, walking the beaches of Daytona, his shirt open, an uncorked bottle of champagne in one hand, two stem crystal glasses in the other. He strolled barefoot in the shallow surf calling to her, endlessly searching for the love of his life – the woman who changed his world during a chance encounter on the very same beach – a woman he changed to be his, or so Susannah always fantasized in her dreams. His lips formed her name and his voice sounded all rich and enticing, sexy way past the word go. As he slowly turned, a sensual smile crossed his features, displaying a perfect set of glistening fangs.

In every dream she ran after him, calling, but her voice drifted away with the waves. She could never seem to catch up. She chased him in vain, running after the fading image of her desire, her love. "Kell!"

Susannah startled awake, sitting bolt upright. She always knew his first name, but was it really the correct name? The cheap sheets stuck to her naked sweaty body. No red spandex dress, no champagne, no sire. She struggled to focus on Kell's image and physical location. The last threads of her dream faded with the final rays of the setting sun. Susannah burst into tears of frustration and anger.

"Where are you? Why can't I find you except in my dreams? Why don't you want to find me?" Susannah sobbed into the bunched blanket on her bed until common sense and emotional exhaustion forced her mind back to reality, the sweltering hotel room and the mess her tears always created.

"I will find you, Kell, my love."

Resolute, she arose and showered. Clean clothes, a couple bags of synth-blood and she was in a much better mood. After loading her things into the car, she checked the address of the Daytona Beach Coroner's office, filled her tank at the local gas station and hit the road. With any luck she would make it to Daytona Beach by early morning.

*****

The previous night had been a semi-crappy evening for Jordan and he returned early to the estate depressed and tired. Slinking off to bed, his day-sleep was frustratingly elusive as he tossed and turned through the day. With the approach of evening, he lay awake, still depressed.

Groggy from lack of sleep, Jordan felt a tingling in his mind that he had never experienced before. Like a kind of Morse code, the tingling turned to an annoying tap, then faded. He pulled a satin covered pillow over his head and pressed the luxurious fabric hard to his face.

Now what?

A power spill from some close coven member who gorged himself a little more than usual?

A message from the Devil himself?

How about the DeVinci Code playing out in his skull?

In any event it was gone as quickly as it appeared, leaving him wide-awake. A remnant scent filled his nostrils. It was not vanilla but a tangy scent filled with spice that lit up his morning arousal.

Stretching, he rose and padded to the bathroom. A youthful face frowned back from the mirror. The image's hair stood on end and a reddish crust caked at the corners of its mouth. Jordan shook his head. No one would want him like this. Not any of the female vampires on the estate, that was for sure, let alone Marisella.

He was a hormonal teen vampire-mess.

Why couldn't his father have waited at least a few years before turning his son and essentially freezing the boy's development? It would be hundreds of years before Jordan would even need to shave. He resembled more of a youth than a man. At ninety that just burned him to the quick.

What little sleep he'd gotten was disturbed by dreams of a blonde woman in a red glittering spandex dress wandering alone along a sandy beach, lost, searching for something... or someone.

But what?

Who?

She kept calling a name. No matter how hard he tried, he couldn't make out her words as the rolling surf and wind tore the sound from his ears. She was gorgeous in a creamy sort of way. The woman had pale skin and her deep crystal-blue eyes were mesmerizing. The eyes alone could look into the soul of a man and find him wanting.

The reoccurring dream was an enigma to Jordan who was more inclined to pursue dark complected women. He preferred voluptuous Latinas with long rich hair, needy hips and red lips. The hair and lips of Marisella. The dream-blonde had only appeared recently, but consistently. It was frustrating in a thought provoking way that took him out of his normal pattern. If he couldn't have the real thing, at least he could pretend with his fantasies.

Now even his fantasies were deserting him in favor of something he did not understand. How many women had succumbed to his attentions? All a poor substitute for what he could never truly have, yet desired above all. What did he desire above all else? Blonde? Dark? His mind was a tangle of questions with no answers.

Jordan grabbed his toothbrush and hit the shower. He was spending a lot of time in that erotically decorated shower lately. He would have to do something about that.

As he washed away the last dried flakes of slumber's crust, he remembered the Beachcomber Hotel had a wine tasting party that night. He had a standing invitation from the owner of the resort, a somewhat affable fellow he had done some private work for.

Dressing more carefully than usual, Jordan checked out of the estate and headed for the Beachcomber. As much as feeding from live beings repulsed him, he did find some redeeming value in the sexual ecstasy he gave and received from the women he used. He was careful to never take more than one donor could afford to give. Later he always erased all memory of the encounter. Not all of his coven peers were careful or sensitive to the needs of the humans they fed from, hence the periodic need for 'work'. Bengie and the other gators in the basin that bordered the estate were well fed.

Screeching to a stop in front of the resort's club, the valet waved a casual greeting and caught Jordan's keys with practiced grace. Jordan was a regular at the Mango Bango, a nightclub located at the Beachcomber Hotel and known for its loud music, exotic drinks and young crowd. It was also known for its more lively and unique offerings available in shadowy corners and bathroom stalls. Drugs, sex, and rock and roll went out in the seventies but drugs and sex made a quick return engagement in a much more varied and creative venue at the club. These days virtually anything was available for the asking at the Mango Bango and that included a little vamp attention. As long as the drinker used good manners and didn't leave a trail of bodies and blood to bother the local law enforcement, everyone stayed happy. Though Metolius owned most of the cops and city officials in the area, flagrant misuse of humans was strictly forbidden.

Rich rust colored silk slacks caressed his muscular legs as he wandered across the crowded club. A darker silk shirt opened to mid chest revealing a pair of pecks and a ripped set of abs that rivaled the latest Hollywood heartthrob. Jordan was a slight teen when Kellan turned his son to the vamp side, but vampirism and almost a hundred years of exercise toned and built his body into a well-packed form he was proud to display. Thick wavy blonde hair and rich chocolate eyes were the only things that remotely resembled his father's features in Jordan's youthful face. His skin tone, brilliant smile and wide, almost voluptuous lips definitely favored his mother's side of the family, for which he was grateful.

He hated the parts of himself that reflected his father's genetics and worked hard to develop a body and personality that didn't remind others of his lineage. At one point he even went as far as dying his hair and wearing contacts. Joining the ranks of the high maintenance crowd was not a comfortable fit for Jordan and his vamp nature fought physical changes that did not enhance its survival. Plus, Marisella once mentioned how she admired his eyes, so natural and brown they remained.

He wore a pair of soft leather loafers sans socks. Stylish with the Daytona Beach set. At six foot six inches, he towered over many of the men at the club. Jordan was definitely a desirable package and drew more than a few glances from the female contingent, as well as several glares from the more physically challenged male patrons in the club. His animal grace only added to the comments he endured from both men and women as he trolled for a safe pick-up.

Jordan spent an inordinate amount of time in selection this particular night.

Why?

He had no clue.

He just did.

Close to morning without having fed, he was feeling the hunger pull him toward less intellectual questions and more toward food.

Accepting a glass of red wine from the bartender, a petite Asian woman with exotic golden eyes and long black hair accidentally, on purpose, bumped his elbow. Then, catching his eye, giggled and quickly apologized in broken English. Jordan favored the woman with a seductive smile, making small talk as his mind searched her thoughts for entanglements and dangerous relationships.

Pulling information from the minds of humans he touched was easy. It was a talent his father shared with him. Jordan learned on his own to be careful with his selection of female companionship for a quick nip. His genetic-based skill came in handy. A lone woman without responsibilities or expectations was the easiest to use, be mind-wiped and sent on her way with a few implanted memories of a one-night stand with a handsome stranger. Unlike his father, Jordan never left behind a little mistake.

The Asian girl was flipping her hair and babbling about some party down the beach as Jordan pretended to pay rapt attention to her ramblings.

The pulse at the base of her neck drew his attention and he fixated on the sultry beat. She was sexually excited and it showed. He traced a sensuous fingertip down her chin along her neck. The blood lust fought to emerge. He clamped a tight mental grip on it and bent to brush her mouth. Open and accepting, her cherry lips eagerly sought his. Her name was Tia or Shia, or something close to that.

Inhaling deeply, Jordan felt his groin tighten, its hardness visibly pushing against the smooth silk of his slacks.

Not even five foot tall, the girl giggled as she maneuvered an accidental brush against his erection. Falsely apologetic, she covered her mouth with a small manicured hand, contriving a shocked look at what she purposely touched.

Jordan stroked her hair and reached to touch her mind, although he doubted he would need mind control to entice this woman toward a quiet and private area. She seemed more than willing to follow him anywhere. As he tasted her thoughts he found foggy confusion and extra amounts of serotonin drenched neurons.

Ecstasy.

The drug was rampant in the Daytona club set. This girl was feeling no pain. In fact, she was feeling only ecstasy and her blood would be like spun honey, thick and sugary sweet.

She would do.

Whispering in her ear, she willingly took his hand, following him out the back of the club onto the deck. It was too easy. Steps lead to the beach and a series of palapas used during the day by sunbathers for shade. At night they were used to hide clandestine encounters of the sexual and drunken kind.

Jordan led the woman to an empty palapa with two canvas lounge chairs. Sinking onto one lounge chair, he pulled Tia, or Shia to his lap. He found her eagerly searching for his lips with her tongue.

She ravaged his mouth forcing her way between his lips with quick circular motions of her tongue. Wiggling to straddle him, she ran her hands beneath his shirt, caressing his chest, giggling at his sigh of pleasure. High on her body's own reaction to Ecstasy, her clumsy, groping hands rambled across Jordan's body in quick movements.

"You likey Tamia fingers, big man?"

Ah, Tamia - that was her name. No matter, Jordan fisted her hair and pulled her mouth to his, devouring her drug induced passion as his blood lust reached for the surface. His tongue danced with hers as he eyed the beach making sure no casual observers strolled near enough to see him feed. Continuing to watch, Jordan slid his lips down Tamia's neck to the juncture at her collarbone and swirled his tongue. The girl squealed softly and wiggled outrageously against his engorged cock. He groaned as she reached to unzip his pants, freeing his huge erection. His teen hormones were in full play and he was ready and waiting.

Tamia shimmied her skirt up and sank her body down, ensconcing him in one quick movement. Her arms snaked around his neck to hold on for the wild ride that was coming. He kissed and sucked at her neck as she rode him, bucking and swirling her hips. She continued to giggle as she worked his body for her own pleasure.

Jordan could feel her Ecstasy soaked mind spiraling toward climax. Waiting for the perfect moment, he sank his fangs into her tiny neck. Sucking in swift gulps, Jordan shared her heightened climax. She came with a jolt of pure passion enhanced by a drug over-stimulated hypothalamus combined with the effects of Jordan's bite.

Tamia sighed sinking deeper into the magic orgasmic pleasure of the vampire's bite as she pressed against his fangs forcing more of her sweet blood into Jordan's mouth. God it was wonderful, tainted and stimulating. Jordan was close to coming himself and held the girl's hips, working his own body with hers. Hot jolts of fire spread from his loins to every part of his body until he was engulfed in flames. Tamia moaned as her breathing slowed and her movements stalled.

Blood loss.

Still Jordan moved closer to his own release, pumping and twisting as he sucked more blood. He was close, almost there. Jordan took one last mouthful and exploded into the woman, one eye on the sagging girl he drained and one on the beach.

She would survive, of course.

He never took too much.

Blonde hair on red spandex flashed at the edge of his vision.

Stunned, he froze abruptly withdrawing his fangs. Unceremoniously, he dumped Tamia from his lap as he stood, frantically zipping his slacks.

It was her!

He was sure.

Red flashed near the deck and he ran after the color, the person. He had to catch her.

She was the woman from his dreams.

Chapter 8

Lust

It is the nature of the animal to lust
A package deal dealt in misplaced trust.
The beauty, the sex, the blood.
On the prowl, a bestial stud.

Vampires play.
The innocent pay.

Mistress of the Dark, Shakikima Malisievahah
Alliance of the Dark, San Francisco, California

Jordan ran through the crowd, searching. The dim lights, swaying bodies, the waiters scurrying about with loaded trays; his vision swam. The loud music dampened his senses. He could not find her.

Where had she gone?

"Manolo, did you see a blonde in a red spandex dress come this way?" Jordan knew the club host well.

"Nah. Mahn. Me tinks I would have seen da wohman in dat dress. No red dress mahn. Why you look for her? Is da mahn on da fever?" The Jamaican chuckled, shaking his head. "Day be da end of us, mahn. Wohmen no good for da head." He sauntered toward the bar. "Come, me friend. Drown your sorrows before da wohman drown your tinkin mind, mahn." He pointed to his head with a sparkling white smile in the center of a very black face.

"No thanks, and Manolo, quit with the jive. I'm not one of your customers. If you happen to see her, ping me, okay?" Jordan spun and headed for the parking lot in case the woman had left the club.

"Okay, okay, man." Manolo shook his head with a low chuckle. "In a bad way, huh?" He watched Jordan hurrying out the door. "Big trouble, Jordi." He downed a quick shot and continued his rounds.

*****

Susannah hit town a couple hours earlier than she expected,

probably due to the speed at which she drove and the fact that, until she was close to Daytona Beach, traffic had been sparse. Checking into the Beachcomber Resort, Susannah figured it was finally safe to splurge, but under an assumed name. If Daddy was already looking, it would take some time for him to realize she wasn't using her own name. He underestimated her in just about everything she did. She requested a spacious suite and completed the paperwork under the name Helga Anderson with a bit of a smug smile. The real Dr. Anderson was back home with the happy newlyweds. After presenting a bright shiny credit card with her picture and Helga's name, Susannah sent her bags up with a Bellhop and parked in the garage attached to the resort hotel.

Once in her room, she slipped into a cute little red number that showed off her curves, drew a brush through her long blonde hair and headed for the club downstairs. It was a dress similar to the one she'd worn the night she died, right here on the beach.

Hoping the music and crowd at the club would cheer her and temper her miserable mood, she hit the club. Out on her own for the very first time in a long while, she was sorely disappointed. A few minutes among pathetic humans whose sole purpose for being at the club seemed to be snagging a quick lay, drinking themselves into oblivion or scoring drugs and she was more than ready to depart the fix. Just a few years ago she would have been one of those pathetic, self-centered party mongers. Amazing how joining the ranks of the undead and saving the world from bad guys colored a girl's attitude toward frivolity and irresponsibility.

Hold up a second, she thought to herself glancing at her reflection in the floor-to-ceiling plate glass windows that kept the dark and damp outside and the cool air-conditioned atmosphere inside.

Irresponsibility?

Frivolity?

Not her thing any longer?

The jury was definitely out on that one. In her mind anyway. She'd run away, in reality, to answer some questions and find the man who sired her because she wanted a fairytale life. She'd faked ID, counterfeited a credit card and now she paraded around in a look-a-like dress she'd worn the night the lover she so desperately sought had murdered her.

The jury was shaking its collective head in her brain.

Prior to leaving the farm, Susannah e-mailed the Daytona coroner and set up an appointment to see him early in the morning. She wanted to see the records of her death for herself. According to her father, the Colonel, neither the detective nor the coroner were overly concerned about finding her murderer - her sire. In fact, someone designed, laid the foundation and constructed some pretty thick brick walls around her case.

Despite dead ends, she knew his first name, or at least the name he had gave her. She knew his face. She wore the scars of his making. His VMD flowed through her veins making her what she was. She would find him.

Frivolous or not.

Irresponsible or not.

Susannah shook off the thought and stepped through the huge stone archway that opened to the beach beyond. A stroll in the sand under the stars would do her good, clear her head. After all, she didn't have to worry about muggers or rapists, even wearing her little red number. Even without her super powers as a vampire, hand-to-hand combat training as a member of the Vamp Squad more than prepared her to handle civilian perps. She was a covert operative for the military, for heaven's sake. She could handle herself and just about anyone else. With vampire power she could handle Godzilla on steroids without even breaking a nail.

She kicked off her strappy shoes and wiggled her toes in the sand feeling the heat of the day in the ground. Her dress sparkled in the moonlight, just as it had that night. She gazed out over the soft waves, remembering.

"Kell, where are you?"

Closing her eyes, Susannah concentrated, reaching out with her mind. But there was nothing there to grasp. Not one single tendril of useable information beyond what she already knew.

She walked up the beach toward the boathouse where she had made passionate love with her handsome stranger – just before he tore out her throat. Well, the sex was good anyhow, that much she could remember. Actually the sex was the best she had ever had, but the end result wasn't anything to brag about. Hopping up on the dock with graceful ease, she strolled to the end watching the lights of boats offshore appear and disappear. Like winking stars, they blinked a secret message in some undecipherable code.

Sadness overwhelmed her for a second or two. Why couldn't she just be happy for Natalia and Yuri? Why did this jealousy, this green monster, have to rear its ugly head and mess with her mind?

Susannah was genuinely sorry she left after the reception and party but it was water under the bridge now. She was on a mission, an important mission.

Guilt inched its way into her thoughts. Damn, she hated growing up and being all mature and everything. Right then and there, on the resort's deserted dock under the stars, she made a promise to herself to apologize to Natalia and Yuri when she returned to Olney Farm, with her own bonded mate on her arm, of course.

It was close to sun-up and she would need to prepare for the day. V-Screen and Vampire No-Doze waited in her room. Her appointment was at seven a.m. and she wanted to be wide-awake. It was unmistakably obvious on the phone that one Ronald Fineblatt knew something about her death. Susannah was determined to find out exactly what the coroner was hiding in his little human mind. He'd virtually choked when she mentioned the name Maddox, then sputtered quick one-word answers to her questions. Posing as a private investigator for a client who wished to remain nameless, she asked all of the standard questions about Susannah Maddox's murder and the whereabouts of the body. When she got to the 'whereabouts of the body' part, Fineblatt's conversation became increasingly incoherent and vague. Keeping the call light and airy, she made an appointment to visit and requested the files be available for her review in keeping with the public access to records under the Freedom of Information Act. It was so easy to intimidate public officials who had something to hide. It remained to be seen what she could actually get out of the man.

Susannah sauntered back across the rough planks congratulating herself on a job well done. Just inside the hotel's lobby, she slid into her shoes and punched the call button on the elevator. Stepping into the car, she turned, intentionally ignoring someone running for the elevator. He was shouting at her to hold the door for him as she intentionally turned her face to the wall. Having had enough of humans for one evening, Susannah punched the button for her floor keeping her eyes downcast, purposefully not acknowledging the man. She couldn't resist a smug smile as the doors closed a fraction of a second faster than the running fellow.

*****

Jordan swore as his leather shoes slid on the marble floor and he smashed his elbow on the closed door of the elevator. "Damn it. I missed her again." He turned to the concierge's desk directly across from the main bank of elevators. "Did you see the woman in the elevator – the one with the red dress on? Do you have any idea who she is?"

Both bellhops standing next to the desk shook their heads.

Jordan stomped across the lobby, fishing in his pocket for money. He folded two crumpled one hundred dollar bills in half waving one in front of each man. Without a word he slipped a C note into the chest pocket of the first man, then the other bill into the pocket of the second.

"One more for her name. Another for information about her business here. Got it?" Both men stared as if dumb struck. "Got it?" Jordan repeated himself with a little more emphasis and a bit of a mental shove.

"Ah, of course, Sir. Ah, who do we, ah tell?" The younger of the two found his voice.

"Just let Manolo know. He'll find me and I'll find you. I don't have to remind you that this is on the down low, right?"

"Of course, Sir." The two sputtered in unison. One headed for the front desk and the other punched the elevator button. They were off.

Jordan was hopeful but never found humans to be particularly resourceful with their limited abilities. However, at this point he was willing to try anything, even human bellhops. Slowly he circled the lobby returning to the club and Manolo.

Who was this illusive woman of his dreams?

Why was she haunting him?

Apparently she was real. He wasn't hallucinating. He, unlike his father, had never killed a human in his vampire existence. There were so many of what his father used to call his small "mistakes".

Jordan had no mistakes.

In order to have mistakes, he would have to have acted completely self centered, immature and irresponsible. That was just not him.

He frowned in frustration, searching for Manolo across the crowded club. The Jamaican man sat near the entrance of the bar surrounded by a bevy of beautiful and hopeful people. Manolo controlled entry to the Mango Bango with an iron hand. The rich and famous knew it was safe to play there. Manolo kept the club environment free of paparazzi but rife with drugs, eye candy or alcohol of choice. He was the ultimate host and he was paid well for his skill at anticipating the guests' needs while keeping their secrets. Manolo was one of the few people who knew about the Metolius coven and didn't seem to mind as long as parties didn't leave a trail of garbage behind. The coven provided him with copious amounts of green printed paper. Under the table of course.

"Yo, Manolo." Jordan wanted help and knew Mango Bango's host would provide.

"Yeah? Wahcha need Jor-*dan*?" Manolo chuckled and waved away the pathetic pleading masses just outside the entrance. "What can I do for you this evening?"

"I saw her again - the woman in the red dress. It was like she was trying to avoid me. She went upstairs but I couldn't catch her. She didn't even look up. What's with that?" Jordan wiped a hand across his face, shaking his head.

"Well now, Jordi, maybe she got a glimpse of da teeth, ya know?" Manolo smiled and pointed at Jordan's pursed lips. Their easy relationship often lead to gentle teasing and Jordan valued the man's humor and acceptance within both the human and vampire world. "Maybe she's a figment of your imagination since you insist on remaining single and unattached. It's da fever, I'm telling ya mahn. You need to get yourself laid, buddy." Manolo had a habit of popping in and out of Jamaican dialect with friends who knew him well. With the club's clientele he was strictly the perfect Jamaican host with the most.

"Manolo, I set a couple bellhops on her trail with C notes. Told them to tell you what they find. She must be staying here somewhere. Text me if you hear anything, okay?" Jordan headed for the door. He wasn't sure where he was going, but he needed air, and the woman in a red dress.

"No problem. Easy enough." Manolo returned to the beckoning throngs at the door. They cheered and begged, welcoming him as if he carried manna from heaven to the starving masses.

Jordan claimed his car from the valet and roared off to the estate well before the morning rays touched the horizon.

He was tired.

He was frustrated.

He was confused.

Actually that just meant he was himself – situation normal, all fucked up. Wasn't that the definition of SNAFU?

That was the definition of his life as well.

*****

Susannah sat in front of the mirror slathering her face, neck and arms with V-Screen. She wouldn't be in the sun long, but no sense taking chances. V-Screen had been around for years but she didn't often need the heavy-duty sunscreen at Olney Farm. The Vamp Squad lived a protected life in their underground facility and had the squad's humans to do things for them during sun-up hours. As a very young vampire, she would have a hard time resisting the need to sleep during the day for many hundreds of years to come. "Vamp No-Doze" helped and she could remain awake a good portion of the day before crashing in the death like day-sleep of a vampire. That was one particular drawback of being a vampire she really hated – sleeping through her favorite soaps. TiVo was actually invented by a vampire for that specific purpose. Humans latched on to it just like they did sunscreen, making millions off vampire ingenuity and labor. Go figure.

"Thank God the old legends about vampire reflections are false," she talked to herself in the mirror as she applied eyeliner and mascara over the V-screen. "I would never get this stuff on straight without a mirror."

All dolled up and ready to impress, Susannah headed for the garage and her car. From garage to garage in a UV protected car, getting around in modern society wasn't that difficult for the contemporary vampire with the necessary resources and money. She punched the CD player and cranked the volume. Shakira blared over the speakers while Susannah sang along and squirmed in her seat to the beat of *Hips Don't Lie*.

Chapter 9

Illusive Answers

The answer is illusive, floating on the wind like diaphanous mist.
Just beyond corporeal reach, but grasped by a mind's casual twist.
Don't lie to me for I will know,
All that is there, deep below.

It is my way, sweet child of mine.
Be afraid! Be aware! For it is time
To seek safe haven, a place to stay,
Because the vampires, walks your way.

Marisella Ferreira, First Female
Coven Metolius, Daytona Beach, Florida

Jordan parked in his usual spot, locked the car with a double beep and headed across the back lawn toward his apartment. Exhaustion and depression showed in his hunched shoulders and slow step.

A hint of vanilla drifted on the early morning air. Jordan paused to inhale the sweetness. Again, he drew the fragrance down into the depths of his body and felt the heat grow. The scent was familiar, actually, more than familiar.

It was the smell that invaded his dreams and lent them the wetness that occasioned the unavoidable dreams of the youthful teen years. Teen years in which he was *stuck*.

The light floral vanilla was the smell of memories for Jordan. Memories so vivid and sweet that the very fragrance meant a kind of innocent love and adoration.

It was the scent of her.

"Jordi." Marisella breathed his name. There was no mistaking the owner of the voice. She was one of the few allowed to call him that childhood name.

A lithe shadow posed, resting against the archway that led to his quarters, a place she graced well. Smoke curled from a menthol cigarette held between two slender fingers. Jordan thought to himself, her nails are always perfectly manicured and always red. Did that mean something or was it his wish?

"Drechell told me about the latest execution. I know those things bother you."

Jordan believed every word that floated from those moist red lips.

"That pig also said he was the one sent to destroy Kellan for disobeying the Master's policy." She stepped closer and, taking him by the hand, drew him into the shadows with her. "Believe me, I did not know until now. Even if I'd known, I could have done nothing. Even now I must tread softly."

Jordan struggled to breath as he stood a hand's span from his ultimate desire. His skin burned with her touch. His mind flared with a fire so hot it melted reason. His body immediately betrayed itself as he struggled to disguise the obvious lump expanding his tailored slacks in her direction.

"S'alright. The old man deserved it." Jordan hissed staring at the apex of her ample cleavage.

"Jordi, he was your father! He did not deserve to be burned alive. We all felt it. No one deserves that!" Marisella lifted his chin with a delicate, perfectly manicured, red-tipped finger. "Drechell is a monster." Her perfect features dissolved into a frown. "You were Kellan's human son. Should you not grieve for him?" Her disapproval was as effective as a cold shower.

"It was four years ago and he was the same kind of monster as Drechell. One monster destroying another – seems appropriate to me. Kellan made me what I am, and yes, he was my father, but fathers don't make their sons into vampires just to simulate some kind of depraved immortal family. I had a life, a mother, a human world. What do I have now?" He fought the shame of tears and lost.

"Jordi, you are but what, eighty, ninety years old? You will get used to our life. It's not so bad." She pulled the young man into her arms in a motherly embrace and kissed his cheek. His blood red tears only added to the luscious beauty of her red lips. "Do you know how lucky you are? We live here in this beautiful place with family around us. Protected."

Jordan knew he could not disguise the motion his cock made in such close proximity to her. He was pretty sure Marisella could feel it as well, yet she still held him close. "Marisella, you may think we have each other, but if Metolius saw you as much as touch me, I would share the same fate as my father. The Master handles problems with bribes, threats and murder. He owns the police and forces those who disagree with him to do what he chooses through brutal discipline or mind control. You sound as if we are one big happy family instead of a depraved cult of blood sucking vampires who hunt innocent humans and feed from them as if they were no more than cattle. You know the stockyard Metolius maintains." Jordan pulled from her embrace overpowering his body's desire to remain. The emotionality of his life was just too much to remain in control so near Marisella.

"I know everything is not as I paint, but I prefer to see the positive side of our existence. I can do nothing about what I am. There are times that I actually think Metolius is correct in thinking we are the next evolutionary step."

Jordan could not miss the falsehood in her eyes as she spoke.

"Someday humans will be kept simply as food or extinguished. They cannot compete with vampires. We are too strong and much more intelligent. Metolius has a vision, an idea for a world where we will walk free and superior. It is not so bad."

Marisella stepped into the glow of the garden lanterns, striking a seductive pose as she drew smoke into her lungs. Her breasts heaved as she blew the gray smoke toward a retreating Jordan. He could tell she did not believe what she professed.

"Who was it that kept saying resistance is futile? Some silly TV program about the future. But they did have a point, and so do I." She threw her cigarette to the walkway and ground the remnants into the pavement with the toe of her black Luciano Padovan boots. "Think about it carefully, Jordan. Metolius is a harsh master and he is also very powerful. He can make or break people, human as well as vampire. I don't want to see you broken again."

This time her words held a concerned softness and Jordan saw the truth in her eyes. She did care about him, if only in a motherly way.

Damn.

"So this is an official warning? Did Metolius send you to talk to me? Or did you just overhear something you thought important to pass along?" He sneered at her words even though he knew her intentions were for his best. It was that damnable need to rebel, to be young and careless.

"Jordan, will you never grow beyond challenging everything in your universe? Did you never learn to listen without prejudice? Metolius is not a benevolent father who will spank you as an errant child. He is the Master. He will have you destroyed without a single thought. I do not bring you veiled threats from him, nor have I heard anything substantial. But I am not blind and you do not always tread lightly with your feet or your tongue. Both can easily be cut off. If you do not heed my warnings, at least be a little more careful of the

First Lieutenant. There are things afoot here within these coven walls. Some may, in the end, be good. But then, some are not so good."

Jordan could not understand her veiled comments.

"Drechell gains power and favor. He detests you. You taunt him. Yet why do you not see the folly in that?" Marisella stepped forward and took his hand rubbing at the scars on his wrist, the only remnants of his last punishment. Metolius had made sure Jordan retained a reminder on his skin. "I nursed and fed you once. It was different then. I am not in a position to do that now." She planted a quick peck on his cheek, spun on her spiked heels and strode towards the manor house.

Jordan watched her sensuous walk as the first rays of dawn burned the sky a deep reddish-purple. Her dark tresses shone with a russet glow as the deep rust colored satin of her clingy dress accentuated the most beautiful figure Jordan had ever seen. He closed his eyes for only a moment, cementing the picture of her in his memory, filling his lungs with her scent.

Memories were all he would ever be allowed to have.

He knew that as much as he knew the sun would rise.

He hated both.

Drechell stood motionless, hidden behind the garden gate. Watching through a small hole in the wood, he grinned as Marisella kissed the brat and then left. He could see that her sexy exit had given Jordan an instant erection. *So... the little boy was growing up*. Maybe he would challenge Metolius for the whore someday. That would be interesting to watch. Maybe he would not live long enough.

Drechell grinned again.

It would be fun to see how far this little tête-à-tête would go. He rubbed his flaccid cock in silence, feeling emptiness where the testicles should be. *Fuck the little bastard*, he thought, as he snuck back the way he had come.

Jordan was completely unaware that the one person who could probably do him the most harm had observed his clandestine meeting. He trudged off to bed more depressed than ever. The woman of his dreams had materialized and then disappeared just as rapidly. The woman he had always desired, above all others, had just warned him to be careful with his place in the coven. What was life, if not one disappointment after another?

The morning rays of hot sunlight broke the horizon as the door to his apartment clicked shut behind him. His bed called and he was ready to sleep away the day. In fact, he was ready to sleep away the rest of his life. To bad life as a vampire would never allow that.

*****

Susannah's tires caught and squealed as she negotiated the tight turns of the municipal garage. It was dark and protected even during daylight hours. As she scanned the lot for an open space, she sought to get a grip on any memory of this place.

It was no good.

There was just a big blank page in her brain. A girl should remember her own death, ya think?

Well, her death she remembered. Everything else was a blur.

Pulling into a compact spot under the sign that said "Employee of the Month", she grinned and shut the engine off, got out and punched the auto-alarm on her keychain. No one would be at work this early, not even the employee of the month. Susannah pushed the call button by the service entrance and waited. Nothing. Pushing the button again she spoke into the speaker.

"Yo, anyone alive in the morgue? I have an early appointment." Nothing.

Susannah, never one to waste patience, pushed the button half a dozen times then knocked on the dark blue metal door.

"S'cuze me, ma'am." A portly man in a brown jumpsuit slid his keycard through the slot, opened the door and rushed on past. Grabbing at the golden opportunity, Susannah followed, slipping through the door before it closed behind the careless employee. Apparently low wages accompanied lack of eyesight and interest.

"Wait. I have a special appointment with the coroner. Can you show me where the morgue is from here?" She smiled sweetly at the man who stopped in front of a janitor closet and was unlocking the door with a huge set of keys.

"You have'ta check in at the front desk. No one is allowed here without an escort. Go up front and ask for Mr. Fineblatt. He's who you need. My shift's over, I gotta go, lady." With that, the man rushed off through a set of swinging double doors.

Susannah could just see the painted stainless steel surface that advertised the morgue in large blood red letters as the doors swung back and forth after the hurried man.

Susannah loved blood red.

"Okay then. No need to bother anyone and Mr. Fineblatt is exactly the man I need." She skipped through the swinging doors,

80

reminding herself to figure out how to v-port when she got back to Olney Farm with her new mate in tow. Maybe her sire would know how and they could travel together! All of those romantic get-aways just waiting for a transporting vampire. Her life would be great as soon as she could find the man she wanted to share it with.

Chapter 10

A Desirous Hope

Could it be, the one I have waited for?
The longing, the need, the love foreswore?
Can I see, through veils and mist,
The one who gave me life's sweet twist?

A thought, a whim? 'Tis my hearts desire,
To search the world over; to find my true sire.
And in his arms, will my life be complete?
Together, from loneliness we shall retreat.

The Poems of Lady Feronda Wellington
Varontage Retreat, North Umbridge, England, 1866

Ronald Fineblatt sat at his desk dreading his seven a.m. appointment. Small beads of cold sweat trickled down his back, despite the air-conditioned room.

Who was this private investigator and why was she looking for information on the Maddox girl's case? The case was over four years old and dead as a doornail, but it still gave him chills. He remembered the girl's body was taken by her father in some absurd theft. When the police followed up, hot on the man's heels, the entire case was mysteriously closed. All evidence was removed and a gag order clamped around everyone's tongue. Serious consequences were outlined in blaring intimidating color if an individual chose to ignore the order.

In any event, the only solid records he had left were the original pick-up order and his standard sign-in sheet of visitors. But, he did have a great memory and that was sharp as a tack.

Both his memory and his brains were expensive. How much he chose to divulge to the private eye depended on her wallet and her looks. He was a sucker for a great pair of legs that accompanied greenbacks. Lots of them. Fineblatt smiled to himself thinking he was not so lucky as to normally end up with a real looker.

A pair of clicking heels drew him from his troubled musings. His ears perked up at the sound.

Susannah took a deep breath, placed the dark rimmed glasses on her nose for a studious effect and toed the door open. "Hello, anyone home? Mr. Fineblatt?"

Ronald Fineblatt had the good manners to rise from behind his desk despite his obvious surprise. The gal that came through the door following a beautifully pedicured toe was definitely a looker. Her long legs were encased in sheer stockings and she was wearing stunning strappy heels. And… she was very young.

He was in luck.

"Ms. Anderson? I'm Ronald Fineblatt. At your service ma'am. Please have a seat." Fineblatt wiped his sweaty palms on his white lab coat and extended his plump pale hand in greeting.

Susannah shook the man's hand then sat in the chair on the other side of the desk, crossing her legs in a slow demonstrative fashion. Already she could feel the coroner's excitement grow along with the length of his little dick. Her ability to "read" humans had doubled during their mission to Afghanistan and it continued to grow under the watchful eye of sister-vampire Natalia. She could now feel human emotions and determine intent with crystal clarity. Obviously, this man was swayed by a pretty face. That would be helpful if he actually knew anything about her death.

"Mr. Fineblatt, so nice to meet you finally. Did you have a chance to find the file on Susannah Maddox? My client will be excited at any new information I can recover." Susannah ran her tongue over cherry red lips leaving a slight sheen behind, on purpose. She was pulling out all the stops and using every tool in the book.

Susannah gave a small sigh and adjusted her glasses, looking over the rims as she leaned forward exposing just a touch of cleavage. Any more would depend on his answer.

"Who did you say your client was?" Fineblatt was obviously fishing for information. She didn't miss his hopeful look.

"I didn't. Confidentiality, you understand. What kind of an investigator would I be, if I ran my mouth all over creation?"

Her fleeting glance a little below his waistline sent Fineblatt's mind racing. Susannah leaned closer and heard Fineblatt's pulse increase measurably, as her tongue did a little circle around her lips. He was so transparent Susannah could feel and hear every thought that crossed the fat little pervert's mind.

This little fellow spent way too much time in his morgue.

Ronald's mouth watered as he eyed the top button of her royal blue satin blouse, praying to God for a costume failure, a loose thread or even a deep breath. "I understand. As a matter of fact, the file has been closed and classified for several years. I did a little research and found not one, but several brick walls. "

Oh please little button, just pop, she heard him pray more fervently as she sensed his mouth fill with more saliva. Ick, sometimes vampire powers afforded a little too much sensory input. Apparently there was more to the story stuck in his revolting little brain.

Susannah took a deep breath that stretched the front of her blouse open just enough to reveal the black lace bra and its clasp between her breasts. "But…?"

She led his thoughts with a sexual prompt.

"Ah, but I do have the original pick-up request for the body. You have to understand this is strictly confidential and I shouldn't even be showing it to you. I could get in a lot of trouble just talking to you about this case."

He slid the form half way across the desk. Susannah caught a mental whiff of Buddha and Allah being added to the growing list of deities to which he prayed as fast as his depraved mind could go. His thoughts told Susannah she had his dick right where she wanted it.

Before reaching for the form with a slow, deliberate movement, Susannah stood up and leaned across the desk. The movement gave Mr. Fineblatt a smashing view of the depth of her cleavage and lacy undergarment.   She couldn't have given a more impressive performance had it been choreographed by the great Anna Pavlova herself.

Fineblatt's heart was near racing and his cheeks were a lovely shade of beet red.

Hitching one hip on the edge of the desk allowing her skirt to ride ever higher on a creamy and toned thigh, she glanced over the form.

"So, Ms. Maddox's body was found on the beach beneath the Boca del Mar Pier. Hum… by a server at the Mango Bango Club. Interesting. Do you know if the woman was registered at the Beachcomber Resort? The Mango Bango is the resort's on-site club right? Pretty swank, so I hear." Susannah leaned over to point out the name of the resort on the form, stretching the two top buttons to the breaking point.

She nudged Fineblatt's mind with a little fantasy in black lace. God bless vamp training - all those hours practicing mental manipulation!

Susannah inwardly winced remembering her petulant behavior

and Elizabetta's patience with her training. There was that guilt again.

"Nah… I mean no, I don't. I only deal with the bodies, not the investigation end." A touch of spittle formed at the corners of the man's mouth and Susannah thought she detected a slight tremor in his voice. "The rest of the file is gone. Sanitized. So this must have been a special case. Closed by judicial order."

Fineblatt looked directly down Susannah's blouse as he licked the drool from his lips. She almost laughed at the man's audacity.

"So this is all there was? Nothing more? Do you recall anything that could help a poor struggling private eye?" Susannah pursed her lips in a seductive pout. To any other male in the universe, her maneuver would have been a blatant warning of purposeful manipulation. However, Ronald was a very lonely, forgotten little man in a morgue full of very unsociable dead bodies.

"Well, there may be a thing or two. Let me think." He smiled into her cleavage again and Susannah clearly felt his overpowering desire to rip her clothes off and have his way with her right there on his cluttered desk. His mind was running a fantasy that she would never allow him to have, but it was powerful bait.

She pouted and heaved a heavier sigh.

"There's more? Really! Is it juicy gossip or just the facts?" Licking her lips on the word gossip, Susanna added a glint to her eye and leaned in, as if sharing a conspiratorial secret.

Ronald was having trouble remembering to breathe. Susannah almost giggled at his thoughts. The yellow number 2 pencil in his hand snapped as he struggled to focus on the words that came from his own mouth. They both knew he should not be telling her so much.

"I kept the log, the visitor's log from that week. The girl's father came twice. The second time he removed his daughter's body. Stole it really. I was out of the office, thank God. He was a kook, nut case from the word go."

Even though she did not appreciate her father's military drive, Susannah bristled at the words Fineblatt spoke.

"Situation was very unusual. Even more unusual was the fact that nothing was ever done about the theft. Internal Affairs rounded up everything they could find. That was it. But they didn't get my log or pick-up form." He tapped a manila folder in front of him on the desk. "Those forms were in my briefcase with me when Internal Affairs raided the place." He smiled like a lovesick puppy waiting anxiously for a morsel.

Susannah could feel his heart pumping dangerously close to a blow out but she pressed on. She desperately needed to know what he kept hidden in his sexed-up jumbled thoughts.

"Mr. Fineblatt, what would it take for a gal to see that log?" The top button of her blouse worked its way loose. At last the satin gaped. She teasingly slid a finger beneath the top flap of the folder.

Oh, God bless who ever made that blouse, Ronald mentally cheered, adding the Roman and Greek Gods to the prayer list.

Susannah strained to keep from laughing out loud. His thoughts skittered across her mind. She heard him pray again.

Just one more button and they would be swinging free. Please, please, please let the puppies come out and play, Fineblatt mentally begged.

Susannah grinned.

"I guess, in the name of justice I could let you have a peek*." That is if you let me have a peek* – his mind was spinning in ever tightening circles, fixated on that second button. *Just one more breath... please God!*

Susannah had to play with this pathetic man. She took a deep breath and held it, flexing the button by microscopic amounts. At last, she pulled a shoulder and... pop!

"Oops!" Susannah gasped with a provocative and completely fake look of horror on her cute little face. After providing a fairly clear view of her black lace bra and creamy breasts, she grabbed the front of her blouse and the log from inside the folder. Turning her back on a thoroughly happy coroner, she quickly scanned the log entries while slowly buttoning her blouse. Besides her father and detectives, a quick scan provided only one other name on the sheet. It was a Kellan Burke the III.

Oh my God – Kellan!

Kellan?

Kell!

It all came back to her along with suitably red cheeks.

It took a great deal to make a vampire blush.

She faced the coroner once again with a sheepish but unrepentant smile. "That always seems to happen at the worst possible times. I am truly sorry if I embarrassed you, Mr. Fineblatt."

Her sire had a name - Kellan Burke the III!

"Ah. No problem. My pleasure. I mean..." The little guy was smiling and stuttering as he realized what he had said. "I mean, well never mind. Can I do anything else for me, Ms? I mean *you*, Ms. Anderson?"

"No thanks. You have been very helpful, Mr. Fineblatt and I am
truly sorry about the blouse thing." With a quick pouty smile and a
wink, Susannah was halfway out the door before she heard his wistful
response.

"Ronald. Call me Ronald."

Chapter 11

And What of Hope's Sweet Scent?

Does hope have a feel, a smell, a taste?
Will it remain in the mind, despite haste?
In seeking the end, an answer, or desire.
Then softly, through life's rough road should retire
That which builds in expectation,
And all that is hope's lamentation.
You mourn the loss of the drive to find
All that is withheld by your own kind.

Andreus Mellina, Historian
Trentino-Alto Adige, Italy, 1904

Susannah pulled her little indigo XKR into the deserted parking lot that overlooked the Smyrna Dunes State Park entrance. The tourists and locals weren't up yet, but the sun had been for a while. She said a little prayer of thanks to Sergeant Miller for installing the intelli-screen tinting on her Jaguar's windows. NASA had come up with the intelli-screen for the space station's main observation window. Embedded microchips automatically detected the level of infrared radiation and adjusted the tinting of the window to protect the occupants accordingly. Heaven only knew where Milo Miller found out about the invention, let alone procured the technology to install it on the Vamp Squad vehicles. It did a great job protecting vampires from sunlight while out and about during the day.

A small niggle of guilt tickled the back of her mind when she thought about the Sergeant.

Susannah had manipulated him shamefully. It was for a good cause, for love. He would understand and forgive her when she had a chance to explain it all to him. That's how adults were supposed to act, to forgive the impulsive young. In the mean time, her car looked really cool and was a safe haven for her in the event she needed to drive during the day.

She shut the motor off with a simple push of the button, pulled a notebook from the stack of papers on the back seat and began to write notes.

- Kellan Burke the III.

- Visited morgue.

- Sire?

- Name she remembered. Brother did she remember!

- And the sex, <u>OMG</u>! Big double lines underscored the 'Oh my God!'.

- Case closed and sanitized.

- All records sealed by judge.

- Name of judge? That was a missing link.

- Pieces collected by Internal Affairs.

- Name of IA agent? Another missing link.

- Father visited twice – Why twice?

- Second time took the body. Weird. Wasn't that against the law?

- In the middle of an investigation? Swiped? Released? Daddy never said. Big whopping missing link. Maybe she should have spent more time talking to the Colonel.

- Body (me) found under Boca del Mar Pier. Under? We were behind the boathouse.

- Drunk (~~stupid me!~~) – foggy memory – not the sex part! Susannah scratched out the 'stupid me' quickly.

- Found by a server at Mango Bango. Name? Missing link.

- Mango Bango at Beachcomber Resort.

She remembered registering to stay at the Beachcomber Resort. They had a special for college students during Spring Break that year. Susannah paused in her note taking. It would be easy to find the name of the manager of the Mango Bango. She had been there last night when some guy tried to catch up to her in the elevator. Maybe she could return to the club tonight and ask around, do private eye stuff. It would be fun as long as no freakoids showed up. She didn't have time to play with humans. She needed to find her sire. Then they would be together and live happily ever after.

Just like a fairy tale princess and her handsome prince, only with fangs.

Cool.

She set her notebook down on the passenger seat and punched up the Internet access on her car's console computer. Her XKR was personalized with extra goodies, courtesy of the government spook department. She loved the fact that she had access to the world at her fingertips. A compact keyboard slid from the center section between the seats as a rich deep voice resembling Sean Connery asked for a command.

"Research and display. Burke, B – U – R – K – E, Kellan, the third." She spelled the name out in crisp letters. The signal bar moved with lightning speed as a graphic of Kellan developed in quick lines. It began with his perfectly coiffed hair, moved to his immaculately tailored suit and ended with his shiny shoes.

It was him!

Her spring-break-midnight-lover-on-the-beach-killer.

He smiled at her from the screen looking handsome and human.

"Nice try, cutie, but those sexy lips hide a very dangerous secret." Susannah grabbed a bag of synth-blood from the cooler on the back seat and slid her fangs into the plastic tubular openings designed for just that purpose. Settling in to enjoy a snack, she listened as the computer digitally verbalized the article next to Kellan's picture.

"*Article one: Kellan Burke III was appointed Vice-President in charge of marketing for Proctor Pharmaceuticals today in a surprising move to improve the companies lagging sales. The private family owned company is the third largest producer of pharmaceuticals in the United States but has shown a significant decrease in competitive sales for three of the last four quarters. Company spokesperson, Marisella Ferreira welcomed Mr. Burke to the office with a sumptuous banquet at the Proctor Family Estate on Friday evening. The company's top executives were in attendance, as well as Mr. Burke's son, Jordan. In a short speech during the festivities, Mr. Burke assured company officials he would, quote, pull out all the stops to accomplish the goal of propelling Proctor Pharmaceuticals into the number one position in sales here and in Canada, unquote. Mr. Burke's previous positions include district sales manager for a large pharmaceutical company in Toronto and as a design specialist for marketing and sales for Mantel Packaging, Inc. Local critics see Proctor's move as a last ditch attempt to revitalize the company and infuse sales with new blood. End of article. Wall Street Journal, March 2004. Next article…*"

Susannah punched the pause button. "New blood, eh? No kidding." She studied the man in the picture.

That was him!

Definitely.

She scrolled through the articles and stopped at the end of the listing. A Miami Herald title caught her eye.

"Kellan Burke, III: Fatal Car Accident Ends in Explosion and Fire," she read aloud. The date on the newspaper was March 27th, only five days after her death. It was the same day her father liberated her body from the morgue.

"No way. No shitting way. Fuck! He can't be dead." Susannah tore the empty bag from her teeth and threw it at the back window over her shoulder. "God damn it. All this fucking work. All the research. All the time tracking this guy down. Putting up with Milo Miller. Aughhhhhh!" She hit the horn with her fist then pounded on the steering wheel several times as she stomped her feet on the floorboard.

"Say a command." Her computer attempted to interpret the noise within the car as a request. Susannah thought about tearing the keyboard from its station and shoving it through the screen but restrained herself at the last moment.

She was an adult, a full-grown vampire now and should not act like a child in the midst of a temper tantrum. Instead she took several pencils from the box she purchased at the office supply store on the way to Florida and systematically broke them into small pieces. Each piece landed somewhere on the back seat.

Systematic destruction helped her reign in her temper. On the fifth pencil Susannah paused, touched the screen and scrolled up again remembering something important.

Kellan had a son.

How could a vampire have a son?

That made no sense at all.

Maybe the kid was an adopted vampire, or a fledgling. If Kellan was dead maybe the kid knew something.

"Research and display. Burke, Jordan, son of Kellan." Susannah sat patiently.

The signal bar zipped across the screen. "One result found." A large spinning number one on the screen accompanied the voice.

"Yeah, yeah. I already know about that one. Refine search and display. Burke, Jordan, Proctor Pharmaceuticals."

Again Susannah waited, tapping a nail against the burl-wood trim of her console panel. Five thousand six hundred and forty-five results popped up for Proctor Pharmaceuticals. Ninety-five included a reference to the name Burke but always Kellan, never Jordan. Sixty-five articles involved the company and various people with the last or first name of Jordan, but no Jordan Burke. She tried again.

"Refine search and display all references. Jordan Burke, Florida." This time she hit pay dirt.

The screen displayed twenty-nine Jordan Burkes, one whose home address was listed simply as the Proctor Estate, Daytona Beach. Under those particular results were sixteen public records of unpaid parking fines and two speeding tickets. Susannah tapped the first record. It showed a scanned copy of the citation noting the location, car, individual and fine. Jordan Burke got a parking ticket for leaving his car in a handicapped parking space at the Mango Bango.

"Holy shit! Now I have a link that actually matches something else. *Yeah* for the Nancy Drew of the fanged world." She patted herself on her own back and giggled. The wheels in her mind began to spin with excitement. *I'll bet the manager at the night club knew Kellan and probably knows Jordan as well,* she thought.

The puzzle pieces were coming together and a fuzzy mental picture was forming. Kellan, loud music, a beautiful night on the beach, incredible sex… Susannah squirmed. Having her throat torn out. Dying. Being dumped under a pier. The picture was becoming more focused and not quite as fuzzy.

"I think I also need to take a closer look at Proctor Pharmaceuticals. If Kellan was a Vice-President, and Jordan lives at the estate, it's possible that Proctor is a front for a vampire coven. Wow, sometimes I even surprise myself." A huge yawn followed her self-discussion with her tech-based alter ego.

Halfway through the yawn Susannah was startled as a jogger ran by and slapped the hood of her car. She could hear the muted words through the excellent insulation of the Jag.

"Yo, wake up in there. The sun is up and I'm running with the gulls."

He could be running with the bulls for all she cared. The sun was definitely up and had been for some time. She should be heading back to the hotel for some shut-eye before she couldn't resist the vampire sleep cycle that was so frustrating for her. It would not be good to fall asleep in her car next to a public park. Someone would report the car and things would go from bad to worse. Besides, a luxurious bed in a hotel was much better than the seat of her car, even if it was a perfect Jaguar XKR with fine leather seats. She started the engine and roared out of the parking lot.

"Take that you nature-loving sun freak." Her tires squealed as she headed for the Beachcomber and a well-deserved nap.

During the short drive it finally hit home – according to the newspaper her sire was dead. No wonder he never came for her.

So how did she survive?

In light of this revelation, what should she do now? Susannah banged on the steering wheel in frustration.

Could Kellan have survived and started a new life somewhere?

Could he have gone to ground to hide or heal? Her memory was so fuzzy. It was time to reevaluate the situation and adapt her strategy.

Proud of her deductive thinking skills and now, a more adult way of handling the world, Susannah considered popping a couple Vamp No-Doze. The pills would allow her to work through the day.

With a little more thought, she decided to tackle the problem of Jordan and Proctor Pharmaceuticals later that night with a fresh mind and a rested body. She was a responsible adult and that meant getting her rest and staying fit so she could do a good job. She was not only proud of herself, but knew Elizabetta and the rest of the squad would be too, when they actually found out how capable she was on her own. Daddy would probably be pissed, but that was his perpetual state, anyway.

She yawned again and ran a red light.

Chapter 12

5 Really Important Lessons for Remaining UnDead

1) Keep your fangs sharp and your gun loaded.
2) Watch your own back.
3) Watch everyone else's back… and front.
4) Never meddle in Coven politics unless you have balls to lose.
5) Never, under any circumstances, piss-off the Master.

Corvell Drechell, 1st Lieutenant
My Personal Rules for Survival
Proctor Manor, Boca Raton, Florida, 1995

Jordan day-slept fitfully, his dreams a crazy mixture of two very different women: one a red-dressed blonde, and the other a sensuous Latina in revealing purple satin wearing leather boots with three inch spiked heels. They danced just beyond his grasp, dashing off to leave him standing empty handed at each turn. He would give chase only to find their images fading before his eyes the faster he ran. He woke at sunset, tired and out of sorts. A quick shower with no shave required. That still tweaked his self-image. He added a splash of 'I'm handsome, irresistible and unattached' cologne. His closet was full of expensive shirts and slacks, but tonight was more for blending in with the beach crowd, without the flash and show.

He grabbed a pair of tan Dockers. Chose a deep blue, short-sleeved silk shirt and slid into his comfortable alligator skin loafers. A glance in the mirror told Jordan he was successful in affecting the casual dress of the local elite. Selecting a slim belt of matching alligator, he finished by adding a large, very sparkling diamond signet ring to his right pinky. The entire ensemble shouted casual yuppie with money, but on the make.

Exactly what he wanted.

Grabbing his wallet bulging with bills and a set of keys, Jordan headed for the Beachcomber. He was determined to spend this night, and every night from now on, scouring the club and beachfront until he found the woman in red that haunted him. Frustrated and now visibly grumpy, he left a good deal of rubber on the driveway of the estate as he departed.

Never once did he notice the black Lincoln Town Car that followed at a quiet, respectable distance.

Corvell Drechell shifted into drive and pulled onto the main road behind Jordan. Where was the punk going? Some clandestine rendezvous with that bitch, Marisella? Metolius would be furious if he knew his woman had a thing for the brat. Providing that kind of information would cement Drechell's position with the Master, once and for all.

Getting in real close was what Drechell needed to affect his plan. He was almost there and taking care of the little Burke shit was an ace card in his deck. Jordan's father should have been offed years ago - it would have taken care of the dad and the kid. At least the kid stayed out of trouble most of the time. His old man was a slick piece of shit though, always on the edge of something. Drechell knew the asshole must have had Metolius by the short hairs. Otherwise, he wouldn't have gained entry into Proctor Pharmaceuticals and the elite circle of the Proctor coven so quickly. What it was, Drechell never uncovered before he was given the honor of roasting the fuck-up to ashes. Just what Kellan deserved, becoming a crispy critter in back of a greasy dive in the middle of Nowhere-ville. The thought brought a fearsome smile to the coven Lieutenant's scarred face.

Drechell concentrated on tailing the candy apple red Viper as it scooted through traffic, weaving in and out between cars and racing through every caution light in the nick of time. Shit! The kid was a skilled driver, Drechell would give him that. Caught by a red light, Drechell watched Jordan's taillights disappear around a corner and swore out loud. With a quick glance for cops, he ran the red light and turned the same corner.

No Viper.

Fucking shit!

Drechell drove down the road slowly, checking each cross street for a sign of the boy's car. The street ended in the parking lot of the Beachcomber Resort. He pulled in to turn around in disgust.

Bingo!

The red Viper was parked next to the entry of the Mango Bango in a space reserved for the handicapped. Drechell drove around the large lot until he found an open space near the exit. So the brat was out partying. About time the kid got used to his own nature and hit the hot spots for a nip or two. Drechell got out, locked his car and headed for the club.

Passing the Viper, Drechell bent and slid a small square package beneath the bumper activating its tiny switch with a flick of his finger. The box stuck to the frame with a soft click. The transmitter was in place and activated. Jordan would not evade Drechell again. Straightening his slacks and tucking his shirttail in, Drechell strolled to the Mango Bango's gaudy entrance.

Jordan breezed through the doorway of the Mango Bango passing a long line of folks all begging for entry. The throng of beseeching women wore various club attire, usually low cut and tight, the tighter the better. Glittery bling covered what their clothing did not. Most of the men wore a variety of expensive but casual designer slacks and shirts. Some even wore suit coats, although it was hotter than hell and the humidity index hit ninety-two earlier that evening.

Jordan enjoyed the hot muggy nights of the Florida coast. His vampire senses tingled with the tiny drops of moisture that gathered on his skin, often trickling down his neck and back in erotic rivulets. He was born in the Louisiana bayou country, born to sweat, and loved it.

His first job of the evening was to check with Manolo. The club manager would have any leads the bellhops might have gleaned. Then his game plan was to cruise the club and beach in a circular pattern, watching for any flash of that honey-blonde hair. The face of the woman who haunted his day-sleep was clear in his mind after yesterday's dream fest. He had memorized his mysterious woman's profile and would know her at a glance. Jordan was amazed that one single person in a series of dreams could have such a clear and persistent memory after he woke, but this woman sure did.

Manolo sat at the end of the bar holding court, determining who would enter his domain. He also decided who would stand outside, praying, or paying for his favor. Jordan waved with a quick smile, as he cut to the head of the line and slipped into the club. Sliding onto the stool next to Manolo, he greeted the manager with a questioning look.

"Any news, my man?" Jordan was hopeful yet frustrated. It showed.

"Jordi, so far nothing. Sorry. But the good news is, there's lots of new blood here tonight. Lots of eye candy." Manolo winked at Jordi. "Maybe you can find something you like?"

"I'm not in the market for just something to my liking. I'm looking for the woman who haunts me, Manolo. Like that voodoo shit you do back in your country. She keeps invading my head. I can't think about anything else. I saw her in the lobby last night." His youthful appearance was slightly marred by the lines of frustration creasing his forehead.

"My country? Yeah, right. You know I'm from Brooklyn, Jordi. So far I've got nothing from the bellhops. But I do have my eyes and ears out. If she comes in, I'll know it." He patted a sulking Jordan. "Ease your mind and have a drink. Trust Manolo." He motioned to the bartender, his fingers moving in a unique pattern that told the woman behind the bar exactly what Jordan needed.

Within seconds, Jordan found a drink under his hanging head. The Bloody Mary was cool and real, although he doubted the blood was from anyone actually named Mary. However, the specially brewed alcohol mixed with the thick red blood provided a quick way to take the edge off his distress. He downed the contents of the glass and motioned for another, quickly emptying the second one as well.

"Slow down, man. You keep slamming those back and the chase will be a stagger, if we do find your woman." Manolo covered the top of his third drink with a staying hand. "Be cool, mahn. Take it easy. We'll find her for you." He turned Jordan's stool around to face the crowd of mingling clubbers and slapped the vampire on his back in an almost fatherly way. "Take youself off now. Come back in a while and see if I have anything for you." Manolo held the drink he'd been covering out to Jordan and pushed him toward a group of laughing party-goers. The women in the group surrounded two men who stood out by their height. It was a three to one ratio and clearly the men were after something more than a one-on-one romp in the hay.

Jordan stumbled toward the group acting as if the alcohol had done a much better job than it truly had. Unless specifically created for a vampire and brewed in the 'old way', alcohol did little for a vampire except tickle the tongue. He heard Manolo behind him holler at the smallest girl in the group. "Martina, me mahn here needs some fine lovin'. Tink you can hep da mahn out?" Manolo's fake Jamaican persona was firmly back in place.

Martina's huge grin was more than enough of an answer to motivate Jordan. He needed to stroll the room and this roving band of luscious women on the make was as good an avenue as any. Causally draping an arm around the grinning Martina, he pasted a friendly kiss on her forehead and was rewarded with a close hug and a subtle grope. Passing the 'fun and frolic' test, he joined the revelry moving across the room like a school of wandering piranha in mating season.

Peering from behind a long line of waving and pleading people lined up at the door to the Mango Bango, Drechel watched as best he could. As Jordan moved out of sight, Drechel shoved his way forward forcing the minds of the human folks he strong-armed, to ignore his presence. At the door he waved Manolo aside and spoke quietly.

"Metolius wants me to keep an eye on Jordan Burke. He just came in." Drechel was a known element and, like most everyone in Daytona, Manolo feared the masochistic coven Lieutenant.

"Of course, Sir. Do come in." Manolo stepped back and unclipped the black velvet rope that held back the waiting masses. No one seemed interested in the fact that a man from the back of the line was being admitted over those who had waited most of the evening. No one even seemed to notice.

This was not good. Manolo hooked the rope in place and stepped back to allow Drechell access. As the Lieutenant disappeared into the crowd, Manolo pinged Jordan and then texted the young man a single name - DRECHELL.

Jordan felt his cell phone vibrate and pulled the smartphone from his pocket. Its light seemed like a beacon in the dim club. He read the name and swore. What was Drechell doing following him? Why hadn't he noticed before? He was so preoccupied with finding the woman in red, he'd lost track of how precarious his life was and the political mechanicians within the coven. It was a mistake that could cost him his life. It cost his father a great car and his pathetic life. Marisella warned him and he had disregarded her words. In light of his tail, Jordan would not be that stupid, or headstrong again.

Jordan pulled Martina toward him and let his mouth slide toward her lips. He whispered to her mind, *let's get some air, baby. Out the glass doors.* Martina giggled and leaned into his kiss as she automatically dragged him toward the exit to the beach.

"Come on handsome, I need air." Martina was moving through the crowd with purpose. Jordan tempered his mental hold and they slowed to an inconspicuous walk. "I hear the beach is beautiful at night. Wanna see?"

Leaving the club, they moved across the sand. They walked like lovers who shared some special secret, heads together and down in flirty conversation. Martina, held enthralled by Jordan's mental grasp, did exactly what the vampire mentally directed her to. Walking toward the hotel, the couple laughed and whispered with their arms around each other. Jordan watched to see if Drechell caught sight and followed. Martina continued to laugh at nothing and whisper nonsense. Once inside the lobby of the hotel, Jordan released his hold on Martina and implanted a thought that would take her to the restroom in a hurry. She would be out of his way for at least five minutes, enough time for him to escape.

Giggling to herself, Martina wandered off to find the ladies room. Jordan headed for the front door. In a hurry, and watching behind him, he felt his phone vibrate again. No doubt an update from Manolo. Reading the small text on his screen, he nearly collided with a couple headed for the same set of revolving doors. Manolo had texted the message that Jordan's woman in red just entered the club and was sitting at the bar downing fruit juice with vodka.

Shit! She was at the club and he could not go back. Jordan texted back, *"Ask her to meet me in lobby. Make up a story. Drechell?"*

Within seconds Jordan read Manolo's answer. *"Trying. Here. Lkng 4 u."* Moving to the secluded corner of the lobby, he sat in a rattan high-back chair with a good view of the hallway connecting the lobby and the club. Any minute now he would see her. Hopefully a face-to-face meeting would explain, or at least bring an end his dream obsession with this woman.

Inside the club, Manolo sauntered up to the new arrival and introduced himself. "Good evening, pretty lady. My name is Manolo. I manage this club. You need something, you see me. Okay?" He smiled and kissed the back of the hand he gently held.

"Why, thank you Mr. Manolo. I'm fine with a couple drinks, then it's off to work for me. I'm a detective and I'm on a case. Anderson, Helga Anderson." Susannah smiled slyly as if she had just uttered the famous line, 'Bond, James Bond.'

"Really, Ms. Helga Anderson. A detective? I may have a lead for you. A fellow out in the lobby would like a word with you." Manolo flipped out his phone and showed her a picture of Jordan. "This is the fellow. He won't wait long."

In perfect character, Susannah looked over her glasses at the picture on the tiny screen. "The blonde fellow in the picture? Been there, done that and I don't think so. He's just a guy on the make and I'm not interested. Thanks anyway but I'm not that easy to dupe, Mr. Manolo." She smiled and tapped the club manager on the forehead with her index finger.

"Nah, pretty detective. I've known this guy for a while. He has information. You should have a talk with him." Manolo wangled, looking overly serious.

"Thanks, but no thanks, Mr. Manolo. I work alone. You don't even know what my case is about, so how can you know your 'man' has information I need." Susannah wiggled a finger back and forth, tisking as she turned back to her drink.

"Because he's the *Man* to go to in these parts, Ms. Helga Anderson. He's *the Man*." Manolo peered seriously at the young woman through the smoke and dim lighting. "Trust me pretty lady, I wouldn't steer you wrong."

"Really? Does that go for all pretty 'ladies' or just the blonde ones? Remember a girl named Susannah Maddox? The girl who was found dead under the pier a few years ago? Did you steer her too, Mr. Manolo? Did she have your help?" Susannah sat on the bar stool and looked directly at the smallish manager. "Well? What would your 'man' out in the lobby tell me about the girl, Mr. Manolo? Or is this some kind of game you play with your patrons here at the Mango Bango?" Adopting a direct confrontational strategy, Susannah cut right to the chase.

"Ah, Ms. Anderson, I can't say, but the man in the lobby can." Manolo suddenly found Susannah's drink irresistible. He focused on the little umbrella that clung to the side of the glass between ice cubes. "You go talk to him and find out." He shoved her drink toward the bartender and signaled for the woman to remove the glass. "On de house."

Finding herself without a drink and summarily dismissed, Susannah sneered at Manolo. Imitating his fake accent with a healthy dose of sarcasm she responded, "I don't *tink* so, Mr. Manolo."

Susannah threw a twenty on the bar, waved off the bartender and strode through the club toward the beach. Reassessing her strategy, but still angry at the way the manager refused to answer her questions, she stepped off the deck onto the beach. Removing her shoes, she kicked a wall of the sand in a high arch and swore to herself. "God damn it anyway. Why can't people just be honest?" With a giggle she thought about her cover name. "Well, why can't other people be honest?"

The question spoke volumes to no one at all.

She was sure Mr. Manolo knew something. He had to have been involved in the cover-up of her death. Maybe he was a vampire. No, she would have seen his vampire aura flashing like a neon sign. Monique had taught her to identify the members of her own coven by their distinct colors. Manolo had no color, just greasy hair and a sleazy handshake-kiss thing. She wiped the back of her hand on her dress.

Manolo made the 911 phone call when an employee discovered her body that night, four years ago. It wasn't that far in the past that he would forget, however Manolo had no reaction when she mentioned the incident, not even a recognition reflex. He was either used to finding dead women, or he was very experienced at handling uncomfortable questions.

She had tried to probe his mind but found a wall. Serious mind probe was not a talent she had developed to an art yet, even with humans. Fineblatt was easy with his overflowing sexual proclivities, but Manolo was different. He almost felt to Susannah as if he was comfortable around vampires and had developed a defensive ability. She could mentally communicate well and tell what people were thinking when strong emotions were involved, but complete thought patterns still evaded her at times especially when the person was aware of what she was trying to do. Too bad Natalia wasn't with her. She would have known everything in the little human's mind in a flash. A stab of jealously danced fleetingly across the neurons in her brain before she could squelch them with her new found self-control.

Where were her #2 pencils when she needed them?

Susannah kicked up a flurry of sand.

"No," she chided herself, "I am a well-trained operative. I can handle this investigation on my own without any help from my father or the Vamp Squad. Damn it! I *will* handle it on my own." Susannah walked the sandy beach as she lectured herself out loud.

Back at the arched entry to the lobby, she paused. That blonde guy was looking for her and she didn't want a repeat of the other night.

So he was the guy to go to for…what?

Drugs?

A hook-up?

Information?

Probably not.

The patrons of the Mango Bango had way too much money and way too little sense, in her opinion. Maybe the blonde guy paid Manolo to set her up. Some guys pictured themselves as the center of the freaking universe and she was definitely not interested. Manolo and the blonde guy could set up some other gal.

Reversing her direction she caught a flash of bile green between the pilings that held up the pier behind the club. The very same pier where her body was found! Someone was snooping around the same spot where she died four years ago, and that someone was a vampire. By the color of the aura, the vampire was a male, a very vile naturist male who obviously fed on human blood. There was no other way to gain the bile green color in an aura without live human blood in the vampire's system.

Susannah crouched behind a palapa and pulled the attached fronds down to cover her own aura. If she could see him, then he might be able to see her as well. Tucked behind a couple chairs and the leaves of the palapa roof, she watched the mysterious vampire sneaking around the pilings. She could clearly see him stop at each huge log and sniff. Like a dog working a scent, he ran his nose up and down.

Searching for what?

Obviously a scent, but the scent of what?

Drechell lost track of Jordan in the club and now hunted by scent alone. He'd lost even that a few feet outside the club. The sand contained too many scents contaminated by the acrid smell of human sweat, sickening sweet sun tan oil, and all kinds of feminine pheromones from the day's sexually over-stimulated sun worshipers. Try as he may, he could not pick up Jordan's trail. Drechell slid a hand up and down the pier then punched it with a fist. The wood cracked and splintered but held. Drechell stomped off toward the club to begin the hunt once again. Maybe this time he could find a clear trail.

Susannah lay down flat against the sand and calmed her thoughts dimming her aura as best she could. She definitely did not want to be seen by the stomping vampire, whoever he was. Despite the limited evening starlight, she could see his face was horribly scarred and she could tell he swaggered to cover a slight limp. Was he a rogue, or a member of some naturist coven in the area? If so, then she was in big trouble. As little as Susannah knew about vampire etiquette, she was completely sure a fledgling like herself would be fodder if caught in another coven's hunting grounds without permission of the Coven Master or Mistress. Fear rose like a red flag firing her aura with an intensity that could be seen from a mile away. Still the vampire stomped toward the club, oblivious to her flashing neon aura behind the palapa. She watched from her hiding place as the man pushed his way into the club and disappeared.

What was that all about? Why didn't he sense her, or see her aura? The fear that made Susannah's limbs heavy, began to recede and she stole off down the beach and around the back of the hotel. The archway entry into the lobby would have to do. She would find a way to deal with the blonde stalker who waited there. After all, she was a highly trained undercover operative. If she couldn't handle one overly attentive human then she didn't deserve to be in the Vamp Squad. With her vamp-enhanced strength and speed, he wouldn't be much of a threat. Out of sight of the club windows, she sped off toward the archway.

Jordan sat in the corner of the lobby, scrolling through Manolo's update. The broken text told the abbreviated story. The woman had been in the club, and then left by the back doors leading onto the beach. Drechell had gone out onto the beach as well. Then Drechell returned alone and obviously angry.

Jordan stood and paced. Were they connected? Was she working for Drechell and Metolius? Or was Drechell following the woman in hopes of finding Jordan? How would the coven Lieutenant know about the woman in red?

Shit.

His mind was running in circles.

No one except Manolo and the bellhops knew about Jordan's interest in the woman. Even they didn't know the entire story. Drechell could have picked up something from Manolo or one of the bellhops, but he didn't have the skill to read minds. He would have had to force them to verbally recount long periods of time and they would have remembered the coven enforcer's actions and mental touch. Manolo would have told Jordan something happened, if Drechell fucked with the human's mind in the club. More likely, Drechell was following Jordan and happened to be in the same place as the woman he sought.

Seriously?

Jordan did not believe in coincidences so closely related. What was going on? Fear grew to tickle the back of his mind.

"Mr. Burke? The woman you asked after was in the gift shop right off the lobby, sir. You said you wanted to know. You said there was another C note in it." The bellhop paused eying the guest who had promised money for information.

"Good work. Thanks." Jordan threw the man a one hundred dollar bill.

"No, thank *you*, Mr. Burke." The bellhop smiled at the huge tip. "If you hurry, she might still be there. Babs is running the register. She may even have a name and room number for your lady, Sir."

Jordan threw the guy another bill and ran for the gift shop. Maybe there was a chance to get some answers after all. As he rounded the corner of the lobby, Jordan pulled up short. Drechell stood near the counter inside the gift shop speaking quietly with the clerk. His back was to Jordan and the woman in red was not there. Quickly, Jordan ducked back behind the corner and trotted the other way.

"Parker, over here." He motioned to the bellhop who was rolling the two crisp one hundred dollar bills into a tight tube.

"Sir?" Parker recognized a lucrative relationship when he had one.

"There is a guest in the gift shop. I don't want to talk to Babs until the shop is empty. Private business, you understand. Would you keep an eye on the shop, and let me know when the guest has left and the coast is clear?" Jordan tucked another much smaller bill into the bellhop's hand.

"Yes, Sir! No problem, Mr. Burke." Parker was off to watch the gift shop.

Jordan closeted himself in his corner and tried to review the facts in his mind. The woman in red had been in the shop. Drechell was in the shop. She had been on the beach, and so had Drechell.

Coincidence or connection?

Why was Jordan dreaming about this woman?

Then she shows up in the flesh and he can't seem to catch her.

How does Drechell know her anyway?

Achhhh! Jordan punched the arm of the chair in frustration. Why wasn't Drechell gone by now? The woman in red was slipping between his fingers once again. He needed to find her, but she was already gone.

His only hope was the clerk.

Precious minutes ticked by as Jordan schooled his mind and body to calm silence. Energy slithered between his still fingers and his brain spun in useless circles. He cast a tight line of mental inquiry toward Martina. The woman was asleep on a toilet in the bathroom.

Perfect.

"Mr. Burke? The gift shop is empty. The last customer left the hotel by the front entrance. Now would be a good time to talk with Babs. She goes on break in about five minutes." Parker was standing just beyond Jordan's chair with his hands behind his back, speaking quietly.

"Thanks, Parker." Jordan slipped the bellhop another bill, then headed for the gift shop. "Keep track of that guy, would ya? Just in case he decides to make a return engagement."

"Sure thing, Mr. Burke." Parker casually exited the way Drechell had left, as Jordan entered the gift shop.

"Babs, how are you tonight?" He had dropped hundreds of dollars in the shop buying little trinkets for Marisella. Babs was a loyal employee of the hotel with exquisite taste in jewelry, often

104

recommending special things that she knew Marisella liked. Jordan had come to know Babs well over the few years she'd worked for the hotel. He actually purchased a set of emerald earrings for the clerk. They were a surprise on her birthday last year, in appreciation for her help, of course.

"Mr. Burke, always a pleasure. How are you this evening?" Babs' smile lit the room with its brilliance.

"I'm good, Babs. I have a question for you. The woman that was in here just a few minutes ago? I think I know her from somewhere, but I am ashamed to admit I can't remember where. Did you, by chance get her name?" Jordan was at his suave best as he leaned on the jewelry case. Still, he nudged her mind just a tad.

"Now Mr. Burke, you know our guest list is strictly confidential." Babs looked down at the case, then back at the man who was always in the market for something from the expensive side. Her simple statement confirmed the woman in red was staying at the hotel.

"I know but Babs, I'm between a rock and a hard place here. I have to keep hiding out when I see her because, well, ya know… a gentleman should remember a woman he has… shall we be delicate here… had a liaison with? It's really embarrassing. Please help me out, I feel horrible, but I can't seem to remember her name. I'm not a cad, Babs and I would hate to have the lady think our little interlude was not memorable." Jordan's eyes actually began to twinkle giving their delicious brown a depth and warmth that no woman could resist. Especially when combined with a subtle mental push. Babs would never feel it, but she *would* capitulate.

"Ah, Mr. Burke, you're such a sweetie. I have no idea why some lucky woman hasn't snapped you up yet. I swear by my mammy, the entire population of single women would give anything for a guy like you." Jordan's act was working very effectively on Babs. She leaned closer. "Well, maybe just this once. So you won't feel so bad. It's the least I can do, for one of my best customers."

"Ah, thanks, Babs. You're a lifesaver. If I am ever in the mood for permanent wedded bliss, I'm coming to find you." Jordan kissed her cheek with a flourish as she slipped a business card beneath his hand.

"Ya know, I think the lady in question needs a little gift from my heart to hers; but you're sworn to secrecy. You can never tell her of my faulty memory, right?"

"Of course right, Mr. Burke. What faulty memory? I have no idea what you are talking about." Babs winked. "Now what would be appropriate, Sir?"

"You've got great taste, Babs. Why don't you pick something out? Whatever you think would remind her of what a great guy I am. Something that says I remembered her after all this time." Jordan was smiling like the cat that ate the rat. "In fact, you pick something. Have it wrapped and delivered to …" He glanced at the back of the card in the palm of his hand. "… Helga? Ah… Helga's room with a little note saying something sweet? And pick out something for yourself at the same time. I owe you for saving my reputation." He was laying it on heavy but it was well worth it. Babs was completely wrapped up in the conspiratorial shopping spree, and being the savior of Jordan's gentlemanly reputation.

"Of course, Sir. I'll do just that. And, I am going to hold you to your promise. A husband like you would make a girl's dreams come true. I shiver to think…" Babs was grinning from ear to ear. She was already contemplating Jordan's gift and the prospect of choosing something for herself that she could, never in a million years, afford as a clerk in the gift shop.

"Okay then, thanks again, Babs. You just made my day. What was she looking for anyway?" Jordan gave the woman a dazzling smile with a quick wink as he turned to leave the shop.

"State map, a new case for her iPod. Nothing big. Have a great evening, Mr. Burke." Babs was turning over pieces of expensive jewelry and reading the tags. She worked on commission and tonight would be her lucky night.

Kellan left the clerk to her task and headed for Parker's station. A state map, huh?

Helga Anderson? That name meant nothing to him. The face was the woman in his dreams, but the name had no memory or connection he could think of. Why would he dream of a woman he didn't know? Wasn't his type anyway? And with a name he didn't recognize? This mystery just got more and more weird with what little information he had gleaned.

"Emille, did Ms. Anderson get a map from you?" The bellhop who manned Parker's station was a Haitian refugee who spoke fluent French and about five other languages. He made the perfect bellman for the international resort.

"Yes, sir. She wanted directions to a little restaurant up the highway, near the state line. I printed her MapQuest directions and let her know that the place she was heading was not a great location for a lady. It was some dive off I-95, just this side of the Georgia line, I think." Emille loved being helpful when he knew he would be generously compensated. Jordan's generosity had a reputation of its own at the Beachcomber.

"Thanks, Emille. Oh, you happen to remember the name of the restaurant?" Jordan slid a Jackson under the man's gloved hand. Emille wore light gray gloves at all times, even in the thick of summer. He was a proper bellman from the old school. However propriety usually flew out the door when green paper passed beneath his gloved fingers. Jordan loved having money, lots of it. Everything had a price and he had the cash to pay.

"As I recall, Mr. Burke, it was a little place call the Sipper. No, wait, Sipper and Tip, I think. Actually, I'm not sure, sir. Sorry. I can look it up for you, Sir."

"Could it have been the Sip-n-Tip, Emille?" Jordan's heart gave a sudden beat.

"That's it, Sir. I can't imagine you'd know the place. It's a real greasy spoon according to the ratings on the tourist map. Didn't even get one star." Emille made a disgusting face. "I did warn the lady, Sir." He made an apologetic motion with both hands then excused himself to help another guest. The twenty had magically disappeared from beneath Emille's gloved hand.

The Sip-n-Tip?

That was where his father was murdered by Drechell and his band of thugs. What did Helga Anderson, his lady in red, have to do with his father and that hole in the wall?

It was time for some answers.

Jordan glanced at the card. Next to the name Helga Anderson was a number. He was betting it was her room number. He crossed the lobby and punched the elevator button.

Room 1846.

Susannah stood on the eighteenth floor waiting for an elevator to take her to the garage. She'd gotten directions to the Sip-n-Tip at the bellman's station and was ready to go. It was a long shot, but it was where Kell, or Kellan, was killed. It was a piece of the puzzle, but what piece she wasn't sure of. She didn't have any clear memories of the little place, but maybe a visit would help settle the fog and jump start her clogged brain.

Now that she knew Kellan was dead, she wanted to remember as much about their relationship and her awakening as she could. If she couldn't have her ideal mate, then at least she could have some memory of him... and her, together. Maybe someone at the diner could tell her what happened that night.

For the first time since she had left Olney Farm, she thought about calling her father and demanding some answers.

Well, maybe asking nicely…

Unfortunately there were as many holes in her file as her memory. If Daddy Dearest had more information, it would have found its way into her file. He was a stickler for correct procedure and an infallible paper trail. When Sergeant Miller snuck her a copy of her file, Susannah was amazed at what little concrete information it did contain. Either Daddy Dearest didn't know… or he wasn't sharing.

The elevator bell chimed and she got in, punched the 'B1' for basement and felt the elevator car lurch as it made its way down to where she'd left her car parked.

Chapter 13

All Roads Lead to the Dead…End, Eventually

The road is long,
With many a blinding turn,
That leads us to you know where
Only he knows when.
But I'm strong,
In mind I carry him
He ain't heavy, he's my Master.

So on we go.
Break rules and I will burn.
No burden am I, to bear,
They'll get there.
For I know,
He would just outnumber me.
He ain't heavy, he's my Master.

Bobby Scott and Bob Russell, Songwriters
Vampire version of: He Ain't Heavy
Recorded by Pyre Records, 1989

Jordan got off on the eighteenth floor in time to hear the doors of the elevator next to his swish shut. He followed the little metal signs that directed him down the hall, to another hall, then to another. At the end of the third hallway was Suite 1846. Helga must be loaded, thought Jordan, her suite took up the whole west end of the hotel.

He knocked, trying to figure out what he would say when he came face to face with his dream woman, at last. What does one say to a live person who has only, up until a day ago, existed in one's mind?

There was no answer to his knock. Next to the double door panels was a small ivory button embedded in a maple frame with a gold metal grid that covered an intercom speaker system.

Jordan pushed the button and could hear a doorbell ring inside the suite. Unfortunately that was all he heard. Impatiently he rang again.

No answer.

Shit!

So close and yet... what? So far?

So close, so close and yet so far – it was the theme of his life lately. The song rattled through his frustrated brain like a rickety train on a downhill slope; unstoppable and repetitive.

The other elevator!

It must have been her leaving for the Sip-n-Tip. If she wasn't in her room, and the bellhop had given her MapQuest directions, she was probably on her way.

Damn, this Helga of his was a slippery woman.

He sprinted through the hallways grabbing at the corners to speed his turns. He hit the down arrow light on his elevator, and stood there. His vamp hearing told him someone's elevator car was seventeen stories down and still moving. Glancing around to see who might be watching, Jordan forced his set of doors open and jumped. He had to get to Helga before she got to her car.

Hitting the bottom of the shaft with the grace of a cat, Jordan pressed the emergency release and the door opened onto the basement floor in the garage. Just in time to see an indigo Jag speed past with Helga at the wheel.

"Fucking shit! I just can't fucking catch this woman," he growled, stepping out of the way of the descending elevator in his shaft. Mentally wiping the security tape which existed somewhere in the hotel behind locked doors, Jordan took the stairs to the main floor at vamp speed. He would catch her exiting the parking lot and jump in front of the car if necessary. He had to catch this Helga woman before she left the hotel or he would be driving all night to snare her.

Without any thought, except the desire to catch a speeding Jag, Jordan hit the front exit and kept going... right into the iron arms of Corvell Drechell.

"Hey, boy! Slow down there. Where're you off to in such an all fired hurry?" His sadistic grin was even more disgusting than usual, given the fact that he only possessed one fang.

Jordan stared at the man, recognition coming just a second too late to wrestle free. As Helga's speeding Jag screeched by, Jordan took a deep breath and held it in complete, unmitigated frustration.

Drechell hauled the young man closer by his shirt and yelled in his face. "I said, where do you think you are going in such a hurry, BOY?" A spray of spit accompanied the word 'boy'.

Jordan shook himself free with a growl, his fangs instantly extended. "Apparently nowhere, Corvell. Is there something I can do for Metolius' number one ball-less wonder?"

Taking a casual step back, Jordan hooked both hands on his hips, framing a cocky stance he did not truly feel.

"You little piece of shit, I'm glad I had the honor of toasting that fuck-up you called a father. I can't wait for the orders to do the same to his whoreson." Drechell sneered as he ground out the words.

"Oh, get a grip Drechell, you haven't got the cojones, and you know it. In fact, everyone knows it, num nuts." Jordan was all bravado praying Drechell would swallow it. He knew Drechell would leave him be in public. Human eyes watched the two men.

The coven's number one enforcer could eliminate anyone for any reason and probably not face a single question. That was, of course, if anyone was brave enough to tattle on the crazy brute. However, even Drechell would not create a mess in public.

"You look like guilt walkin', boy. You have something going on here, and I'm gonna find out what it is. You can pull the wool over on some, maybe sneak a little smoochy-smooch in the garden with that bitch, Marisella, but you can't con a con. I know a sneaky piece of shit when I smell him, and you are one ass-leaking piece of shit, Burke. Save us some time and just fess-up, boy. Or maybe, I could beat it out of you? What da ya say, huh?" Drechell was inching forward as he spoke.

"I have no idea what you are talking about. I think all those knocks you've taken, in the name of loyalty to Metolius have damaged the piece of garbage you call a brain." Jordan took a step toward his car and pressed the unlock/auto-start button. He was only a few feet from his vehicle. "Why don't you take a vacation, Drechell? Rest up and think about everything Metolius has taken from you. Then, if you can find the balls, come after me. Any time, any place." Jordan waved the other vampire off. He turned his back and strode away in a move calculated to seem as if he had nothing to hide, and was bored with the entire situation. He knew he was sauntering on thin ice.

"You son-of-a-bitch. I'll get you. Maybe not today, maybe not tomorrow, but I will get you. I'm on your scent, boy. Your ass is mine." Drechell was screaming at the young man as Jordan stepped to his car and slid into the driver's seat.

Before closing the door, Jordan yelled back in defiance, "You wouldn't know what to do with my ass, or anyone else's, Corvell, you got no balls. Remember?" Jordan slammed the door and burned rubber backing out. He aimed the car directly at a fuming, spitting Drechel and gunned the engine.

"You're dead, boy. Dead and burned. Ashes, punk!" Drechell

jumped aside as Jordan's car sped past.

Jordan was hoping Drechell would get out of his way, before the car hit the man. The coven enforcer's vampire speed would be enough to carry Drechell over or around the car. It would also allow him to jump onto the roof or back of the car and hang on. He may even have the strength to rip the top open and climb in. That would be a real bad scene. Jordan guessed Drechell would not do any of those things in the parking lot of a resort hotel with any number of witnesses. Drechell was dangerous, crude and foul mouthed, but he wasn't dumb.

Jordan's hands gripped the wheel with super-human strength leaving permanent indentations in the rubber cover as his car sped clear. He slowed to make the turn and saw Drechell in the rear view mirror standing in the parking lot, a middle finger of each hand raised in salute.

Jordan smiled.

His rouse had worked, thank God! He was a great poker player with one hell of a bluff. But poker only cost money when you lost, not your life.

Entering traffic at normal speed, he worked the GPS on his dash, searching for a restaurant called the Sip-N-Tip.

"Searching…" the female voice told him. "Recalculating…Sip-N-Tip Restaurant, one hundred thirty-nine miles to destination on right."

"Thank you, my little British babe. I-95 all the way to the Yulee cut off and bingo, the Sip-N-Tip, on the right." Jordan hit the thruway and put the pedal to the metal. His Viper settled to the pavement, tires hugging the road as the digital read out on the speedometer moved through eighty mph.

"Here I come, Helga, ready or not." With any luck he would overtake the woman and her cute little Jag. Jordan cranked the tunes and activated his Fuzz Buster. No need to play chase with the local men in blue tonight.

*****

Susannah sang along with the latest album from Shakira, her all-time favorite singer. She'd been hooked on the Columbian belly-dancing singer since the Afghanistan mission. Susannah learned to emulate the singer's moves as part of the squad's cover as Tajikistani entertainers. As a sort of present for her great work, Sergeant Miller purchased several CDs of Shakira's songs, as well as her instruction video on belly dancing. Completely blown away by the performer, Susannah stashed the CDs for her road trip before she left. Now, Shakira's Oral Fixation tour played their mixture of Latino rhythm and modern lyrics over the enhanced speaker system of Susannah's Jag.

The Sip-N-Tip was another fifty-six miles away according to the satellite imagery on her console computer station. If she kept her speed up, she would be there about an hour before closing time. What she would find was as much a mystery to her as it probably was to anyone. The people working there wouldn't know her from the next speeding tourist, and certainly hadn't ever met her. She would be surprised if they remembered Kellan's death or could tell her anything of value about the fire. However, she would leave no stone unturned in her search.

"So little Miss Detective, what are we looking for at the shady dive where the notorious Kellan Burke the Third was killed?" She spoke to her reflection in the rear view mirror, squinting as she interrogated the blonde who squinted back.

"Ah, that is the million dollar question. I plan to use my superior deductive skills to answer two rather tough questions. Number one: *What was Mr. Burke doing at a dive like the Sip-N-Tip* and, two: *Why was he killed?* Oh, and the second two: *Who killed him*? And the third two: *Why didn't someone do something to save him*? No one just leaves a Maserati in a parking lot, where it explodes and burns the car, literally to ashes. With its occupant beside the vehicle."

Susannah thumped the stack of printed reports on the accident. From the police reports that didn't jive, to the six different newspaper articles that all reported their own versions of what happened. Nothing matched or fit. Even the insurance report looked contrived. There were more holes in the police report than your standard kitchen strainer. Anyone with a speck of common sense, and primary reading skills, could tell right off the bat, the report had been fabricated. And not well at that. The officer's signature at the bottom was so scrawled it was unrecognizable. Some of the original evidence listed was faded by water damage in very specific spots on the paper. Almost as if someone had blotched certain areas on purpose. There were no evidentiary remains to log and Metolius Pharmaceuticals had taken custody of Kellan's ashes, in the name of his son. The ashes were scattered in the ocean, supposedly. No mention of a wife or ex-wife or family, other than a son named Jordan who now, not surprisingly, lived at the Proctor estate outside Daytona Beach. The illusive son kept a low profile, except for tickets. She couldn't even find a picture of the boy. Zero and zero just don't equal two, and too many coincidences made for a dirty crime. Something was certainly rotten in Denmark. Susannah giggled as she strung the clichés together in her mind. Sometimes this detective stuff could be real fun.

The CD player clicked, and the next album began with Susannah's favorite: *Hips Don't Lie*. Kellan's mystery slid by the wayside for a few minutes as she sang and rocked her hips in the seat behind the wheel. The dark highway had little traffic after midnight and Susannah weaved her car to the music as she belted out the words.

Thirty-two miles to go.

Jordan saw the taillights ahead zigging and zagging, before he was close enough to recognize the car as Susannah's Jag.

"Jesus, somebody had a little to much to drink tonight. That's all I need is to get into an accident with a DUI on a deserted stretch of highway," he thought, and slowed his vehicle leaving about a quarter mile between the swerving car ahead and himself. He watched carefully, waiting for the car to skid off the road but it seemed to stay on the pavement, making equal timed zigs and zags. After a mile or so, he realized the car was creating an intentional pattern. That was really stupid at... he checked the speedometer, ninety-five miles per hour.

Jordan sped up, closing the distance once again.

Hot damn! It was a blue Jag!

Obviously the driver did not notice a car on her tail because she continued her weave for several miles. Finally the Jag straightened out and slowed near the small diner ahead. The neon sign was still lit and the glaring letters spelled S-I-P-I-T-I-P. The two other sides of the N were burned out making it look like the name of the diner was really SIPITIP. Susannah's car pulled into the gravel parking lot and slowly circled around the back of the building.

Jordan pulled up to the front door. Entering the building just as Susannah's car came around the back corner, Jordan quickly slipped through the door, and quietly seated himself in the last booth near the end of the bar. The place was empty and the corner was dimly lit, providing a great view of the diner's entry.

The waitress for the establishment was behind the bar with her hands deep in soapy water, singing to the country western song that blared throughout the diner. She hadn't noticed him enter.

Now all he had to do was wait and watch. Jordan slumped partway down in the seat and leaned against the wall, almost disappearing into the shadows.

Susannah came through the same door as Jordan. She immediately wiped her hand on her jeans, examining the grimy handle she had just released with a disgusted look on her face. She strode to the bar, glanced at the stool before sitting, then carefully perched on the cracked and stained vinyl seat. Drawing a napkin from the folded stack in front of her, she spread the white paper out then folded her hands on top of the long wooden bar and waited patiently for the waitress to notice her.

After a few seconds she cleared her throat.

After a few more, she coughed a little.

When the waitress didn't budge, Susannah picked up a swizzle stick from the container and sailed it across the distance, so it landed in the woman's soapy tub. It floated there on the greasy water.

You would have thought she had discharged her service weapon. The startled waitress spun with a squeal. "Oh my Gawd, girl. You scared the living bee-jezuz out of me. I just didn't hear you come in," she yelled.

Susannah raised an eyebrow and pointed to the headset and mic she wore.

"Oh yeah. Sorry. Name's Minnie. What can I get for ya, honey?" She removed the headset with froth covered hands leaving soapsuds along the sides of the long bright red hair that was piled at least twice as high as her head. She looked like a bit player in a Carol Burnett vignette from the sixties, crossed with Amy Winehouse.

"What's with the ears? Not your kind of music?" Susannah motioned into the air as Tammy Wynette twanged *Stand By Your Man.*

"Nah, I love country. It's a karaoke headset and mic. I'm practicing to be a star. Soon as I get me a demo cut, I'll be on my way. Would you like to order dinner or just somethin' to wet your whistle? We got a cook till 1:00 AM and serve until 2:00." Minnie smiled and tugged gently at her, now very obvious and very high, hairpiece. Her southern accent was thick enough to cut with a knife.

"Just a Coke, please. Lot's of ice, if you don't mind." Susannah took another napkin and spread it in front of her so she could let her elbows rest on the disgusting bar. The wood was dark with eons of stains, several unidentified sticky spots and one glump of who knew what, stuck to the customer's side of the rounded edge of the bar.

Minnie plunked down a Mason jar filled with ice and what appeared to be Coca-Cola foaming over the top. "Hotter than Hell on bar-be-cue day out there, ain't it? Should be, when the sun goes down it gets cooler, not hotter and stickier." Minnie wiped a forearm across her damp forehead. "And my shift don't end till after 3:00 AM. That lazy Buck left me with the morning dishes. His fat ass is good for nothing, know what I mean?" Minnie spoke quietly and shot a dark look toward the kitchen. Obviously Buck's fat ass was still around.

Susannah pressed the cold jar to her lips and took a small sip. It tasted flat. Not at all like when she was human. It had none of the satisfaction or coke burn she had loved as a teen. But it was tolerable. "As a matter of fact, Minnie, have you got a minute? I'm a detective, a private eye. I'm on a case right now, looking into the Burke murder a few years back. Did you work here then?"

"Oh, hell yeah! I've been here since I was sixteen, workin' for that asshole, Buck. Goin' on thirteen or so years now. I was workin' that night, and I sure do remember the mess afterwards. Had a couple of guys in here for dinner. I was servin' em up some good old fashion chicken fried steak with fries and gravy." Minnie shook her head and looked at the ceiling, remembering. "Right in the middle of dinner, that black boy up and ran out yellin' about some car on fire, and a man burnin' in the back parking lot. By the time Buck got his huge ass in gear the car was almost done, and the man was ashes. Buck damn near fell off the porch. He was scared shitless, and pulled the handle right off the damn tap out back. There was water runnin' everywhere. Flooded the storage room and soaked all our potato flakes. We didn't have hash browns for a week. Whew yee! That was some night." Minnie slapped her leg and did a little jig. "More excitement in one night than I seen in all the years I worked here. Except for the one night some bikers came through with an albino chick riding a cherry Harley. I remember-"

"What about the guys that were in here having dinner? What did they do?" Susannah interrupted Minnie's little trip down memory lane before she learned something that she really didn't want to know.

"Ah shit. That black boy skipped on the bill. I remember that, clear as day. Came out of my salary, it did. I think the older guy with him took off with the ice cream truck, and the nig-"

"Wait a minute. What ice cream truck? Who had an ice cream truck?" Susannah asked wide-eyed.

Jordan listened intently from his hidden corner across the room. His vamp hearing allowed him to hear as if he were sitting next to Susannah and the wacky waitress. An ice cream truck? That had never been mentioned before.

"Yeah. The two of them turned up in an old beat-up ice cream truck. Had a huge box in the back. Never got a name or license plate.

They booked before the fire truck got here with the police. I bet they was into somethin' that they didn't want the cops to see, and I'd give you ten to one, there weren't no ice cream in that truck. The cops put out an 'all points' but nothing ever came of it. They didn't have anything to do with the fire anyway. They was both in here eatin' when the car went up." Minnie rolled her eyes. "Never did find out what happened. The cops came back a time or two. They scooped up what was left, took their yellow tape and disappeared. Never offered to clean up or fix nothin' either." Minnie adjusted her slipping hair again. "This thing gets heavy after a while, ya know." Minnie winked as she removed a long bobby pin and reinserted it higher on her head.

"So the police didn't ever explain what happened, how the fire started, or if it was set?" Susannah was digging for answers.

"Nah. They said it was private stuff. Couldn't tell nobody. Buck never saw nothin' and neither did I. I think that's why the boy ran. He saw something for sure. Buck was raring mad, and tried to find out the story because he wanted to sue for getting the plumbing fixed, ya know. He never got nowhere – all dead ends. Then one day he came back from town, all quiet and white like a ghost. I think, real scared. Said not to talk about it any more, or he'd have to fire me. So I shut up. I hate this job, but it's the only one I got til my big break. Did I tell you I'm gonna be a star?"

"I'm sure you will be, Minnie. So the guys took off in an ice cream truck with a big box in the back? Anything else?" Susannah slid a twenty across the bar, and winked just as Minnie had, a minute earlier.

"Well, yeah. Actually, the box was a coffin I think. Well, it had that shape, ya know. Weird, an ice cream truck tot'n a coffin but hell, now-a-days you see everything. Take that albino on the bike, she was one hell of a rider and the guys wouldn't say boo to her. She was like some great white queen with her ridin' harem and…" Minnie was off on her albino story.

"Minnie, thanks for the soda. What do I owe you?" Just as Susannah was fishing for change, Minnie noticed the slumping young man in the corner.

"Oh my goodness, I didn't realize I had another customer. Could you wait just a sec, honey? I'll be right back." Minnie dried her hands on a towel and scooted around the bar toward the customer in the corner booth.

Susannah turned to see who had come in and caught the slight greenish aura of the man in the booth. Her fangs extended of their own volition and she hissed deep in her throat. The guy was the same blonde stalker in Manolo's bar, but he was a vampire. From the color of his aura, he was obviously a naturist vampire.

One who fed from humans!

Chapter 14

The Power of Suggestion

In the world of the vampire, suggestion is command.
You can fight it, hate it, but by his hand,
Will you do his bidding, and follow his course,
At the end his way, is naught but force.

And force he does, to make a way,
For all that seems luscious, and promiscuous play.
But behind the curtain, the vampire does wait,
Controlling and crafting, the victim's fate.

Selinna Canova, Author
The Thoughts of a Victim's Sister
Bozeman, Montana, 1998

"MINNIE, COME BACK HERE NOW." Susannah slid from the stool keeping her back to the bar. Her fledgling ability to command humans, weak humans anyway, was put to good use. The waitress stopped dead in her tracks, spun and walked back to stand mute and dumb-founded next to Susannah.

Who are you and what do you want? She psyched the vampire in the corner, sure he would understand and hear her. That was another little skill she recently picked up working with her sisters on the Vamp Squad.

Jordan's eyebrows rose, as he stood slowly and spoke to her. "I don't want any trouble. I've been trying to find you. I was at the resort, remember? You were in the elevator."

Stay where you are. Don't come any closer to me, or this woman. You need to leave. Get out, and don't cause any trouble here. I'm not from a Naturist coven, and I won't let you hurt this human. Susannah crouched, ready to defend Minnie if need be. She calmly pulled a Beretta Cougar 8000 from her handbag. *These bullets are especially designed for our kind. You don't want to test your immortality today, buster. Now, back off and get out.*

"Look, Ms. Who-Ever-You-Are, I don't want any trouble. I just want to talk. What's wrong with that? I think we have something or someone in common. We have a connection that I can't get out of my mind, or my sleep for that matter." Jordan was inching forward but froze at the sight of Susannah's specially designed gun. It wasn't a standard Beretta, and he could smell a distinctly offensive odor emanating from the gun's magazine.

Garlic extract?

You've got to be kidding!

Yeah, and what, or who would we have in common, Mr. Who-Ever-YOU-Are? Susannah didn't relax her stance but noticed the man's graceful movements and handsome face. She was ready for anything. She had her combat training under her belt, and was a certified undercover operative. She could handle Mr. Blonde and Sneaky.

"How about we figure that out over your soda. My name's Jordan Burke. You still drink soda?" Jordan stood his ground and let the name sink in. He could see he hit pay dirt. The name meant something to her, but he had no idea what. "Can we start with your name? Maybe I'll recognize it. Is it really Helga Anderson?"

"You're Kellan Burke's son?" Susannah was stunned.

"And you are?"

"Sus...Helga Anderson. You promise to leave these humans alone?" Susannah spoke out loud now, but was not going to let her guard down until she had his promise of no feeding off these people. No matter how desperate she was to find out about her sire, she would not allow that.

"Well, Sus-Helga Anderson, I'm not hungry, and for your information, I only feed with permission. I'm not an animal, contrary to what you techno-modern vamps believe. Just because we choose to live the way nature intended, does not mean we treat humans like Big Macs. We don't scarf the special sauce whenever we feel like it, and toss the wrapper aside. I use other sources of blood as well. Now, how about that talk?" Jordan flashed his winning smile that usually had women falling at his feet. He held out both hands as if to demonstrate his openness.

"Alright, fine. But I'll be checking up on you Mr. Burke. And we sit in the open. I face the door and I keep my gun available." *Minnie, go to the kitchen, then bring us both a Coke, heavy ice. Smile and act as if nothing weird has happened and we are normal customers who came in for a cool drink.* Susannah mentally programmed the waitress who blinked, and walked toward the kitchen.

"Nice trick, Ms. Anderson. Where'd you learn how to do that? I sense you are not very old. What thirty years as a vampire? Forty?"

Jordan sat at a table in the middle of the room facing away from the door and gestured to the seat across from him.

"Where are you from anyway? I wasn't aware that Metolius has allowed any other covens to encroach on his territory." Jordan noticed how slender and feminine the woman's hands looked curled around her Beretta. His groin tightened, despite the danger in which he found himself. When had firearms become sensual?

Susannah gave the young man a speculative look. "I'm here on business. I work alone." She tried the line from some grade B detective movie; 'I work alone'. Right! The man's casual sprawl and laid-back manner was engaging, not to mention, in the full light of the room, his slow sensual smiled tickled her core.

"You don't look tough enough to be a rogue."

"Looks can be deceiving." Susannah shot back.

"Well, I know you're not old enough to protect yourself from the likes of Metolius and Drechell. So what are you after besides trouble? It's dangerous asking about my father's death." Jordan leaned forward and took the soda from a quiet and reserved Minnie who still wore a blank look, as she moved through the restaurant.

"I'm checking out the story for a client. Cheers." Susannah toyed with her soda and took a sip just to prove she could. "What do you know about your father's death?"

"Everything. You're not a very convincing liar, Sus-Helga." Jordan snickered at the phony name. "Come on, what's your real name? You can trust me."

Just as he finished the corny statement, Susannah suddenly flew from the chair and assumed the crouch and aim stance once again.

"Trust you? A vampire that feeds on anything and everything? And brings along a friend for reinforcements? You think I'm crazy, Jordan Burke?" Susannah hissed. "Tell your friend to stay the hell away or I'll take you both out."

Her upper lip curled back in a snarl over instantly appearing fangs, and she was growling at the intruder advancing on them from the doorway. Susannah's first thought was the man's aura was the darkest bile green she had ever seen. Her second thought, was that he looked exactly like the profile of the guy under the pier.

Jordan turned just in time to see Drechell streak across the floor, grab the blank faced Minnie by her fake hair piece and sink his fangs into the woman's neck. "He's not my friend, or any reinforcements I called. Let's get the hell out of here, fast!" Jordan was on his feet dragging Susannah toward the door at v-speed despite her gun.

"Wait, what about Minnie and Buck?" Susannah dropped her gun on the floor as she reached to catch her balance, stumbling after Jordan.

"Too late for them now. But not for us, if we move it." They hit the door about the time Buck came out of the kitchen, meat cleaver in hand and started hollering. He didn't holler long. A piercing howl ended any noise from inside the diner.

Jordan hit the auto start on his car and released the doors. "Get in!"

"No. I have my own car." Susannah felt herself v-ported into the passenger side in a split second as Jordan appeared next to her. "My pur..." Her purse appeared on her lap as the car's tires spun and the Viper leapt across the pavement.

"My gun..." The gun she'd dropped immediately appeared in her hand.

"Use it if you have to, but preferably not on me. I find it hard to drive with bullet holes in me." He pushed the barrel of the gun away from his chest.

"You'd not be driving long with these bullets, Mr. Burke, I assure you." Susannah tucked the gun into the side door pocket and reached for the seat belt. "Are we being followed?"

"I don't think so. But then again, I have no idea how Drechell found me in the first place. I didn't have a tail when I followed you out of the Beachcomber Resort in Daytona Beach. I'll keep an eye out though."

"You followed me? I didn't..."

"Why were you weaving all over the road anyway?" Jordan was curious about everything this woman did. Said. Thought. Dreamed. Wanted...

Oops! Bad road to follow, he thought with a grimace, then turned his concentration to the task of driving.

"Shakira; *Hips Don't Lie*. My favorite. I didn't see you following me. Do we have a tail? Who is that guy? I've never seen such a vile aura around a vampire in my life." Susannah shivered recalling Drechell's color. He definitely needed a diet change. "Poor Minnie. She wanted to be a singer, a star."

"How effective is that little gun of yours?" Jordan was looking in the rearview mirror at a black Town Car that just appeared. It seemed to be gaining on them.

"Very. It's been tested and proven effective on very strong vampires." She patted the gun in its little pocket on the door. "Your

Drechell is following us, right?" She twisted in her seat and glanced at the speedometer. "Can we out run him?"

"Hello! This is a Dodge Viper, in case you didn't notice. Of course we can out run him, for a while. On the other hand, sooner or later we need to stop for gas. Vipers aren't known for their fuel economy. How good are you with that gun, and why do you hunt vampires?"

The edge in Jordan's voice was clear to Susannah. He was obviously afraid of what she did, and how she did it.

"I don't hunt vampires. I work for the government, Mr. Burke. I just have access to some unique weapons, and some other little toys that make my assignments easier." She was trying to sound sophisticated, in control, instead of scared out of her mind, stuck in the car with the son of the man who turned her into a vampire, and on the run from a nasty naturist vampire who liked to feed on humans. "How do you know this guy's name?"

Jordan considered her question, and wondered just how much trouble he would get in for discussing coven business with an outsider. It was probably a moot point, and too late for him anyway. Drechell had seen him with Anderson. Associating with other covens, or rogues, without permission, was forbidden. With a long disgusted sigh, he decided that honesty was the best policy, since they seemed to be in the proverbial swamp together.

He looked in the rear view mirror. The alligators were closing in for the kill.

"He's the enforcer for my master. I belong to the Metolius Proctor Coven and Corvell Drechell is Metolius' First Lieutenant. He's a real animal. If you trust me on nothing else, trust me on that one. He, and some of his henchmen, killed my father right back there at the Sip-N-Tip. But you knew about that already, didn't you? You were nosing around asking questions. Mind if I ask why, one more time?" Jordan glanced at the young woman of his dreams. What was their connection. But why had he dreamt of her?

"Mind if I ask why you're chasing me, and why you want to know my business, *one more time*?" She was playing along well, considering the fact that her nerves jangled and her stomach continued to flip.

"Quite honestly, you appeared in my dreams a couple weeks ago and I can't seem to get rid of you. When I saw you at the resort, I thought I'd see what the story was behind your appearance in my life, both sleeping and awake. Now you." Turn about was fair play.

Well, Susannah thought, at least she had landed in the dream world of a hunk, instead of some guy like the one who was following them. His blonde good looks and dark chocolate eyes made her stomach flip in a different way. "My client has questions about your father. I'm following leads. That's all." Susannah smiled sweetly.

Well, …" Jordan waited for a name, hoping Sus-Helga would fall for one of the oldest tricks and fill in her real name for him.

It didn't work.

"Yes…"

"Well, Sus-Helga, can I just call you Helga or Sus? It's weird putting the two together. They really don't work for me. Were your parents fighting when they named you?"

"It's Helga, Helga Anderson." Susannah was sticking to her original alias until she figured out this hot mysterious hunk who drove like a NASCAR racer.

"Well, Helga. You don't seem like a Helga. I've swallowed a lot of things in my lifetime, but I don't think I can take swallowing the detective one. Want to try again? Maybe a little more truth would help. And if you are a detective, you might want to get that little peashooter out and handy. We are about to have company." Jordan pointed behind him at the Town Car close enough now to identify the driver's face. Obviously Drechell was hell bent on catching them and was pushing his car to the max.

"Shit! Why is he following us, or rather you?" She was full of question-answers to his questions. This game was getting her nowhere, but she wasn't giving anything up yet.

"What was it you were doing at the Sip-N-Tip?" Jordan queried again.

Susannah was losing patience with Jordan's persistent question-answers as well. He was playing the same game as she, in his own way. They could dance around each other all night at this rate. The frustration was building and she realized she was getting nowhere at over a hundred miles per hour.

"Alright, fine! I came to Florida to find my sire, the vampire who turned me. Then I find out he's dead and his son is following me around like some crazed stalker. And some maniac is following him. Satisfied?" Susannah unbuckled her seat belt and shinnied around to face the gaining car as she aimed her gun at the guy in the Town Car.

"You're Susannah Maddox? Holy shit!" Jordan swerved at the declaration. "You're the reason they cooked my old man. What the fuck! Hey, hey, hey, don't shoot out my back window." Susannah could tell by the look on Jordan's face that he had been shocked by her true identity.

"You're supposed to be dead. What happened? Where'd you go? And how? Your body was at the morgue then gone. How'd you survive on your own? Wait a minute, that's impossible. I mean, you're existence is impossible."

"Well, obviously not impossible because, here I am. I did survive, obviously, and further more I have no idea how. That's why I'm here. I didn't even know your father's name until I took a field trip to the morgue. Go figure. Can you put the top down at warp speed? I'd like to take care of the garbage following us. The air is beginning to stink." Susannah knelt backwards on the seat watching Drechell approaching. "So why is this guy chasing you?"

Jordan stepped on the gas to put some space between Drechell and the Viper. A quick glance at the speedometer told Susannah they were moving through one hundred twenty mph.

"Fair is fair. I guess I owe you an explanation since I put you in danger. He wants to kill me, but hasn't found a reason yet. He's been keeping me under surveillance for a while now. I just figured it out recently."

"How recently, Jordan?" The question was pragmatic. Susannah was in a somewhat pragmatic mood, all things considered. She double-checked the mag on her Cougar 8000. The mag was full, the gun was cocked and she was ready to play for keeps.

"Ah, tonight." He glanced in the rear view mirror. "And no, I can't put the top down in flight, unless I want it to be permanently down, or gone, actually." Jordan flapped his hand like a fluttering wing. "Drechell has never liked me, or my father. He was fairly jovial about burning the old man. He wants to do the same thing to me, but Metolius won't order it unless I step out of line."

The black car was now about a quarter mile behind but seemed to be gaining once again. What did Drechell have in that thing anyway? Jordan put the pedal to the metal.

Susannah could see them pull slightly away. She chose not to look at the speedometer.

"So what did your father do that was so bad? And why doesn't it bother you that he was burned alive? That would piss me off a lot, even though my father and I don't see eye to eye on most everything. He's still my father." She watched Jordan's face for answers.

Jordan chewed the side of his cheek for a few moments, then answered in a voice deep with hurt. "What if your father was the one to turn you into a vampire? What if he waited until you reached your teen years, then drained your body of blood in some feeding frenzy turning you into a monster? How would you feel about him then?" Jordan kept one eye on the road and one on the rear view mirror.

"The cut off to Fernandina Beach is just up ahead. If you can take the exit without being seen, we might just lose this guy." Susannah had twisted back around in her seat and was working the GPS on the dash as they talked. "In point seven miles, take the ramp right. Then stay right. It winds around and down onto a frontage road that parallels the beach. Looks like a tight curve but I have a feeling you can handle it."

"Bet your life I can." Jordan accelerated around a curve and moved out of Drechell's sight just before the exit.

"I *am*." Susannah watched for the exit. "There. Go! I can't see him behind us."

Jordan maneuvered the Viper like a pro, taking the curve on two wheels but maintaining control.

Susannah held on and managed to keep from screaming her lungs out. He drove like a bat out of hell. Around the dunes and down onto the frontage road they sped.

Racing along the frontage road between the beach and the occasional house set back against the dunes, Susannah searched for a place to park and hide for a while. She needed to calm her nerves down. She needed Jordan to answer some questions.

Two miles down the road they found a small driveway that led to a beach house with covered parking. It looked like the place had been recently vacated. No furniture could be seen through the large open windows and there were no lights on around the property. The nearest home was more than a thousand yards down the road. It looked to be dark as well.

"Jordan, pull under the carport. We can hide out for a while and catch our breath." Susannah didn't realize she had been panting and her knuckles were white from gripping the gun so tightly. "Look, we can close those bamboo shades and no one will see the car. If we don't use any light, we shouldn't be seen."

"Good idea. Keep that gun handy just in case. I still can't figure out how Drechell found me the last time." Jordan pulled into the covered area attached to the house and quickly shut down the engine. Opening the door, he took a deep breath, for effect.

"I might know," Susannah replied, as she slithered from the car onto her back on the ground. "Have you got a flashlight in your fancy-dancy car?"

"Coming right up. Detective and *mechanic*, Susannah Helga Anderson Maddox?" Jordan handed her a tiny Maglite that lit up the undercarriage of the Viper.

"Nothing here. Let me check the back."

Rolling onto her hands and knees, she crawled around to the rear bumper. Jordan paused and leaned against the carport beams for a moment, before untying the bamboo shades.

Susannah noticed Jordan was just as unsteady as she was. As she heard the shades fall, Susannah's warning was loud and clear from behind the car. "Uh oh. Better get ready for company."

Susannah crawled out from beneath the bumper and straightened. In her right hand she held a small box with a micro antennae and a red flashing light. "Me thinks Drechell didn't use his nose to find you." She twisted the metal box until it gave way with a resounding crunch. The red light dimmed, then died altogether.

"Me thinks he won't do it again." She pulled the pieces apart and threw them against the cement foundation of the house connected to the carport.

"I don't think it'll help us right now. He probably already has a fix on the car. Do we stand and fight or slink away like shadows in the night, Susannah Helga Anderson Maddox?" Jordan was relieved to know that Drechell used regular human technology to trace his movements. At ninety, he still didn't know all the powers that existed in the world of vampires. It was not too big a stretch to think some older vampires had extraordinary tracking skills.

"Okay, you can drop the Helga Anderson stuff. You know my real name, and who I am. So tell me why you think I am responsible for your father's death." She stood in the shadows, arms crossed over her chest.

"He turned you without the master's permission. In our coven, no one turns a human except Metolius. He controls our access to food and the rules we live by. He provides us with a safe place to live and keeps the cops and city officials on the payroll to prevent issues from arising. One vampire, one master. No questions, no mistakes. He runs Proctor Pharmaceuticals from the estate – it's wired for everything. Most of us work for the company, or do other jobs for the coven. It's a great set-up. In return we have what we need, as long as we obey. Occasionally we are asked to prove ourselves in some disgusting manner. But generally, it's a good life and, for the most part, we respect the humans around us. Most of us feed only with permission." Jordan tried Marisella's line on Susannah.

"Do you think Minnie and Buck gave their permission?" Susannah was visibly upset by what happened at the diner.

"Drechell is another story. He's a loose cannon. He serves a purpose so Metolius keeps him around. Drechell will have to answer for the mess back there, at some point." Jordan was careful to phrase his response. He knew full well, Drechell would probably kill them both, and skate without anyone even knowing. He would simply blame the deaths on Jordan and the mystery girl he was running away with. What a story.

"You don't believe that any more than I do." Susannah scoffed. "I guess that means we stand and fight, or at least I will stand and fight. You do whatever you're comfortable with."

Jordan was amazed at the naiveté of the young vampire who stood next to his car, vowing to fight one of the most powerful and dangerous vampires he had ever known. It had to have been naiveté, because he was sure she wasn't that stupid. She did have a heck of a set of cojones though. He found that almost hotter than her voluptuous body and knock-out looks. His eyes trailed a path from her red poutty lips to a well-endowed chest. God she was gorgeous! His eyes continued down to a slim waist and legs that went all the way to the ground, and then some. His teen hormones nearly jumped out of his pants and attacked the blonde woman who stood, strategically calculating their next move.

She was a mystery. An intriguing and stimulating female, to say the least. She also seemed to have some unique powers and weapons at her disposal. If she really was his father's last little mistake, she turned what? Four or five years ago?

It didn't jive in his mind.

She knew about evasive techniques, found the tracking device under his car, operated a GPS like a pro, and kept her cool in the midst of a car chase. Who was this woman, and what did she really do? Was she truly a government spy kind of person, or was that all part of her phony cover?

As far as Jordan knew, few humans were aware that vampires really existed and lived right next door. He was fairly sure the government did not have a clue about vampires. The appearance of this young woman, in fact, her mere survival and continued existence without a coven made him rethink his knowledge base. How had she gotten involved with his old man in the first place?

Suspicion ate at his libido with the effectiveness of an ice cold shower.

Options flashed across his mind. Outcomes, too.

"I'd just as soon make a stand, but before anyone starts shooting, can we make sure which side all of us are on? That little toy, as you call it, isn't a standard gun. I certainly wouldn't want you to mistake me for one of the bad guys. We're in this together, right?" Jordan crossed his arms over his chest and looked as stern as he could. "I can't go back to the estate now, if Drechell remains alive. He's a crafty old bastard and violent as hell. With him it's not even bite first and ask questions later. It's more like, an all out assault, no questions asked, unless you want another all out assault. He's pure viciousness in loafers."

"How can I be sure about you? After all, you just said I was the reason your father got killed." Susannah took the same stance and squared off.

It was a vampire standoff at the OK Corral.

She glared at the man across the car.

"I guess you just have to trust me." Jordan adjusted his stance in an attempt to look more intimidating.

"Oh, puh-leeze. You've said that three times in the last two hours. Each time I hear it, I find myself in deeper trouble than the last. Trust you? Not on your life, or mine." She turned scanning and listening. "Speaking of which, isn't that the Town Car coming down the road?" Susannah slid behind the bamboo screens and waved Jordan down.

He crouched behind the car and peeked over the foundation between the bamboo and cement blocks. "Shit. He got a fix on us for sure. All right, if you don't trust me then how about a truce for now. Deal?" He was whispering as he kept his eyes on the approaching Drechell.

"Deal. But you fuck with me, and I'll do more than burn your ass." Susannah snarled, trying to form a strategy in her head. Nothing was coming to mind except a shoot out at the Fernandina Beach corral. How fast was this older vampire? What kinds of powers had he developed in the years he'd been an enforcer? Would she even be able to keep her own thoughts and actions under control in light of what some vampires were capable of?

Elizabetta often talked about different vampires having different powers, not the least of which was mind control. Did mind control work on other vampires? She hadn't gotten Yuri to teach her to v-port before she left. It would have been handy. *Damn*, she mentally castigated herself, *I should have paid more attention to my training, and less to my iPod and QVC.*

"What do you know about this Drechell? Powers? Speed? Weapons?" Susannah was stretching for something – anything.

"He's lightning fast. Well, actually faster than lightning. He only has one fang, and no, uh, balls." Jordan snickered.

"Come on, Jordan, give me something I can work with. I don't give a shit if he has four balls, unless he can kill us with them. What else do you know?" Whispering Susannah silently crawled to the other side of the carport as the Town Car slowly drove by the driveway, missing their car completely.

"He carries a flame thrower for executions. Uh, you know, I've been around him for years and I hardly know anything about him. Weird." Jordan looked blank. "I've never thought about Drechell in that light. I was just always afraid of catching his eye. He's good at intimidation, and usually has a couple of henchmen with him. As for any special power, other than his speed, I have no clue." Jordan seemed in his own world and they were about to engage in the fight of their lives!

"Yo, Jordan! Think." Susannah scrunched down as the car rounded the bend and disappeared. "This is a dead end road. He'll be back. We need a plan."

"Like what? Tea and scones? I've never had to fight another vampire, especially not one like Drechell." Jordan's face was white and he was wringing his hands as he sat on the floor of the carport. "Your gun? Will it kill him outright, or just wound him enough for us to get away?"

"Definitely kill. And I am a great shot, even at vamp speeds." Susannah stood and proceeded to go through the unlocked cabinets that hung off the wall near the back of the carport. "Hah! What do we have here?"

"What?" He was at her side in a flash.

"Fertilizer and grass seed, gasoline and two cans of 10/40 motor oil. Canning jars, charcoal briquettes, flower pots, lids, old newspapers, the list went on. "Yes! Okay, now we're cooking with gas."

"What? You want to change the oil in the car, plant grass, have a bar-b-que and can something?" Jordan shook his head, then froze squinting off into the inky distance. "He's coming back."

Susannah grabbed a couple jars and lids, the small plastic jug of gas and one of the oil cans. "Watch, then do."

She punctured the lid of the canning jar with a fingernail. "You gotta love vamp nails. Never break, never need a manicure, or a can opener!" She poured about a quarter cup of oil into the Mason jar then added twice as much gasoline. Susannah added a lid, rolled the mixture carefully around the jar watching as the sides coated with oil. Reaching toward Jordan, she tore a piece of cloth from his shirt and then stuffed the strip through the lid's hole and into the mixture.

"Voila! Now make some more." She grinned, squatting over her creation on the floor. "Hurry."

"So, where'd you learn to make a Molotov cocktail?" Jordan knelt, and began rapidly assembling several more improvised bombs. Vamp speed was handy when you needed a bomb in a pinch.

"Deranged childhood, or special forces training. Take your pick." Susannah moved on and was efficiently folding what looked to be origami boxes from the stack of old newspapers.

"You were in the Special Forces?" He looked at the lithe blonde skeptically.

"Nope, but Dad was. I hung out with military types all my life. I didn't have a choice; they were my babysitters, best friends and my father's subordinates. Go figure." She had already constructed five paper boxes as she spoke, fingers working at lightning speed. "Most kids had Legos and dolls. I had HAZMAT and G.I. Joes – the real ones. Watch and learn."

Susannah filled each box with fertilizer then folded the top in and tucked the edge to complete a package of the nitrate-based stuff. Kneeling next to the car, she sliced through the supple leather of the passenger seat with her extraordinary nails, and proceeded to grab handfuls of foam and cotton stuffing.

"Hey, my seats! Shit." Jordan didn't stop Susannah but did complain loudly. His car was part of his self-concept. Both the seats, and his image were being shredded at the moment.

She quickly soaked the small clumps of stuffing in motor oil then tucked them into the specially folded edge of each deadly package. The stuffing stuck out just enough to catch a flame.

"Hand me the box of matches, next to the briquettes. Up on the right." They appeared in her right hand as she was pointing. "Nice trick, Mr. Burke." He could V-port like Yuri. Tearing the matches apart she inserted a couple under each glob of soaked stuffing.

Jordan watched in fascination "Ever been to Oklahoma City there, little missy?" He drawled.

"That's sick." She carefully picked up each package and headed for the backdoor of the house. "Come on. He's not far from the driveway. Got a light?"

Jordan grabbed his hastily made Molotov cocktails VERY carefully and tiptoed after Susannah, marveling at what a great ass the woman had. He corrected himself – a great ass, and… a very lethal ass. He'd seen people on the news throwing Molotov cocktails, but had never considered making one. Or using one.

Vampires weren't especially fond of fire. The bomb packages Susannah constructed in under a minute were even more amazing. Maybe she really did work for the government. Or maybe she was an undercover vampire terrorist. Whatever she was, Jordan said a silent thank you for it, and followed her into the house. Drechell was pulling into the driveway. Their car had been discovered.

"Put the packages against the wall in the living room by the front door. Hopefully he won't smell the accelerant if we keep him busy." She was darting around placing her explosive newspaper boxes unobtrusively by the walls.

"Accelerant?" Jordan followed her lead.

Drechell was getting out of his car.

"Gas and oil. Don't you know anything? Hurry! Then get over here and make out like lovers."

"What? Make out? Why…" Jordan was confused and instantly excited.

What was wrong with him? His body had gone from fear, on a scale of 8 to excited at 10. He shifted the growing hardness in his pants.

"Shhhh! Here. NOW!"

Jordan v-ported to the sound of her agitated voice. She pulled him onto the floor and slammed into a lip lock that set his mind reeling and lit his body up with the force of a nuclear explosion. The blood in his veins turned to molten lava and sparks flew before his eyes. Every nerve screamed.

Drechell will watch for a while. You said he has no balls… he must miss this kind of thing. Men always seem to enjoy vicarious sex lives through others. Why do you think the porn industry is so huge and successful? Susannah worked her lips and tongue as she sent the mental message to Jordan.

Not enough of the message filtered through to the tiny part of his brain that remained sane and cognizant. Jordan heard sex and porn. It was enough for him. He could scarcely breath, let alone comprehend the mental communication. His brain had gone into its 'seduce and ravish' mode and there was no turning back. Teenage hormones raced through his body, driving him to ignore everything but the need to have this woman who held him in a death grip with her body and her lips. His mind may have directed him to seduce and ravish, but he was the one being seduced and ravished. His body was out of control, negating anything but the glorious feelings that assaulted him in wave after wave of pure ecstasy.

His cock leapt to life, warring with his instinctual desire to run, to survive. He tried to remind himself it had to be mind over body, but the body just wouldn't let the mind have its way. He groaned and sunk his tongue deep into Susannah's mouth as he pulled her tight to his chest. The cold belt buckle of her low-rise jeans scraped his skin where she had torn his shirt away for fuse. Her knee brushed his thigh and he groaned again as rivulets of electricity stabbed his belly and twisted his guts with a pleasure never before experienced. His mind was on fire with lust. Heat raged through his body. He felt his fangs grow, delicately piercing Susannah's lip. He tasted her blood, and growled like an animal in rut.

Don't lose it Jordan. It's working! Drechell's got to be watching through the front window. I can hear his approach, and it's not slow and steady.

Lose it?

Lose what?

Jordan slid himself between Susannah's thighs, massaging his need as he swirled her blood on his tongue. It was the taste of heaven, and he wanted more. He growled low in his throat and laved at her lips.

I need my hands free to light the fuse. Be prepared to run. Susannah was aware that her kisses had ignited an unusually passionate response in Jordan. In any other situation it would have been endearing, but she was trying desperately to assess Drechell's approach while keeping a lid on Jordan's lust. Not to mention, his lust was having a disturbing effect on her own libido. She shoved her emotions back against her skull and swallowed hard. Above Jordan's sensual groans she could hear Drechell's footsteps on the wooden porch.

Jordan was aware that Susannah was communicating, but had no idea what she was telling him. In fact, he couldn't think enough to even care less. His senses spiraled into a tornado of desire that revolved around finding a way to touch her skin, smell her scent, taste her essence. He couldn't get enough. He tore at her blouse, feeling the satiny fabric give way. His lips slid down her neck. He buried his face between her firm, full breasts.

Oh God! Black lace.

His favorite.

He drew deep lungfuls of the most amazingly wondrous air. Tasting her in a way he had never experienced before, he memorized every tangy element of her scent. This wonderful woman held him to her as if he was the last man on earth, and she wanted him beyond sanity. This was a kind of out of control he had never experienced before. It shook him to the core. On some level he grasped for control but his hand found only a firm mound of the most delightful breast. Its nipple pebbled at his touch. Susannah's quick intake of breath sent him spiraling into a chasm of erotic pleasure. He ached to rip her clothing from her delectable body and sink himself into her as deep as he could. He burned to bury himself in her delicious heat. He craved her tangy blood...

Wait for my signal then run. Out the back.

Jordan?

Susannah was aware the second the front door began to move. *Wait for it. Wait. JORDAN!*

Jordan howled and pulled Susannah tighter to him. He ripped at her belt in desperation.

He needed her.

He wanted her.

NOW.

Susannah flicked a match in her hand, lit two cocktails. She tossed them, one after the other, over the top of a sprawling, growling Jordan.

In a flash, the first hit the floor behind Drechell exploding in a fiery splash against the door. It effectively cut off his exit. Drechell was fast, but unprepared for an attack... and thinking with a sex-drenched mind. He was not fast enough. The other jar broke against a flailing arm, as Drechell tried unsuccessfully to fend off a fate he had experienced once before... and feared most of all.

In less than an instant, Drechell was engulfed in flames. Howling in agony, he dropped to the floor, writhing and rolling, trying to put out the scorching flames. It was useless. Susannah made sure of that when she mixed the cocktail's contents; gasoline would ignite and flame out quickly but oil would cling and burn.

The screaming animalistic sounds finally shook Jordan from his lust-induced reverie, enough to become aware of what was happening around him. He shook his head like a drunken man waking after a three-day binge.

Finally free of his tight embrace, Susannah bounced to her feet, fired three rounds into the flaming vampire, then grabbed Jordan's chin with her free hand. "V-port us, NOW!"

Jordan blinked, and they were gone in a flash, literally. What was left of Drechell, before he dissolved into a pile of ash, fell against the wall igniting several of the makeshift fuses that stuck out of their deadly newspaper packages. The house, carport and Jordan's bright, shiny red Viper disappeared in a colossal explosion that lit up the night.

Susannah's purse appeared at her feet, somewhat charred but intact.

They stood behind Drechell's Town Car, shielded from the falling debris, watching what remained, burn to cinders in the white hot flames.

Strangely enough, the sound of the surf seemed to fill the dead silence following the detonation.

Jordan looked down at Susannah. He still held her in his arms, hesitant to let her go after the wild rollercoaster ride of imminent danger mixed with uncontrollable lust.

Susannah smiled sheepishly, shaking her head.

Jordan took a deep breath and held it to clear his head. He didn't need to breath but sometimes it helped straighten his brain. Everything happened so fast; the danger, the sexual excitement, the confused mixture of the two. Then there was Susannah and his uncontrollable reaction to her. Jordan closed his eyes and tried to comprehend what had happened.

"Sorry about your car." She leaned against the much taller man who held her. He looked so sad with his eyes closed, a frown marring the beauty of his blonde features. She figured, like most guys, his car was a very important part of his image.

A Viper was a hell of an image enhancer.

"I really loved that car. It was a chick magnet." Jordan laughed and hugged Susannah close. "But life trumps car any day."

"Nah. I thought the seats needed work." She smiled and settled against his chest. There was no heartbeat to hear, but that didn't bother her much. She was used to her own intermittent heart rhythm.

"Not funny, Susannah Helga Anderson Maddox. You owe me. But not for the car. For saving your hide!" He watched the flames already dying in the quiet night. "I hope Drechell didn't have the keys to the Town Car in his pocket."

A volunteer fire department siren sounded against the crackling fire and softly rustling surf.

"What? Not in this lifetime buck-o. If anything, you owe me!" She playfully slapped at his cheek as if to wake him for some long coma. "Uh-oh, time to depart the fix, Mr. Burke. That is unless you have a plausible explanation for our little weenie roast. I do believe a different kind of company is on the way now." Susannah pulled away and ducked inside Drechell's car then smiled up at Jordan. "Drechell wasn't very imaginative." A set of keys dangled from her fingers.

She tossed the keys to Jordan and slid from the driver side to the passenger side. Jordan tossed her smoky purse in the back seat, hopped in and fired up the car. He backed out of the driveway and turned toward the dead end.

"If we drive all the way down the road then turn around, maybe someone will believe we were down on the beach, heard the explosion and came for a look see. What do you think?"

"It sounds plausible. Do you think there will be enough left of the Viper for someone to identify the car?" Susannah grabbed for her purse and rummaged through the ruined handbag for her cell phone. "How are you going to explain your car? Drechell? Especially when you show up in Drechell's land yacht?"

Jordan wrinkled his brow and thought for a few minutes as he drove. "Drechell was at the Mango Bango tonight. So was I. Maybe, yeah, we switched cars. He wanted to borrow mine for... he hooked up with a babe and wanted to impress the woman. Yeah!"

"Well, you only have one problem with that theory. That is, if you were telling the truth about the guy's anatomy. Ah, no testicles, right? Why would he hook up with a woman, if he couldn't, you know?" Susannah looked quizzically at Jordan. "If your story is going to float, it has to be probable." At least he was trying. Respect for this son of her sire rose a notch.

"Well maybe he just wanted a snack, in an out of the way place." Jordan was reaching.

"Why would he drive all the way up here, to a beach house he didn't own? Then end up disappearing in a mysterious fire, when the house and car went up in smoke? If there's one thing I have learned in my business, when you lie, keep it as close to the truth as possible. It works better, and you have less chance of forgetting what you lied about." Susannah was thinking.

"And what business did you say you were in, again? Detective? Government what? It's about time for you to come clean. We're both in this up to our fangs now."

They had reached the end of the road. Jordan pulled over and parked with a clear view of the ocean and the road. They sat quietly for a few minutes before Susannah let out a deep sigh.

"Alright. I do work for the government, and it's classified. So I can't tell you everything. And you can't tell anyone anything I do tell you. Understand? Anyway, that's not why I am here. This has nothing to do with my work. I took a sort of 'leave of absence' to answer some personal questions. I wanted to find my sire and figure out why he abandoned me." She looked down at her neatly folded hands laying quietly in her lap. "Now I know that he didn't leave me all alone. He was killed trying to follow me. Probably trying to get to my body before I woke, all alone. I don't remember much, but what I do know, was how horribly afraid and cold I was. The hunger was overpowering, and I didn't know what happened to me. I was in the dark for a long time. Then, I think they kept me sedated for a while… my father and the rest. Most of it's a blank."

"How does your father fit into this disturbing puzzle? I don't understand." Jordan was curious about Susannah's father and the 'they' she talked about.

"My father is Colonel Frank Maddox. He is Special Ops for the Army. From what I remember, I came down to Daytona Beach for Spring Break, my first year in college. He didn't want me to go. He said it was too dangerous, but I was a rebellious teenager. Actually, I was a rebellious child all together. Anyway, long story short, I came, I drank, I died. When I finally woke up, I was in a vault with a woman, a vampire named Elizabetta. My father made a deal with the military to recruit vampires to be operatives. That was after he convinced them that vampires existed, and had skills that could be valuable in certain situations. He heads up the project, and we all live together now as a family, vampires and humans. It's a mixed coven, ya know, a new form of integration." Susannah giggled. "Without Martin Luther King. We go on missions and help out in ways normal humans can't. It's all very hush-hush. Elizabetta told me he did it all because of me." She paused and snuffed a little.

"He could never tell me what happened before he recovered my body from the morgue. It was quite the shock when he learned I was a vampire. Well…" She giggled again. "It was quite a shock just to accept vampires as real, let alone face the fact that his now his kid was one."

Jordan physically felt her pain and confusion. How was that possible? He'd never felt another vampire's emotions before.

Susannah continued, "there has always been this huge black void and I needed answers. We don't have the most communicative father-daughter relationship in the world, if you know what I mean. So here I am with a handful of answers, and a zillion more questions than when I started out on this little road trip. My main goal was finding my sire." Susannah hung her head leaving out the part about wanting to find love as well. It was a moot point after learning Kellan was dead.

Jordan could tell that Susannah lived with this pervasive sadness for a long time. Her very posture screamed 'injured goods'. He pulled her to him and held her tight. Maybe the closeness would mitigate what he needed to say. "I hate to be the one to tell you this, but… nah. Never mind." Jordan kissed the top of her head tenderly. He was beginning to realize they had a lot in common. His old man did a lot of disgusting things, but turning this girl and leaving her alone? She could have become a raving animal, never fully awake, not fully dead… for eternity. Doing something like that was akin to complete disdain for everything, human or vampire.

"No, tell me. I want to know everything." She strained against his arms to look up into his eyes. "I need to know, Jordan." Hope was etched across the pain in her gaze.

"Even if it is not something you would like to hear?" He paused for a few seconds, just looking into the depths of hurt he saw in her glistening blue eyes. This would hurt even more, but she wanted to be told the truth.

"Yes. I can handle it. I'm a big girl."

"Fine. If my old man was following you, it was to get rid of the evidence, i.e., you. Not to bring you into the fold. He used to call the women he accidentally killed while feeding, his 'little mistakes'. He was fairly adept at cleaning up after himself, but in the last ten years he'd become more and more careless. Your body was the one that got away, so to speak. He was frantic to find you before Metolius found out. He left me a crazy message on my phone the day he went chasing after you. Now that I have all the pieces, I understand. My father was the true definition of a monster." Jordan kissed Susannah's head again, as if the chaste kiss could take away the hurt of what he had to say.

"He couldn't have been that bad, Jordan. How could you say that about him? He was your father." A blood red tear slid down her face and Jordan sucked in his breath. It smelled so heavenly and lay there waiting for his tongue. The depth of her sadness and her warm blood ignited his senses again. He felt his cock respond. Jordan pulled her closer, settling her under his arm against his chest, trying to control the teen hormones he would be stuck with for many hundreds of years to come. His next words were chosen carefully and he knew they would tear open his own heart, but Susannah deserved the truth of it all.

All of it.

"How could I say that? Susannah, he kept my mother prisoner for seven years, feeding off her until I was old enough to pal around with him as a teenager. Then he turned me and watched as I fed and drained her. My own mother! I couldn't control myself. I didn't know what was happening. He burned her body in a public dump, in a bayou outside Lafayette. He taught me to feed off of humans, to treat people as if they were nothing but food for slaughter. I never liked it. I'm ninety years old. I still hate the thought of what he made me. He was warped, sick, and he wanted some kind of perverted family. So he made his human son a vampire and a killer."

"I'm so sorry, Jordan. I…" Susannah fell silent, satisfied to sit, wallowing in her own self pity while Jordan sat next to her, consumed in his own hate for his father. They made a great couple. Like any young people parking by the beach. They appeared to the casual observer, like lovers in the middle of a secret tryst, instead of two people in horrendous pain.

So it was no surprise to either of them when the policeman who knocked on the window, had a huge smile on his face. He motioned with his flashlight for Jordan to roll the window down. Susannah scooted to the other side of the vehicle looking appropriately embarrassed at being caught in a clandestine embrace on a deserted beach, at the end of a country road.

"Hey you two, your parents know where you are?" The officer seemed to be a nice fellow, and a little embarrassed himself at catching two young lovers on the beach.

Jordan answered, going along with the officer's assumptions. "Of course, Sir. We're at the movies." He smiled back with an over-exaggerated wink.

"Any chance you heard an explosion a little while ago? A house about a half-mile back blew up and burned. How long have you been here?" He kept his eyes on Jordan, refusing to see any underage female in the expensive car. That would only add to his paperwork for the night.

"Actually, Sir, I kind of had my mind elsewhere, if you know what I mean. Wow! Look at the time. I should get Helga home before her dad skins me alive. Is the road open, Sir?" Jordan was playing it to the hilt.

Susannah kept her eyes downcast, acting embarrassed at being caught necking at the beach. She giggled a little and squirmed on the seat, but did not look up.

"Yeah, but there are two fire engines parked on the side of the road. Just be cautious, and get this little lady home safe and sound. It'll make my job easier. Have a good night, if it hasn't been already." The officer returned to his patrol vehicle and Jordan pulled away as fast as he could, hoping the officer wasn't running a license plate check. The car was a business vehicle registered to Proctor Pharmaceuticals.

"Nothing like getting caught watching the submarine races." Jordan tried to add a little levity to the atmosphere.

"Where are we going? If Drechell's out of the picture, can you return to your coven, and still be safe?" Susannah was confused at what her next step would be. She had some of the answers she had sought though they weren't the ones she hoped to find. But now there was the question of Jordan.

"I guess. I don't have anywhere else to go. I have no idea if anyone could hear Drechell die. When Drechell cooked my dad, Metolius made sure everyone in the coven felt it. But that was arranged ahead of time. If I go back to the estate, I will know immediately, one way or the other. At least there, I have a place to live and a job, sort of. If I tried to leave without permission, Metolius would have someone hunt me down and drag me back, just so he could have me executed as a lesson to the others. He rules with a tight hand."

Jordan steered the Town Car onto I-95 and headed south. They drove all the way to Daytona Beach in silence. There was nothing left to say for the time being as a kind of depression settled over the occupants inside the car.

Chapter 15

Nothing but the Dawn

When there's nothing left but the cold dawn,
And reality sinks, as the night does fawn,
It's last velvety fingers over a mind,
Lost to all, but its own kind.

And what of that kind, so secret and brutal?
Is there no hope, a purpose found futile?
To bring together young love with its first,
Enough passion to make hearts burst.

Not in this world, not in this time.
One man, one master is the line,
That has been drawn for eons past,
The way of vampires, all laid fast.

Monique Alys Merchant, Vampire
Diary of a Mad Vampire, 1796

Susannah sat quietly on the passenger side of the car. Her heart went out to the man who drove, despite his connection to her sire. What he'd said about his father was pitiful.

He was definitely in a bad place.

His future was iffy at best. She knew it was mostly her fault.

His face was drawn and pale as he drove toward the dawn, hands gripping the leather covered steering wheel for dear life, obviously at odds with himself and his world.

A mental battle of her own raged with her mind, as well. Everything she planned for her perfect little world was dead. Gone. Burned to ashes. Nothing was left for her now. Plan A didn't have a plan B for 'just in case.' It never occurred to her that she would not be successful in finding her sire, hitching him to her heart and returning home with a husband to live happily ever after. Just like Natalia and Yuri.

She was so sure, so cocky, so damn smart!

Right.

She never meant a thing to Kellan. Unfortunately, she hadn't even had the maturity to understand it. Her stupid little girl fantasy would make a great country western song: Susannah definitely had her beer goggles on while planning this disaster. Or maybe more akin to the childhood song about bear dancing. Only she had been dancing with a monster on the beach. The only thing that got left behind was her body, torn and drained of life.

The realization stunned her.

"Jordan?" He jumped as she broke the silence, "Why did your father take such a risk with me? I don't understand. After I was dead, he came after me. I remember him calling my name. He promised we would be together. Do you really think all he wanted was to get rid of me? You said 'he had to take care of his little oops', right?"

Jordan sighed as he let out a deep breath, not even realizing he'd been holding it in again. "Yeah. Susannah, I don't want to hurt your feelings, but you have to understand what a creep my father was. He used people, and threw them away. Like they meant nothing. He was a master at manipulation. That's what made him such a marketing expert. And, such a freaky disgusting asshole. One minute he was sweet as spun honey. The next he was a diabolical maniac. Maybe it was the drugs. I don't know."

"Come on, drugs don't work on vampires. You should know that." Susannah wasn't going to swallow some story about a druggy vampire. She knew better. "Our bodies don't assimilate drugs the way human bodies do. Drugs have no effect."

"CE does. It's a wonderful little substance that was developed in Yugoslavia in the sixties. Made its way to the U.S., and Proctor Pharmaceuticals in the eighties. It's been around for a long time. I think my father was addicted. If Metolius had any idea that dad was using, he'd have killed the old man long ago. It is strictly forbidden because it is so addictive, and causes such a loss of control."

"Kind of like coke, or crystal meth? What does 'CE' stand for?" Susannah was intrigued.

"More like opium, crystal meth and ecstasy combined. CE means Crysillus Extract. It is highly addictive. Just a couple uses and you're hooked. It provides an incredible euphoria, and enhances vampiric powers for the length of time it is in the vampire's system. Some say it makes you feel the human in you again, but so much more powerful." Jordan talked while keeping an eye on the road. "That is something many vampires would die for. As the drug wears off, the vampire's power decreases and the person descends into a black depression. Vampiric powers decline to almost human levels for a short time. The more a vampire uses, the longer the decline lasts."

Susannah's brow wrinkled. "I can see how using it could be extremely dangerous."

"After a while the addict can't even feed without it. My father wasn't there yet, but he was on his way. I found his stash once. He hit the roof. He tried to convince me that Proctor was researching a cure for the addiction, like methadone for alcoholics."

"Maybe it was true." Susannah studied Jordan's face as he answered.

"Are you kidding? I never believed anything my father told me. His life, his personality, his existence... it was all a lie; Besides, Metolius has never done anything benevolent. If a project does not have the potential to make a ton of money or increase his power and control, he's not interested. I think Metolius was increasing the drug's reaction, not finding a way to help addicts. Dad was his big marketing executive but everything about my old man was fake." Jordan hit the steering wheel with his fist. "He had this big story about being gifted with vampirism after serving an ancient vampire until this fellow, Callicius was his name, chose to die in the light. It was all a bunch of bullshit. He got bit while fucking a whore in an alley, in the slums of Chicago. I found out when the woman showed up at our house in Louisiana, hungry and needing a place to hide." Jordan's features twisted into such rage Susannah thought a vein in his forehead would pop.

"How'd she find your family? Did you know she was a vampire?"

"No, I had no idea that she or my father were vampires. He was really good at hiding his true nature. He traveled a lot for his job; at least that's what we all thought. I didn't know any of this until much later, after I was turned. My father actually let his sire feed off my mother until she was strong enough to move on. Then, get this, he took her to a deserted stretch of beach and left her there, just before dawn. That's the man who made you. The one you wanted to find. Nice picture, huh?"

"I'm so sorry, Jordan. I had no idea. I don't know what to say – I had a completely different picture. Now after meeting you and... well, I am afraid I've created another mess where someone else will get hurt. Damn." She shook her head sadly. " I don't know how to get you out of this mess I've made. We're almost back at the Beachcomber and it's close to dawn. I..." For once Susannah was at a loss for words, sabotaged by her feelings about someone else for a change. It was an uncharacteristic and uncomfortable feeling. She just looked long and hard at the man next to her and said nothing.

"It's not just your mess. I had a hand in it as well. I was thinking, Susannah, about my dreams. You began your search for my old man, about the same time you started appearing in my dreams. Then you showed up here, and I knew you were real. Maybe this connection we have is a physical link. Maybe, it has to do with the fact that my father turned us both, but I don't really know. We have *some* connection though. Are we like brother and sister?" The thought rolled in the pit of his stomach like a solid glump of oatmeal. Not a good feeling, especially after their explosive kisses.

"Nah, believe me on that one." Susannah sighed thinking about Natalia, Yuri and that last kiss as well.

"You mentioned auras. I don't see them. Is it because you are a techno-modern vamp, you know, no drinking live blood, and all that?"

"Jordan, I've only been a vampire for a few years. There is so much I don't know. Here's the turn." Susannah pointed to the sign that identified the ramp off I-95 into the northern section of Daytona Beach.

"How did you survive all alone? That's not supposed to be possible. When Drechell reported back to Metolius about cooking the old man, he said there were no other bodies or live vampires around." They pulled into the hotel parking garage.

"Look, why don't you come up to my room and we can figure some of this out. I need to make a few calls. You can spend the day on my couch. At least you'll be safe for one more day." Susannah stashed the gun in a specially designed pocket in her ash-covered purse and motioned to an empty parking space. "I need to call my Dad."

"Your Dad? He knows about you? I mean, I know you said you told him and all, but really? Is he a vampire too? I thought you were making this stuff up as you went. Detective, government spy, all that James Bond stuff. You mean to tell me, it's all real?" Jordan was now intrigued enough to spend the day on a hard couch instead of his king sized bed at the estate. Pulling the vanity mirror down, he ran a hand through his disheveled hair and brushed off his pants. There was nothing he could do for the torn shirt or smoky smell.

Susannah snorted. "Yes, no, I mean, ah some is, some isn't. Let's get up stairs and maybe I can straighten it out for you. For your information, my father's still human." She cringed at the slightly snotty tone of her last sentence.

Susannah noted Jordan's reaction and felt a tinge of guilt at her comment. "I didn't mean it that way. I just meant… Oh shit, my mouth is always getting me into trouble."

Jordan got out of the car and scrunched up his nose at her across the top of the Town Car. "Bully for you. But my Dad could bite your Dad." He stuck his tongue out in a typical childish fashion. He completely understood Susannah's problem. He had his own set of unique problems concerning maturity and behavior. His groin tightened at the thought.

Susannah laughed. "I really am sorry. I was nineteen when Kellan turned me. Sometimes, my teenager side comes out a little more than I like."

"Oh, puh-leeze. Like I wasn't?" Jordan made an effeminate gesture with his hand and did a girlish strut to the elevator. "Coming, girlfriend?" Susannah dissolved into a fit of giggles and ran to catch up. This young man had some very endearing qualities, and he didn't blame her for everything, unlike her own family.

The doors to the elevator opened on a well-groomed couple headed for the tennis court, racquets in hand. "Excuse us, ma'am." Jordan spun and dropped his pose. "I mean, ah, Sir."

The couple looked at the floor and walked by quickly.

Tennis at sunrise? Susannah breezed past Jordan laughing so hard she started breathing and was having trouble keeping the snorts out of each breath. Bouncing against the back of the elevator, she held her stomach and doubled over gasping.

"Come on, girlfriend." Susannah wiggled a come hither finger at him.

Jordan slid between the closing doors in the nick of time.

"I think you're getting more fun out of this than you should. Good thing I didn't know those folks. I am kind of a fixture around here. *I* have a reputation." He looked a little sheepish as Susannah went into another fit of giggles.

"Oh, Gawd. I can't breath." She held her hand to her chest and gulped at the air like a guppy struggling for oxygen, which she truly didn't need as a vampire. It was still fun to joke and act carefree, for a few minutes. She half suspected her silliness was a reaction to the night's events, a kind of decompression.

"So? Serves you right." He punched the eighteenth floor button.

"Push eightee – how'd you know what floor I'm on?" Susannah was still grinning, her cheeks sore from laughing so hard.

"I just missed you, before you left for the Sip-N-Tip. One minute earlier and I could have avoided learning about Molotov cocktails and fertilizer bombs." Jordan sighed with a false wistfulness. "But that would have been such a shame. I kind of liked the fireworks"

"Sip-N-Tip? Oh shit, my car? We forgot to go back for my car! It's still at the restaurant." On the ride home she had been so engrossed in Jordan's life story, she hadn't remembered to pick up her car. "Man, I wonder if the cops are there yet? I can't believe we just ran and abandoned those two people in the middle of the night." Susannah paused and pressed her forehead against the wall, all fun and frolic gone with the thought of Drechell's slashing fangs, Minnie, the budding country western singer, and the cook, Buck. In one night they all lost their lives. Because of her.

"I'll get Manolo to have someone pick it up for you and bring it back here. I'll have to make the call from your room. My cell phone was in the Viper." Jordan pulled Susannah from the elevator, planted a kiss on her cheek and smiled. "It could have been much worse. We could be ashes as well." He kissed her tenderly, almost as if she meant something to him.

"Those lips of yours are deadly when I am trying to think." He pulled her into his arms for a tight hug as they walked toward her suite at the end of the hall. "If I hadn't come to my senses when I did and v-ported us…"

"Well, other than the two dead innocent humans, the night wasn't as bad as it could have been, right? If I can get my car back…" Susannah froze, pulling them to a stop.

"We'll get your car back. Manolo has connections and no one should be due at the restaurant until noon or so. I think we can clean up this mess before anyone knows. At least I hope so."

"A mess, Jordan? Two innocent people are dead because of me. You're in trouble up to your neck. Minnie and Buck's deaths were wrong. It's a tragedy Proctor should pay for. Drechell was his pit bull, and your master should never have let that dog off its chain."

"I know, Susannah, but there was nothing we could have done. Drechell would have just killed us outright, then gone right on killing the humans." Jordan ran a hand through his filthy hair. "I can't make it right or change the events of the night. All I can do, is try to keep you and me from being destroyed. How about I make that call. Open says me." Jordan pointed at the door lock.

"That's sesame. Just give me a second." Susannah fished her room key card from the smelly purse, as the doors opened and they walked into her suite. " Nice trick. How long did it take for you to learn how to open a woman's room without a key? Maybe I should call you Handy Randy." She took one step and gasped.

On the coffee table in the middle of the room, stood a huge bunch of pale pink roses in a crystal vase, tied with a lovely gold bow. Next to the vase was a cream colored satin box with a matching bow, holding a small envelope beneath the ribbon.

In a flash Susannah had her gun in hand, her back pressed to the wall beside the door. She pressed a finger to her lips in an attempt to hush Jordan, as she surveyed the room suspiciously.

"Hold on, I do believe I can explain the rose garden on your table." He reached across the opening and lowered the barrel of her gun with one careful finger. "Holster that thing, please."

"I'm not expecting anything, or anyone, Jordan. Get back until I clear the room." Susannah was all serious and professional.

"I'm pretty sure I can explain *this*." Jordan emphasized the word 'this' as he strode across the cushy rug and pulled the little envelope from the jewelry case. Flipping it open, he slid the card out and smiled. Babs had done her job admirably well. He wondered how much it would cost him. No matter, he was sure she'd had fun and also rewarded herself just as admirably.

"What's this all about?" Susannah slid her shoes off, closed the door and joined Jordan. "I believe that is addressed to me, Mr. Burke."

She plucked the card from his hand and studied the writing. "Apparently it's from you. Nice."

Susannah dropped her purse where they stood, and grabbed the box from the table. Tearing off the ribbon, the lid popped open revealing a gorgeous tanzanite pendant and earring set.

"Oh my Gawd, it's more than nice, Jordan. It's tanzanite and diamonds. My favorite! You couldn't have known. Now I am confused. When did you do this?"

Susannah stared at the jewel case with an open mouth. In typical ferret mode, she was immediately distracted by the shiny baubles. Without waiting for an answer, she ran for the bathroom with its giant mirror behind the granite counter. Susannah plucked the necklace from its case and held it up.

"Jordan, its fabulous. Come see." Susannah hastily attached the earrings, pulling back her grimy blond hair with a plastic clip from the large Coach make-up case that lay open on the counter. Turning her head, she watched the earrings go from deep violet to aquamarine, then to periwinkle blue, "These are perfect triconic trillion cuts. Look at the color. Jordan?" He appeared in the mirror behind her. "Will you hook the necklace for me? Look at how the diamonds reflect a touch of the color. They're perfect."

"And they go well with the dirt and ashes in your hair."

Susannah made a funny face at the man who was as dirty as she.

"I especially like the lovely 'eau de bomb blast' you are wearing. It so compliments the earthy smell of smoking purse, and scorched shoes." A rose appeared in his hand. He drew it down her neck and across the ash smudged shoulders of her blouse. "I find the combination so… igniting." He flashed a devastating smile and planted a kiss on the tip of her ear just below some soot, but above the outrageously expensive earring set.

Babs had exquisite taste in jewelry. That was for sure. He would have to remember to tell her how he appreciated her assistance. The roses were an unexpectedly delicate touch. Jordan picked up the receiver next to the toilet and called Manolo's cell, leaving a message to procure Susannah's car and leave it in the garage. He mentioned a clean-up crew and some unexpected left-overs, then hung up.

Enthralled by the new baubles, Susannah didn't even notice his quick call. "Wow, these have to be at least a karat each and the pendant, humm… probably a two point five. Set you back a pretty penny, I'll bet." Susannah was doing a Vanna White in the mirror, calmly assessing the size and weight of the jewelry. Her assessment was critical and exacting.

"Okay, Susannah Helga Anderson Maddox, detective, spy, jeweler, what else?" His little gift didn't have the effect he expected. Usually, women who accepted his small gifts, did not assess their value out loud, or with quite as much accuracy. The events of the evening somehow became lost in the twinkle of diamonds and tanzanite.

"Oh, Jordan! I love it. Gift, bribe or promise?" She spun and threw her arms around his neck, looking speculative. "When did you select these? I don't understand how…"

"Neither, unfortunately. I needed your room number so I made up a crazy tale about having known you from before. I couldn't remember your name and as a gentleman, I…. The gal in gift shop was helpful when I wanted a small gift to go along with the name." He smiled and hung his arms around her hips.

"Small gift. Not! This must have cost upwards of three thousand dollars. The 'gal in the gift shop' has some idea of small. You should take it back and explain that size matters."

"No, you keep it. It is, after all, your favorite. And my credit card company will love my generosity, and romantic nature. I told Babs to pick something for herself as well. I can't wait to get the bill." Jordan winked. "It was worth it to find you somewhere other than in my dreams."

"Oh yeah, and end up knee deep in hot water, involved in a high speed car chase, and almost killed blowing a guy up along with your beautiful car." Susannah frowned and fingered the necklace with obvious guilt. Jordan's honest answer about the gift was surprising, but did nothing to deflate Susannah's excitement and appreciation of the jewelry. That was the job of guilt.

Jordan had to laugh at the teenager-woman wanna-be he held. She obviously wanted the trinket around her neck, but felt obligated to give it back due to her part in the circumstances they now found themselves in.

"Oh yeah, but..." he mocked her, adding a little extra sarcasm to his voice, "I got to make out with an incredibly beautiful woman. Even if it was just as bait. Well worth it in my book."

A soft pink tongue that tentatively licked wonderfully voluptuous lips captivated him. He was losing his mind and just possibly his heart. He couldn't take his eyes off the tongue and then... he did lose it – the mind part.

"Your kiss certainly came with a bang, Mr. Burke," Susannah whispered looking up at him from a coy little pose. She pulled him closer and stood on her tiptoes. "In that case, I'll keep your gift and simply offer my undying gratitude. And this."

Her lips met his in a gentle kiss that had just as much impact as the first one. His body exploded. Only, this time the building remained standing and the only flames that ignited were in his groin. He moaned and lifted her to him, crushing her against his chest as his tongue sought an opening.

"Susannah," he breathed into her welcoming mouth.

What hold did this woman's lips have over him? His cock tightened and grew of its own accord. A little voice in the back of his brain whispered that four-letter word he had not heard since his last human day on earth.

"Jordan," she breathed back, before his brain spun out of control again.

Susannah never felt the kind of power his kiss played across her mind and body. In a flash she was melting against his rock hard chest, gasping for a breath she didn't need, as their tongues fought for dominance. Her arms tightened around his neck with a mysterious will she'd never acknowledged before. Her nails dug into his flesh, eliciting a sensual growl that drew her passion even higher. She felt her fangs extend with excitement, as she breathed the scent of Jordan's sexual arousal.

He settled her against the counter as she tore at his shirt, needing the feel and taste of his skin. Like an addict needs a fix. What was left of the shirt came away in tatters as her hands roamed his muscular shoulders, learning every inch of his chest through her touch. Susannah closed her eyes and sank into the sensations.

Jordan's knees buckled. He leaned into Susannah for balance, feeling her pressure against his engorged cock. His body was completely out of control and he'd lost all power of reason and sanity just seconds before. He ripped the blouse from his blonde nymph, marveling in the perfect form of her neck and breasts. The black lacey contraption that kept him from what he wanted, fell away as his hands worked the hooks from experience and memory. Her scent was heady and intoxicating. He could not get enough. Gulping great lung fulls, Jordan felt her aroma spur him on, the taste solidifying his desire. His body vibrated with power and need as he fought to keep the blood lust associated with vampire sex, at bay.

Susannah's hands worked the button on his pants as her tongue laved at his lips. A fang caught, just for a split second on the edge of his mouth and she tasted his blood. A rush of quivering pleasure assailed her senses, and she fought the overwhelming need to take more. Instantly, a picture of the guard she accidentally killed in the caves in Afghanistan flashed before her eyes. She froze for an instant, as the memory assaulted her brain.

Immediately, Susannah pushed back from Jordan.

"I can't. I can't control it, Jordan." Panting, her eyes burned blood red and she shook on the precipice of losing control. All she could focus on, was the tiny drop of blood that seeped from a puncture wound on the outside of his lower lip.

Jordan did not want to let go. His mind and body were on fire with the racing hormones of a teenager but in a very experienced ninety-year old body. "It's okay, you can't hurt me, Susannah." He licked the droplet provocatively sliding a finger down her neck to rest between her creamy breasts. Her nipples called to him, pert and pebble hard. He leaned down and slowly took one into his mouth.

Susannah fell back on the counter crying out in pleasure. Holding his head with both hands, she pulled him closer. "Oh God, Jordan. I

can't take your blood. Don't let me take warm blood from y...
Ahhhh!" Her mind reeled and her body convulsed with a release like
none she had ever had.

"Jordan!" She screamed his name as she had screamed his
father's name, years before.

Susannah tore his pants in a wild effort to unzip the Dockers he
still wore. She shoved them impatiently to the floor. His briefs went
next, floating to the black tile in shreds. Her hands found his hard
cock and stroked the tight smooth skin as he continued to suck at each
nipple, one after the other. His tongue sent spasms of electricity
through her body, taking her even higher, even closer to danger... to
blood lust.

Jordan withdrew his lips and blew cool air across Susannah's
nipple. He smiled as she cried out and grasped him tighter. He slid
her jeans down and toyed with the lace panties she wore. They
matched the bra that lay on the floor with his torn clothing.

Every gesture, every move, was reflected in the mirror behind
Susannah and he marveled at her perfect figure and cream skin, pink
with excitement.

She was adorable.

Cute.

Sweet.

Beautiful.

No, gorgeous!

Sexy.

Hot.

She was everything all rolled into one. He pulled her to the edge
of the counter and lifted her to him, slowly settling her onto his
throbbing sex.

"Uhh, you're so tight, so wonderfully tight." He was on the edge
of orgasming already. God he hated his teen body. "Don't move or
you'll make me come."

"Isn't that the idea?" She breathed in his ear and wiggled her hips
outrageously. Locking her legs around Jordan's back, she moved her
hips in a small circle watching Jordan's face. He was straining to
maintain control and the artery at his neck pulsed, tantalizing her
beyond the ability to resist.

She sunk her fangs into his skin and sucked.

Jordan gasped as the combined pleasure of sex and Susannah's
bite hit him, all at once. He spun and slammed her against the
bathroom door, pounding into her as she drew his blood. The door

splintered, wrenched from its hinges he held her tight, pumping into her with each mouthful she took from him. His fangs appeared and he slid them against her naked shoulder, unable to resist the frenzy of passion and blood. His mind and body exploded as he sunk his fangs into her flesh, sucking the nectar, rich with raging desire and thick with passion.

Susannah felt Jordan climax. She felt his sweet bite and her body burst into a million shards of crystal, each tiny piece vibrating with a jolting energy of its own. The feeling swelled and burst into bright flashes before her eyes. Swirling in a mass of cataclysmic sensations, she collapsed against his body as her fangs retracted from his neck. Her tongue caught the last drip before her eyes closed and a warm, sweet darkness enveloped her.

Susannah's arms hung limp as he took one last mouthful and released his bite on her shoulder. His legs shook as if he would collapse at any second. Jordan leaned his back against the edge of the shower and slowly slid to the floor, still buried within Susannah. Taking her with him to the floor, a tiny trickle of blood slid down her shoulder to the tip of a breast. The drop hung, quivering, suspended on her pink nipple, swollen from his earlier ministrations. His tongue darted to catch the drop as it dripped from her skin.

Susannah shuddered in his arms, the necklace and earrings twinkling with her movement.

"Wow. If I'd only known what tanzanite could do." Jordan panted, licking his lips and planting a kiss on Susannah's head.

"Mmm," she mumbled, cuddling against his damp chest.

Jordan felt the cold, hard tile beneath his bare ass and tried to adjust to a more comfortable position. "Uh, Susannah?"

"Mmm, huh?" She wiggled dislodging his cock and he groaned at the loss of contact.

"Susannah, I have to move." His sweat soaked skin was beginning to chill and cold from the bathroom tile. It was seeping into his bones, reducing the vampire's naturally cold body even more. His feet were crossed and tangled in the Dockers that captured his legs. Though vampires healed quickly, pain was a feeling that still coursed through the body with the same strength as it did in a human.

"Um, huh." She burrowed her head in his shoulder with a satisfied sigh and began to softly snore against his skin.

It made a cute puttering sound and Jordan chuckled.

"Okay then, I guess it's up to me. He lifted her from the floor in a less than fluid move and carried her into the bedroom. The lost

Dockers dragged around his ankles making it necessary to take small, uneven steps. Thank God she slept, snoring through the entire process because Jordan caught sight of them in the full-length mirror. They looked like refugees from some natural disaster, instead of young lovers.

His legs still shook and he wasn't sure if he would make it to the bed.

Why was he so weak?

He had never been that way after sex before.

Of course, he'd never had sex with another vampire before.

The only other vampire blood he'd ever tasted was Marisella's. That was only when he was injured, and too weak to feed for himself. Her blood made him stronger. He had healed quickly after that.

But, this exhaustion was something new he did not understand.

Jordan deposited Susannah under the covers and sat on the edge of the bed to think. His mind was sluggish and he felt like he had run a thousand miles. Susannah murmured in her sleep and he turned to watch the beauty, still wearing her necklace and earrings, as she lay peaceful and content.

Jordan was dog-tired. The sun was up and he needed sleep. He lay back against the pillows to think about what he should do.

Go back to the estate and face the music?

Run?

Go somewhere with Susannah?

He closed his eyes in frustration. The pillow was so soft. Susannah burrowed into his shoulder; a contented smile playing across her sleeping features.

Chapter 16

Consequences of Living

The living, live until death.
The dead live forever.
So it is said, so shall it be…
Unto eternity.

Callicius Verillius, Gladiator, Vampire
Sparta, 1192 BC

Susannah cuddled closer to the cool body beside her. For the first time in years, she felt an overwhelming sense of contentment. The Egyptian cotton sheets of the hotel bed caressed her skin as she lay, slowly waking to the night's call. She could hear Jordan's slight snore and knew he slept soundly. Twice, her cell phone had vibrated on the nightstand, sending up a racket that would wake the dead. Well, it woke her anyway and she was technically dead.

It felt so wonderful to just lie there.

Her phone rattled again.

She resisted moving.

She especially resisted looking at the caller ID. It would be her father, Elizabetta or one of the Vamp Squad staff. She'd been gone for four days now. That was twenty-four hours longer than protocol allowed. Someone was tugging on her electronic leash. Susannah was surprised she was given that much leeway, considering her father was the commander of the Vamp Squad, and responsible for tracking all operatives at all times. She didn't tell anyone she was leaving and purposely remained out of touch. Her mission was personal, and her business.

Hers alone.

Now that it was a complete bust, she lay in bed thinking about what she should do next. She hadn't found her sire. Well, she couldn't have found him. He was dead. Actually dead and destroyed. But she did find his son. He was dead too, but still among the living.

She sighed.

Alive? Dead? These days it was a matter of perspective.

This dead thing was becoming confusing and over used in her

mind.

Jordan was a vampire, just like she was.

A teen made vampire just like she was.

He was a truly misunderstood teen vampire just like she was.

And he was hot!

She glanced at the sleeping figure of Jordan Burke, son of her sire. More than hot, he was incredibly sexy, buff hot. Like People's Sexiest Man of the Year times a thousand, hot!

Susannah licked her lips and stole another glance at his naked form, relaxed in day-sleep. There was more there than just lust. Her heart flipped in her chest. Uncle Rob's words flashed across her thoughts.

When you least expect it…

Susannah eyed Jordan; his features were child-like in sleep, his hair and face still smudged with soot. She smiled to herself. Wow! It had been an amazing twenty-four hours. Was it the Burke genes, or was sex with all vampires just plain mind-blowing? She was a virgin as far as sex with her own kind went. She had absolutely nothing with which to compare their tryst in the bathroom.

Jordan rolled over and threw an arm across Susannah. He sighed and smiled in his sleep, obviously as content as she.

Her cell phone vibrated again, rattling across the glass top on the nightstand, ending her contentment with its noise.

"Shhh!" She grabbed the phone and hit the green connect button. The screen showed the capital letters MVS2, the code for Monique's private line. So Frenchy was tasked with finding Miss Susannah, Operative on the loose.

"Hey, Frenchy. What's up girl?" Susannah answered her phone as if she were in her quarters, not four states away and in bed with a hot vampire lover.

"Cheri, are you alright? Everyone is worried. Mauvaise petite fille! Your father is out of his mind, and Elizabetta is spilling smoke from her ears. Even MorningStar has commented! Where are you?" Susannah could tell Monique was really worried, but her sister vampire's voice was tinged with curiosity as well. "Possibly, did you find some play thing and have been so enamored to have forgotten your family? Shame on you, sister!" The seductive giggle gave Monique away every time. She wanted to know details.

"I'm fine. I just needed to take some time for myself. You know, grow up. Find myself. Please tell everyone not to worry. I'm okay." Susannah winked at Jordan, who had awakened and now watched her talking from his pillow.

"So, Cheri, you will be home for dinner then?" Monique was hunting for clues. Susannah watched the time on her display. No more than two minutes, or they would have a fix on her without having to really work for it.

Not good.

"Hey Frenchy, let me call you back. I've got something on the stove." Susannah pushed the red disconnect button and tossed the phone on the chair a few feet away.

Something on the stove?

Couldn't she have come up with a statement a little more in keeping with her personality? She was just too distracted by Jordan's sleepy smile. He really was irresistible, with his hair a mess and those yummy brown eyes watching her every move.

"Morning, handsome." Susannah smiled and snuggled into Jordan's outstretched arm. She fit perfectly against his shoulder.

"If I look anything like I feel, handsome is not a word I would associate with me. Daddy looking for you? And who is Frenchy?"

"You sure wake up curious, Mr. Burke. Frenchy is my sister, sort of. My father has called twice, and his Lieut…, ah, friend, has called as well. Obviously they figured out I would answer Monique's call so they made her dial me. Never the slow one, my father."

"He keeps pretty close track of you. What is this about something on the stove? You eat cooked food as well as drink soda? Ick. I don't even like to smell food cooking – brings back painful memories of the ribs my mom used to fix before…" Jordan closed his eyes.

"I know. There are a lot of things I miss about being human, not the least of which is a quart of Ben and Jerry's Triple Chocolate Raspberry Ripple. Especially on a real bad day." Susannah sighed wistfully as she licked his skin and smacked her lips. "Nothing like comfort food."

"You little tease, you!" He pulled her on top of him and took to her lips like they were a slab of ribs smothered in bar-b-que sauce, licking and sucking the tender juices.

Immediately, Susannah settled a knee on each side of his hips and undulated against his erection as she returned his eager kisses. "Wow, when you wake up, *you* wake *up*!"

Her hands roamed his hard chest playing with the ripped muscles, tracing their patterns on his flesh. His skin was cool and smooth, not how she remembered his father's. Of course, Kellan was older and more mature. His chest was covered with soft blonde hair that felt like velvet. Or, at least that was what she recalled through the alcoholic blur of four years ago.

Her mind began to tingle as Jordan's tongue wound around hers and sucked. She could feel a repeat of the bathroom scene coming on, complete with the overpowering blood lust.

Embarrassment lashed at her building libido.

"No!" Susannah sprang from the bed and stood a few feet away, a hand covering her mouth to hide fangs that began to descend.

"No Jordan, we can't. I mean, I can't." She hung her head focusing on her toes in abject disgust. "I don't know how to control the blood lust every time I get excited. I was in Afghan…, well, I was doing a job and ended up getting carried away. I once killed a man. I can't let that happen again. You know I belong to a coven that does not approve of feeding on human blood." Red tears began to trickle down Susannah's face.

Jordan sat up and motioned for her to sit on the bed next to him. "It's okay. I don't understand why you bother, but it's okay." He patted her hand in a brotherly fashion – not at all what she expected from him. "I have never lived the way you do. It's natural for our kind, Susannah. Like sex, it's who and what we are."

"Not me. It's not who I am. I can't…" The tears flowed freely.

Jordan found her lifestyle confusing and frustrating. He didn't know what to say to her. It was like they were from two different countries. More like two entirely different religious backgrounds. It definitely placed a damper on his evening wake *up*. "I have to go anyway." He was obviously disappointed but willing to give Susannah the space she needed to gain control. "If it's okay, I'll grab a quick shower and be out of your hair."

"Where will you go? Will you be safe with your coven? They must have figured out about Drechell by now. What will happen when you return with his car?" Susannah followed a naked Jordan into the bathroom, her string of questions running together without time for his answers in between. "More importantly, what are you going to wear?" She pointed to his pile of filthy and ripped clothing. They lay in a jumble on the bathroom floor next to his shredded briefs.

"I don't know, Susannah. Maybe some hot water and soap will clear my head and I can think of something. I'm not sure, but I think Metolius knows when something happens to one of us." A grin erupted from the frown he had worn a second before. "Think he'd notice if I returned naked? Seriously, even though my father wasn't from his line, he still knew when the old man fried. Metolius is seriously old and very powerful." Jordan walked around the glass divider. He turned the water on to heat up and stuck his head out of the steam. "Maybe you could write me a note? Like my mom did in school when I was absent. How about that?"

Susannah sat on the counter next to the sink, and watched the perfect specimen of a man through the glass. She'd never really paid attention to a man in the shower before. It was intriguing. Jordan moved like a dancer in a classical ballet, fluid and supple. He worked the shampoo into his hair and scrubbed vigorously, stretching and preening like a cat after a nap. He seemed to enjoy the hot water and steam.

"You gonna come out to breathe?" Susannah heckled from the counter, enjoying the show.

"I loved the heat and humidity when I was human. I still do. I was born in Louisiana, the hotter the better." He continued to enjoy the steamy water.

Susannah continued to enjoy the show.

Soon she couldn't help herself. Drawn from her front row seat, she slid in behind Jordan joining him in the misty hot shower.

His body was covered with a film of white froth, and his hair stood in a clump of foamy soap. Her hands ached to slide all over his skin, playing with the slippery coating. She touched his wide shoulders and skimmed her fingers down the center of his back, feeling each bump of each vertebra under his skin. She followed the trickles of water that ran with her touch. Susannah's hands paused at his rump, savoring the next move.

Would she be able to maintain control if her hands roamed farther south?

She slid her arms around his waist and fondled the soft film of hair that grew in a circular pattern around his navel. Her fingers followed the flow and moved lower.

Jordan leaned back against her wet breasts and moaned, loving the slick film between them and the feel of two soft mounds pressed to his back.

"The name 'prick tease' must have been invented for you." A gritty growl escaped his lips as a shudder passed across his shoulders and down muscular legs that now strained to hold him up. "Susannah, how can you play like this? Don't you know what it does to me?"

He turned to face her, his eyes a deep blood red. A fleeting smile crossed his lips showing brilliant white fangs completely distended. "You're not the only one that seems to have trouble with self control when we're together. This… thing we have…is so totally unexpected. A simple touch and you can really blow my socks off. It's weird." Jordan raised an eyebrow and shot her a puzzled look.

Completely stunned by his choice of words, Susannah paused as Uncle Rob's statement came back to haunt her for the second time that morning.

Nope, it had to be a coincidence.

She wasn't in love with a man she had just met!

It was impossible and completely, what?

Unexpected?

A shiver ran down her spine.

Love at first sight?

Impossible.

Completely caught off guard, Susannah did what she did best; ignored the serious and fled for self-satisfaction. She slowly shrugged a sensuous shoulder and slid to the smooth tile floor of the shower. She loved the scent and taste of the man who now towered over her, sending a spray of fine water across her body. Her soft tongue touched the tip of his growing ardor and she heard Jordan moan with pleasure as he struggled to keep his balance. She circled the tip of his cock with her tongue, and then took him deep into her throat. Now it was her turn to groan with pleasure as his taste consumed her senses.

She wanted him deeper, harder, more of his taste and scent. She breathed in his smell mixed with sweet soap, steam and the spray of the shower. Closing her eyes she immersed herself in a fantasy of taking Jordan this way on a grassy bank somewhere in the bayou. She imagined the Louisiana heat and humidity bearing down on her naked body as she worked her oral magic. For once she focused on giving pleasure, rather than taking her own.

"Susannah, my little teasing nymph." Jordan fisted her hair and pulled her tighter to him. The water poured over them as she sucked and laved his cock. He groaned and murmured words of passion until a shudder passed through his body and he growled her name over and over.

Her strategy was working. She was maintaining control while her pleasure built slowly. She squirmed against the tile floor, pulling Jordan down with her to the cool wet tiles. "Don't let me go. I don't want your blood, just your… body." She almost said *love*, but caught herself before she could make that mistake.

Susannah forced herself to focus on reality; she was engaging in sexual pleasure in a hotel shower with an incredible stud.

Nothing more.

But there was more somewhere in the back of her mind that fought its way toward her tongue. She pressed her lips together to keep from making some crazy confession she would most likely regret later.

Crawling over Jordan's long body to find his lips, they stretched out on the tile. The luxurious shower would accommodate at least a party of five, and she found plenty of room to play in comfort. Jordan was more than willing to let her play. Slithering up onto his chest, she lay atop her lover, planting tiny feather kisses across his jaw and cheeks. She was careful to avoid his neck and the veins that throbbed with enticing excitement. They were too tempting for her still.

"Jordan, I can't get enough of the taste of you. My blood is on fire. My head is spinning." She lowered her lips closer to the carotid pulse calling to her. Red warning signs flashed before her eyes. She pulled away with a small cry, scrambling to the side of the shower to crouch against the glass. "Damn it."

"What?" He raised his head from the tile to look at Susannah pressed against the glass, resembling a whipped puppy trying to escape its master.

"I can't do it without biting you. I won't do that. It's wrong." She plopped down, sitting with her knees drawn up, arms wrapped tightly, holding herself in check. "I'm sorry."

Jordan sat up and took her in his arms. "Like I said before, it's okay." He planted a kiss on her wet forehead, took a deep breath, then stood to finish his shower with a deep sigh. "Come up here and let me do your hair. It's so luscious, like spun gold. I love the way it feels in my hands."

Susannah could tell he was thoroughly disappointed, yet he would not push her beyond her comfort zone. Surprised, but frustrated at the same time, she marveled at the man who held a hand to pull her from the floor. How many of her past boyfriends would have acted so honorably, in the wake of her mixed up crazy behavior? The answer was easy and immediate.

None.

With a very teenage flounce, she stood and turned to face the wall as Jordan pumped shampoo into his hand. He lathered her hair slowly, paying close attention to every inch of her scalp. He worked the soap like an expert, massaging as he went. It felt heavenly, and oh so sensual. She could feel his body against her back.

What if?

Susannah wiggled her ass cheeks against Jordan's cock, feeling his stiffness pulse against her. She slid her hand behind and stroked his length. Jordan's strangled groan cemented her decision. Bending just a little, she guided his manhood to the right spot and slid her hips back to ensconce him completely. As long as she kept her mouth away from his neck, she might just keep herself from biting him in uncontrollable lust.

As their rhythm built, Jordan reached around to cup her breasts with both hands, messaging her nipples and creating ripples of sensual pleasure that caused her muscles to clench drawing him deeper. His lips sucked at her neck and covered her back with hot kisses.

How could one man's kisses on her back make her entire body shake and quiver for release? She pressed against the length of him and rode his cock until an orgasm drowned her senses, leaving her limp and weak.

Jordan held Susannah against his chest as her muscles pulsed and clenched in the throws of orgasmic pleasure. It was all he could take. Exploding into her with a deep growl, he slid them to the floor and sat holding her on his lap in sheer exhaustion. For a few moments they cuddled under the pelting hot water, just enjoying soapy bodily contact in the afterglow of fantastic sex.

"Why don't I go back to the estate with you, Jordan? It would make your story more plausible, then if there is trouble, I can help you escape. I could corroborate last night's adventures. I'd really love to see where you live. The Proctor estate? You said Metolius allowed other vampires into the coven." She was burbling her words through the water as Jordan placed her head under the shower and began rinsing the shampoo from her long tresses. "You could say I was looking for your father and found you instead. That part is true." Susannah choked on the water and coughed. "Maybe, I could be checking out the coven to see if I wanted to join." She was reaching for anything to make their dicey situation better, even if it meant walking into the snake pit.

Jordan had to laugh as he stood and planted Susannah on her feet. "Your naiveté never ceases to amaze me. You don't go shopping for a coven, silly." He flopped her hair into a loose bun and planted it on her head with a childlike pat. "Covens take vampires. Whether they like it or not. Or you end up like my old man. With Metolius, maybe worse."

"Well, what if I just showed up as your girlfriend? Besides, I'd like to do a little recon on that drug you mentioned. CE? Right?"

161

Susannah turned to face Jordan, naked and wet with her hands on her hips.

"Susannah," Jordan grabbed her around the waist and pulled her close to him. "No way in hell will you get yourself tangled up with CE. Not even close to it. Understand? Don't touch it. Don't try it. Don't talk about it. That is, unless you have a death wish."

Susannah could tell by the deep tone of his voice and the intense look in his eyes that he was serious and concerned about her curiosity.

"Don't you be silly! I never did drugs when I was human, and I don't intend to start now. I just think there might be more about this drug than you think. The idea of killing two birds with one stone makes sense to me. What happens to humans if they take it?"

Susannah's cheeks were turning red with the heat of the shower. She pulled from Jordan's arms and rinsed quickly. Stepping from behind the glass, she grabbed a towel and continued the conversation.

"Jordan, tell me what you know about CE and I promise I won't ask at the estate."

"Of course you won't ask at the estate because you are NOT going to the estate. It's not safe for you. In fact, it's not safe for you to stay in Daytona Beach either. If Drechell communicated any part of what went on last night, we're both dead meat." He enunciated his words carefully as he rinsed and followed Susannah. "I'm not strong enough to sense anything this far away from Proctor and the estate, but when I get closer, hopefully, I will know a little more about what the master knows. That doesn't mean I can predict what he will do, or even know all of what he knows. This is risky business, Susannah. If I survive, I will be lucky." Jordan threw his wet towel on the floor and stomped into the bedroom. "I won't let you get drawn into this mess. I can't. Metolius has big plans for this country. He thinks he is a visionary."

"But Jordan, you don't understand. I have certain skills…"

"It doesn't take any skill to die. You've done it once already. Wanna make it permanent? Metolius Proctor's coven is huge. He has his fingers in all kinds of stuff, not just pharmaceuticals. He owns the cops and most of the politicians in the area. His influence grows with every election. He sees the future of this country as some new home for vampires. Somehow CE plays a key part. Nobody will be allowed to get in the way of his plans. He has his own personal army of enforcers. You'd be lucky to make it out of Daytona Beach let alone across the state border, if he didn't want you to." Jordan was pacing the floor as he spoke. "You got your vampire life from my old man, so

162

let him give you the lesson of his death; don't cross Master Metolius! End of conversation."

"But, Jordan, I can-"

"NO YOU CAN'T! Don't even think about it. Just pack your bags and go home to Daddy and whatever it is you do, Susannah Helga Anderson Maddox." Jordan tugged a dry towel tightly around his hips looking at his stained Dockers and torn shirt on the floor. "Shit. I'll have to call downtown for new clothes before I leave. No sense giving the whole ballgame away at the onset." He rummaged through his pockets for a wallet and car keys, then paused at the bathroom door.

"For your own sake, don't follow me to the estate. Please." The sincerity in his eyes was enough to keep Susannah from arguing, but she was not ready to let the subject drop. She watched Jordan sit on the bed and dial the clothing shop on the main floor.

"All right. I won't follow you, but I'm not ready to go home yet. Maybe tomorrow." Susannah was stubborn and pouty. "I have a couple more things to check out before I head north. Maybe we can have a goodbye drink. Tomorrow night? I should be ready to leave by then. How about it?" She stood in the bathroom doorway wrapped in her own towel.

After a few quick words, Jordan crossed the room in a flash. Gathering her face in his hands, he kissed her forehead then her earlobe, pulling her toward the bed before he realized what he was doing. "As much as I would love to… the answer is no. Go home before it's too late, Susannah. This is not a game, it's your neck." He slid his fangs along her skin breathing deeply, then moved quickly into the bathroom, slamming the door behind him.

Susannah stood alone in the middle of the room, half naked and chilled. What just happened?

She dropped the towel and tugged on a pair of comfy sweats anticipating the delivery of Jordan's clothing. How had they gone from hot lovers to opponents, or whatever they were?

What were they?

Was Jordan's concern more than just worry about Metolius or was there something more? If it was more, then how could he so easily send her packing?

She was confused.

Jordan was headed back to the estate despite the fact that he would probably be called to answer for the death of Master Metolius' first lieutenant. He knew how dangerous it was, yet he was going anyway. He wouldn't talk about CE. He didn't want her asking any questions either. According to him, it was too dangerous.

Well, he just didn't understand.

She could handle herself.

She was a well-trained undercover operative.

She'd been to Afghanistan, blew up the Taliban and came out alive.

How much more dangerous could some old vampire be?

A chime announced the bellman loaded with a zipped suit bag, shoebox, and plastic bag of sundries. Susannah tipped the man and knocked on the bathroom door.

"Stuff's here."

Silence dominated the room as Jordan dressed and gathered his things to leave. With a quick peck on the cheek, he reaffirmed his earlier statement. "Don't fool around here, Susannah. This place killed you once. Don't let it happen again. I don't have a choice, but you do." He shook his head before walking out, leaving behind an angry and frustrated woman.

More than frustrated and confused, Susannah's little demons began to dance in her mind.

She stomped into the bathroom.

Huh!

No one was going to tell her what she could, and couldn't do. She stripped, leaving the sweats in the middle of the room. Flouncing through the bathroom, she grabbed her make-up kit and stared into the mirror.

Sexy or sweet tonight? Which one would get her the most information about this mysterious coven and its little drug?

After all, Danger was her middle name.

Detective girl was her game.

Chapter 17

Invincibility of Youth

The young never seem to understand,
The ways of the world have a heavy hand,
In the lessons of time and place,
Oft leaving behind an empty space.
Where once stood a youth in prime,
The waste of young life - such a crime.

Illianna Nightshade, Philosopher, Vampire
Macedonia Prima, 425 BC

"Ms. Merchant, a response?" Colonel Maddox stood stiff as a rod. He gazed out the tiny window of the farmhouse that disguised the entrance to the subterranean Vamp Squad complex.

Monique knew he'd spent a good portion of the day watching the road that led through the woods to the main highway. She found his 'straight as a rod' posture at odds with the flannel shirt and baggy jeans he wore as cover when above ground at Olney Farm.

"Ah, Colonel, she said she would call me back. Apparently she was ...cooking?" Monique looked suspiciously at Susannah's father, as he clenched and re-clenched his hands. His eyes never left the road.

"Did she say where she was?" He asked the questions as if it were an order.

"No, she did not. In fact, I am sure she was counting the seconds, Sir. She hung up just before two minutes. Susannah knows that we could have pinpointed the location of her cell phone, if she unceeded that amount of time. I believe she wants to be d'isolement, alone for a while." Monique was worried about her little sister as well, but had an idea what the young woman was up to.

"That's ex...ceded, madam. Sgt. Miller can find her anyway. It will just take a little longer." Colonel Maddox stomped across the kitchen toward a cellar door. A secret panel in the cellar concealed one of the many entrances to the complex below.

"I believe she knows that, Sir." Monique took his place at the window, straining to see through the cloudy dark afternoon. "I also believe she has her own agenda. A private agenda."

165

Maddox paused before the open doorway to the cellar stairs. "Ms. Merchant, my daughter is nothing, if not intelligent. And she has never cooked a thing in her life, or death." He clomped noisily down the stairs.

Monique tried not to giggle at a father's obvious frustration. It was a toss up, whether he was more angry at an operative's insubordination, or a daughter's misbehavior. He was not used to being thwarted by anything, let alone a daughter. All things compounded, she was curious how the Colonel would handle Susannah's return. Still she pretended to watch for a pair of blue tinted headlights in the rising fog, knowing full well her sister was not going to appear any time soon.

Colonel Maddox hit the Operations Command Center doors with his fist, slamming the swinging metal door open with a loud bang. Sergeant Milo Miller jumped in his seat. Already Susannah's cell phone records glared in lime green script on the sergeant's monitor. The Colonel did not have a clear view of the screen and had no idea Miller anticipated his visit... and request.

"Sergeant, pull up my daughter's cell records. I want to know the location of her last call. About five minutes ago." Maddox was all business and Miller knew the faster he worked, the sooner Maddox would calm down. His daughter had been gone for nearly four full days. Colonel Maddox was not a patient man when it came to Susannah. Apparently, he wasn't willing to wait any longer to find the girl and get her back to the safety of Olney Farm. Sergeant Miller was well aware Maddox thought he knew his daughter well. The Sergeant was sure Maddox figured she could only be in some kind of trouble, as usual.

Miller concentrated on the task in front of him.

"Done, Sir. Working on the location now." Miller's fingers flew across the extended keyboard.

"How-?"

"Monitoring all communications in and out of the facility, Sir. My job." Milo smiled to himself. He was monitoring the security cameras from his consol and listening in on the Colonel's conversation with Monique. The newly healed belly dancer tattoo on his right arm undulated, as his fingers tapped the keys in rapid succession.

"Do you-"

"Florida, Sir. Triangulating as we speak. One moment, Sir." Milo worked the screens, pinpointing coordinates and reducing the areas of search. He rarely bothered to look up when engrossed in a search.

"Sergeant, is there some-"

"No, Sir-"

"-reason you have an answer, before I even get the question out?" Maddox walked behind the Sergeant's monitor and watched the progress, his arms tightly locked across his chest.

Miller shifted in his chair, uncomfortable with the Colonel behind him. He was uncomfortable with anyone behind him, let alone an angry father who was also his commander.

"Just being efficient, Colonel. Bingo. Daytona Beach. Downtown area. On the beach. Probably a resort. Stand by Sir, I'll have it in a second."

Miller was multi-tasking on the fly as he worked two monitors. One screen showed a satellite location with a dot for the position of Susannah's phone. The other was a road map of the same area.

"I have an address, sir. Longwood Drive and Ocean Shore Boulevard, Sir."

"Where-"

"The Beachcomber Resort, Sir."

"Miller, let-"

"Yes, Sir." Miller responded without looking up. He was already pulling up the hotel registration records.

"Miller, damn it! Let me at least get the question out before you give me the answer. It probably doesn't do anything for you, but it helps *me* keep up with the conversation. Can you-"

"No one registered under Susannah Maddox, Sir."

"Mil-ler?" Maddox growled as he drew out the Sergeant's name in exasperation.

"Ah, sorry, Sir. You were going to ask me to check the hotel registry. I did. No Susannah, Sir. However, there is a Ms. Anderson."

"So?" Maddox didn't get the connection right away.

"Helga Anderson, Sir." Now Miller did look up, waiting for the Colonel's light to come on. The Vamp Squad's leader was usually faster on the uptake, but dealing with anything involving his daughter had an unusual effect on the Colonel. With Susannah it wasn't ready-aim-fire. It was more like ready-fire-aim. Working the issue probably slowed his brain due to the amount of energy it took to control his temper at the same time. Miller smirked to himself, but carefully hid the expression.

"Doctor Anderson is in Daytona Beach with Susannah?" Maddox

was not making the connection. But it had very little to do with just his daughter and everything to do with fighting the irresistible urge to throttle the Sergeant. Miller did that to some people and the Colonel's frustration button was glowing brilliant red. His daughter was a thousand miles away, involved in who knew what, and his Sergeant seemed interested in Helga Anderson.

"No, Sir. Obviously Ms. Maddox has taken her undercover training to heart and is using a false name." Miller tried to keep the sarcasm out of his voice as best he could. He'd never seen Maddox this slow. "I imagine she has counterfeit identification and is operating under the name Helga Anderson." A tiny trickle of sweat appeared on the tan skin of Miller's forehead.

The Colonel didn't seem to notice.

As Miller was providing answers for the Colonel, he was putting two and two together and coming up with some answers of his own. So, the little snippet had used him to set up a personal scam. He'd better figure out what it was before his part in her escapade was discovered.

"Orders, Sir?"

"No, not right now, Sergeant. Find out anything you can about what my daughter is up to, would you? Let me know when you do. And thanks, Milo."

Wow, the Colonel actually knew his first name! *Great way to stay under the radar, stupid,* Miller mentally chastised himself. He took the Vamp Squad position a few years back, sight unseen. Then, he needed to be underground for a while. His last unplanned escapade had almost landed him in the brig. The fact that Colonel Maddox used his first name was disturbing.

What else did the Colonel know about him?

How much had slipped into his file?

Somewhere, once upon a time, there had been a lonely sixteen year-old general's daughter pining away for the handsome soldier who professed his undying love. Disappearing after he had done a little more than just profess his love, Miller did what he had to do to save his hide. Which directly related to the need to disappear and stay underground for a while. General Pantterdyck had a long memory and an even longer reaching arm in this man's army. His little girl was his pride and joy. He would have killed any man who hurt the young woman, at least any man he could catch. Milo was a slick operator, but not slick enough to escape the General's grasp. Since homicide was against the law, Pantterdyck gave him a choice. Which was why he jumped at the opportunity to join the deep cover operative group without a lot of background information up front.

Since his assignment to the squad, humans had been the least dangerous of the individuals he dealt with. So, Susannah's sweet smile and earnest questions manipulated the ultimate manipulator?

She'd conned the con.

He was slipping.

So, what was sweet little Susannah and her cute fangs up to?

Milo shuddered at the thought of those fangs. All of the vampires he worked with gave him the creeps, even sweet Suze. He took great precautions to make sure he was never alone with any of them, despite the Vamp Squad's strict prohibition on biting humans or drinking warm blood. Though he hid it well, he still didn't trust the vamps. One never knew when a vampire would change her mind and cross the line. Once he'd had a pet rabbit he raised from a baby and after three years of loving and caring for the cute little white bunny, one day it bit him for no reason. The next evening his family had rabbit stew. He would never trust an animal again.

In his book vampires were animals.

Truly, fangs and hormones were not something to mess with.

A shaky hand adjusted the plastic collar he wore beneath his ACUs. No sense taking chances. Vampires were not human and he was not about to become a meal for some hungry thing that saw him mainly as a food source.

No way, not this sergeant, he thought with a smirk. Somehow Susannah had gotten under his skin though. He thought back on their conversations and the seemingly simple favors she manipulated him into doing for her.

"Milo?" Dr. Anderson and Monique Merchant stood in the doorway. "Did you find Susannah? I am very worried about the young lady." Helga Anderson joined the Vamp Squad about a year ago and was studying vampires as a government sponsored project. Earlier in the month she took delivery of a truckload of records and partial research projects from the Nazi days. After just a few hours in the archives she was ecstatic over the information found. Apparently it was just the surface of what information the old moldy boxes contained. She and Elizabetta planned to dig in after the wedding when Susannah abruptly disappeared.

"Yes, ma'am. She's in Daytona Beach." He responded watching the three screens he now worked with quiet efficiency. He loved the access he had to technology. This job was cherry. He simply had to ask and it appeared.

No budget queries.

No red tape.

No security constraints.

Cherry.

"Ah, mon ami, any idea why she is there?" Monique appeared behind the Sergeant and ran a finger down the back of Milo's neck.

"Ms. Merchant, please don't do that." Miller spun in his seat and ended up facing Monique's lovely décolleté, neatly tucked into a very tight and very revealing pink sweater.

Monique giggled and took a tiny step back. "Cheri, I would never hurt you… on purpose. And if I did, I guarantee that you, mon amour, would thank me for it, and beg for more." She bent and flicked her tongue across the tip of Miller's nose. "Oui?"

"No! Please, ma'am. I'm just doing my job here. Nothing more. Nothing. Understand?" That trickle of sweat found it's way to his collar. He hated fearing this incredibly beautiful woman, but he could not get over the fact that she had fangs and drank blood. The synthetic version of blood the vamps in the complex lived on was developed in the 90s, but in his book, blood was blood. To the French vampire, Synth-Blood-In-A-Bag was the vampire version of a MacDonald's happy meal.

"Monique, leave the poor young Sergeant to his business there. Obviously he doesn't appreciate your more unique, and abundant assets." Helga laughed as she strode across the room to join the Sergeant and the vampire. "So what are you finding with all of your nefarious, high-tech skills?"

Helga noticed the Sergeant's obvious nervousness.

"Something more than Monique is bothering you, Milo. What's up?" Helga had a sensitive way of getting the Sergeant to spill his guts.

"Dr. Anderson, before Susannah left, she wanted me to help her find some information about her death. I wonder if that had anything to do with her little excursion? I certainly hope not. I don't want any trouble. Why Daytona Beach? What's there, other than really bad memories?" Miller was pulling up all kinds of information about the area and people.

"Who knows? Did you ask her father?" Dr. Anderson was watching the Colonel through the glass window of his office. The man was pacing back and forth. "Maybe I should have a talk with Maddox. He seems agitated."

"Good idea, with Ms. Merchant please. Maybe the three of you can figure out why Susannah would go to Daytona Beach alone, without telling anyone." Miller smiled at Helga with such a hopeful look the doctor almost laughed. She was well aware Miller did not wish to be alone with a female vampire, especially Monique

"Of course. Monique?" Miller watched the two women whisper to each other as they crossed the Ops floor to Maddox's office. Safe again, he wiped the sweat from his face and settled in to work on the current mystery. Other than the location, there was little information about Susannah's death and how she became a vampire.

Miller's skill as a strategist was keen and honed to a fine point, but his ability to ferret out information from a myriad of public, as well as classified sources, was phenomenal. It was also dangerous. It landed him in no small amount of trouble on several occasions in his past.

Frustrated at the slow refresh response on three of his screens, he pulled another terminal into his semi-circular workstation, then settled into his own mini-command center for a long night of searching. He felt comfortable in his silicon-castle surrounded by computer banks and screens, as he kept an eye on the two women in the Colonel's office.

"Frank, you mean to tell me you have no idea why your daughter has run off to Daytona Beach? It's not even close to spring break." Helga watched her questions slide off the Colonel as if he were made of teflon.

That was, until she mentioned spring break.

Then he visibly blanched.

Monique sighed. "Ah, so that is it, mon ami. She returns to the place of her birth as a vampire, no?" The French vamp patted Colonel Maddox on the shoulder. "What is a father to do?" Monique was playing her part to the hilt. With the inside information Monique had from Susannah's note, she quickly figured out the parts her sister left unsaid.

"Susannah was turned in Daytona Beach during a spring fling, right? Is that it, Frank?" Helga sat in the chair by the door and thought for a moment. "It becomes clear to me now. She left after Natalia's wedding, didn't she? Elizabetta mentioned her concerns to me about Susannah. Your daughter seemed to be having trouble with the emotionality of their ceremony. I believe Susannah has gone to find her sire, possibly a husband as well. Do you know who turned your daughter, Frank?

"No, I have no idea. When Ted and I retrieved her body, we drove straight to Maine. She was, ah, not in any condition to, ah, well, you know. She had just awakened in a coffin, for God's sake. She didn't know anything. She didn't even recognize me for a long time." Maddox collapsed into the chair behind his desk, head in his hands. "We opened the coffin and she tried to attack me. Ted, well, he knocked her out before she could, you know." The Colonel was avoiding eye contact with Helga as he spoke. "This is very hard for me. I wasn't myself back then. I didn't know anything about all this." He pointed at Monique. "By the time I started asking the right questions, the doors were closed. Everyone was tight lipped. I could never find a paper trail. The coroner disappeared for a while. It was a better cover-up than what my own government can manage, when they want to."

"Of course, it was a very strange beginning, to a very unique time in your life. I understand. So Ted was there, too? Maybe he remembers something. Mind if I have a chat with him, Frank?" Helga was being extremely sensitive, well aware that Colonel Maddox rarely spoke of his daughter's beginnings as a vampire. The pain he endured thinking she was dead nearly killed him. Then having to come to grips with the fact that she had actually been reborn as a vampire was the final challenge to a very stressful time in his life.

"Ted has gone home, Dr. Anderson. His mother is very ill. He wanted to visit before things got much worse. She has lung cancer, Helga." Monique had become a kind of *Information Central* at Olney Farm and somehow knew where everyone was at any given time with no effort at all. Everyone talked to Monique. Everyone except Milo Miller.

"I am sure you have his cell phone number, Ms. Merchant." The Colonel smiled at Monique knowingly.

"As a matter of fact, cheri, I do. I also have the number of his Highness, Prince Nicolas Sarkozy, and many, many more." She smiled coyly. "But I suppose you are simply interested in the number of Ted, no?" Monique pulled a crystal covered, hot pink phone from her hip pocket. Scrolling down, she tossed it to Helga. "Please, soyez mon invite, be my guest."

Helga hit the send button and waited. When she was transferred to voice mail, she left a quick message for Ted to call and flipped the phone back to Monique.

"Dead end for now. Thanks Monique. Frank, are you sure there is nothing more you can tell me about Daytona Beach, and Susannah?

Any connection at all?"

Colonel Maddox stared off into space for a few seconds. "There was a fire at a diner where we stopped for dinner, but I don't think it had anything to do with us. We left before the fire department arrived. I didn't want anyone checking on the load we carried. Know what I mean? When I think about it, we never followed up on the fire to make sure." He looked blank for a second, trying hard to remember the sequence of events of that tumultuous night. He wasn't proud of the way he had behaved, or his lack of usual military efficiency. "I don't believe I was at my best back then."

"Well, maybe Ted can shed some light on this little mystery. You need to get some sleep, Frank. You look exhausted." Helga smiled at the man she had come to know as a friend. They were close to the same age and both lost their spouses tragically. Both raised children alone. "I think I'll check with Natalia and MorningStar to see what they know."

"Yeah, Doc, you're probably right. No sense borrowing trouble. I think I'll catch a bite to eat first. Thanks, Helga, and you too Monique. I don't often say it, but I really do appreciate what you both have done for my daughter." Colonel Maddox was unaccustomed to baring his soul and made a hasty retreat before anything more could be said.

On his way through the Com Center, he paused. "Sergeant Miller, find anything and you'll-"

"Yes, Sir. In your quarters. Right." Miller didn't even look up as he responded, fingers still skipping across the keys at warp speed.

"On the line to me in my quarters. Right." Colonel Maddox shook his head mumbling to himself as he passed through the doorway. "God I wish he wouldn't do that."

Monique watched the Colonel leave in silence. She needed to find out how long Susannah planned to be gone. Things were getting out of control here at the farm, and now Miller was hot on the trail. She caught a glimpse of Helga's calculating look and shrugged with a sheepish smile.

Monique knew Helga suspected there was more to the story. Monique wasn't ready to spill her information until she really needed to, and hopefully Susannah herself would be back to explain her behavior before that happened. Sisterly secrets were one thing, but worrying an entire group was another thing. Monique was also painfully aware that her little sister had a way of getting into all kinds of trouble, with little or no effort.

*****

Susannah really didn't have anything left to do in Daytona Beach but just couldn't leave, yet. It was a matter of honor, as much as stubbornness, mixed with a little hope that she might get to see Jordan one more time. After the way they parted, it was a long shot. Shit, he could be dead by now, for all she truly knew. But as the saying goes, hope springs eternal.

She had come so far. Yet, now she knew all of her best-laid plans had literally gone up in flames more than four years ago. Kellan was dead, and she would never know her sire.

It was a dirty rotten shame.

Life was so unfair.

Damn.

Jordan had returned to the estate and probably walked into a lion's den. She understood he just wanted to protect her. What a guy. Hopefully, he was still a live undead guy. At the thought of Jordan her heart did a little flip.

She flopped on the bed and lay there staring at the ornate ceiling. "Damn, damn, damn! Why can't anything ever work out for me?" She kicked a couple pillows across the room and punched the mattress. Slapping a bag of synth-blood on her fangs, she hung backwards over the edge of the bed, letting her wet hair dangle onto the rug. She was hungry and drained the bag in seconds. The synth-blood was not half as enticing or satisfying as the blood she had taken from Jordan, but her guilt overshadowed that enjoyment. She still felt dirty and shameful. It was like sneaking alcohol from your parent's bar in high school – definitely taboo but just so…

"Damn, damn, damn!" She threw the empty bag at the pillows across the room and slapped a second bag to her teeth.

Her cell phone chimed. She grabbed for the crystal-covered phone as it vibrated off the nightstand. Caller ID showed MVS2 again. Monique.

"Shit." She punched the green button. "Monique, I said I'd call you back." Susannah tossed another empty bag at the pillows and missed.

"Susannah, do not hang up on me again, sister. Everyone is worried about you. Your father is cooking, and has set Milo on your trail. Is what I think going on, going on?" Monique was persistent and would not be put off.

"That's steaming, Monique. Who's listening?" Before she said anything, Susannah wanted to know who was on the other end of the line.

"No one, now talk! What are you really doing, and why are you in Daytona Beach?"

"Well, it didn't take you long to figure that out, did it? My guess is one Milo Miller had a hand in it, right? Make that a keyboard." She was mildly miffed. Miller was not supposed to have figured it out so soon. Maybe she underestimated the quirky sergeant.

"Of course, chéri. He is just so bright, and talented, and horribly afraid of all of us. It's cute. He actually sweats when I am in the room. Of all the reactions I desire from men, sweating in fear is generally not one of them. However, with Sergeant Miller, it is just so-divertissement, how do you say?" Monique giggled.

It was good to hear her voice and her perpetual happiness. "Entertaining, Monique. You have a warped sense of humor, Frenchy."

"Alright, back to you, my little sister. Spill the peas."

"That's beans, not peas, Frenchy. Okay. I came down here to find my sire and answer a few personal questions. You probably figured that out from my note. I'm coming home tomorrow. Tell my father not to worry. I'll explain everything when I get there. It was a stupid mistake. But you don't have to tell him that particular part." Susannah knew she could trust Monique. They shared some very secret secrets over the last few years. Susannah probably knew more about Monique than anyone else in the coven. They were as close as real sisters and truly enjoyed each other's company, and their secrets, of course.

"Did you find your Kell? What is he like? Tell me everything! I want to know les détails." Monique was intrigued.

"Shit, Monique, you know me. If it weren't for bad luck, I'd have no luck at all. He's dead. Dead and burned. His coven had him killed right after I was turned. I did meet his son, Jordan. That was cool. He's a real hotty, that one. But it's not going to go anywhere. He's a naturist vampire, Monique." Susannah was trying to gloss over the details, despite Monique's excitement.

"So, did you do the hotty, chéri? Come on, I want details, mon chéri!" Monique could barely contain herself over the phone. Her voice quivered with sensual pleasure. Monique's tendency toward voyeurism often got the best of her.

"I'll tell you everything when I get home tomorrow. You'll just have to wait until then." Susannah giggled and sat up in the middle of the bed. "Right now I have to get packed, and take one last shot at the bar downstairs. See if I can scare up anything else about Kellan, or his coven. I'll call you before I head north, okay? Give everyone a hug for me, even Miller. That should make him squirm. Ciao for now." Susannah hung up on purpose, without listening for an answer or comment from Monique.

She bounced off the bed and dug for something unique to wear that would tease and entice. It was time to be Helga Anderson, girl detective for one more evening. She found a tiny black sheath with rhinestones up and down the low neckline. The dress had no back and very little front. It was perfect.

She pulled a pair of strappy black spiked heels from her suitcase and tried them on. The effect was striking. Her sultry five foot six inch height suddenly became an elegant and sophisticated five foot nine. With kohled eyes that twinkled bright blue, and just enough bling to catch the attention of whomever she wished, Susannah looked like an international model. She was ready to hit the Mango Bango with a flare. Grabbing a rhinestone wrist clutch, she buckled the tiny purse to her arm, and inserted a platinum credit card in the name of Helga Anderson. Running a pick through her damp blonde hair, she flipped it upside down, then added a little spray for height.

Perfect!

Just enough messiness to be chic.

She was ready.

And so was the Mango Bango.

The club was hopping with a live band, pounding out the latest new age singles. People of all colors, sizes and shapes crowded the floor and crammed into booths that ringed the dance floor. The low lights created individual shadowy refuges where groups sat close, plying their trade, working their game with complete and secure anonymity. At first glance, nothing seemed to connect the patrons except the music and fancy drinks that cost way more than they should have. However, in reality, the common denominator was definitely money.

Susannah flashed her key at the manager and strutted toward the bar. The hubbub continued, but all eyes noticed the newcomer. It was exactly what she wanted.

"How about a Bloody Mary, with straight O negative." Susannah winked at the bartender and hitched a hip up on the stool. She did not miss the quick looks exchanged between the woman behind the counter, and the manager lounging at the end of the long bar. Susannah dazzled the woman with a brilliant smile and a little mental nudge.

A light hand slid to her elbow. "I be introducing myself once again, lovely lady. My name be Manolo, and I be da boss mahn in dis establishment, if you recall."

Susannah pulled away from the man's touch, but favored him with a seductive look. "I'm Helga Anderson. But you probably remember that as well?" She stuck out her hand.

"Ah, Jordi did give me the heads up. And you have the blessings of the Man, I would bet. Just let Delilah here know what you want, and she will provide it. If not, you let me know. I will serve you personally." Susannah smiled as Manolo signaled to Delilah with two fingers in a v shape. Obviously Manolo was used to serving vampires in his club. That was an interesting little piece of information to catalog and evaluate later. He must have known Jordan well to drop the phony accent with Susannah.

Exactly how much of this town catered to the Proctor Coven?

"One O negative Bloody Mary coming up." Delilah shoved a tall glass toward Susannah. The ice tinkled and melted, thinning the coagulating red stuff. It smelled horribly rank to Susannah but she put the glass to her lips anyway. Actually drinking any of the stuff was impossible, but she needed Manolo to know what she was, so she did the best to fake a sip. She could feel his eyes on her as she pretended to drink.

He moved closer and Susannah stood her ground. "Jordan asked me to run a little errand. It is safely parked for you, in the basement." He slipped Susannah a valet check and smiled. "Enjoy the evening, pretty Miz Susannah."

Taking her glass with her, Susannah wove her way through the undulating throng on the dance floor, without spilling a drop of her drink. The huge sliding doors were open to the beach, and she could feel the cool damp air blowing through the opening. The smell of sea and sand drew her. A small table next to the doorway was vacated just as she approached. Susannah took custody of the table without a second look. It was a great place from which to observe the dance floor, and most of the rest of the club.

The floor was crowded, and its hardwood planks heaved with the weight of too many people. As the band wound up some foot stomping beat, Susannah watched the different groups intermingle. They would divide and return to their respective seats, covetous items secreted away to be shared at a more private time. It seemed everything was available at the Mango Bango.

Good thing Metolius owned the police.

Watching the crowd, Susannah wondered if he owned the ATF, DEA and FBI as well. When she was sure Manolo was engaged with the crowd of wantons praying for entry, Susannah dumped half the contents of her glass into the potted palm behind her stool. It would do for now. She would have loved to be right where she was, only with Jordan in the seat next to her. She imagined him to be an elegant and superb dancer.

It wasn't long before the sounds, scents and thoughts of the crowd began to eat away at Susannah's control. The acrid smell of sweating bodies became overpowering. The sounds were way too loud. The rhythm of the music reminded her of a heartbeat she no longer felt. Even the slip of clothing she wore scratched and hung heavy on her skin. As a human she partied away the nights when she could.

But now?

Now she wasn't human and partying seemed so futile, something to be left to the empty headed starlets and the likes of Paris Hilton and Lindsay Lohan. She had more important things to accomplish in her life.

*****

Jordan pulled the Town Car into the front parking lot of the Proctor estate. How he could possibly convince Metolius that Drechell forced him to switch cars, and then took off with the Viper? He was worried that Metolius could pull the real story from his thoughts with ease. He knew Metolius could never read his father's thoughts, but Jordan was not as talented or old as Kellan. Maybe it had something to do with the fact that Metolius had not created his father. Jordan didn't have a clue, but erring on the side of stark fear wasn't a bad idea.

He shut the engine off, left the keys in the ignition, and sped toward his quarters with vamp speed. He was too tired to v-port since he hadn't fed for a while. He needed time to perfect his story and practice it several times as well. Maybe then he would have a chance.

Slipping into the apartment complex behind the main mansion, he swiped his electronic key and ducked quietly through the doorway.

So far, so good.

His vamp-vision allowed him to see without the lights and he found his bedroom without a problem. Flopping onto the mattress, he curled around a large pillow and began to develop his alibi.

The third scenario was the best.

He stuck with it.

Replaying the plot in his mind, he actually visualized Drechell's words, clothing, actions and attitude. He reviewed the parking lot and the people around them, imagined the club and his conversations with patrons and Manolo. Then sent a quick IM to the club manager cryptically explaining his quick departure. Weaving the story until it was a truism in his memory, he thought it just might work.

When he was sure he had the evening reprogrammed in his brain, Jordan rose and tossed the sack containing his old clothing into the fireplace. With the gas jet on high, the singed shirt and pants were incinerated in moments. With his enhanced sense of smell, he could detect the burned fibers and the ash as well as Drechell's death scent. But, after several minutes in the fire, there was nothing left to find amid the fake burning logs.

Jordan hit the shower. He would need to scrub Susannah's scent from his body although he was loath to lose the connection to her. It kept him in a perpetual state of semi-excitement which was a pleasant mind-set. His countless sexual encounters left him empty and wanting of something more. Like the lingering taste of a great wine or the scent of expensive cigars, her presence in his mind and on his body kept his libido engaged and charged.

As he stood beneath the heavy spray of hot water, he systematically recalled the contrived events of the evening. Over and over he replayed the scenes, burning them deeper into his memory. Planting new neurological pathways scrambled the truth and splintered facts with false pictures and meandering tracts. All the time, he prayed his mental game would work.

When he could no longer detect Susannah's scent, he scrubbed with Irish Spring soap one more time. The soap smelled horrible to all vampires, but was very effective at extinguishing any scent but the wild fresh smell of the highland spring and sunshine. To Jordan it was more like swamp cabbage, but it did the job.

Jordan had been home all of two hours when he stepped from the shower… and came face to face with Damien Malvenien, Drechell's number one thug, and best buddy.

"Holy shit, Damien, what gives?" Jordan grabbed a towel and wrapped it around his hips. "What the fuck are you doing in my bathroom, you little fairy. Get the hell out of here."

"Where's Corvell? He followed you last night and didn't come home. Now his car is out front and I can't find him. Where is your car?" The effeminate vampire sprayed spit at Jordan, as he screamed the questions in his face.

Damien was out of control.

"How the hell should I know? Drechell took my Viper. I didn't feel like telling him no at the moment. He better get it back here in one piece. Said he was hooking up with some meat at the bar. Guess he wanted to impress the snack. What are you now, his babysitter? How'd you get in here anyway?" Jordan's eyes glowed red with anger as he stalked Damien across the room, backing the smaller vampire up toward the door.

When he wanted to, Jordan was a force to be reckoned with. It was a genetic gift from the old man.

Damien sneered. "Metolius wants to talk to you. He sent me to get you. Put something on and hurry up. I don't want to keep the Master waiting, fuck-up. If he gets too agitated, you just may get the same thing your dear old dad got."   Damien motioned toward the door.

"What does he want? So now you play messenger *and* mini-me bully? Coming up in the world, I see. Bite any little boys lately?" Jordan disappeared into the bedroom and came out wearing a pair of jeans, casual tee shirt in forest green and a pair of athletic socks. He slipped into worn tennis shoes, then motioned to a fuming Damien. "After you, Queen of the Vampires."

Damien barred his fangs with a growl. It sounded like it came from a Chihuahua. Damien tore at the door handle. "I'm just waiting for the day Metolius gives us the word, dog sucker. Then I'll have my fun watching you join your father.   And it'll be slow, trust me." Damien retracted his fangs and stomped through the door. "He's waiting in the billiards room. Got a nice crowd gathered."

Jordan's heart sank.

If the Master was playing pool with Marisella, surrounded by his lieutenants and counselors, it was going to be an inquisition.

Obviously, Drechell's presence had been missed. Jordan could only hope the alibi he constructed was solidly planted in his mind and he could hold his own against whatever information the Master already possessed. If Jordan was due for some kind of punishment, he wished it would not be meted in front of Marisella. The thoughts of the last discipline flew through his mind; the pain, the embarrassment in front of his peers, the jeers and social isolation. Marisella's interceding with

Metolius on his behalf quite possibly saved his life. That part wasn't so bad, but the rest was more than humiliating.

Just the mention of being summoned to the billiards room struck fear into the souls of Proctor coven members. Metolius had a habit of playing pool while he played with the mind of the individual summoned to appear. Jordan had observed the master spin philosophical tales that had no discernable application to the issue at hand. Then he'd patiently wait, while the vampire on the hot seat became more and more confused and fearful. Sooner or later, the poor individual would confess to anything or implicate himself in some way, out of pure frustration or bewilderment. Next came the cowering in abject fear at the realization of what the individual had done.

Jordan went over his story one more time. With a fresh eye.

No mistakes.

He was solid.

He would remember correctly. He pushed his mind into sociopath mode and slipped into the compulsive liar suit that projected total belief in anything he confabulated. Wasn't that how humans beat lie detector tests?

He could do it.

He had to do it.

The Proctor mansion was an incredible world of English country-style opulence and modern convenience, cleanly disguised beneath dark hand polished woods and ornate furnishings. Even the small private theater was subtly lit with Windsor crystal sconces, and furnished in hunter-green leather. Each seat had its own hand tied fisherman-knit afghan. It was a world created by Metolius' money, and the mind of a powerful vampire who loved England of the 1800s.

The billiards room was located just off Metolius' main conference center, through double hand-carved walnut doors. Each door depicted one of the Master's favorite Greek tales of the ancient Gods. The face of each hero resembled Metolius himself. Carved wainscoting circled the entire room, its base illustrating the crest of Proctor Pharmaceuticals repeated in relief. That was an interesting parallel in the life of the very old individual. Proctor Pharmaceuticals crest was the same crest that graced one warrior's shield in ancient Greece.

The French doors that lay open were specially designed to slide on rollers, opening the entire side of the room to the cool breezes of the Florida evening. Just outside was a marble patio with huge Grecian vases overflowing with bright red blooming bougainvilleas. Through the open doors, Jordan was lead by a gleeful Damien.

181

Around the open room, cozy groups of chairs circled small marble tables. Each table was lit with a Spanish Ironwork lantern topped by stained glass Tiffany shades. Across from the doors, high arches with brass fittings added a kind of old-world look to the shelves of a French bar that boasted just about every kind of alcoholic beverage brewed by man and vampire.

Cautiously, Jordan surveyed the occupants, naming the key players in his mind. Bertrand de Derecho, better known as Bert the Brute, sat with his gang of perverts sipping a mixed drink, looking smug as ever. Callius Crendula lounged with his group of henchmen across the room. Nervous and high-strung as usual, Cal's eyes darted from one occupant to the other, taking in every move, every breath. Mallory Matiesse curled next to Marisella on an expansive divan, her legs drawn up beneath her, casually watching the game between Metolius and Ignacias Trenchertt.

Mallory and Marisella were friends, but at arms length. It was common knowledge throughout the coven that Mallory was assigned as Marisella's personal bodyguard when Metolius made Mari First Female. Everyone also knew Mal was the Master's watchdog and spy. She accompanied Marisella everywhere, ensuring his First Female remained loyal and devoted.

Trenchertt was the one voice of reason and sense in the coven. Jordan respected the priest and Knight of the Templar. Everyone did. His history was unique among most vampires. Seems Trenchertt could never justify the brutality and slaughter he witnessed as a soldier of God in the 1200s. When it was Ignacias' turn to die for the Lord during a particular gruesome Crusade, he chose immortality as a vampire instead. A man of God who became a man of the Dark, Ignacias Trenchertt never let go of his moral beliefs in the face of what he became. He continually badgered Metolius to soften his ways and to treat humans with respect. He and Marisella seemed to be the only moderating influences with Metolius in this modern age. Still, the estate remained a treacherous swamp of politics and power games.

Jordan waited patiently in the doorway for an invitation to enter. Protocol was everything when Metolius was surrounded by watching eyes and listening ears.

Damien cleared his throat, a ballsy move to be sure.

"I am aware you have accomplished your task, Mr. Malvenien. Now do something you have little talent for, Damien. *Be patient!*" Metolius lined up for a shot while Trenchertt stood behind the Master smiling broadly.

"Take your best shot Proctor, for soon I shall smite thee with the might of the Knights Billiard." Trenchertt was one of the few in the coven who could not only match the Master's power and skill, but also beat Metolius at just about every game in which they engaged. He was the only one who could joke at the Master's expense.

The actual table on which they played was carved from one giant piece of Brazilian Blackwood. It had come from some decimated South American forest and weighed almost a ton. Highly stylized, the sculpted sides showed a tangle of beautiful naked bodies reveling in obvious orgy. The red felt of the playing surface was pristine after almost fifty years. Two matching ornate crystal chandeliers hung over the table providing ample light for the game and the players. Jordan always considered the table a masterpiece of overdone porno in an endangered species of wood.

"Do tell, Ignacias. Now shut thee mouth so I may do so." The Master's humor was dry as a bone and crackled from his pale lips. White hands gripped the cue with feminine efficacy as he mentally measured the play, knowing full well he would soon lose to his friend. He shot and missed by a fraction of an inch, then swore in some long extinct language.

Trenchertt let go with a belly laugh as he quickly ran what was left of the table, and bowed to the Master. "Master of my world, but misser of the ball! This is the one hundred and four thousand, six hundred seventy second game, Metolius. When we reach fifteen hundred I shall play for real. Then you shall see such a challenge, as hath never before challengeth thee."

Unable to challenge the knight's talent and skill with a cue stick, Metolius found fault with what was left him. "Ah. Ignacias, when will you update that archaic language you always use? In this age it is so passé and unimaginative! Challengeth? Really, my poor priestly vampire. Do get with the times."

Metolius hugged a suddenly rigid Trenchertt.

Mentioning Trenchertt's religious beginnings was always a sore subject with the man.

"Take for instance, our young Mr. Jordan Burke here. I understand he has devised some little scheme of his own which has come to our attention. Somewhat enterprising, but troubling just the same." Metolius tended to use the royal 'we' when he brought individuals before him for questioning.

The hackles rose on Jordan's neck.

"How shall we handle this, my friend and advisor?" Metolius waved Jordan into the room and pointed at an empty straight-backed chair near the bar.

"And what scheme would that be, Metolius?" Trenchertt calmly placed his cue in the rack and turned to face Metolius with a questioning look.

"As Coven Master, I am ashamed to say, I have no idea. What I do know is, my first lieutenant is missing but his automobile has mysteriously returned. Young Jordan's automobile has just as mysteriously disappeared. However, he seems to be here, safe and sound. I have been told there is a woman involved. Possibly a new young female vampire, of whom I have yet to make the acquaintance." Metolius paced the floor with slow intent; his thin pale hands clasped behind him like some lecturing professor at an Ivy League school. His immaculate velvet smoking jacket and silk slacks accentuated every step.

"And what has young Jordan to say about this?" Trenchertt took a seat on the divan next to Mallory, unceremoniously shoving her aside.

Mallory barred her fangs and growled at the ex-priest, but made no real move against the huge man.

"I have called him here to explain, Ignacias. That would be your suggestion, would it not?" Metolius paused in front of an obviously nervous Jordan.

Trenchertt leaned back, slouching comfortably with his hands behind his head. "Then let the boy speak, before he has a heart attack." Ignacias chuckled and crossed his ankles.

"Jordan?" Metolius motioned to Jordan to begin.

Jordan shifted nervously in the chair, tucked his hands beneath his legs like a kid in trouble, and shifted forward. "I'm not sure what you want to know, Sir. Drechell found me at the Mango Bango and demanded that I give him my car for the evening. Said it was a chick magnet, and I owed him. He took the keys out of my hand and threw his at me. That was the last I saw of him. I spent the day with a friend, then came back here. Next thing I know, sweet cheeks here…" Jordan waved carelessly at Damien who still stood near the open doors, "was in my apartment when I stepped out of the shower. A little awkward, yes. He demanded I come here. He said you wanted to see me, so here I am." He sat back and tried to act casual, but suitably concerned.

"Ignacias? Truth or dare?"

"Far as I may tell, he speaketh the Lord's truth, Metolius." Trenchertt shrugged and recrossed his ankles.

"There is no Lord involved. You can sense no deception in his words or thoughts?" Metolius scrutinized his friend, only trusting Trenchertt's answer so far. Metolius survived several thousand years because he trusted no one.

Metolius took nothing at face value.

"Metolius, you know I believe the Lord is involved in all things. But no, I sense no deception in this young man, or in his words." Ignacias was never one to let a slur pass without refute. Metolius and Trenchertt had kept this verbal baiting contest going for almost a thousand years.

Interesting... Metolius could not read Jordan's thoughts just like he couldn't read Kellan's mind.

This might work, Jordan thought!

He forced himself not to take a deep breath.

"Fine, Priest. Now, Jordan, what about this friend? Possibly a female vampire? An outsider?" Metolius probed.

"Yes a female. Yes a vampire. Not an outsider. At least I don't think so. I don't really know. She's more like my stepsister, sort of." Jordan was hedging. He dragged out the conversation, wanting to give Susannah as much time as possible to get away from Daytona Beach before Metolius knew the truth.

"So now you decide who is and who isn't a member of this coven? As if you are Master here?" Metolius screamed at Jordan. The Master's face was inches away in a v-flash, fangs barred and claws extended. Metolius' eyes were silvery red and dangerous as he stared at Jordan.

"No, I... no, Sir. I mean technically I..." Jordan was stammering, afraid to move, but so wanting to run.

"Metolius, give the child room. He obviously has something to say, but can not speak with your nose in his mouth." Trenchertt stood and calmly approached the enraged Master. "Let him speak. You can bite his head off later." All archaic language immediately dropped in favor of clear and concise speech. Obviously Jordan was in trouble and Ignacias did not want to see the conversation end in a blood bath.

"Of course, Ignacias. You are, as always, the voice of reason in this insane world I seem to have made for myself. Do explain yourself, Jordan." Metolius backed away and resumed his calm pacing.

One minute Metolius seemed an animal ready to attack, the next he appeared to be a benevolent father, searching for the truth in an errant son.

It set Jordan's teeth on edge.

"The girl, well woman, is the one my father turned, before he was killed. Her name is Susannah. She came looking for her sire, my dad. She didn't know he was dead. She found me instead." Jordan smiled sheepishly at Trenchertt, afraid to look at Metolius. "So I figured, I don't know, she was one of us. Right? That's the way it works, right?"

"I could see how you would assume that, young man." Trenchertt joined the Master pacing back and forth, half in mocking jest; half for protection of Jordan should things escalate again. He had a secret stake in the young vampire's welfare.

"What do you think, Metolius? The boy's logic has some merit."

Metolius paused in mid step. "So this girl, this Susannah, was progeny of Kellan? Hummmmm. Interesting. She should not have survived. That is a tale I would like to hear." Metolius assumed a thinking pose, complete with hand on chin.

After a moment of seeming contemplation, Metolius spoke. "So, go and fetch your young woman, Jordan. I should like to meet her and introduce her to her family. We owe her that much." Metolius moved to the center of the room, arms open wide, pleading his case to the audience. "She must have had a very difficult life so far. It is time she join her true family, and begin to live as one of us. After all, she belongs to me by birthright."

Jordan looked from Metolius to Trenchertt, then to Marisella.

Metolius smiled solicitously.

Trenchertt's shrug indicated a judgment well intended.

Marisella's agreeing smile was as cold as ice. The fierce look in her eyes betrayed her security as First Female.

Jordan immediately recognized the anger burning just below the vampire's pretty exterior. He quickly figured out Marisella thought Metolius was trolling for a new First Female. Susannah!

"Ah... I'd be happy to, except damn, she left." Jordan snapped his fingers and stood to leave.

"Left? And why would she do that, considering you spent, I assume, the evening cavorting and the day sleeping together?" Metolius was more than interested in what Jordan and Susannah had been up to. The Master licked his thin lips, as if salivating over a scrumptious treat.

"Well, you could call it cavorting." Jordan tried to heat his mind with their sexual encounter, in case Trenchertt was sensing his thoughts. It wasn't difficult. "I didn't exactly split on good terms.

186

She was angry and told me she was leaving. Going back where she came from, since my old man was dead. I think she was after answers. I had none, so she left." Jordan felt the color rise in his cheeks.

"Ignacias? Truth or fiction?" Metolius seriously doubted the boy's story.

"Hard to tell with these hormonal teens, Metolius. He could be telling the truth, and just embarrassed about being caught en delicato. Or he could be covering something. Knowing Jordan, its probably a sweet boy-blush. Nothing more." Trenchertt was reaching out to Jordan's mind and knew the boy was covering up something, but was not sure what. Celibate since he accepted the cloth, sexual thoughts always turned his stomach and colored his ability to discern the truth.

"Master, what about Corvell, Sir? Ask him what happened to Corvell. I think he knows more than he is telling." Damien took a chance and interrupted Trenchertt. His squeaky voice floated into the mix.

"You were not asked to speak, you little worm. You might have Drechell by the cojones, or what ever there is to hold," Marisella's lip curled as she spoke of the Master's brutal lieutenant, "but you have no reason to speak in the presence of your betters." Marisella hissed at Damien who cowered by the door. "Leave us now, worm!"

"My dear, calm yourself. This little maggot has a point. There is something suspicious here. I would like to get to the bottom of it. So the girl may have left. But where is Corvell? He does not stay away this long, as a rule. Jordan?"

"I hope the asshole is ash by now!" Jordan spoke with enough vehemence to communicate his true feelings about Drechell without exposing any particular knowledge. "All I know is, I better get my car back without so much as a scratch, or I'll be really pissed."

"Definitely the truth, Metolius. His hate of Corvell is a palatable thing that I can feel, even from across the room." Trenchertt laughed at Jordan's response. "It doesn't take my kind of gift to feel that, and with little wonder. Probe his mind if you do not trust my judgment."

Metolius shot Trenchertt a dark look. "You know as well as I, old friend, Jordan's line is not of my making." It was the only open remark Metolius ever made concerning his own abilities. Apparently Metolius could not read the mind of any vampire he did not create.

Jordan trusted the comment only as far as he trusted Trenchertt, but was relieved to a certain degree.

Why had Trenchertt taken a chance on revealing Metolius' short coming, in front of the coven and his First Female?

Possibly there was more afoot than Metolius' schemes?

Jordan discretely glanced at Marisella and thought he caught a slight nod. He took great pains to never allow his gifts, or vampiric talents, to be known as they continued to developed over the years. It was more survival instinct than a planned strategy, but it served him well. No one alive, or dead, knew the extent of Jordan's abilities.

"But, Master," Damien wheedled, "Corvell never stays out without letting me know where he is. Something has happened. I felt it. I know Jordan has something to do with it."

"The only thing you can feel is Drechell's dick up your ass, you insignificant leech." Marisella was off the couch and had a well-manicured hand clamped around Damien's scrawny neck in less than a heart beat. "Suppose I put you out of all our misery, Malvenien. If Drechell didn't need you as a playmate, I'd find a hungry alligator, and see him well fed tonight."

Jordan raised his eyebrows, just a hair.

So, Damien was Drechell's bitch!

That explained a lot.

Unfortunately it blew a giant hole in Jordan's story. Drechell would not have wanted to pick up a female, if he was gay.

Shit.

Possibly shit.

But then again, even Drechell had to feed. He didn't have much mind control with humans, and women tended to fight less.

"Ah, please do not soil such magnificent hands, my love." Metolius calmly removed Marisella's hand from Damien's throat and kissed it, less than gently. "Drechell often used females to feed, but always saved his more amorous pursuits for his little Damien. As repulsive as you, my heterosexual lovely, may find it, the relationship seems satisfying for both of them. I am not one to judge the needs of a male. Or Drechell, for that matter." Metolius chuckled at his joke at the enforcer's expense.

Marisella made a gagging noise and Metolius placed a pale hand beneath her chin, raising her face to plant a chaste kiss on her luscious red lips. "Diversity, my dear. It is a new age we live in, remember? But then, it is not so different than the ancient days." He chuckled again, depositing Marisella back on the divan with a soft pat, and a knowing look toward Mallory.

"Jordan, where was Susannah going when she left? Has she been adopted by another coven? Or is she just rogue, living on the streets, as it would be?" Metolius concentrated on Jordan once again, as

Damien slunk away, rubbing his neck.

"I have no idea. She didn't really say. I do know her human father is aware of his daughter's species alteration and seems to be okay with it. And her sister called… while we were in her room. That's all I know. We were otherwise occupied, most of the time." Jordan blushed again.

"Then I suggest you find out if she is really gone. If not, then bring her back. She needs to meet her real family. I think we have a lost child out there who needs to be found." Metolius motioned to Marisella and Trenchertt. The interrogation was over. Both high-ranking vampires followed the Master out of the room.

Jordan took a deep breath and shuddered. When did he start that bad habit? Oh yeah… when he met Susannah.

He had to stop it. Most vampires only breathed around humans.

Susannah…

He was in serious trouble if Susannah was still around. Metolius would have little to say if Jordan could not find her. The Master may let this incident pass, if there was no woman to be found. But if she was still at the resort, he would have to produce her as soon as vampirically possible.

That was double trouble.

Marisella would not appreciate it, if Susannah were to return with Jordan and catch the eye of the Master. Jordan's heart was torn. Marisella risked her life and place in the coven to help Jordan. He had no interest in repaying her with betrayal.

It was a no-win situation if Susannah was still in Daytona Beach.

Jordan could feel the quicksand closing in around his heels. He said a silent prayer that Susannah took his warning seriously and left.

Damien hid behind a vase just outside the billiard room, listening. Jordan was ordered to get the girl! Good. Damien knew his lover's disappearance was somehow tied to Jordan and this new vampire, Susannah.

All he had to do was follow them.

He would find the connection.

He would find his Drechell.

Chapter 18

Pedigreed

What is a family, but a group of people who had no choice?
Except, with the vampire, he has a voice,
In the dynasty, in the creation, in sharing of his deed.
With vampires it all comes down to one thing…
Pedigreed.

Petcha Dragonesceu, Gypsie Vampire
Transval Province, 1552

It was too much. Susannah was beginning to realize the sensory overload dulled her reflexes and thoughts. She rode on a fevered beat that carried her mind away like the thrumming vibration before a storm. She had to get away from the sounds, the feels, and the smells…

"I thought you said you were leaving." Jordan clenched her elbow and rasped in her ear. "You need to get out of here. Now. For your own good. And mine. Go. Don't come back." He was snarling and she could feel fear in his every word. Immediately her brain re-engaged… along with her teenage rebellious nature.

"Don't push me around, Jordan Burke. You left. Why did you come back? Leave me alone." Susannah was angry at being ordered around. She snarled right back at him.

On the other hand, she was secretly excited to see him and squirmed in her chair nervously.

"We're being watched. Metolius knows something is up. He sent me here to get you, but I don't think I am alone. You have to leave. Now." Jordan was dragging her through the open doors of the club.

"There are no other vampires in the club. I would be able to see them, stupid. Let go of my arm, Jordan." Susannah pulled away and faced him. She didn't know if she should punch him, or hug him.

Maybe both?

The weight of his words finally sunk in and her mind clicked into high gear. "You went back to the estate? Did someone question you? Why are you the one who was sent to get me, Mr. Burke? Obviously you are here, of your own free will." Susannah stood her ground, hands on her hips, glaring at Jordan. "Is this some kind of gentle kidnapping? You didn't want me to go to the estate, and now you are here to take me there. You are a fickle vampire, Mr. Burke. Or maybe just a tool..."

"Keep moving. Susannah, this is serious." Jordan couldn't believe she was just standing there, staring at him. As if he wasn't risking his life to get her away from the long reaching arm of the Proctor Coven before it was too late!

"Right. And I'm supposed to just take you at your word? Believe everything you say? Without any explanation? Come on, Jordan." She was still hurt he would not let her help him, or go with him to the estate. It was rejection in her book. She did not do rejection well. It brought out her true childish nature, in spades.

With the last word out of her mouth, she turned to go back indoors, back to the club, when she noticed several glowing auras that had not been there a moment before. Four men, surrounded by neon lime halos, were crossing the crowed club. Headed right in her direction.

"Okay, so maybe I was a little hasty with the judgment thing. We should take a walk, like on the beach, like right now." Susannah left her drink on the picnic table and ducked through the patio enclosure.

Jordan was glued to her heels. "A little faster would be good, Susannah." Jordan hissed in her ear as he grabbed her arm and half dragged her toward the boat dock.

"No, not the dock, Jordan. Been there, done that. Got the fangs to prove it." She stopped and flung her arms around his neck. "V-port us to my room. You can do that right? Quickly."

Without even thinking, Jordan transported them directly to the living room of Susannah's suite...

Right into the arms of two more waiting thugs.

Bert the Brut laughed, his gloved hands immediately slipped one side of silver and titanium handcuffs on the restrained Jordan.

While the silver in the cuffs burned his arm, they did something even worse to him; they severely limited his powers. Jordan knew he could not escape by v-porting with an arm encircled by silver. Nor could he break the titanium metal covered in silver.

He struggled but to no effect.

Their options were dwindling. Rapidly.

Before she realized what was happening, Susannah's wrist was quickly enclosed in the other side of the cuffs. She winced. The silver touching her skin made her nauseous and itchy. Her vision blurred for an instant, but it cleared quickly. She, however, could still hear Jordan's thoughts and see the auras around her.

Susannah knew that feeding on synthetic blood reduced the vampiric reaction to sunlight. Apparently it dulled her reaction to silver as well. She was still uncomfortable. She had somewhat of an idea what silver would do to Jordan and mentally reached out to him. He was hissing and Susannah could feel his mind was a blur of pain and confusion.

Obviously he was in much worse shape than she.

"Get these things off me right now. I don't know who you think you are but-" the tall man struck her across the mouth. She could feel blood trickle down her lip. It tasted of fear. Her own.

"Shut the fuck up, bitch." Bert laughed as he spit the words at Susannah, then licked her chin tasting the blood there. "Ack! That shit sucks. What the hell have you been feeding on? Dead animals? Damn. Anybody got some Listerine?"

"Serves you right, ass-wipe." Her sarcastic retort earned Susannah another slap.

This time Jordan growled and bared his fangs, his eyes an angry red despite his pain.

"I said, shut the fuck up, BITCH!" Bert raised his hand again. Susannah hit him as hard as she could with a mental blast.

Bert staggered back in surprise.

She was still learning to alter air pressure by creating a kind of physical punch, but hadn't perfected the technique. She mentally sent a quick little thanks to Yuri for his patience and training, though she had been a less than stellar student. The punch did not carry the power she wanted yet, but it was somewhat effective with Bert.

"What the hell?" he grunted.

"Bert, cut it out. Damien said, just make sure we bring them back to the estate. He didn't say to beat the shit out of the girl, ya know. Man, you gave her a fat lip." The other guy was wary and warned Bert off.

"Yeah, yeah, it'll heal before we get out the door, dumb-shit. Come on." Bert shot a dirty look at his cohort. "We're just making sure you both come back to meet Proctor, like the Master ordered. Move it." One man on each side of the handcuffed couple, the group marched toward the elevator. Bert draped his coat over their cuffs.

If you can hear me, nod your head Jordan, Susannah mentally communicated.

Surprised, Jordan looked at her and nodded slightly.

Try thinking something so I can see if I can hear you.

I'm dead meat if Damien gets to us before Metolius. Jordan stared at the glaring buttons on the slick black elevator panel, as he tried to think as loud and strong as he could.

Why could he hear her with silver on?

Okay, got that one. Who's Damien? And what can he do that Metolius can't? Susannah was trying to get a picture of who these men were, and how they fit into the game plan. *Think of the individuals so I get a mental picture, with the name.*

Damien, believe it or not, is Drechell's lover! Why didn't you just leave? Don't you understand how powerful Metolius is? Jordan was shaking his head as if to clear some fuzzy thought, or settle a dizzy spell. *He thinks we are connected with Drechell's disappearance. When I got back, Damien had gone to Metolius and told him about the car. He doesn't know for sure what happened, but he felt Corvell die. I'm sure of it. I made up a story in my mind and practiced it because Metolius has a reader"* Jordan framed a picture of the knight in his mind. *Ignacias Trenchertt is almost as old as Metolius. He can sense truth and falsehood. Metolius uses him to test members of the coven and to sentence vampires who lie or break the rules.* Jordan shook his head again.

Stop moving so much. Just think to me. Susannah shot at Jordan. His lips were moving as he formed mental sentences.

I'm sure Trenchertt knew I lied, but didn't say anything, maybe because he and Marisella are tight. She probably told him to protect me. I don't know. I'm so confused. The silver, it doesn't affect you. How? He stumbled and Susannah jerked to catch him, succeeding in only causing him more pain.

It has an effect, but not as strong as someone who feeds on live, human blood. It's a metal thing, iron and silver. I have different powers than naturist vampires. Perks of the lifestyle! Maybe you should convert. So give me your story. I'm not sure if I can hold up under this Trenchertt guy, but I'll give it the old school try.

As they rode handcuffed together in the back of Bert's big yellow Hummer, Jordan did the best he could to mentally fill Susannah in on his alibi. He could think to her and hear her response, but not read her thoughts. The one sided conversation was a little frustrating but he got the hang of it quickly.

They practiced back and forth in silence as the swamp passed by and Susannah tried to mentally alleviate some of Jordan's discomfort. She had mentally joined with Natalia on their Afghan mission to help heal Yuri after a firefight. Now she tried hard to remember the way her sister vampire helped Yuri recover from his deadly wounds.

After several attempts, Susannah finally felt the fire in Jordan's arms. She siphoned off some of the pain, allowing him to relax a little and concentrate more effectively. Not for the first time, she made a mental promise to pay more attention to her training in the future. She also said a little thanks to her instructors for as much as they had given her.

Susannah was making a lot of mental promises to herself lately. It felt an awful lot like growing up.

In too short a time, the estate loomed ahead. Its private road lined with weeping willows and overgrown swamp vegetation was impressive. In Susannah's mind it was beautiful and terrifying at the same time. Rounding a sharp curve, the driveway followed a man-made canal for about a quarter mile, then opened onto a vast lawn set with two small ponds. Beyond the last pond, the mansion rose three stories, in Victorian majesty. Built with huge slabs of pink marble and gray stone, Susannah thought the main building more a mammoth castle. It would have looked right at home somewhere in the countryside of regency England.

She couldn't help herself and blurted out, "Oh my God, it's breath-taking. This is where you live? The Proctor Estate? Wow!" Mentally she nudged Jordan. *It's not hard to act excited about meeting the Master that lives here. This place is fabulous!*

Obviously you didn't look closely at the ponds back there, did you? Full of hungry alligators that take care of our little garbage problem. The culls are kept captive in what used to be the stables. They appear great from the outside, but don't look to close. It's not a pretty sight.

Culls? What are they? In typical teenage fashion Susannah was excited despite the danger ahead.

Culls? It's what we call humans that are kept for food. They are happily drugged out of their minds and live like animals in stalls. Jordan was suitably embarrassed even mentioning the coven's disgusting stable. It was something he truly hated about the way Metolius operated, taking downtrodden humans captive, keeping them for food.

Ick. You, ah, dine there? Susannah was aghast.

No! Never. I can't stand to think about it, let alone go there. We're here. Be careful and don't think about anything except the story. Don't take a chance. If you think Trenchertt is getting into your mind, think about sex. He was a priest and doesn't have a good grasp of the difference between sexual excitement and lying. Guess it reads the same in his head so he can't tell what the person is truly feeling. Jordan sent a mental giggle and blushed. *It works every time for me.*

"Come on you two. Get your asses out of the car and march. Damien is waiting." Bert lifted Susannah by her arms and Jordan fell out of the Hummer behind them, still connected by the handcuffs. He hissed in pain as his skin tore against the silver.

"Bert, go easy. They still have to see Metolius. It won't do if they're all beat up. Come on man. I'm more afraid of Metolius than that faggot, Damien." Bert's buddy was concerned with good reason and trying to mitigate any damage that might show on the girl.

"I thought we were supposed to see the Master?" Susannah stammered.

Bert grabbed her hair, pulling her face close to his. "Damien first. He has the right." Still holding Susannah's hair in a fierce grip, Bert growled, then suddenly released her. "Damien might be gay as a fruit cake, but Drechell was a good enforcer, afraid of nothing. If you two shits had anything to do with his disappearance, I'll be the first to let Damien share your carcass with his pets. He has one gator that's totally white, and vicious as hell. I like to watch Damien feed the thing." He leered at Susannah. "I like it so much I gotta go fuck something afterward."

"Man, you are a pervert, Bert, but what the hey. Let's get this over with before Metolius catches wind of what we are doing. If he finds out we might as well jump in that pond with the gators. It would hurt less." The smaller vampire was waving Bert on.

The two thugs dragged Susannah and Jordan along the gravel walk around to the back of the complex, toward a workshop that stood in a clearing. Several alligators lay on the grass snoozing in comfort, completely ignoring the two-legged animals that walked among them. Damien stood in the doorway leaning against the moldy wood.

"Welcome to the Proctor Estate, Miss." A maniacal smile split Damien's features. His yellow teeth were chipped and his fangs were somewhat shorter than expected. Susannah wondered if gay vampires normally had short fangs, or if it was just that this guy was on the petite side. She suppressed a giggle.

"Damien, you're in deep shit. Get these things off me." Jordan struggled in the handcuffs. "Metolius ordered me to bring Susannah to him, not to you. If he catches you, your ass is ash for sure." His wrists had begun to bleed from the tight metal and continued struggling. The skin on his arms looked burned and cut, acutely painful.

Susannah could feel his agony through his thoughts. It hadn't gotten alot worse, but it hadn't abated either. He wasn't healing at all beneath the metal.

"Oh yeah! Brave little dog sucker. Metolius ordered this. Metolius ordered that! Fuck Metolius. I want to know what you did to Corvell, and I *will* find out. Know what I mean, Verne?" Damien imitated the hillbilly, Jim Varney, his favorite southern comedienne.

Typical of Damien; small mentality, dumb humor. With the upper hand, Damien acted all in control of the situation and much bigger than his five foot height. Tugging on a thick chain, he moved out of the way as an enormous albino alligator lumbered out of the little building, its jaws snapping at the metal leash. Its fat white legs clawed the ground with heavy footsteps.

Susannah gasped, then let out a tiny shriek as the gator turned toward her. Pale pink eyes trained on her legs, the gator's head too heavy to rise much higher. The mammoth creature opened its gaping maw with a horrible hissing growl, then lunged, hauling hard on the chain held by the diminutive Damien. Susannah pulled back, dragging Jordan with her.

Damien let out a self-satisfied chuckle as Jordan moaned in pain, the silver cuffs burning deep into his flesh as he jumped to keep pace with her. The gator sniffed the air smelling fresh blood and hissed again. "You like my little pet, huh? He loves the taste of pretty white meat. Maybe your tongue will loosen if you watch my Bengie here, taste your girlfriend. Just a little bite? One leg, no?" Damien let out the chain he held, link by link teasing both the gator and the vampires.

The white alligator continued to growl and haul on its leash, a hopeful look in the cold eyes. Inches away from Susannah's feet, it snapped and twisted, working to get to the sweet smelling meat just inches away.

"Have thee parted from thy wits, my little friend?" Ignacias Trenchertt stepped from behind a huge weeping willow bordering the swamp's thick green water. His hands confidently set on his hips. He stood tall and strong like a knight of the Round Table. His long brown robe was emblazoned with the red cross of the Crusades in which he'd served. "Mr. Malvenien, were you not awareth the Master hath requested the presence of yon children? I would bet my faith you'd not cross the Master's will."

His smile reminded Susannah of a grinning wolf. She shivered at the cold breeze that blew across her skin with his soft words. Susannah could imagine Trenchertt never raised his voice. It was not required. His very presence commanded respect. When he spoke, all listened, probably even the master.

"Trenchertt, mind your own business. What difference will five minutes make? These two rats know something about my Corvell, and I want to know."

My Corvell?

God, Jordan was right.

Damien and Drechell? A couple? Susannah's mind spun just a touch and she tried hard not to go visual on that particular revelation.

Damien continued his lament. "Trenchertt, Corvell had something on Jordan. He was following the little shit," he wrenched a thumb at Jordan, "and now he's missing. So is Jordan's car. Don't you think those two things are related? Come on Trenchertt, let me have a go at 'em, then you and Proctor can have what's left. Come on." Damien wheedled and pleaded. It was an ugly sight that turned Susannah's stomach. Would there be a chance she and Jordan would be left in Damien's hands?

"'Tis not my decision, but 'tis your choice. Think on it well, Malvenien, for should thou chooseth not the Master's will, I shall be honor-bound to taketh thy head." Again Trenchertt spoke softly with a benevolent and dangerous smile. His giant arms lay at ease across his chest as he sighed. "Think thou well. I am a man of God and liketh not the taking of a life. Even one such as yours."

The threat was clear and Susannah could see Damien blanch whiter than his normal pallid color.

"God damn fuckin' piece of shit. Take 'em then. But Proctor better find out what the hell is going on before, his head rolls right into yon swamp. Can't let shit go, or it comes back to bite you in the neck." Damien sneered and tugged the huge alligator back. With a pathetic growl, he dragged the animal into the shed.

"Come, children. We shall attend the Master, forthwith." Trenchertt stepped in front of Susannah, waved his hand across the cuff and smiled as they fell to the ground.

Now that was power!

She heard Jordan sigh in relief as the cuffs released. Susannah took the huge knight's extended arm and stuck out her tongue at the retreating Damien.

"Thou should, alas, hold thy tongue rather than extend it to thine enemy, child. Tis less of a chance to lose it from thy lips." Trenchertt chuckled at Susannah's immature action. He drew her toward the main house, locked tightly on his arm. Jordan shuffled after the two, rubbing the bright red stripes around his wrists, the only evidence left of being restrained by Damien's special cuffs.

"Sorry. He's such a fruitcake, don't you think? Dangerous, but a real fruitcake." Susannah smiled winningly at the knight with whom she walked willingly. One quick glance from beneath her lashes told her he was not in the least turned by her smile. "So, are you really a knight, like in Arthur and Camelot? Knights of the Round Table type stuff?"

"*Was* a knight, yes. A Knight Templar, as a matter of fact." Trenchertt murmured crossing himself as he traced the red symbol on his chest.

Susannah turned and touched the red fabric with implied reverence. Having never met a knight before, she was trying to act the part of a girl impressed by the lore and prestige of heroes long gone.

Trenchertt gently removed her hand. "And a priest, child. Do not ply your sweet trials upon my frock. I am less inclined to temptation than young Jordan who, it seems is easily swayed." Trenchertt leaned his head toward Susannah with a secret smile.

He was feeling for her thoughts and the tenor of her soul. Immediately she felt the tendrils of power surge in her mind. She was ready for it and smiled back sweetly looking, directly into his seemingly kind eyes.

"And the truth shall set you free, Sir Knight." She filled her mind with erotic thoughts and vivid scenes of Jordan in the throws of ecstasy. Her body tightened at the thoughts and she could feel her womanly moisture begin to dampen the lace panties she wore. Weaving the feeling into her mental fantasy, she immediately felt Trenchertt's mental distaste, and hasty withdrawal.

"And so it shall, my child." Trenchertt's smile turned stony. He looked away, obviously embarrassed and unwilling to tempt his ability to delve further into Susannah's preoccupied, pornographic mind.

"And so it shall." Never one to let a man have the last word, Susannah could feel Jordan mentally warn her.

Jesus, Susannah. Quit! He is one of the strongest vampires I have ever met. Stop the spoiled kid shit, please. Concentrate and be serious or Metolius will have our heads. Jordan kept his eyes down as they walked.

Don't sweat it, Jordan. I have this thing under control. Whoops! Susannah stumbled on an exposed tree root and clutched at

Trenchertt's iron arm.

Okay, okay!

They walked toward the back deck that led directly to Metolius' main office. Jordan's neck was covered with sweat. Rivulets had begun to trickle down his back. He quit rubbing at the wounds on his wrist minutes before, and little was left of the marks the silver cuffs made. *Watch your thoughts with Metolius and Trenchertt. They will both be looking for the slightest slip up. We are suspect to begin with, so just be serious, okay!*

Puh-leeze - I got it. I got it. Now stop worrying. I am a professional. We'll be fine.

Now, on what she considered a full-blown mission, Susannah was in control and at her cocky best. She gave a mental shake and reigned in her overconfident arrogance. No more mistakes of the Susannah variety, she chided herself and took a deep breath to still her nerves. At Trenchertt's backward glance, she thought the better of releasing the unneeded oxygen.

Watch it Suze, just play the part girl. Her self-warning came as a bit of a surprise.

They climbed the six marble stairs to the small, private patio and could hear heated discussion from within through the open French doors. A woman's voice was raised in anger while Metolius' voice drifted melodically toward the approaching group.

Like the overpowering smell of the southern gardenia, Susannah felt his voice envelope and smother all other words and thoughts. With a pressure that clawed at each neuron, it drove her mind and body toward paralysis. Closer to the door, Trenchertt drew Susannah who now walked with stilting movements.

Jordan, used to the affect of Metolius' voice placed a gentle hand at the base of her back to propel her forward.

Oh my God! What kind of a monster is this Metolius? Susannah was immediately scared out of her wits, all machismo gone and seriously flushed! She resorted to little pants to still her mounting nerves.

It didn't work.

Just keep your cool. Marisella is arguing with him. It always makes him seem worse when he is angry with a woman he thinks he possesses. She is brave to argue with the Master. Jordan took Susannah's free hand. *Stay physically connected. It will make our thoughts work better. Well, at least my thoughts. I think we will be stronger together. We're supposed to be lovers anyway, so let's act like it.* Jordan sent her calming thoughts tinged with erotica emotions.

The strange combination of eroticism and fear seemed to somehow work. Susannah internalized the calming sensations and buried her fear beneath the sensual thoughts that ignited a smoldering fire somewhere behind her bellybutton. She licked her lips and stole a glance at Jordan.

He projected a cocky grin, and winked as he squeezed her hand. Susannah couldn't help it.

She giggled like a giddy high school girl in her first romance, excited, but scared out of her wits at the same time. It was an intoxicating combination.

Just outside the French doors, Trenchertt paused. "Have a care as to that cute tongue, child. The Master is not as easily entertained as I." He dropped her arm and stepped back, pushing Susannah and Jordan through the doorway ahead of him.

Immediately Marisella and Metolius ceased their argument, smiling together in a contrived welcome. "Come in, come in." Metolius motioned toward the young couple. "Jordan, do introduce me to your young lady." The Master's brilliant smile paled against his even whiter skin.

The stone tile beneath Susannah's feet seemed to hold her to its hard surface with a death grip. She could not move.

Jordan pulled Susannah in front of himself and circled her with his arms. It was more to hold her in place and demonstrate ownership than a warm embrace. "Master Metolius Proctor, this is Susannah Maddox, progeny of Kellan Burke the Third, of Proctor Coven. Susannah, our Coven Master, Metolius Proctor and his First Female, Marisella Ferreira." Jordan formally introduced Susannah.

"Pleased to meet you, Sir, Ma'am." Susannah clawed her way out of the temporary paralysis that held her rooted to the floor. She smiled and projected a blast of romantic feelings toward Jordan.

He smiled and squeezed her waist affectionately obviously enjoying her mental push.

Metolius rose from the low couch on which he had been sitting with Marisella. Their vehement arguing immediately sidelined for a time. "So this is the sweet thing who has captured your heart, Jordan, my boy. And, no wonder. What a lovely child, she is." Metolius crossed the spacious office, took Susannah's hand in his pale effeminate fingers and raised it to his cold lips. He breathed in her scent as he planted a wet kiss in the palm. "Welcome home, my child." He bent slowly, peering into her eyes as he kissed first one cheek and then the other.

Jordan held her tight in place, still and unmoving.

Susannah froze as Metolius kissed her cheeks. He loomed above her, posturing for intimidation. Eyes closed, she played and replayed her first kiss with Jordan, over and over. It stilled the nausea in her stomach at Metolius' touch and helped block out the abject fear that threatened to consume her entire being. The scent of long dead flesh filled her nostrils, threatening to choke her mind and soul. Had Jordan not held her so close, she would have turned and run for her life.

In Susannah's limited vampiric experience, Metolius smelled like death incarnate. He stood tall, at least six and a half feet, wispy and effeminate, but horrifyingly monstrous at the same time. Pale with a thinly emanating strength that held one enthralled, she concentrated on Jordan's touch to keep from loosing her grip on reality and her sanity.

His long burgundy smoking robe hung loose clearly displaying the white silk pajamas Metolius habitually wore. A sort of Hugh Heffner of the vampire world, the deep rich velvet of his robe contrasted hideously with his white pajamas and paper white skin. Susannah was struck by the corn-silk hair that hung to his shoulders, glistening white in the artificial light of the office.

"Welcome, my dear. Please call me Mari. We are all family here." Marisella moved around Metolius to take Susannah warmly in her arms. She winked at Jordan. Susannah felt Jordan purposefully release her to Marisella and relaxed a bit. The First Female's hug seemed genuine and truly welcoming. "We must plan to spend some time getting to know one another. Jordan is like a son to me, aren't you dear?"

Jordan winced and shrugged as Marisella deposited Susannah back into his arms, away from Metolius. "My pleasure, Ma'am." Susannah was finally at a safe distance from the Master, at least for the moment.

"Such a sweet amigita no, Metolius, darling? She will be a wonderful addition to our little family. Jordan, why do you not show her around the estate, then you may join us in the billiards room?" Marisella was keen on getting Susannah away from the Master as fast as possible. His eyes were beginning to change from the normal frigid silver to a warm reddish-orange. It was a dangerous sign and definitely time to remove the temptation with pretty blonde hair.

Susannah was more than ready to be removed.

Trenchertt cleared his throat. "There be a small matter of security, Metolius. Damien seems to think our children here, have some knowledge of Drechell's absence. He may not be amenable to their wanderings."

"Then, by all means, do go with them, Trenchertt. I seriously doubt Damien will be a problem with a somewhat overgrown knight in tow. Now go, before I demonstrate my horrible lack of self control and ask you two to join Mari and I for a little fun." Metolius' eyes were deep red now. His head hung low, shimmery hair veiling his face. The solicitous smile had deteriorated into a sneer and he eyed Susannah with a hungry stare. Spittle formed at the corners of his thin translucent lips.

Marisella held tight to his hand, pulling him toward the couch and away from the young couple. "Go, Jordan. Trenchertt, go with them." Marisella sunk into the couch and pulled Metolius toward her neck and the firmly pulsing vein that stood out in the glaring light. Susannah realized immediately that Marisella was forcing her heart to beat as a distracter to keep Metolius' attention while Jordan and she made their getaway.

"Marisella?" Jordan asked tentatively.

"Go now, Jordan." Marisella mewed, grasping Metolius' hair and drawing him to her.

Susannah saw the woman wince as Metolius sunk his fangs into her neck and began to feed. At the horrific sight, Susannah stood frozen in place, unable to move on her own. She did not even feel Jordan and Trenchertt drag her from the room and into the sparkling, starlit night.

Chapter 19

The Path of One

The path of life, is a path of one.
Beyond birth, genetics, and the grace of the Son.

We follow our hearts toward frolic and fun.
Of what end? A body planted 'neath the dun.

The end? The middle? The beginning anew?
Only we discern what is really true.

Marisella Ferreira, First Female
Coven Metolius, Daytona Beach, Florida

Monique was in the hot seat once again.

The rest of the Vamp Squad sat around the conference table just watching. Colonel Maddox was purple with rage, and containing it less than well. In fact, he was shouting at the top of his lungs.

Sergeant Milo Miller sat behind his self-constructed helm, calmly operating the technical equipment, following, as best he could, the ranting and raving of his commander.

Elizabetta Zoeltel, Mistress of the Vamp Squad Coven, sat quietly listening at the far end of the room, her exquisite hands clasped tightly in her lap.

"I can't believe my daughter would act *this* irresponsibly! After everything we've been through as a team, I thought she actually learned something. That'll teach me to have expectations, now won't it?" His fist hit the table.

Yuri and Natalia, cuddling together as usual, jumped.

"Colonel, calmez vers le bas! Susannah said she would be home tomorrow. She will soon be checking out of her room at the Beachcomber. That means she will soon be on the road, and on her way home. Est ce correct, no?" Monique squirmed as she modestly crossed her legs. The fact that she did not flaunt her sensual nature spoke volumes. She was extremely uncomfortable.

"You spoke to her and did not order her to come home immediately? Very poor judgment, Ms. Merchant, very poor. Miller,

203

any way to find her current location?" Monique was close to tears under the Colonel's verbal barrage while Maddox stood to pace back and forth in front of the techno-active computer projection on the huge whiteboard at the head of the room.

"Not immediately. She somehow disabled the commercial tracking device in her car. However, I may be able to locate her vehicle if she uses the specialized search engine on the computer I installed before she left. That's a big if, Sir." Sergeant Miller was displaying a visual of Susannah's computer screen and the new search engine.

"So, what if she used it already? Can you find it then?" Maddox was not the least bit computer savvy... and not the least bit embarrassed about it.

"Ah, no Sir. The computer has to be on and the search engine functioning at the same time I am looking for its signal. Kinda like hearing a radio – it has to be on, right? Get it, Sir?"

"Okay, so when Susannah turns on her car, you can find her. Start looking." Maddox slammed the desk to emphasize his order.

"Sir? She has to have the computer on, not necessarily the car itself. I have an auto search up and running twenty-four/seven, Sir. Nothing yet. She must not be using the computer." Milo actually made eye contact with Monique. "Ms. Merchant, have you tried calling her cell again?" Milo's ever-active fingers automatically pulled up Susannah's cell records. No new calls had been received or generated from her number in eight hours.

Elizabetta interjected, "Possibly she is a little recalcitrant, eh? Maybe a little embarrassed as well. She is still a very young woman. She is in search of her identity and learning how to live as one of us. She has only been gone for four and a half days. That is not a horribly long time to be out and about, Frank. Monique assures us she is on her way home. It cannot hurt to wait until she has returned, before you decide to clip her wings and ground her for life." Elizabetta smiled at the angry Colonel.

As soon as the words were out of her mouth, she realized her mistake. The Colonel's face turned a deep red and the veins on his forehead popped out, visibly throbbing. He marched to the sliding doors that separated the conference room from the Operations Command Center. Opening one side with crisp military precision, he walked through the doorway and proceeded to take the handle with him. The handle tore out of the sliding door with his vicious yank. Elizabetta could only shrug and shake her head as the handle clattered down the middle of the room accompanied by a string of curses and loud stomping.

"He is concerned about his daughter," MorningStar's quiet comment washed away the military veneer, and said it all.

Though Susannah was a member of the Vamp Squad, she was first and foremost, Maddox's daughter. Everyone on the squad knew he would move heaven and hell for his little girl, if he needed to. The mere existence of the Vamp Squad was a testament to the lengths of which Maddox would go for his daughter's safety.

All eyes focused on Milo Miller slumped behind his command screen. The smartboard on the wall of the conference room projected pictures as he searched with inhuman speed.

He did not need to see their faces. "On it ladies. Result in twenty seven point three minutes." He was glued to his monitors. No one had requested a search, but no one ever had to with Miller. He wasn't a vampire, but he was a very uncanny human being.

MorningStar, of all the vampires, laughed out loud. "Can you not see he is connected to this thing called Internet, as I am connected to the earth and the wind? It is part of the sergeant's..." the Native American vampire was at a loss for words and looked quizzically at Elizabetta for help. A woman of a very different world and time, MorningStar simply shrugged.

"So how can we help?" Natalia asked loud enough for everyone, including the preoccupied Miller to hear.

"Under control. I'll hit the all-call if there is anything new. Thanks for asking, Ms. Vyrubova. Correction, Mrs. Milassoviech." Miller's fingers continued to fly as screen shots flashed by at inhuman speed.

"I just feel so helpless, sitting here doing nothing." Natalia hugged her husband close. "Maybe we should go down there and see what's going on."

"That, my darling wife, would be a mistake. Susannah has been so emotional lately. There are some things a young girl must do on her own, including making her own mistakes. To become an adult is not an easy task, but something we must all do at some point." He kissed the woman in his arms soundly. "She is a vampire as well. What can happen that she cannot handle? And, if the trouble is too much, I have faith she will ask for help. She can be fiercely independent and doggedly stubborn, but she is not stupid."

"Faith in Susannah? That is a stretch for me, but I hope you are correct." Natalia shook her head.

The couple rose and moved toward the door. "How does he do that?" Natalia blew a kiss toward Miller as she followed Yuri out of the conference room.

"Ya nee zni-yo, no idea, my love." Yuri patted Natalia's rump as she scooted ahead of him.

"Mystery of the techniverse." Elizabetta followed the couple with a heavy sigh.

MorningStar gave Miller a quick look as she set off on her own with purposeful strides.

Monique was the only one who remained behind. She pulled a chair next to Sergeant Miller's computer and settled in for the long term.

Miller stalled.

"Ah, don't you want to go with the rest of the, ah, ladies?"

"No, I shall remain and help you. I should have done more to get Susannah to come home. Or at least find out the information we needed. Susannah is my little sister. If anything happens to her, I shall never forgive myself." Monique tucked her feet beneath her and set her chin on her knees. "What can I do?"

"Um… nothing really. I just have to run these calculations and make sure the search frequencies are correct. It doesn't really require help, Ma'am. I'm fine alone, really." He paused to look at her, then quickly looked back at his screen. Making eye contact was something in his book to avoid. In his opinion, one never knew when a vampire would use *those* skills to hypnotize a guy, and do all sorts of weird things!

"No, no. I shall stay and watch. What do I look for?" Monique smiled sweetly and patted Milo's arm.

Milo flinched.

"Ms. Merchant, this is kind of a one man show, if you know what I mean. I punch in the figures, and then just wait. No need for you to hang with me and be bored." Miller was trying to convince Monique to leave him to his computers. He found it hard to concentrate without distraction… or self-defense around Monique.

"Sergeant Miller, why do I frighten you so? We have virtually lived together for over four years now and still, you are vierge dans un bordel. Innocent, oui? I know I tease you unmercifully, however, now is time for gravité, to be serial. I have a very bad feeling. What has Susannah gotten herself into? I believe she may be in difficulté, more than she can handle. And not like Yuri, I do not think she will request help. Il est une question de fierté. The pride, oui? And I think, love.

She must find a way to love herself."

Monique hung her head and frowned with worry. The computer dinged and numbers began rapidly appearing, line after line. "What is happening?"

Milo shifted away from the vampire who moved closer to the screens. "That is serious, gravité, oui?" Miller smirked at his French interpretation. "The computer is searching for the last entries from Susannah's computer when she was using the search engine. Crap, I should have installed double redundancy in the tracking device when she took delivery of her new car. I just didn't think she'd pull anything so soon. I thought she'd tell me when she found what she was looking for. Not just go off on her own."

"No, no. Do not blame yourself. None of us thought her capable of leaving so suddenly, without telling anyone. It is not your fault."

"Yes it is, Ms. Merchant. I helped her look for this Kell fellow. I helped her hack into the city morgue files to research her own death. I know she was frustrated when we hit one dead end after the other, but…I thought she was just, like trying to find her roots, so to speak. I didn't think she would take off, or anything. I used to think I was so good at figuring people out. She was one step ahead of me all along. Shit!"

"I do not understand why Susannah has no tracking device in her car. Is that not standard for us all?" Monique chewed on a nail as she watched the sergeant.

"Her car just came in a few weeks ago and she was so keen to get the new computer system installed, I had no idea she would skip out on me before Dr. Paulson in IT finished the special accessories package. It included the upgraded tracking device. The standard one was not tamper-proof. Obviously. It's not like we use On-Star, you know."

"Oui, oui. This I know as well as my little sister. When that child wants something, she can be very persuasive, especially with men. Like I said, do not blame yourself. Colonel Maddox will do enough of that for us all!" Monique watched the two computer screens as the text flew by. "You have no extra-ordinary power that I can sense, Sergeant. How do you follow this scrambled mess that flies by? It is impressionnant, for a human."

"Lots of practice and a certain knack for recognizing data streams and key words. I cut my teeth on computer screens. My mom was one of the best con artists in all of Illinois. She could plant a *sneaker bug,* then follow a *sink and snatch* before the *wag* was even aware of her electronic presence. Once, she took the British Common Exchange for over six million pounds. In through a back door she found while writing code for a simple spreadsheet program. The CEO himself actually apologized to her, when he had to let her go." Miller spoke without taking his eyes off the flashing monitors. "Seems they ran into a serious and unexpected lack of funds. She had a good laugh on them. She met my dad while setting up an offshore account for her take. It was love at first heist when he took her for a couple cool million himself."

"Your mother was a thief? Is that not, repoussant, repulsive to a son?" Monique was intrigued by the specialized words she did not quite understand. She had no idea Milo Miller was from a family of criminals.

"Mother, father, uncles, cousins. My sister is the biggest con of us all. She's an attorney in D.C. She writes and audits defense contracts. Now there's big money under the table." He laughed and paused a screen. "Got something here. Take a look, Ms. Merchant. I do believe we have found an artifact."

"Ah, do call me Monique. I promise, cross my heart, I will not bite you, Sergeant. What am I looking at? What is an artifact?" Monique patted Miller's arm and ignored his obvious flinch again.

"An artifact is a buried *trace* data stream. The last time Susannah used her computer in the car, she was researching a company called Proctor Pharmaceuticals, and a fellow named Jordan Burke." Miller scrolled through the file's meta-data tagged with Susannah's trace. "Bingo, Ms., I mean, Monique." Miller shook his head at the familiarity of a first name for the sexiest vampire on the squad. "Jordan Burke is Kellan Burke's son. Kell short for Kellan, possibly? Name ring a bell? Here's a newspaper article about the father's death. Damn, have a look at that car! Now that boy had some kind of money to afford a car like that."

Monique blanched at the name Kell, but read the article as Miller ranted about the expensive foreign car. Kell was too close to Kellan and she had given up believing in coincidences, a long time ago. Just as she got to the bottom of the article, her cell phone vibrated and she jumped.

"Ooh, I so love that little buzz." She pulled the phone from between her breasts and pushed the connect button. Ted's name and number appeared. "Bonjour, cheri. I am so glad you have called. How is your mère? And how are you?"

After a few moments of catching up, and the news that Ted's

mother was doing as well as could be expected, Monique asked about the night he and the Colonel drove Susannah's body from Florida.

Ted recounted the tale as best he remembered. When he mentioned the fire and a fancy car, Monique interrupted. "Do you recall the kind of car, cheri? It is important."

"Of course, Monique. I would never forget a cherry Maserati Quattroporte Sport GT, metal-flake black with smoke windows! Gawd, I still have wet dreams about that car. Such a waste. I almost cried, watching those guys torch the fellow and his car. I think it was some kind of hit. The Colonel and me, we beat feet out of there, ya know, we had Susannah in the back. In her coffin."

Monique was bouncing up and down on her chair. "Ted, just a minute." She motioned to the car in the picture. "Sergeant, what kind of car is that in the picture?"

"Just a sec... it's a Maserati of some kind. I recognize the hood ornament. Why?"

Monique's smile widen. "Ted, mon ami, you are a wonderful man and I will kiss your face a million times when next I see you. Au revoir." She hung up and squealed. "We have made the connection, Sergeant. Susannah's Kell is Kellan Burke the III. She went to find her sire, but found his son instead. Where is this Jordan living?" She affected a surprised tone with just a touch of excitement. The information wasn't really news to her, but the specifics of the whole picture were slowly becoming clear.

Miller scrolled through the articles then paused on the one that talked about Jordan Burke and his move to Proctor Estate. "He lives at the Proctor Estate in Daytona Beach. Gee, let me see, Kellan Burke worked for Proctor Pharmaceuticals. Burke died in a mysterious car explosion at the same time Maddox and Ted were retrieving Susannah. Actually, in the same parking lot where the truck was parked. His son now lives at Proctor Estate. Only a moron wouldn't see that connection. How did we miss it? I'm going to bring up the Proctor website and do a little digging. That teenage terrorist you call your little sister, will not get the draw on me again." Miller hunched over his keyboard and retreated into his world of the electronic hunt.

Monique slid from her chair and quietly took her leave. She knew that posture and look. It told her there was no point in remaining with the Sergeant. He would be oblivious to the world until he found what he was looking for, or burned a few motherboards in the attempt. As the broken door slid closed behind her, the little smartphone in her bra vibrated again. The caller ID window showed SVS5.

It was Susannah!

"Ma cheri, where are you? The world is tilting here. Your father is in a smit. We are all concerne'."

"That's snit. Hey sis, listen, I won't be back tomorrow. I'm visiting some relatives down here."

Monique pushed the key to record their conversation as soon as she heard the word 'sis'. It was their private code for *something's up*.

"I found my missing cousins. They want me to hang around for a while and get to know the family. Remind Dad to feed my bird, and keep an eye on my flowers. Maybe water if needed." Susannah used the pre-arranged code words that spoke volumes. 'Feed my bird' actually meant set a trace on my phone. 'Keep an eye on my flowers' was code for set up satellite observation. 'Water if needed" said to send help, if it looked like it was needed. Susannah would have only used the code is she was in the middle of something serious, or in deep trouble.

Monique was immediately alert. "Okay, Susannah, at least you are with family, so we will not worry. I'll be sure and take care of things. You know how Dad can be with your pets." Monique banged on the window of the conference room and waved frantically at Miller. She pointed at her phone and mouthing *Susannah*.

Miller was on it in a flash.

Monique watched the timer on her phone as she continued the sisterly chat. She had to keep Susannah on the line at least two minutes for Miller to immediately locate her signal and pinpoint the location. "So, are you having fun, little one? I miss you so. I should have gone on vacation with you. All I have to do here is dishes and cleaning. Your father is such a tyrant, and there are only cows to talk to. Tell me, are the men on the beach handsome, and strong, and ooh so tan?"

"Oh yeah, I'm having a blast. I loved dancing at this little club, the Mango Bango. It's in the hotel, I stayed at. A great place! They fix a hell of a Bloody Mary. The manager is a sweetie. He did card me though. Hey, gotta go sis. Call you later. Tell Dad not to worry. Love you guys."

Three and a half minutes!

They had a location.

Monique ran back through the door.

"Did you get it? Here, listen." She played back the entire conversation. "What do you think?"

Miller dashed into the OCC, followed by an excited Monique. He punched the green complex intercom button. "Code red, conference room immediately." Miller's announcement would bring the others back to the conference room to evaluate the new information and listen to the recording.

"She was giving us a lot of information. How fast do you think the Colonel…" Monique was cut off by the Sergeant's answer.

"One and a half minutes." Miller smiled as a red-eyed Colonel came busting through the door of the OCC in shorts and a khaki tee shirt.

Monique stared at the Colonel's face. Maddox had contracted an instantaneous full-blown cold or had actually been crying! His eyes were a lovely bloodshot color and his nose was a rosy red.

"What have you got, Sergeant?"

"Trouble, Sir. Contact from VS5. Coded; requested phone track, satellite surveillance, and support if situation warrants. VS2 recorded critical intel during conversation." From the Operational Command Center, Miller could see Natalia and Yuri had entered the adjoining conference room trailed by Elizabetta. Dr. Anderson and MorningStar trotted down the hall behind Captain Devlin, who limped along with the help of a cane. Monique waved them toward the conference room with an excited smile. The Colonel and Miller were the last to join the group and take their chairs, transferring control of the computer terminals back to the console in the conference room.

Apparently their newest addition to the squad, Lieutenant Previn wasn't in quite as big a hurry. His chair remained empty.

Miller quickly pulled up the information he and Monique discovered, displaying it on the enormous smartboard, at the front of the room. "Ms. Merchant, you seem to have a handle on this thing. Would you do us the pleasure of a briefing, please?" The Colonel was concealing his own excitement as he invited Monique to spill the intel.

"Oui, Sir. Susannah called my cell phone at twenty-two thirty-seven hours. Coded conversation requested a phone trace, satellite surveillance and backup if there seemed to be a problem. She kept the connection long enough to give us a location and a little more information. What history Sergeant Miller and I found is also very interesting. It leads me to believe she went to Daytona Beach to find her sire, Kellan Burke the III, who is décédé. She located his son, Jordan who lives at the Proctor Estate of Proctor Pharmaceuticals. She told me she was visiting family, new cousins, indicating, I believe a coven. Kellan's coven, to which Jordan belongs. She was registered under an assumed name at the Beachcomber Resort, which is also the home of the Mango Bango nightclub. Since Susannah mentioned the club by name, along with the drink 'Bloody Mary', I believe this club is a safe haven for Jordan's coven. She mentioned being carded in the club, so obviously the manager knows of our kind. He could be an asset. She said he was 'sweet'. Susannah's last instructions were to 'tell my dad not to worry' which actually means the opposite. Then she signed off with 'love you guys'. The plural ending means get the team involved." Monique paused.

"How do you know this Kellan Burke is, or was Susannah's sire?" Captain Devlin was jotting down notes with a huge smile plastered across his face.

"Sergeant Miller accessed Susannah's art…"

"Artifact. A data trace stream." Miller automatically supplied the words.

"…and found she had been researching Kellan Burke's history. In our… sisterly talks," Monique winked at the Colonel, "Susannah told me she remembered only the first name of her sire. While in Daytona Beach, her computer files show she downloaded several articles. One of which documented Kellan's death in a car explosion on the day Ted Vanderloss and the Colonel were originally transporting Susannah to Olney Farm. I contacted Ted and he remembered the fire and the car, a…"

"Black Maserati Quattroporte Sport GT." Miller pulled up a picture of a man and his sexy car. He continued to fill in the words for Monique like a well-practiced comedy team.

Colonel Maddox smiled at the conversation that flowed without breaks by two individuals supplying the words. At least he wasn't the only one Miller did that to.

"It was Kellan Burke and his car. He was following Susannah when he was dispatched, most likely an asesinato."

"Hit," Miller translated the French word for assassination as Monique reviewed notes on a paper in front of her.

Miller continued from there. "Considering the evidence and Susannah's cryptic call, I would submit, Sir that Susannah has been discovered by Kellan and Jordan's coven. They are probably related to the Proctor family and located on their expansive estate outside Daytona Beach. Proctor Pharmaceuticals is most probably an active cover for the coven. Kellan Burke was Vice-President in charge of marketing at the company before his suspicious death. Now Jordan lives at the estate. The triangulated locator signal of Susannah's cell phone showed the same address as the estate. What we do not know, is the implication of her presence there, Jordan's part in this event, and whether Susannah needs assistance."

"Sergeant, set up-"

"On screen, Sir."

"-satellite … Miller?" Colonel Maddox glared at the Sergeant who was watching the screen.

"Sorry, Sir. At sixty-five percent, this is the estate." The picture momentarily fuzzed then cleared. "Infrared shows forty-seven signatures at ninety-eight to one hundred degrees and twenty-five at less than eighty degrees. That would indicate forty-seven humans and twenty-five vampires currently in residence. If you look at the red shadows, human sigs, the majority are clumped in a single area near what looks like a large structure, well behind the main building. Several of the vamp sigs roam the grounds and some human sigs are grouped in a single section of the main building. Those in the outbuilding are in rather close quarters. A dorm? A bunch of cubicles? Unsure."

Elizabetta sat forward with a small gasped and covered her mouth with a delicate hand.

"Ms. Zoeltel?" Colonel Maddox motioned to the Coven Mistress.

"An office? No. They keep culls. My God, how inhumane." Elizabetta shook her head. "I wonder if the Council of Elders knows of this coven and their ways?" Disgust replaced the look of shock on the elegant vampire's face.

"Culls? What are culls?" Captain Devlin twirled his pencil nervously.

Lieutenant Previn, the missing member of the squad, just joining the group, sneered from the door. He leaned against the door jam, arms crossed over his chest. "Humans kept for food. They are usually chained in pens or heavily drugged. Family tradition for naturist vampire covens. Nice relatives, huh?"

Captain Devlin coughed softly. "Previn, join us please. You may be able to add something useful." Devlin motioned the Lieutenant to his empty seat.

Previn took his seat next to Monique and smiled viciously at the French vampire.

Monique slid away from the Lieutenant.

Miller glared at Previn from behind his console. "Nothing good, I'd wager." Miller mumbled just loud enough for everyone to hear. Miller feared the ladies but also maintained a healthy respect for what they did for the government in Afghanistan. They had earned his respect.

Previn simply detested the women and took every opportunity to let it show.

"Ladies and gentlemen, back to the issue at hand," the Colonel grumbled. "Let's listen to the recording and then develop a support plan if VS5 requires assistance. Sergeant, is there anyway to figure out which one of those blue blips is my daughter?"

"Not at present, sir. If she uses her cell phone again, I can tag her, then we will be able to follow from that point on. After Susannah spoke to Monique she shut her phone off, Sir."

"Alright, you all know your jobs so I won't presume to tell you what to do. Please keep in mind," he quietly added' "from a worried father, that Susannah is an operative, as well as *my* daughter. Let's not screw the pooch on this one, okay?" Gruff to the end, Maddox rose and strode out of the conference room.

"Well, that's the most loving thing I have ever heard the Colonel say." Natalia smirked.

"Be nice, my love. He is a soldier. He means well. He just can't quite climb out of the military uniform."

Natalia poked Yuri in the ribs. "Soldiers, they all stick together." She kissed his head. "To work, my soldier love."

Chapter 20

Of Fight or Flight

We are all but animals under the flesh of civilization,
And it is the mind that defines our realization
Of the animal's need to fight, or take flight.
In the presence of one who instills such fright…

And still we drench ourselves in false logic,
Hiding the fact of proof anthropologic.
Society's veneer is but rule by might.
A boon, a blessing, in the vampire's sight.

Marianne DuPries, Poet
Essays of the Human Condition
New York, 1984

Jordan and Susannah strolled across the meticulously manicured grounds of the Proctor estate hand in hand, like the teen lovers they could have been. Should have been… in another world. Jordan pointed out different buildings and sights, while Susannah giggled and preened at each opportunity. Trenchertt kept a respectable distance, but an obvious presence. Susannah could feel his mental probing so she kept her mind on Jordan's handsome figure and filled her head with sensual thoughts.

It wasn't difficult. Jordan cut a delicious picture. His casual Dockers and polo shirt fit as if they had been specifically designed for the hot body they covered. His blonde waves hung almost to the wide shoulders that easily carried the weight of her safety. His rich chocolate eyes missed nothing as they wandered the meandering paths. Pausing at the rose garden, Susannah noticed the approach of a human.

"Company? Human," she mouthed quietly.

"That's Metolius' secretary, Almaund. Smart and human. Very smart. He misses nothing. Be careful." Jordan pulled Susannah closer burying his nose in her sweet smelling hair, letting the waves of lust fill his mind. His groin tightened and he felt Trenchertt's mental touch withdraw.

Susannah felt it as well and giggled. A Knight Templar? A

sword-wielding hero of centuries past? Intimidated by love?

How cute!

"Bad boy, big bone." She breathed as she let the feelings overwhelm her. The ease of their connection was scary and exhilarating at the same time. Susannah tapped the top button of his slacks suggestively and circled her hips invitingly. She could feel his sex grow with obvious pulses as she wiggled suggestively.

"Sir, the Master has arranged for Miss Susannah to be quartered in the guest suite at Proctor House." Almaund handed Jordan a swipe card encased in a small paper pouch. It was emblazoned with a gold P encircled by filigree scrollwork. Almaund inclined his head to both and retreated as quickly as he had appeared.

"Well, it looks like you will be a guest here for a while." Jordan kept his voice edged with excitement, but conveyed his worry to Susannah with his eyes. This was not a good thing.

"Wow! This is so totally cool. I'm going to stay at the big house? How fantastic is that! We can see each other every day, every minute…" Her lips sought his in a kiss that exploded within both their minds, smothering the edge of fear. It was amazing… and doubly good in case Trenchertt continued to monitor them. Their connection rattled her senses and played havoc with her mind.

Like a wild fire, a powerful surge of lust flowed from Susannah to Jordan and back again. This unexplainable bond they shared was almost scary in its intensity. One minute they stood calmly talking. The next, she wanted to push him to the grass and rip away the clothing that separated their hyper-sexed bodies.

Could this be anything like what Yuri and Natalia felt?

Was her and Jordan's DMV that close it wanted a physical connection and ignited their minds and bodies when they touched? Susannah caught Trenchertt's wince out of the corner of her eye. *Serves the old bastard right for tapping into our thoughts and emotions. Vampiric voyeurism! Huh…*

Jordan disengaged Susannah from his embrace and held her at arms length. "I can't think when you do that." He was telling the Lord's own truth! A wide smile split his gorgeous features. "But I like it."

That made Susannah giggle again.

"Maybe you should think about retrieving your things from the hotel. You may want to have a change of clothes and your car. Although," he stepped back raking his eyes over her, "naked is always good, too."

Susannah took a swipe at Jordan for the blatantly outrageous statement, then dissolved into a fit of giggles as she fell into his arms at Trenchertt's approach.

Jordan turned Susannah in his embrace to face the Knight, his hands locked just beneath her ample breasts pulling her blouse taut for a clear view. One thumb absently caressed a nipple as he smiled at the strained expression on Trenchertt's face.

"If you two can restrain yourselves for a few hours, I think it would be a good idea to fetch Susannah's things. I shall assist." Trenchertt bowed.

"A knight to escort me and mine. I am honored." Jordan had to bend with Susannah, affecting a kind of double bow as both of his hands cupped her breasts.

Susannah purred. She didn't have to try to play along. Their foreplay had her wet and ready for Jordan's advances. Straightening, she placed her hands over his and closed her eyes, a dreamy smile clearly apparent to Trenchertt, who, was apparently clearly disgusted.

"Honor or not, I shall attend thee. I would be grateful for a little less emotional entanglement." Trenchertt rubbed his temple and sighed. "It is taxing, as you may well understand."

It was an opening Susannah could not let pass. She bounced off Jordan, taking Trenchertt's arm. "Sir Trenchertt, have you ever thought of getting a little on the side, so to speak? I am sure it would help with your stress level and cure that little pain near your temple. Well, anyway it always helped my father."

Trenchertt froze like a marble statue. Susannah, still locked arm in arm, jerked to a stop. "Mistress, what young woman speaketh of her father in such terms? Does not your generation have the least speck of respect for their elders? I stand aghast."

And he did. Rooted to the ground where he stopped.

"Ah, Trenchy, come on. It's the new millennium." She tugged at the knight's arm without success. "A good three-way is all the rage these days." She was affecting the perfect Gen-X attitude. The more blatant sexuality, the better. "Stress will kill you, ya know. Better to let off some steam with the 'new generation'. I promise it will help that little pain." She glanced seductively at his crotch while she squeezed the muscle in his upper arm, then licked her lips invitingly.

Despite almost a thousand years of watching human nature, witnessing horrendous battles, despicable acts of genocide, and sadistic cruelty, Susannah's behavior was more than the poor knight could handle.

It was also exactly what Susannah wanted.

No one had treated Trenchertt this casually since he had taken up the cloth! Not even that seventeenth century queen who had a kingdom to lose. "On second thought, Jordan, I am sure I can trust you to escort Miss Susannah to retrieve her possessions and return here safely. I shall remain behind and ensure no trouble follows." He peeled Susannah's hand from his arm and strode purposefully toward the shed where Damien spent his free time. "Return post hast, children. I shall be vigilant."

Susannah skipped to Jordan and planted a loud smack on his cheek. "Free, free, free at last." She grabbed his hand and tugged the astounded young man toward the parking lot. "Works like a charm. Intimidation is a wonderful thing. Big guns or aggressive sexual advances - gets em every time."

Jordan just shook his head and followed the only woman who had ever caused Father Sir Ignacias Trenchertt, Knight of the Templar to back away and run scared.

"To my chariot, knave. We shall departeth this fix." Susannah had her mind set on running, as far and as fast as she could. And taking her newly acquired boy toy with her.

She gave herself a mental shake, once again. Jordan was more than a boy toy, more than a friend with privileges… but…what actually was he? Her heart gave a couple quick beats all of its own accord.

Her heart beat?

On its own?

It was time to run.

Focus on the run, she told herself.

Safe haven was Olney Farm. By now her team had probably figured out she was in way over her head.

Smart-ass verbal battles with ancient knights was one thing.

Survival was another.

It hadn't taken her long to figure out Proctor Estate was not a safe place to play girl detective without back-up. Reality at the estate was just a little too biting.

Jordan hit the auto unlock and ushered Susannah into the front seat of Drechell's Town Car. He switched on the radio and tuned to a station with a hard base rhythm. He cranked the sound until he could feel the beat in his bones.

"We can't just take off, Susannah. We wouldn't make it to the end of the parking lot. Metolius has this town wrapped up. Why do you think you could die a horrible death and no one looked twice at your body or the records? How do you think everything was confiscated and your case was shut? The Master owns the police, the judges, the resort, hell, he even owns me. If I so much as smell like I want to escape, I'm dead meat." The noise of the radio made hearing difficult and overhearing impossible. Those listening electronically would be incapable of distinguishing voice from beat. Those listening vampirically would not be able to shut out the blaring base.

Susannah cuddled close to Jordan's lips and settled in to whisper. "There has to be a way, Jordan. I won't leave you without a safety net. I wouldn't do that to you. And I won't let Metolius turn me into some plaything either. I saw the way his eyes changed. I also saw the way Marisella reacted. I am not dumb or naïve in the least. How would you feel watching Metolius feed off me, or worse?" The wheels in Susannah's mind were spinning at warp speed. The picture was terrifying.

Why *did* she care what happened to Jordan so much?

It was unexpected?

It *was* unexpected.

She was beginning to think she was channeling Uncle Rob.

"If it ever came to that, I would already be destroyed. Metolius never overtly takes what he thinks belongs to someone else. He simply dispatches the opposition and consumes the spoils." They stopped at the gate for a delivery truck with the ominous P scrolled on the side. The name Proctor Pharmaceuticals formed a black circle around the letter.

"Another delivery of heaven for the culls. God I hate this place." Jordan pounded on the steering wheel.

"What's in the truck?" Susannah casually waved to the driver as the truck lumbered on by.

"I told you not to ask about it here at the estate." Jordan gunned the car and turned onto the main road leading into Daytona Beach. The base pounding out through the radio set his teeth on edge. "The unwilling become the willing with a little Proctor magic. Enough said."

Susannah was not easily put off but they had bigger problems to consider at the moment. "Why don't we just pack up my stuff and take off in my car? We can go to my home. You'll be safe there and my, ah, family can help with the rest of the problems. They're a unique group with some very unique skills."

"By now your car has probably been bugged and wired for

tracking. Your things probably have half a dozen tracking devices hidden in them. Undoubtedly some kind of control device has been installed to shut your car down if we head in an unacceptable direction. I am sure we are being watched as well. Metolius is an extremely resourceful man. Now he has his eye on you." Jordan shook his head, "We have no choice. We have to return to the estate or we will *be* returned."

"Jordan, pull over at that gas station. I need to use the bathroom," she hollered above the music.

He gave Susannah a curious glance but pulled into the parking lot.

"I'll be back in a flash, baby. Mommy has to pee." She giggled and ran for the toilet while dialing her cell phone. As soon as the door closed behind her, she engaged the black sound device carefully hidden on the side of her phone. No one would be able to listen in on her conversation as the tiny chip emitted a signal frequency that matched and cancelled her own. One ring and the voice of Milo Miller could be heard clearly.

He didn't even let her say hello. "So, the prodigal daughter calls in. We have issues to discuss, little lady. I am not pleased at being your dupe." Miller's tone was as clear as his message.

"Sergeant, I have a situation here. I need a car with accessories at the Beachcomber Resort on the top level of the parking lot in one hour. Accessories for two, departure plan and airlift. Copy?"

It was close to 1:00 a.m. They had to make their escape and find cover before the sun rose.

"Copy. Pre-authorized and on the way. Strategic departure and pick-up point will be in the console computer. Agents Wilson and Barkley will run interference. Then we will *talk* Ms. Maddox." Miller placed just a little too much emphasis on the word *talk* for Susannah's liking, but she knew she would have to do a lot of penance for this little caper.

Provided she and Jordan survived.

Her whole trip to simply find love had turned into a goat-fuck. She needed help and apparently help was on her menu.

Thank God, the Squad and the US Government!

"Copy. And, thanks, Milo." She paused for a second, not knowing exactly what else to say. She'd really messed up royal, but help was still on its way.

"Don't thank me. I believe in tough love, Ms. Maddox. If it were up to me, you'd be getting yourself out of whatever mess you're in." He paused for a split second. It was enough to tell Susannah he did care what happened to her. "Be safe. Out." The line went dead.

Susannah flushed the toilet, stashed her cell phone and returned to the car. At least she had a plan. Should she share it with Jordan, or just wing it and hope he kept up?

"Everything come out alright, sweet thing?" Jordan rolled his eyes toward a yellow hummer parked near the side of the road behind them.

Susannah got the message.

"Yep. I just need one more thing." She smiled and pointed to the cell phone in her bag. Jordan nodded.

"And what would that be?"

"A kiss from you, baby." Susannah wiggled across the seat and set her lips against his ear making a smooching sound for the carload of eves-droppers behind them. *Help is on the way,* she mentally communicated, *Daddy is sending a car with some toys included. We have a location for an airlift out of this place. Just follow along and we may get out of this thing alive. Think your answer and I will listen to your thoughts. That way I'll have hearing by the time we get to the resort.* She reached and turned the blaring music down to a tolerable level.

Why didn't we do that back at the estate? Jordan frowned trying to add facial expressions with his mental conversation. Susannah thought it was cute but unnecessary. His mental communications came with their own emotional frequency. But of course, he wouldn't know that if mental communication wasn't one of his gifts.

Because, I have no idea who can do what I do. At home we can hear everything that goes on most of the time. Makes it very hard to lie, ya know! Susannah giggled and cuddled up to Jordan as he pulled onto the road once again.

You amaze me. That must be some home life. Is that why you made the crack about your father's sexual proclivity back there with Trenchertt?

Oh, ick NO! That would be like peaking through the door when your parents are doing it. That's even too sick for a vampire. Anyway my father is human. Only the vamps psych. Psychically speak. Susannah kissed his ear again. *The more we communicated with our minds, the easier it seemed to be to keep the connection and psych both ways. It's weird, but our powers seemed to be in sync and growing. Does that happen with your coven?*

Not likely! Metolius covets power. He's not the sharing kind of guy. We're almost at the resort. What's the plan? The closer they came to the Beachcomber the more tense Jordan seemed.

There'll be a car on the top level of the garage with enough fire power to start a mini revolution; our specialized kind of guns so only shoot to kill. We should have all the information we need inside. Two agents, Wilson and Barkley will run interference. I've worked with Barkley before, but not Wilson. Barkley is about six feet tall and has flaming red hair. For an undercover agent, he is hard to miss.

Jordan pulled into the parking lot and took the first open space. They would have to walk across the grounds but that would give their observers the idea that they were not in a hurry. Casual like, not on the run. Susannah held Jordan's hand and swung it like a child wandering playfully.

Any other time, any other place, he would have loved her playfulness. Every once in a while she would stop, jerking him around to catch a kiss or grope a body part. Despite the seriousness of the situation, he was so hot by the time they found the elevators, he could hardly breathe. He could tell Susannah was feeling the same as she sent him mental moans with every kiss, which only served to amp up his jumping libido.

The overly tricked-out yellow hummer parked on the street, away from the couple but well within eyesight. Metolius' men weren't even trying to be subtle.

The elevator was empty so Jordan took advantage of the privacy to return the sex play Susannah started hours earlier. He captured her in his arms and dragged his lips along her temple, breathing in the sent of arousal. She lifted her lips to his and he plundered her mouth. Soft mewing sounds drove him on as he pulled her closer rubbing his engorged sex against her thigh. "You taste like heaven, my own personal heaven." His mind was on fire for her and he didn't think they would make it to her room.

"I can't seem to get enough of your lips." He mumbled against her mouth as his tongue circled hers. She was everything wrapped in a moment, pressed against him.

He was a drowning man.

At the fourteenth floor, a rather plump woman got on. "Just get a room, please." She glanced at the couple with distain, then punched the fifteenth floor. The tiny fur ball on a leash at her swollen feet yapped in agreement.

"Got one, Ma'am." Jordan mumbled as he continued to take everything Susannah offered.

His mind tumbled in the feelings that tore as his body. Was this a game she played or was there more? Like at the beach house just what? A day before? He could not resist this woman of his dreams, her touch, her taste, her smell. He growled and pressed her deeper into the corner of the elevator. Feeling the length of her against his body sent shivers up and down his spine.

The woman promptly departed on the next floor with a snort and a yap. Both Jordan and Susannah laughed as the doors shut on the obviously disgruntled woman and the little mop on the leash.

"She probably hasn't gotten any in a decade." Jordan whispered in Susannah's ear while she tried to shush him.

"Don't be nasty. Everyone can't be vampire-perfect, ya know. Here we go. Are you ready?"

All too soon they were at her floor.

The elevator chimed and opened to the eighteenth floor. The way was clear to her suite as they quickly covered the distance. *Only think to me, Jordan. No verbal talk unless it is sexy, okay? Keep things casual.*

It was hard to believe this woman could capture his mind and body with a couple kisses then get right down to the point – the business point. How did she do it? Jordan shook his head to clear the heat that continually fired his mind and hormones.

She pulled the key card from her pocket and efficiently swiped it in the lock. "I have to make sure I didn't miss anything, baby. It'll only take a few minutes. Why don't you turn on the TV and catch up on your favorite game?" Susannah was stalling for time, opening and slamming drawers and rummaging around in the bathroom, anything to make noise and waste time. The car wouldn't be in place for another ten minutes.

All of a sudden, Jordan was behind her in the mirror. "We could have one last private little shower, sweet thing. I really liked the first one we shared. Just think of how much water we would save at the estate." He ran his hands up and down her sides, watching her reaction in the mirror.

Susannah reached up and ran her hands through his hair, pulling his head to her neck where he proceeded to rake the flesh with his fangs. She gasped and shuddered with sensual energy. How long could she keep this up without exploding from the pent up need that coiled ever tighter in her core? Every touch sent her closer to losing control. Every little comment played out a dozen fantasies in a flash of sensual thought. Her body was on the verge of demanding satisfaction. Every nerve tingled with anticipation. She remembered reading some sloppy romantic novel in high school that mentioned exquisite torture. Now she understood the complete meaning in no uncertain terms!

"Won't we be expected back at the estate right away?" Her brain finally re-engaged. A plan was forming.

She still had a recording of two voice specialists imitating sex on her phone from their mission in Somalia. If she ran the fifteen-minute dialog they would have extra time to get to the escape vehicle. They'd be on their way, while their tail was listening to what the thugs thought was Jordan and Susannah having a great time. Damn, audio pornography came in handy in a pinch. She would miss that phone!

"Are you kidding? You've been teasing me all day and I am up for a quickie, literally." He took her hand in his and guided it to his aching groin.

Susannah purred at the feel.

"Nobody will miss us for a while."

Susannah winked at him. *This is perfect. I have a voice recording we can use to get the hell out of here.*

The shock on Jordan's face was precious.

Susannah had to cover her mouth to keep from giggling. She pulled him over to the bed making a big noisy deal of bouncing Jordan onto the mattress. She grabbed her sleek little phone and pointed to the menu. Susannah scrolled to a file labeled "Noisy Sex".

"Oooh baby, come to mama. I need some honey." Susannah bounced on the bed a couple times, ruffled the covers then hit the play button.

The recording began with soft moans and muffled sounds of kissing and more rustling covers.

Jordan looked stunned as Susannah silently waved him off the bed and pointed to her suitcases. *Leave them. Let's go while the getting is good.*

There is no 'getting' and it is definitely not good. Why is it when we have these...moments, our lives are in serious danger and there is always somewhere we need to run to?

Susannah could clearly feel the emotional whine that accompanied his psyche.

Jordan tiptoed to the door and scanned the hall through the peep hole. It was still clear except for a tall red haired man who stood patiently at the corner of the hallway, waiting. Obviously waiting for them. *I think Barkley is out there. Have a look.*

Susannah peered through the peephole in the door and nodded.

That's Barkley. See what I mean about the hair. Definitely a give-away. Let's go. She covered the door latch with a towel and opened the lock.

The recording had increased in volume and it was obvious some lucky couple was headed for one hell of a joint orgasm. Creaking bed sounds and panting mixed with moans and soft screams filled the room.

Jordan shook his head in mock sadness. *That could have been us. But NO! We have to escape. Damn bad timing.* He swatted Susannah on the butt as they quietly left the room and softly closed the door behind them.

It's just a recording. Two guys in separate sound booths. Trust me, they are professionals, not lovers, and there was very little enjoyment. Just a paycheck. She blew him a silent kiss as they approached Barkley standing in an open elevator. He was waiting for them with a serious expression and a finger to his lips. *Believe me the real thing is much better.*

And how would I know? Jordan's mental picture felt a little peevish.

Come on, you'll survive. Try to keep up! Susannah was already trotting down the hall.

The man in a dark suit with a wire in his ear, waved them on to the elevator. Even escaping certain punishment or death did nothing to improve Jordan's attitude. He really needed to make love with Susannah. No woman ever had that kind of effect on him. Two days of togetherness was like a miraculous gift from heaven he could not get enough of. Despite the explosion, imminent danger and a hell of a pickle they were currently in. He was already having trouble picturing himself without her.

A danger signal buzzed through his brain. He recognized the red flag but couldn't keep the smile from his lips. The thought of a 'forever' kind of thing tickled the back of his skull.

Susannah waved to Barkley with a signal that questioned what floor they headed for.

Barkley punched the twenty-first button and handed Jordan a manila envelope. He pointed to instructions written on the front in scrawled script.

Jordan nodded in response to the directions. Apparently a specially outfitted black Caravan was parked next to the stairs across the causeway on the twenty-first floor of the parking garage attached to the hotel.

Susannah signaled the 'okay' to Barkley and took the keys and cell phone he held out. The door slid shut as silently as it opened and Barkley went to work, a small black wand in his hand.

Once both Susannah and Jordan had been cleared of bugs, the agent whispered, "Wilson's downstairs with a blue suit in case of trouble. No time to install the kind of computer uplink you're used to so there's a satellite linked laptop on the back seat. Appropriate accessories are behind the passenger seat with twenty hot mags for each gun. Bluetooth enabled parrot device with all the possible numbers you may need already loaded. Clothing's in labeled gym bags in the back and…

"Whoa, whoa, whoa." Jordan pushed the stop button on the elevator. "A blue suit? You mean a police officer?" Jordan blanched. "Susannah, Metolius owns the cops in this town. We're dead. This isn't going to work." Jordan punched the wall with his fist.

"Hang on, Jordan." Susannah turned to the agent, "Barkley, call your partner. Find out what's going on, and give me your throw down."

Barkley reached down, pulled up his pant leg and handed her the gun in his ankle holster. "Glock twenty-six, nine mil special loads. Should work fine in a pinch." He shrugged apologetically and pressed his earpiece. "Eighteen-nine to one-nine, location?" The radio was silent. "Eighteen-nine to one-nine, Wilson what's your location?"

There was no response the second time.

Immediately, Susannah knew Jordan was right.

They were in big trouble.

She hit the button for the twentieth floor and prepared for a firefight. "Jordan, stay behind me and be ready to run for it. Wilson is probably a goner. Sucks to be him and it's too bad. Barkley, you got our back?"

"Yep. Who we fighting here? Terrorists? Insurgents? The FBI? Please tell me it's the FBI because I love putting those bastards down." The glee in Barkley's statement didn't surprise Susannah. Among federal agents, it was common knowledge the FBI ranked right up there with pig slop and horse shit.

"Much worse. My kind, gone astray. Shoot everything that moves unless you want to end up as an appetizer. They won't die with standard ammo, but our specials will take them down, or at least slow them down. Then get yourself out of there, pronto. Got it?" Susannah knew Barkley was aware of the existence of vampires. He'd worked with the squad before. However, she had a sneaking suspicion he still thought of her kind in the Bella Lugosi venue. Real vampires were much more dangerous and devious.

The elevator doors opened silently and they headed down the hall to the stairwell. Susannah in the lead, Jordan in the middle and Barkley bringing up the rear. As they climbed the stairs, Susannah cast her senses ahead and felt three vampires at the entrance to the causeway. About twenty feet of concrete and glass spanned the area between the garage tower and the actual hotel complex.

Unfortunately, it was wide open and clearly visible.

Hopefully their reception committee was small and not expecting company quite yet. The element of surprise would be extremely helpful. Again, unfortunately, the element of surprise was difficult to come by with the cops on the dole.

Susannah tried her newly developing mind control. She affected a bored and lazy sentiment, then directed it at the men who stood near the causeway entrance. She had no idea if it would work on anything but weak-willed humans, let alone her own kind. But she had to try. They were in a pickle. She made a quick silent promise to train harder when she got home.

If she got home.

It fleetingly crossed her mind that, once again, she seemed to be making a lot of those kinds of promises to herself lately. Why hadn't she paid more attention and taken her training more seriously?

It was a moot point as she prepared for battle.

"Cal, how long do we have to wait? Bert said they were fuckin' up a storm down there. Sun'll be up in a couple hours." A large man in biker leathers, complained loudly. He wore a gold chain connecting a ring through his nose to a ring in his ear. "You know I can't take the UV. Sunburn messes up my tats. Damn." He kicked the wall leaving a cracking hole in the plaster.

"Shit Willy, don't wreck the place. We gotta stay put in case they come for the car that Wilson mentioned. Ya gotta love having that wimp on the payroll. Back in my previous life, federal agents had loyalty and much bigger guns. Did you see what that little shit was packing?"

Cal laughed. "Right, but you was runnin' moonshine with Boots Malone. Elliot Ness was the real pisser. He had good toys to track ya then."

"Them was good days. We got so many different agencies now they chase each other in circles! Shit, you can't tell the good guys from the bad guys. Most times there ain't no difference." The biker vampire hung his head. "How the hell do we tell who's who anymore?"

"The real bad guys have fangs, stupid." Cal slapped the biker on the back of his head.

"I'm going over to see what Sal and Bert are up to with the car. Just fire a few rounds if you see 'em and I'll come runnin'."

A might ADHD, Willy couldn't sit still for long. Waiting was painful. He strode across the causeway and disappeared into the parking garage.

"Big, God damn, good for nothing, mountain of shit. Willy! Willy? Fuckin lazy bastard." Cal perched on the edge of the windowsill and set his gun against the glass to wait.

Susannah whispered to Jordan, "Can you v-port us both to them then grab the gun before he figures out what's going on?" She would have communicated mentally but wanted Barkley in on the plan. "I'll take care of Cal and you'll have a gun. I think there's only three in the garage."

"Sure. You think you can take him?" Jordan was just a little surprised at himself for even asking. After all, she had somehow arranged their escape and staged the sexed-up diversion. He was beginning to believe she could do just about anything. That red flag waved pathetically in the back of his mind, but he ignored it. This woman was just way to hot... and capable.

"Of course." Susannah smiled brightly at Jordan.

His cock did a little jump.

"Barkley, you're our backup. Do I need to reiterate, shoot anything that moves?"

"No ma'am. I'm on it. Let's go."

Susannah suppressed a little giggle. His enthusiasm was sort of cute. Nowadays, the small select group who were an extension of the Vamp Squad Support Team, didn't get to use their weapons very often. Any excuse was good enough for the trigger-happy agent to expend a couple rounds of the taxpayer's bullets.

As soon as we disappear, head out." Susannah wagged her finger. "And please don't shoot us. We're the good guys, okay?"

"Disappear? Ah..." Susannah and Jordan disappeared and right on cue a mildly surprised Barkley stormed through the door.

Cal had just enough time to look up and recognize Jordan before Susannah struck his throat with a vicious chop, then knocked the choking man to the floor. Jerking his head sideways, she broke his spinal cord in one quick move.

Barkley appeared, panting behind Jordan who stood with Cal's Glock in his hand. "Is he dead?"

"Technically he has been for a long time, Barkley. But no, he'll regenerate. However, not in time to be a problem for us, I don't think." She made a crunching noise with her tongue and twisting her hands in front of her.

Agent Barkley got the picture.

"Let's get this thing done. Sunup in sixty-four minutes. I want to be inside and protected." Susannah hunkered down and sped across the causeway with Jordan in tow. Barkley stood his ground still panting. Waiting for her signal.

Low to the ground, she peered around the corner. *There's one under the car, one by the back hatch, and a Biker dude taking in the scenery. Where does Metolius come up with these guys anyway?* Susannah waved Barkley across the causeway. *Jordan, can you v-port a device?*

I can only v-port what I've touched before. And I have to go with it, or it has to go with me in most cases. Sorry, babe.

Okay, you take Willy and I'll take the guy under the car. Barkley crouched behind them. "Barkley, can you take the Biker dude? We can handle the rest."

"Yes Ma'am. There are 13 bullets in this clip. Will that be enough?" He was serious about the firepower question.

"Long enough for us, I hope. Get in the van as fast as you can. Ready?" Susannah and Jordan crouched waiting for Barkley to catch his breath. "Go."

Bert was talking on his cell phone, his back was to the group as they rushed the scene. Jordan took him out with a well-aimed blow to the back of the neck. Susannah caught Sal's groin with a hard stomp as he tried to shinny out from under the van where he was obviously trying to attach something. Barkley rounded the corner of the van and proceeded to fill Willy full of hollow-point forty-fives. The biker vampire spun, revealing the huge exit wounds and promptly collapsed in a pile of bloody tissue and ripped leather. Catching sight of the holes, Susannah knew he would be down for a while. She hoped it would be long enough.

"Let's go." Barkley had already punched the auto-start and was automatically unlocking the doors.

Sal lay half under the car in a tight ball holding his precious family jewels. Thank God, like humans, pain could incapacitate even a vampire for a while. Jordan dragged the moaning vampire out from under the van and emptied his gun into the man. He gave Susannah a high five before hopping in after Barkley.

Just as Susannah turned to get into the driver's side, a bloody, and very angry Willy grabbed her by the hair. She turned on him, grabbing the chain that connected two very sensitive parts of his body, and yanked. The chain came away in her hand, small hunks of flesh still clinging to the two rings that used to connect his nose and earlobe.

Willy screamed and swung for the woman in front of him just a second too late. As a swift knee to the groin sent him to lay next to Sal in companionable agony, Susannah jumped into the back of the van. Jordan, now in the driver's seat, gunned the engine.

They were on their way.

"Mr. Burke, if you slow down and drive a respectable speed we may not be so noticeable." Barkley mentioned casually as he reloaded his gun in the swerving lurching van. "We may have another reception waiting for us at the exit. No sense advertising our approach any more than we have to."

"Ah, yeah. Right. Susannah, check the back. You said there would be some very special weapons."

Stretching between the two front seats, she hit the phone button on the dash. As the list of preprogrammed numbers were announced, she rummaged around in the back of the van. The digital voice said Olney Farm and Susannah lurched to punch the red dial button. A busy signal buzzed over the radio speakers.

No luck.

"No kidding. These guns, or whatever they are, are fabulous. Man, Barkley take a look." Susannah passed a sniper rifle with an attached night scope forward. In the back seat, she fingered something that resembled a machine gun but with a strip of shells containing a plastic center filled with what looked to be liquid silver. "Damn. This could be lethal in a big way." She grinned in the rearview mirror.

"Trouble!" She warned from the backseat as they approached the exit gate. "I've got no change on me and looks like our night security guard is glowing a puke green. Guess we'll have to run the gate."

Jordan stomped on the gas and crashed through the single restraining bar, wood splinters flying everywhere.

"That was Bert back there. He sure recovered fast. They'll know in short order that we have escaped." Jordan spoke calmly from the driver's seat. "We won't get far. There's probably a tracking device underneath us remember?"

"Take care of that in a minute. Right now let's make some room to maneuver."

They were off down the road and headed for North Federal Highway.

"Barkley would you read the protocol in the glove box please." Susannah was busy scanning the road for a tail or possible police intervention.

Barkley removed the document from the glove box and read out loud. "Two options, Ms. Maddox. An address that a Mr. Ted Vanderloss has established in the west section off Ridgewood Avenue, or proceed on to Patrick Air Force Base southeast some forty-five miles. Barkley grabbed his seat as the van swerved and Jordan pulled off the road behind a car wash.

"Jordan would you do the honors?" She smiled sweetly pointing to the floor of the van. "Grab the tracking device and stick it to the bus right over there." She pointed at a public bus that was gassing up at the station next to the carwash.

"Yeah, sure. Good idea." He was gone in a flash and back even faster. "Done deal. Let 'em chase a bus around all night."

"I vote for the closest safe haven. What about you, Barkley?"

"Madison and Sixteenth it is, Ma'am." Barkley input the data and the GPS automatically plotted the map.

"Exit, turn right on Baker. Drive two point four miles then turn left on Sixteenth Street," the digital British voice directed.

"What's at Madison and Sixteenth?" Jordan looked across at Barkley and the moving map.

"Titto's Place is what the protocol directive says. Other than that, I have no idea. We are to call ahead." Barkley searched the SUV's database and found the number for Titto. The device automatically dialed the number.

"Susannah?" She immediately recognized Ted's voice.

"Ted! Thank God! We're coming in on the run."

"We'll be ready."

"Roger that."

Chapter 21

Safe, Say You...

When life is the question, safety is the answer.
Cavemen had it right! A large club, as it were.

Who to trust, what to think, where to go?
To protect, to bring down, a life to show.

Safe say you?
Only in your dreams!

Marianne DuPries, Poet
From: Song of the Heart
New York, 2001

"Colonel, Ms. Maddox is on her way to the checkpoint. Barkley and a young man are with her. Ted checked in. He is waiting with, what looks to be a small mountain named Titto." Miller's voice over the intercom stopped Maddox in mid pace.

"On my way." He punched the intercom button and trotted toward the Operational Command Center. As he hit the door, Miller was ready with a report.

"Sir, Susannah is one point six miles from Checkpoint Tango. Reception includes Vanderloss and six thugs from his hood. Sorry Sir, six temporarily sworn agents from the local area. She has called in and preparations are complete. At present there is no tail. Van and occupants are clean. No facts yet on the kind of trouble she is in. We suspect the young man with her is Jordan Burke."

Monique uncurled her legs from beneath her and stood, announcing her presence, which the Colonel had overlooked in his haste. "Colonel Maddox, Susannah is on her way to safety. Whatever has happened, she will be okay once inside the garage." Monique patted the Colonel's arm. "Do not worry. I would trust Ted with my life. He is very resourceful. This will work out très bien." She tried to sound optimistic and positive.

"Ms. Merchant, how long have you known my daughter? Four years? Do you really believe 'things will work très bien? Sergeant

Miller, get a line through to Tango. I want to know everything that happens. Do we have an eye there?"

"No eye, on speaker phone now, Sir." Miller turned toward the speaker. "Hey Ted, Colonel Maddox is here. He wants a blow-by-blow of the situation." Miller had the speaker open and broadcasting before the Colonel could reprimand him for jumping ahead on his own.

"Yo Milo, what's shaken? Suze'll be here in a couple minutes. My man Titto and his boyz are ready and waitin'. No problema, mahn. We got the situation under control."

The three in the situation room could hear the garage door screech open and a car enter. The engine shut down and the next sound was Susannah squealing as she obviously hugged Ted. The garage door screeched shut with a bang.

"Suze, babe, let go! You're strangling me. Sir, the van is..." Ted's words were cut short as the place erupted in chaos. After much clatter and hollering, the line went dead with a resounding crack.

"Shit! Re-establish communications, Miller. NOW!" Maddox bellowed. They were blind and deaf.

"Trying, Sir." Miller's fingers flew with no success. "No can do, Sir. I have two other numbers for the location but I think they may be too busy to pick up at the moment. We'll just have to wait until they contact us. Sorry, Sir. I'll keep at it though."

*****

Just as Susannah thought things had begun to look up, a burley Sal materialized next to the van with Willy in tow. Barkley was the first to die, his throat torn out by Willy's slashing fangs before anyone realized what was happening. Titto pulled Willy from the Federal agent's body and twisted his head from his shoulders with a Samoan tribal yell. Ted kept his anti-vamp rifle on Sal.

"Freeze, sucker!" Ted grinned. "I always wanted to say that."

"You can't stop me, nigger." Sal v-ported into the van and tore the gun from Jordan's hand. "I owe your bitch one." He slammed Jordan in the back of the head with a set of titanium knuckles, a strike that would have annihilated a human skull.

Titto's boyz surrounded the van and Susannah went for the gun. "Ted, use the silver net! Hurry before he v-ports out." Susanna dove for the rifle as a mandoor at the front of the garage splintered into a million pieces. Three more of Metolius' soldiers came through the

233

ragged gaping hole.

"Nobody breaks the Greaseman's door!" Titto charged the first man he could find. Huge hands closed over the vampire's head with a sickening crunch and the vamp went down. At the same time, Titto's boyz tore into the intruders. The mammoth Samoan humans worked together, double-teaming it, as they proceeded to rip, smash and otherwise destroy the other two vampires that were dumb enough to trespass on Titto's, aka the Greaseman's, property. Body parts flew in all directions. Within seconds, the fight was over, or at least stalled for the moment.

That left Susannah standing inches from the van, her rifle pointing directly at Sal's head. "Don't even try it. You won't like what this little baby can do. How'd you find us anyway?

Sal grinned, holding up the chain Susannah had ripped from Willy's face. "Like finds like, baby. Willy wanted his jewelry and his tissue back. Too bad he lost his head at the last minute. Never was one to use it anyway. Ciao." Sal snaked an arm around Jordan's neck.

Susannah fired a fraction of a second too late. The bullet lodged in the seat that held Sal just a half a heartbeat before. "Shit. He got Jordan. God Damn it. I should have just offed him without the nice talk!"

Ted placed an arm around Susannah. "We'll figure something out. First we have to get you back to Olney Farm. Titto, you be okay?"

The mountain of a man grunted as he dropped Willy's decapitated head into an incinerator at the back of the shop. "No problem, man. We clean up nice and pretty. Gotta fix my door, damn suckers made a mess fuh sure." He picked up a four by eight sheet of plywood in one hand and a sledgehammer in the other. "Guess I can nail it shut for now. You gotta get that little lady outta here."

"Just as fast as I can." He hit the redial on his cell phone and waited to reconnect to the situation room.

"Ted? You guys all right? We heard a fight start, then the line went dead." Miller was on the other end of the line talking just a little too fast for his usually calm self.

"Dropped the phone when the fun started. Sorry, man. Suze is fine. Barkley's dead but we lost the boy. Vamp got him before we could move. We took out four. But one did that thing Yuri does. He just vanished and took the kid with him."

"Ted? Maddox. Tell my daughter she has some explaining to do and high tail it back here. I'm sending a chopper for you. Rendezvous in fifteen at the following." Maddox reeled off a set of coordinates and hung up.

"Did he ask how I was, or anything?" Susannah's timid question made Ted want to laugh at the bizarre relationship between the Colonel and his daughter. Love/hate didn't even come close to describing the wild young woman and her straight-laced military father. There was no father-daughter pair in the world, farther apart than those two.

"No, but he was upset. We gotta go, Suze. Titto, a pleasure man. Those kids of yours sure did grow up handy! Love ya man." He and Titto did the male grab-hug thing.

Susannah thought she heard a vertebrae pop in Ted's back but wasn't quite sure.

"Car's in the back, Suze. We're on the clock and it's countin' down, kiddo. Let's go."

They ran out the back and were driving toward the rendezvous point before Susannah had time to gather her thoughts. "Wait Ted, I can't leave without Jordan! They'll kill him now. We have to do something. What about Barkley? I hardly knew him. He died helping me. We can't just leave his body in a garage. I feel horrible. This is all my fault"

Ted shot Susannah a sobering look. "Yes, it *is* your fault, no argument there." Ted glanced at the young woman who rode beside him catching her wince at his harsh statement. Ted spent too much time in the 'joint' to mince words. "Titto will take care of the vamps and your father will arrange a pickup for the loyal agent who died in the line of duty. SOP, you know that. Your father did ask me to relay a message earlier; he said you have some explaining to do. I suppose that's a given at this point."

"Great. That's just peachy. Run home to Daddy and get grounded." She stamped her foot on the floor of the car.

"Grounding is for when you stay out past curfew. It's for when you take the car without permission or get caught smoking. Not when you are responsible for getting several people killed. When are you going to grow up and act like something other than a self-centered little girl?" Close since her turning, Ted was as frustrated as the rest of the team with Susannah's continual self-centered behavior. To be fair, he was also aware of how hard she tried during training and their missions. It just seemed things with her always got screwed up somehow. He was as frustrated as the rest of his group. But he also understood on a personal level, how unfair and unsympathetic the world could be for a mixed-up young adult.

He'd lived it.

Ted earned some hard lessons in his hood and in prison.

Thinking back, he could have used a sympathetic ear and a shoulder to lean on. What he'd had was a gang and a cell with a ten-ton baby Louie for a roomie. However, just out of a vamp fight, having lost an agent, Ted was more inclined to be impatient and unsympathetic than lovingly supportive of the young vamp's habit of causing chaos. He took a deep breath and stilled his need to take out his frustration by hollering at her. What the hell did she think she was doing in Florida without support anyway?

Susannah stared at the floor and remained silent. She figured she had some kind of lecture coming. Ted was like a real father to her. He was straight with his criticisms, but also warm and helpful with his praise.

When had things changed with him?

Susannah knew the answer before it had completely formed in her mind; when she messed up on the last op, despite the efforts of the entire Vamp Squad!

She felt a self-promise coming on.

Ted's attempt at stilling the verbal barrage failed. "After Afghanistan, I though you had this spy shit figured out. I guess I was wrong. You've compromised the security of the squad, endangered my friends, put some unknown vamp in total jeopardy, and fucked up my first vacation with my family in three years. I hope you're happy, young lady."

He couldn't help it.

He was on a roll and moving right along.

"Ya know, your father has built a world around you because he loves you and wants you to be able to live a decent life, *in safety*. And what do you do? Run off on some fairy tale love quest for the guy who killed you."

Susannah was stunned.

Did everyone know why she left Olney Farm on this little jaunt?

"Monique told me all about it when they recalled me from leave. How stupid and immature is that? I think…"

"All right, I get the point, Mother Superior." A tiny tear formed at the corner of Susannah's eye and she hastily wiped it away. She hated tears – especially vamp tears that left their mark in red stains. "Believe me, I get the point. I just don't know what to do about it now. I think… I think I'm in love with Jordan and it's not a fairy tale.

I can't let him die, Ted. I have to do something." Her confession fell on deaf ears. Ted didn't even blink. "Not to mention there's some stuff I found out at the Proctor estate where Jordan lives." She continued to try to drag a little investment out of Ted. "It's a cover for a coven of naturist vampires. There's some kind of drug business going on. They keep culls Ted! And I am sure Metolius will make a lesson of Jordan and then kill him. It won't be nice! I just can't walk away from this."

She wasn't getting anywhere.

Taking a deep breath, Susannah took the ultimate step. "You're right. I am responsible and I accept that. But I still have to do something. I really do think I love him, Ted." The last statement was a whisper. It finally got Ted's attention. Unfortunately, not the kind of attention she wanted.

"Save the report for the team. They will want to know everything. Personally, at this point, I don't want to listen, Susannah. Right now I just want to get you back to the farm before some other group you've insulted or pissed off, comes after us. You may be immortal, but I've only got one life. A life I'd like to keep. Apparently hanging around you is not the best way to do that right now."

That said, Ted drove in silence to the pick-up rendezvous with a sullen Susannah riding along quietly. At the rendezvous point they boarded a Pave Hawk helicopter for the short hop to Patrick AFB, then a quick flight back to Maine. Colonel Maddox deployed the Vamp Squad's G-5 early on in the operation.

The Gulf Stream jet was adapted for use by the squad, shortly after their return from Afghanistan. It now sat on the base's tarmac, full of fuel, awaiting the two operatives. It was amazing what an unlimited budget could do for an experimental and very secret anti-terrorist group. Thanks to the enormous booty from the Afghanistan mission, the government didn't even blink at the Colonel's purchases, or the need to make expensive adaptations.

Susannah was not surprised that Ted accompanied her north. Was it a free ride back to the farm? Orders to make sure she actually got home? She knew the answer to that question. She could tell Ted was extremely disappointed and not opposed to letting it show. He was not letting her out of his sight.

Appropriately chastised, Susannah remained silent the whole way home, dreading the confrontation to come but resigned to accepting it.

It was close to noon when Ted and Susannah arrived at Olney Farm. From the private airport, their three-car motorcade pulled directly into the barn to protect Susannah from the direct sunlight. A concealed entry near the old-fashioned paddock took the group two stories down and connected directly to a passageway that ended in an immense subterranean garage, connected directly to the situation room and business section of the complex. Their footsteps echoed ominously in the steel reinforced tunnel as the two walked toward an uncomfortable homecoming. Susannah, exhausted and hungry, stumbled and Ted took her arm firmly.

"I really don't want to be here," she mumbled.

"No shit, Suze, but ya gotta face the music. Remember, there is a young man whose life may depend on what decisions the squad makes in the next few minutes. If you really care, prove it. Make an effort. Get a grip."

"That's not fair and it's not what I meant, Ted. Jordan is all I can think about right now. I just really don't want to face my father in front of everyone. He can be merciless. I'm the only one here who has a dual role, daughter and operative. Sometimes Father Colonel doesn't consider that. I can't take away the fact that I am his daughter. He can't seem to see it at all, unless I do something wrong." Susannah frowned. "I don't expect you to understand. I should be back in Florida helping Jordan escape."

"Give us a minute." Ted nodded at their escort. He pulled Susannah to a stop, as their escort walked on ahead. His temper cooled, and now a real burst of love emanated from his rich dark eyes. "Then show your father you can be a responsible operative, and a grown woman. Walk in like you're a professional with value. Turn off the emotional stuff for now. Be VS5 until the business is over. Then, when you two are alone, be Susannah Maddox and stand up to him as a young woman would with her father. Don't let him do the 'bury the feelings part' and then run from you. It takes two to communicate, kiddo." Ted ruffled her hair as if she was a ten year old again and smiled. "I know you're capable of it. I watched you back at Titto's. You got it goin' on girl. Now you just have to keep it goin'. Let's do it." With a quick hug, Ted waved the way and Susannah moved ahead.

It was good to have her old Ted back, warm and supportive. He was right. She could do this, then for once, settle things with her father. In private.

With a weak smile, and one deep breath she really didn't need, Susannah entered the situation room ahead of Ted. Nodding to her father, she took her appointed seat.

No one said a word.

The silence was so thick you could cut it with a knife. Ted came through the door with a thumb's up for Miller and a smile for Elizabetta.

Colonel Maddox cleared his throat.

Susannah recognized the black look on his face.

"Report."

Susannah straightened in her seat and took another deep breath "VS5 report for the record." Susannah tapped the key on her console.

The Colonel's eyebrows rose at his daughter's professional tone and willingness to immediately go on record.

"During an unauthorized leave of absence, I came into contact with a naturist coven of vampires. My sire's previous coven. Kellan Burke the III was my sire and is deceased. He was destroyed by his coven for turning me without permission. His biological son, Jordan, also a vampire of the coven run by Metolius Proctor the so-called Proctor Coven, provided that information." She paused and took another deep breath before continuing.

"The Proctor Estate is the coven's nest location where they keep culls as a food source. The humans are drugged while being slowly drained until they are of no further use. The bodies are disposed of in the swamp that surrounds the estate. Daytona Beach is currently a very vamp-friendly area. Jordan, my, ah... informant, was taken captive as we affected our escape. He is in certain danger. Jordan conveyed to me, Metolius Proctor owns most of the law enforcement officers and judges, as well as a handful of politicians in the local area. He rules his coven with an iron fist. My actions may have already ended Jordan Burke's existence." Susannah looked directly at her father without blinking. Though it was difficult, she maintained eye contact.

"There is more. During my interaction with Jordan and the coven, I learned that Proctor Pharmaceuticals is producing a drug called Crysillus Extract, or CE. It is highly addictive for our kind. According to what little information I could obtain, when the drug is administered to vampires, it provides an incredible euphoria and enhances vampiric powers for a while. There is said to be a return to a human-like feeling for some that use the drug. As the drug's effect begins to fade, the vampire's powers decline to almost human levels, followed by a black depression. After a while, the addicted vampire can't even feed without using the drug. Addicts lose control in the wake of starvation, becoming wild animals that kill, but can't feed. Between euphoria and starvation, the individual goes insane. I am sure this is something that warrants closer investigation." Again she paused, looking at each of the members of her coven. "For obvious reasons."

"Proctor is making and dispensing the drug. I personally think, he will use this drug on techno-modern vampires, like us, or possibly competing covens. His plans, according to my inside sources, are to place coven-friendly politicians in high offices to begin slowly taking control of the political structure of the country. I believe he has a vision to create a home nation for vampires, with the human population as a food source. Jordan called it Metolius' *Vision of the Future*."

Elizabetta interrupted Susannah's report. "We cannot, by accord, encroach on the territory of another coven without permission. However, I think it prudent the Council of Elders to be informed of this Proctor's schemes. Is there no one in this coven willing to ask for our intervention?"

Susannah raised her hand, staying Elizabetta's comments.   "I suspect two individuals at the estate; a very old Knight Templar named Ignacias Trenchertt and a woman, Marisella Ferreira are allies. I cannot confirm this for sure. They seemed to afford Jordan and myself a certain amount of protection from Metolius, when possible." Susannah paused to consider anything she had left out. Holding up her hand and counting on fingers, she continued. "I believe I have abandoned an individual to certain death. There exists a valid threat to national security if Proctor continues with his drug production. Metolius' personal plans for our nation are a national security concern, in and of themselves. Humans are being retained against their will and systematically exterminated." Susannah held up four fingers, then pointed to her fifth. "Slowly. Very slowly." She looked directly at each member of the team, one after the other, gauging her statement.

"Vamp Squad involvement is requested and, in my opinion justified. If, for no other reason than to liberate the culls, I mean human beings fed on against their will. End of report. Questions?" Susannah took a gulp of air and relaxed a bit.

Elizabetta smiled, proud of the way Susannah took charge and provided an excellent, honest report.

Ted shot her a thumbs up under the table.

Natalia poked Yuri as if there was some secret bet she won, and Monique stared open-mouthed for at least a few seconds before anyone thought to ask anything.

"VS5, do you have the location of your informant?" Miller was impressed, but without the open mouth.

"I believe he has been taken to the Proctor estate. I cannot confirm it at this time. One of the coven vamps was able to v-port, which was how Jordan was taken captive." Susannah's response was professional and without emotion, just as her father liked it, but it was taking a toll on the worried young woman.

"Is Proctor aware of our location? Does he know of the existence of the Vamp Squad?" Maddox pinned his daughter with an icy glare.

To her credit, she did not flinch but answered with a steady voice. "Not at this time. Jordan and Proctor know my real name. It was unavoidable after you identified my body for the record. Jordan knows I am an operative working for the government. He is aware that my father works for the government as well. Beyond that, is anyone's guess. I met several of the coven members but have no idea what powers those individuals possess."

"Just how did young Mr. Burke find out you work for the government?" Maddox was containing his anger well. How long he could maintain was in question.

"I dispatched Proctor's First Lieutenant, a vampire named Corvell Drechell. I blew up a house along with a nice shiny red Dodge Viper, in the process. Jordan was with me. It was a little hard to cover up since I constructed some explosive devices, on site, and in a hurry." The smug young lady smiled sweetly at her father. "McGuyver style, homemade of course. It's not something the normal young woman, or vampire for that matter, would know how to do."

"Great. Anything we need to clean up?"

"Nope. It was a very effective fire. I do not believe..." Susannah's personal cell phone played the theme song from Phantom of the Opera. "That is Jordan's ring. That's weird; his phone was destroyed when the Viper burned. Stand by."

The order was out of her lips before she realized how much she sounded like her father.

Natalia winked at Yuri. "Jordan has a personal ring. Hummm? After only four days?"

Yuri smiled at his bride knowingly. There was more to the story than Susannah was telling. But the ring – it was telling volumes.

"Jordan?" Susannah answered with excitement.

"No Susannah, this is Marisella."

Susannah immediately punched the speaker button so the rest could listen. "I saw Sal return with Jordan this morning. Metolius is in conference with the coven soldiers and Jordan is in a chamber in the basement. Ignacias had a phone programmed for me with Jordan's data package. That's how I could contact you. He said he had a feeling about you. He said maybe you could help. I have no idea how, but you know I love Jordan like a son. I cannot simply sit by and watch something horrible happen to the boy." There was a catch in her voice at the last statement. "I think Metolius will have him killed after what Sal told everybody. Something about a fight in some car garage."

"Whoa, Marisella. I'm at home with some friends. Funny you should call since we are discussing the situation right now. Can you keep Jordan's phone handy, so I can call you back?"

"Yes. Only Ignacias knows I have it. If you can do anything to save Jordan, it has to be soon. Adios, me hija."

Susannah looked around the table at each of the members of the Squad, then at her father. "Marisella is dead on. Metolius will execute Jordan. He's big on visible lessons. No one is allowed to cross him and survive. Marisella is First Female of the coven." Susannah looked hopefully at Elizabetta.

"Well, Colonel Maddox, I believe that constitutes a formal request for intervention. For the record let it be noted." Elizabetta smiled at her surrogate daughter to continue.

"I am responsible for this man's capture and I will be responsible for his death, if we don't do something. Please..." Susannah's last word was more a pleading statement than a request. She kept her eyes on the cell phone on the table.

"Please?" She whispered.

Chapter 22

What's Love Got To Do with It?

What is love but a jumble of emotions that tangle the mind?
In one fell swoop, the heart is captured, caged, entwined.

Seeking freedom or delving much deeper,
Logic and thought gone, so much the weaker.

So in the end do we choose, or are we chosen?
Caught in the turmoil and angst of emotion.

Brighter men than I have sought a solution
But Tina Turner gave absolution!

What's love got to do with it?

Dobey Randal, Biographer
Love's Life Lost
San Francisco, 1921

Jordan sat in a straight-backed rigid chair as Ignacias Trenchertt probed the young vampire's mind and soul. Jordan tried to set his mind aflame with thoughts of Susannah, to build a wall of brick and fire. However, each time he tried, fear overrode desire. He could not hold the mental image. Like worms creeping throughout his gray matter, the tendrils of Trenchertt's mental investigation slipped in and out, around and through, searching for fact, falsehood and memory. Had Jordan held any sense that he would survive, this personal affront would have been intolerable. He grimaced as Trenchertt approached his father's memories. He kept that part hidden from the world, buried beneath an exterior of bland disinterest. Closer, the pressure-like feeling built then, missing the mark all together, instantly disappeared.

Jordan opened his eyes to a smiling priest and the pronouncement that he was not guilty of betrayal, only stupidly following juvenile hormones.

Metolius nodded, then smiled. Lust was something the Master understood. It had been Metolius' downfall, many a time. In fact, the

Master missed a good portion of the Reformation while his body lay interned beneath several tons of rock - the result of a failed relationship and a vengeful lover. In Metolius' case it was certainly true that there existed no fury greater than the wrath of a woman scorned, in Hell or on earth. In all those lonely, dark years beneath a mountain of rubble, he did not learn his lesson. Metolius' libido too often ruled his mind still. In all fairness to the boy, Metolius found sexual desire an acceptable excuse for the young, randy vampire's suspect behavior. The Master nodded at Trenchertt's proclamation.

"Did I not try to tell you, darling? Jordan is simply a boy gone wild in the candy store. You, of all people, have to admit little Susannah is a delectable morsel. She has swayed our Jordan, but not turned him away from his family. He simply needs a little direction, not a cell."

Metolius wrapped a fist in Marisella's rich dark hair and drew her to him. Holding her face within inches of his own, he growled, "Never involve yourself in the politics or discipline of this coven. I may be forced to show you the error of your ways, my dear. There is only one Master and it is I."

"Darling, you know I would never interfere with your leadership." Immediately aware of her mistake, she whispered seductively, "There is only one thing I want from you and I get that on a regular basis." Her delicate fingers stroked his face gently. "I just know how it is with young men and cute, but inexperienced girls. Jordan is finally sowing some wild oats, that's all. You are not so old as to forget how that is." She sent wild, seductive thoughts to the Master as she encouraged his body to respond to her ministrations.

Seduction was her gift.

She used it well.

His hand slid from her hair to her breast and she knew in that simple gesture, her distraction had worked.

"Come, my love, let us play at being young once again." Metolius lifted her from the divan where they lay together watching Trenchertt do an impression of a lie detector. "Trenchertt, release the boy and …"

Sal burst through the door followed by an enraged Damien. "That little shit burned my Drechell! He killed your First Lieutenant, Master!" Damien pointed a lacquered fingernail directly at Jordan. "He killed my Corvell, my…" Tears streaked Damien's face as he wailed. They made a red mess on his silky shirt. "I have the right to see him burn." Damien fell to his knees in front of the Master, grasping the hem of his robe pleadingly.

It was a disgusting display of pathetic emotionality.

Setting Marisella on her feet, Metolius stepped from the disheveled vampire's grasping hands. Eyeing Damien curiously he asked, "Have you proof beyond tears and childish cries?"

Damien stood and wiped his face. "Yes, Master. The police found what was left of Jordan's car at a house up north." He snuffed dramatically before proceeding with his tale. "I questioned the officers and the firemen. One policeman said there was a young couple necking nearby. In a Town Car! With a Florida license plate ACF 079. My Corvell's license plate. The officer sent them home thinking nothing about it. Shithead and his bitch were there, Master! They must have done it. I don't know how, but…" His tears fell again streaking the pale pink silk shirt he wore with long red marks.

Metolius eyed Jordan as he spoke. "Damien, where is this officer that I may hear this for myself?"

Damien took a step backwards with fear in his eyes, wringing his hands. "He, ah… Master, I was a little rough on the man. He couldn't remember all of the details so I, ah…well. I forced his mind to open. He's dead, Sir. But he showed me. I SAW!" Damien fell to his knees, hands clasped as if he prayed for the Master's decision. "You have to believe me, Master. He killed my Corvell. I swear it."

Marisella kicked the kneeling man against the wall. "That is no evidence, darling. This little worm would say anything to hurt Jordan. He is a hateful…"

Marisella could not get the last words out before Metolius' hand struck her across the face with enough force to kill a human woman. She flew across the room and landed on the couch where minutes before they cuddled in foreplay.

"You would take a side in this issue when you have been warned to keep your silence in the administration of my coven? If you advocate so strongly for young Jordan, perhaps I should re-evaluate your place as First Female. Leave us, Marisella! You have much to answer for." With a wave of his hand, Metolius dismissed his lover and mistress.

Marisella wiped the trickle of blood from her nose and rose to leave. "Darling, I…"

"Leave us now!" The Master's screeching voice made even Trenchertt jump as Marisella fled the room. Damien cowered against the wall, silent tears flowing in wide red streams down the man's face.

"Speak, Jordan. Speak of this incident." Metolius' hard stare pinned Jordan to his chair.

"Metolius, perhaps I could..." Trenchertt saw the entire mess moving rapidly towards complete chaos. He saw no one alive in the end. No one except Metolius Proctor.

Just as it had been for two thousand or more, years.

At the sound of Trenchertt's voice, Metolius rounded on his friend of several hundred years. "I have had enough of you, Sir Knight. You and your pompous ways and archaic language! You have pronounced this young man innocent, yet I have another who says he is guilty. I think therein lies something rotten, no? Perhaps something that wears the cloak of the clergy, my friend? Or perhaps the silk of a lover?" Metolius backed toward the bar and removed a sword from its decorative hanger. "Speak Jordan. In any event you will burn, boy. I will not risk the coven's security for either of you." He waved the sword madly back and forth between Jordan and the knight.

"This sniveling slug," Metolius pointed his sword at Damien, "has executed a human without permission. I am displeased."

Sentence pronounced, he swung the sword with skilled practice. In a flash the head of a still slobbering Damien rolled to the floor. He leveled the tip at Jordan. "Speak!"

Jordan had enough. If he was going to die, then it would be with a clear conscience and a clean heart. Susannah had made a difference in his pathetic life and he would not be destroyed without standing for something. She was safe – gone from his life, but her love and strength remained.

"I didn't ask to be made a vampire. My old man did it out of some perverse sense of wanting family with him. I have always hated what I am. This place is exactly why I hate what I am. It is hell on earth with the devil at its helm. Sure, I took Drechel out, or I should say, we took Drechel out. And you know what? I'd do it again, a million times. The bastard was a filthy piece of rotten shit. He killed my old man and liked it. He threw it in my face at every chance. You all did. Marisella calls this a family. Well it's only a family of depraved, torturing, blood sucking leeches that have to live off innocent humans because you've never allowed another way."

Jordan took a gulp of air and continued; in for a penny, in for a pound. He knew he was going to die anyway. "Susannah showed me something different. She showed me love. Caring about something besides power and your own perverse desire. She showed me that there is life beyond living off humans. Killing whatever resists your depraved ways." Running out of steam, he hung his head.

"Oh, the little chit that escaped and left you here to face this fate? Curious. I wonder if you will still see her as some delivering angel when you burn in the morning sun? Or," Metolius grinned evilly through his paper-thin lips. "Perhaps you will burn together when I have tired of her. Did I fail to mention I have sent for your Susannah Maddox? Oh yes, young Jordan! Your little girl will soon be on her way to me, cradled in the loving arms of some of her own family. Kissing cousins, so to speak."

Metolius lowered the point of his sword and waved at two of his soldiers standing at attention near the door. "Take this thing from my sight. Place him in a secure chamber. No one is to see or speak to him. I am done with this for the moment. I shall be in my quarters possibly interviewing candidates for a new First Female." He waved an effeminate hand toward Jordan.

"Metolius, really. Marisella has been a faithful First Female and lover. She does not deserve this." Trenchertt spoke softly as the two henchmen dragged an unresisting Jordan from the room.

"Ah, Ignacias, I trusted you once. Was I wrong to do so? Did I make a mistake?" A smiled played across pale, thin lips.

The question hovered between them.

"No, Metolius, you did not make a mistake. I have served you faithfully for many years. Even during the times when you tested my faith, my loyalty, even my strength. I simply like Marisella. She has been good for you in her own way." The old Knight affected what he hoped Metolius would think was a brotherly smile. Like two old friends, siblings through the centuries. "You have to admit she has her good points."

"Ah yes, her good points. But what are good points without trust? I fear I have come to distrust the woman and so it is time to replace her with one more malleable. I have existed for a very long time Ignacias. Never have I found a woman who is as faithful, or loyal as you, my friend." He patted the steely arm of his friend good-naturedly, trust restored between them. "But for the moment I think I shall rest. This," Metolius waved his hand across the room, "business has been somewhat taxing. Perhaps I shall allow Marisella to service me one last time."

Trenchertt stood silent as Metolius wandered towards his private quarters. He hoped Marisella would survive the 'one last time.'

Their plans depended on it.

Plans were secretly put into place over several painstaking months of quiet communication and company manipulation. If Marisella was destroyed before things came to fruition, his life would be forfeited as well. He withdrew his cell phone and hit the speed dial. Perhaps with enough warning…

*****

Jordan lay at the bottom of a cylindrical cell chained over a painted symbol of the sun. The twenty foot deep stone cell was open to the sky and he could count the stars that passed across the opening as the hours passed by. Chained spread-eagle, he had nothing better to do until the sun rose. Then the only thing left was to die.

Jordan pulled on the metal and felt the burn of silver. Of course, it was the only metal that could hold a vampire. It just added insult to injury. Would his jailers close the hatch when the sun rose? Was this a fear tactic or a final death sentence?

He wondered how it would feel and how long he would live. His father was burned alive. Jordan could only imagine he died quickly. That's what Drechell told him. His old man screamed for several moments before the car's gas tank exploded enveloping everything for yards around in flames.

Guess the old man got off easy compared to what Jordan now faced.

He pulled on his chains again and growled in anger. Pain shot through his arms, but he didn't whimper. Those days were past. There would be no Marisella to comfort him.

What would Metolius do to her for taking his side?

Lines of worry wrinkled his forehead as he lay contemplating the lengths to which Metolius could, and would go to prove a lesson. He felt for the coven's First Female. She was the only one who ever cared about him.

Thank Heaven Susannah got away. She would be safe back at her home by now. His groin ached at the thought of the beautiful young woman he'd fallen in love with.

Love?

Had he really fallen in love, or were the feelings just another trick his hormonal teen body was playing on his mind?

At this point in his life – the end point, he had no time for tricks. At last he was sure his love for Susannah was the real deal.

An image of her face swam before his eyes. In his mind he relived every minute they spent together. Too short a time, but no less real for its duration.

Yep, it was love, pure and simple.

And yep, he was going to die, pure and simple.

He couldn't even cry about it. His dying would kept Susannah safe and that was the true test. He was willing to give his life for the woman he loved.

A smile played across his lips at the thought. He never did a noble thing in his life and yet… here he lay counting the stars, thinking of his love and preparing to meet his end in the fire of the sun. If it hadn't been so serious, it would have seemed almost comical. He lay back on the cold stones feeling the grit of ash - those who had gone before him. There was nothing to do now, but stare at the universe… and wait.

"Susannah, Susannah, wherefore art thou, Susannah?" Jordan could not help the chuckle that escaped from his lips.

Did Romeo laugh in the face of death?

Considering the situation he currently found himself in, Jordan let his mind wander. He and Susannah were a kind of new age form of Shakespeare's star-crossed lovers. In life and death, truly in love. Well technically, only in death truly in love. They were both dead long before they fell in love. But only he would perish for it.

Did Susannah even love him?

He thought he had seen something in her eyes.

An emotion that flashed across her beautiful blue orbs?

Love?

It was a question that would never be fully answered for him.

He would never be completely sure now.

He would never see the answer spoken from those lovely lips.

A tear trickled down Jordan's cheek.

Where was all his nobility now?

*****

"This is not something I ask for myself." Susannah stood, placing both hands squarely on the table, even though she was dog-tired. They'd been debriefing for hours. "It is something I ask in the name of humanity and for an innocent that has become embroiled in something he had nothing to do with."

Previn sneered. "Right. There's a nest of blood sucking vampires preying on the Daytona Beach community, young girls like you used to be. You want to commit the resources of the government to go rescue one of their own? Just goes to show you, *all* vampires stick to their own. When it comes right down to it, you are all the same!" The Lieutenant slammed his coffee cup down on the table in disgust.

"Enough, Previn." Elizabetta's eyes were bleeding red with anger. "You've been with us long enough to know what differences lay within our race. Your own issues cloud your judgment in this. If you can't be helpful, be somewhere else." She waved the Lieutenant off with a calm smile, fangs extended as a kind of punctuation mark at the end of her statement.

Lieutenant Previn stood with a huff looking toward his Colonel for support. Maddox did not so much as twitch. The atmosphere in the room was on the verge of going ballistic. Previn grabbed his cup and stomped out of the room.

The desired effect gained, Milo Miller smirked behind his console and mouthed the words 'Thank you, God' for all to see.

Monique blew Miller a loud kiss.

Everyone relaxed.

"Shall we continue? Time is of the essence." Elizabetta motioned towards a standing Susannah. "Since this is your mission, what is your opinion on how best to proceed, VS5?"

Susannah's jaw dropped open.

Natalia let out a stifled gasp.

"Ah... I'm not sure. It's a bigger picture than just rescuing Jordan. Here's the thing – Metolius has a plan, long range though it may be, he seems to be very patient. I believe he wants to work within the human system to subvert the government and make a homeland for vampires. He has the money and the brains. He also has the time. He has already made Daytona Beach vamp friendly and owns the cops, the politicians, the judges... practically everybody. If he can be successful there, then when is the state of Florida next? Then on and on, etc. To who knows what? There are several inter-related problems we face." Susannah clasped her hands behind her back and paced back and forth.

Just like her father.

"He is extremely old and powerful. A naturist who feeds off humans, as I have said before." Susannah swallowed, bringing up the distasteful subject again. "Yes, he keeps culls so humans will be in and around the estate. Possible collateral damage. He has a huge pharmaceutical empire to provide the necessary tools to chemically deal with any threats, without anyone noticing. I also believe he is experimenting with CE in order to keep any vampire resistance addicted and down to a minimum.

MorningStar spoke in a low, calm voice. "On a positive note, probably not all of the vampires in his coven like his plan. Most assuredly not all humans detest vampires, as well. Not everybody thinks like Previn. Thank the Spirits."

Susannah continued with a nod of thanks to her sister vampire. "After Marisella's call, I no longer doubt her assistance. If we have her help, we probably have Trenchertt's as well. That is still a speculated guess on my part." With that comment, several individuals at the table murmured consent. "Right now I just want to get Jordan to safety then we can deal with the rest of the stuff!" Susannah sat down dejectedly.

"Miller, bring up a satellite view of the Proctor Estate." Maddox and the team listened as Susannah ran through a description of the grounds. She pointed out how the estate was organized and what buildings held humans. A plan was coming together.

"Milassoviech, alert the av-group, choppers and the G-5 crew. Dr. Anderson, would you please see to the necessary provisions the team may need in light of the human element and possible injuries? VS group, get on the plans. We bug out in 2 hours. I'll go upstairs with the Intel and get the appropriate clearances and airspace. Miller, make sure…" Maddox's order was interrupted before he finished.

"Scheduled a sat black-out within one hundred miles of mission location, Sir." He didn't bother to look up as his fingers flew. "Sorry, Sir." Miller mumbled as an aside.

When the plan was fairly complete, Maddox headed for the door. Pausing behind his daughter's seat, he placed a rough hand on her shoulder and gave a slight squeeze of approval. More emotion than the Colonel wanted to demonstrate, he left as quickly as his stiff military legs would carry him. For a moment the only sound that could be heard was Milo's tapping fingers.

Susannah let out the breath she didn't know she had been holding. She looked up… into the smiling faces of her team. What she saw moved her heart to beat…twice.

It was time to get to work and they had one hour and fifty-eight minutes left until departure. With a fairly clear semblance of a plan, everyone just had to put the pieces together and make the picture work. For the team it was child's play. Actually, it was anti-terrorist, undercover operative play. It was the opinion of most of the V-group that when the toys came out, so did the fun.

"Okay then…?" Susannah looked down the table as everyone spoke at once.

Chapter 23

Belonging

Humans, and vampires alike need to belong.
It feeds the soul and makes us all strong.
Yet given a choice of none or bad,
We choose the bad, true but sad.

So therein lies the point of life,
Free will can cut, like a knife.
Bonds that hold and tie to one
Sever in the light of the morning sun.

Love holds true without ties,
Clings to hope, before one dies.
In the end as it be told
Love is all that we truly hold.

Frescia McCallister, Song Writer
The Ties That Hold
McCallister, Scotland 1861

It was twenty-hundred hours on the dot when the team departed Olney Farm. Two specially designed helicopters lifted the group from a quiet glade behind the last hay field and sped them south. The Vamp Squad, split between the Sikorski S-90 and the accompanying Pave Hawk HH 60G, went over the plan for the third time, communicating on secure radio channels between the choppers. The Gulfstream V admirably fitted with a medevac unit and v-trained medic team launched from its private airfield a few miles away. It would land at the Daytona Beach Community Airport and standby, in case it was needed.

Susannah was all serious operative now, immersed in the role of mission coordinator for the first time. Most of the humans remained behind at the farm for their own safety. No way could humans face a small army of vampires and be expected to survive. Although Colonel Maddox and Captain Devlin refused to remain behind, Miller, Previn and Dr. Anderson were just as happy to be tucked away in the secure situation room of the farm where they could monitor the team's progress via satellite feed.

Four Special V-Force soldiers, vamp trained and well-armed, rode along in the Pave Hawk with the Colonel and Elizabetta. Their liquid silver ammo and flamethrowers contained high-powered garlic concentrate mixed with the newest form of super-Napalm called NP2g.

NPg, the g standing for garlic extract, was developed during the WWII years. Hitler, attempting to create a super army of vampire SS officers, needed an efficient way to dispatch his failed experiments. The modern form of napalm for hunting vampires was NP2g; twenty percent benzene, thirty percent gasoline, forty-five percent polystyrene and, most importantly, five percent garlic extract. The sticky brown goop burned like the fires of hell and smelled like Greek pizza. Another brain-child of their IT support group, the Vamp Squad laughingly called their specially designed flamethrower the SuperSoaker-g.

Susannah and the rest of the squad flew alongside in the S-90. MorningStar was the only one who refused the ride. She effortlessly flew beside the S-90, obviously enjoying her communion with the wind and the noisy mechanical bird.

"One more time." Susannah's voice crackled over the frequency. "Let's go through it one more time." All around groans could be heard as the team's broadcasts stepped on each others' signals. "We can never be too prepared. By the numbers."

Monique covered her mic and yelled to Natalia over the engine noise. "Was not Susannah the one who complained so bitterly about practicing before a mission? Now she encourages it? Something has changed our little sister, oui?" Natalia and Yuri smiled their responses and listened to the mission review through their comm units. "Possibly I should join our Native sister." Monique waved to a grinning MorningStar outside the helicopter.

"One: AVS1 touches down between the main house and the stables. Max, Tank, Bear and Blue Boy deplane covering the humans in the stable with Elizabetta and Dad. I mean Colonel Maddox." Susannah heard Monique giggle through the radio at the unintentional slip.

"Two: At the same time AVS2 touches down on the main lawn in front of the mansion. Team members deplane. Natalia, Yuri, and MorningStar provide cover as Monique and I head for the west end of the main house. The solar cell is located between the waterfront and the main tennis court. According to Marisella's text and Miller's satellite recon; the cell is a twelve-foot deep cylindrical structure with stairs on two sides. Originally used as a kind of meditation garden, Jordan should be chained in the middle. The chains are silver, which won't hurt us but has a negating effect on a naturist vampire's powers. Expect Jordan to be weak and in pain. Questions?"

The team had gone over the plan several times, so the fact that Susannah posed the question about *questions,* tickled Elizabetta no end. She nudged Colonel Maddox and mouthed the words *you should be proud.*

Susannah continued, "We have the vamp and human count, so be on your toes. Master Metolius is a cagey fellow and extremely strong and fast. No humans take on the Master, got it guys? Trenchertt and Marisella will not protect Metolius, but the rest of the coven will no doubt fight. Once we have Jordan safe and sound, we bug out, ASAP. Questions?"

The comm line was silent. "Okay. I think we have it. Our ETA is four hours twenty minutes from now. Watch check on my mark." Susannah paused and checked her new watch, a gift from Uncle Rob. "Mark."

Natalia mentally communicated to Monique. *She even does a time sequence check. What has gotten into the girl? In Afghanistan, she didn't even wear a watch, let alone be concerned about watch check. Didn't she lose her watch in Somalia? I am impressed. This Jordan must be something.*

Oui, oui! Our sister was malheureux! Despondent I think, when we moved more slowly than she desired. This boy's life must mean a great deal to her. I am pleased to see that she finally accepts responsabilité. Like watching a babe grow to womanhood. I find myself so satisfaisant! Oui.

Yuri, unable to miss the directed communication between Monique and his wife, frowned. *Susannah is not a baby to coddle and watch grow up in our midst. She was an operative before this crazy chaos and she has much to atone for when it is over, if we all survive.*

Yuri, my love, do not be so hard on the girl. She only wants what we have, my love. Can you blame her for looking? Natalia kissed her husband of five nights.

Nat, I was a soldier and still am. Yes I can blame her for endangering the entire squad and being irresponsible with others' lives, including this boy Jordan.

Phew! Men! They will never understand the voyage du coeur. Monique closed her eyes and relaxed into the leather seats.

*****

Milo Miller sat comfortably in his little techno-command center monitoring the communications between the helicopters as they raced toward Florida and a date with a real mean vampire. He slouched in a relaxed manner that Dr. Anderson had not seen before.

"Milo, you almost look comfortable, I must declare." Helga picked up a wide semi-circle of clear plastic. "Don't tell me you still wear this thing under your uniform?"

"You betcha, Doc. No bites on this man's neck." He stretched displaying his clean-shaven skin. "When the ladies are gone, I feel so free and … Hold up there a minute."

A little light on his console flashed and a beep sounded from the loudspeaker above the screen.

"Company, Doc. Have a look."

Helga stepped behind the console and peered at the checkerboard screen. "What? I don't see a thing."

"Watch, right…there." Miller pointed to a small square on the screen labeled Camera one-A.

"I still don't… Oh no! Who are they?" Helga stepped back as one of the intruders took aim directly at the camera and fired. The screen went gray with static. "He shot the camera!"

"Yes Ma'am. I don't believe they're friendlies, Doc." Miller hit the comm link button. "Miller to Maddox."

Helga could hear the response as well as Miller.

"Maddox. Maintain Radio silence."

"I think you're gonna wanna hear this, Colonel. Tangos. I count six at one-A. Took out visual. Headed in."

"Shit." Maddox swore over the radio. "Handle it, Sergeant. We're too far away to be of any help right now."

"Are they vamps, Milo?" Susannah's heart sunk.

Obviously, Proctor had come after her.

"Beggin' your pardon Ma'am, but I didn't check their teeth and I can't see their color the way y'all can. Should I ask when they knock?" Miller's fingers tickled the keys as he followed the tangos' progress. He monitored the security screen as systematically, each camera along the gravel road that led to the house turned gray with static. "Sorry Suze. Gotta go. It's going to get real busy here in the next few minutes. Out."

Miller took a key from around his neck and unlocked a clear

Plexiglas box that covered a large red button. As the box came away, he hit the button and smiled. "It's my 'Easy Button', Doc."

Sirens blared and doors began to close. Throughout the complex Helga could hear and feel the entire place closing up. Above them, steel shutters slid into place securing the windows and doors of the small farmhouse. Within seconds, what was left of the human staff assembled in the situation room and the complex was protected, closed up tighter than an oyster guarding its precious pearl. A humming sound vibrated through the floor as Milo grinned at a clearly frightened Dr. Anderson.

"UV lights, Doc. Had them installed last summer. They're strong enough to turn night into day. If the tangos are vampires, it'll slow them down a bit, but not forever. We need a plan." Milo motioned to Lieutenant Previn and the ten frightened humans in the conference room as he tucked the plastic piece around his neck and straightened his tie. He tapped the intercom, "Four tangos above. Two around. Probably vamps. I'm open for ideas, folks."

Ten people shook their heads. Previn's slow smile was enough to scare everyone in the room.

"Sergeant Miller, deactivate the arsenal storage lock. We need to arm ourselves immediately. This time the shoe's on the other foot. It's time to hunt some blood suckers." Previn issued the order as if in command. He *was* the most senior officer left in the facility.

Helga immediately covered Milo's mic. "Under no circumstances do you open that vault, Miller. Previn only has an inkling of what we are up against. I'm not ready for extensive human loses on our own turf because of some overly hateful lieutenant." She released the mic.

After a few seconds, the good doctor smiled. "Actually," Helga tapped her head, "Milo, I do think I have an idea. Can you get me a secure line to this number please?" She scribbled something and handed the sergeant a yellow sticky note with a long series of numbers on it.

"International number, Ma'am. Romania?" Miller dialed the number and handed the phone to Helga.

"Orsova, Sergeant. I think we need more help than we have here if, we want to survive those vamps out there and," she pointed a low finger toward the conference room, "Lieutenant Previn in here."

Miller shook his head and spoke into the mic. "Ah, no can do Lieutenant. Don't have the password." The Sergeant snickered to himself as he watched Previn slam his fist into the wall.

Not just once, but twice.

"Hope the bastard breaks all his knuckles," Miller murmured under his breath to a grinning doctor.

*****

Marisella paced the cold tile floor of the quarters she shared with the Master. She was fuming as a deep cut in her lip closed up and began to heal. How dare that ancient pervert hit her like that! It wasn't so much the pain, as the humiliation. In a fit of anger he beat her in front of some of his henchmen. They laughed and cheered him on. Even that little bitch, Mallory giggled with every fist, every kick. Marisella barely made it to their room before she had collapsed.

She was First Female of the coven and CEO of Proctor Pharmaceuticals. No one, not even the great Metolius Gallcius Proctor, warrior and conqueror, could treat her like that.

She would gouge out those cold silver eyes with her bare hands!

She would tear his paper-thin skin from his emaciated body!

She would…she would… she froze at the sound of the heavy wooden door as it scraped across the floor.

Ignacias Trenchertt slipped through the opening and then eased the door closed. He held the handle as it quietly clicked shut, then silently slid the lock into place. "Marisella, I was sure you were hurt too badly to be up and moving so soon." Trenchertt pulled her to him in a bear hug.

"Ignacias, please. I may seem fine on the outside but my ribs still work to mend. My back is covered in purple bruises. Please be gentle." She smiled at the knight who towered over almost everyone and had never learned his own strength.

"Ah, forgive me, Mari. I was worried quite beyond myself for you and for this little girl of Jordan's. Metolius has discovered her home and sent soldiers to bring her here. Apparently she was not quite as smart as Jordan thought. She registered at the Beachcomber under an assumed name, but listed her real address. He intends to use her harshly. Possibly, if she is malleable enough, make her First Female when Jordan is done for." Trenchertt bowed his head and crossed himself. "I fear all we have planned is done for, as well. Metolius no longer trusts you and he has begun to suspect me. We have worked for so long. For what? Your destruction? Jordan in ashes? We, nay, the *world* cannot allow Metolius to continue on this road to dominion. He must be stopped."

Marisella placed two fingers over his lips. "Shhh! Ignacias.

257

There is time yet. Not everyone in this coven supports Metolius. He has punished too many, for too little, in these past years. Everything is in place at the company for our take-over. Metolius has no idea I have prepared the way for his end. A new day simply requires the death of the family patriarch. Between you and I, it will not be difficult to lead this coven to a better way. Only a few of Metolius' men will object. I am sure any resistance can be handled quickly and quietly." She removed her fingers and strained up to see the gentle smile of the big knight. "It has always been your dream to bring this coven to the light, Sir Knight. It is time to cease the use of drugs and culls. Now is the chance. We must seize this window of opportunity before we are found out. I have no wish to join Jordan in his cell."

"How? Metolius celebrates with his soldiers. He works himself into a lather. He must in order to take Susannah as his own when she is returned to him. He is too proud to show his failing libido in front of his men. He will not leave the party, I think. You know better than I, his ancient member requires more and more attention to rise to the occasion." Trenchertt turned to peer out the window into the night, embarrassed by his own statement.

"Of course. That is why I must be destroyed in the end, Ignacias. When I discovered the truth about the Master, I knew I would never be left alive to tell of his impotence. What Metolius does not understand is that there are those among the coven, and on his own Board of Directors at the company, who have guessed the truth of it. With a little help the seeds of knowing were planted long ago." Marisella shrugged her shoulders as if she had no knowledge of how the discovery was eventually made public. "He cannot hold this coven or the company much longer. His own people begin to doubt Metolius' strength and leadership. That is the fallacy of rule by might, Sir Knight."

"It will be sun-up in a few hours. I fear we can do nothing to save our Jordan. He languishes in the solar cell, chained in silver. If Metolius does not order the roof doors closed soon, he will meet the sun. I only pray Susannah is not returned to us before Jordan walks the path home." Again Trenchertt crossed himself. "I do not think we will be able to save the boy, Mari."

The tortured words were finally out.

"We must, Ignacias, we simply must. Think. How can we lure Metolius here? What will draw him from his revelry?" Marisella began pacing the floor once again. The split in her lip had faded to an angry red line and she walked without a limp now.

"The only thing that would drag him from his celebration is if you were dying. He would come to see for himself your death and decomposition. In the end, he would want to see the body, the ashes…"

"Of course, Sir Knight! You are a genius! You must go and tell him. Tell him he inflicted too much damage and I am close to death. That will bring him running! If not to watch, then to complete the job. Go. Hurry."

"But, Mari, what will you do when he comes? You can not fight him."

"No, Ignacias but I can distract him while you take his head." Marisella smiled sweetly.

"He is not that stupid, Mari. If he senses a trap, he will kill us both. What if he brings his henchmen with him? We would not stand a chance. I can fight with skill, possibly take several to my God with me, but I do not know if I can kill Metolius. He appears frail but he has tremendous strength. He has been feeding all night from a host of virgins. The Master is close to out of his mind with lust. Lust can easily turn to violence in less than a heartbeat." Trenchertt pressed a finger to the fading red streak on her lip.

"It is our only chance. If you tell him I am close to death, he will come to make sure of it. You must convince him quietly, so he comes alone. He would not kill me in front of his men. I am too popular with the coven members. Do not forget, I have protected many from his heavy hand. I believe he will be so relieved that I die, unseen and quietly, he will come alone to ensure his desired end. You need only follow as is proper for his friend and advisor. You have been witness to worse over the years, yet you still serve him. He would not give your presence a second thought."

"You may be correct, Mari. You may be correct." Trenchertt was thinking, preparing himself to appear truly sad at this woman's imminent passing. "I go now to tell my brother of the sad happenings here. May God help us both if he does not believe me and this plan should fail."

He watched silently as Marisella took Metolius' ancient long-blade dagger from its sheath near the desk and tucked it carefully beneath the cushions on the divan next to the bed.

"This blade has ended the lives of thousands of humans and vampires alike. Now it will bring the end of its Master. It is fitting." Marisella climbed into the massive bed she shared with Metolius. Pulling the covers to her neck, she nodded to a departing Trenchertt.

259

"Tonight, Sir Knight, a friend shall die. Either Metolius or myself, it is up to you now." She closed her eyes and tried to look pathetically ill and close to death.

With one last sign of the cross, Trenchertt headed for the billiards room and the escalating orgy a floor below.

*****

Miller watched the security cameras as one by one, the UV lights exploded in a shower of sparks then darkened completely. "Five down and two to go." He flipped on the infrared scanner as the last light went down. "They're at the farmhouse door. They are definitely vampires and the steel won't hold them long."

"Hello, Fiona? How are you, my dear?" Helga spoke quietly into the receiver.

"Door's gone. They're in. Being careful. Woops. Camera four-C down. Make that four-C, D, and E down."

"Yes, dear. We have a small problem here. Uh huh." The doctor continued her casual conversation as if their deaths were not imminent. "We sure could, sweetie. Any chance the Council would send an extra …"

Helga squeaked as a faerie vampire appeared in front of Miller's console flanked by seven huge vampires, all dressed in black and armed with a host of vicious looking, rather archaic weapons. Fiona's contingent filled the command center from shoulder to shoulder and wall to wall.

"…hand?" The little flame-haired vampire smiled sweetly as she spoke in a lilting voice. "How about a fang or two? Possibly a khopesh, a mace, or my favorite, the Sword of Andraste? How about a claymore? They work nicely in a pinch." Fiona floated a foot above the floor encircled by her billowing red gown held tight with a black leather corset. Attached to the metal-studded leather belt hung a vicious daca and a cell phone in its matching red case. Fiona was incongruence wrapped in leather, blood thirst and femininity. But for her diminutive size, she might have been a warrior out of some sci-fi fantasy illustration of medieval times. "We come to help. Where's the party, lovely Doctor of humans?"

At her appearance, Miller croaked, jumping up and back against the wall. The largest of the vampires who appeared with Fiona hissed and bared his fangs. The Sergeant's eyes rolled back in his head as he slumped to the floor, unconscious.

"What is wrong with him?" Fiona glanced casually at the crumpled figure of Sergeant Miller.

"I believe your…escort, the big guy, scared him." Helga shook her head with a smile. "He'll be alright."

"Is he afraid of vampires? What *is* that thing on his neck?" Fiona bent and plucked the dislodged plastic collar from around the Sergeant's neck.

Helga covered her mouth and chuckled, drawing a curious glance from Fiona and two of her guards. "It is his fang protection, Fiona. He wears it to keep vampires from biting his neck." She could barely get the words out without fully laughing at the Sergeant's little plastic contraption.

"He truly believes this would stop one of our kind? Silly human." Dropping the collar on the inert Sergeant, she turned to view the gray monitors. "So, what is this threat which requires our assistance?"

With a wave of her hand across the console, the individual video screens came to life and the lights within the farmhouse came up revealing six very surprised vampire soldiers attempting to sneak around in a room that, a second ago, was dark. Immediately one of Metolius' soldiers leveled his gun and fired, sending a hail of bullets into the lights and cameras, to no effect, of course.

Fiona twittered in her faerie fashion and nodded to her men. Three of the seven disappeared only to immediately reappear on the monitors in the room above.

Helga watched the screen as a bloody massacre ensued. Metolius' soldiers were no match for the Council's Guard. Watching alongside Helga, Fiona appeared to jump up and down in mid air as she clapped her hands and laughed outrageously. The Librarian's faerie-vampire wife seemed to enjoy gore and delighted in watching her henchmen decimate the intruders.

"Watch Paolo, he is my favorite! He has dispatched three already." Her girlish delight was somewhat gruesome, however, Helga was not about to criticize the woman. She came from the Council of Elders to rescue them. Miller groaned and stirred on the floor behind her. The rest of the staff remained silent and still. In the situation room all eyes were wide with fear.

The only human who seemed comfortable in the presence of Fiona and her guard, was Helga. Lieutenant Previn avoided eye contact and stared at his notebook, scribbling things as the encounter continued. The vehemence with which he scratched his notes was not lost on Helga or Fiona. The doctor watched to see what the little vampire would do and was completely relieved to see Fiona ignore Previn's insulting behavior. The man was incorrigible.

"Oh pooh! All done. And so quickly. No fun at all." Fiona pointed to the monitor. It showed ashes of the six unlucky losers settling into piles on the floor. Her three guards returned in a flash of red. "Is there anything else, Human Doctor? Emilliano does not know I am gone and he will be gruff with me if he finds I am missing. He seems to think I have a penchant for getting into trouble. Pah!! I think it more that trouble gets into me. Ah well, do you require anything more of me and my lovely Guard?" Fiona patted Paolo's bulky arm damp with a red wetness, then delicately licked her fingers clean.

Helga blinked. "Ah, no I guess not." Over the last year, she and Fiona had built a kind of long distance friendship around the sharing of some very interesting information. Though they never met face to face until today, the little Irish vampire was a fascinating creature, despite her unique habits and love of revolting gore.

The doctor did not have to force herself to take Fiona's tiny cold hands in hers. "It is wonderful to finally meet you in person. Please give my warmest regards to your husband, Fiona. And I do thank you for your quick response. I must admit, I am flabbergasted at how quickly..."

Fiona giggled and to Helga's surprise, took the doctor in a fierce hug. "We are even now, human, although I do not know what a flabbergast is, I am happy you have it. I shall remember this small diversion as... possibly... fun. We should do these things more often." Fiona whispered the last sentence in her fairy like voice and instantly disappeared along with her fearsome contingent. A high-pitched giggle echoed throughout the complex for several seconds after she vanished.

"Is she gone? Where did they go?" Miller croaked from the floor. His eyes fluttered as he tried to make sense of what happened and what he missed while he lay unconscious. His hands frantically searched his throat. Finding not a single hole in his precious tissue, he calmed.

Doctor Anderson sighed. "Back from whence they came, I suspect. Let me help you up Sergeant. I believe you took quite a hit to that invaluable noggin of yours. We need you ship-shape. Our particular threat has ended, but the mission is not over."

Miller climbed from the floor to his chair and was texting the team. "I'll let everyone know what happened and the outcome. Miller wiped his eyes. "Um, Doc, what did happen?"

His blank look was comical.

"Milo, just say Fiona came to the rescue. The danger has passed. We are hale and hearty. Leave it at that. They can have the long version when they return."

*****

"Five minutes to touchdown. Any last questions?" The tension in Susannah's voice was palatable. The frequency was silent. They'd made good time with a twenty-five knot tail wind. The AVS1 and AVS2 cruised at over one hundred and ninety knots with their over engineered design and mammoth engines.

The squad's maintenance crews were composed of the brightest and best geekoids of the business led by a short round fellow who could only be described as a cross between Yoda, Bill Gates and Chuck Yeager. Melvin Paulson physically and mentally contained the patience and build of Yoda, the technical genius embodied in Bill Gates and the outrageous and uncontainable daring of General Yeager. He was a perfect fit for the Vamp Squad. He worked amazing feats with transportation vehicles. Hence two very special helicopters that traveled at incredible speed for rotorcraft, with the maneuverability of Fury's Gazelle on steroids.

"Switching to stealth mode. Radio silence in three, two, one." The pilot of AVS1 coordinated the flight's timing and switch to silent running. Susannah smiled sheepishly at Monique who returned a bright smile with a thumb's up for good measure.

This was it.

In less than two minutes they would be in the thick of it with no turning back. Susannah took a deep breath and checked her gear, one more time. She felt for the cargo pocket and squeezed the short handled bolt cutters that lay concealed; ready to free the man she loved.

If they were in time.

It was still at least an hour until dawn. If everything went according to the plan, Jordan would be safe in her arms well before the dangerous rays of the sun touched his cell.

Through the small windows of her chopper, Elizabetta watched her fledgling daughter with welcome surprise. It was truly rewarding to see Susannah this way - professional, responsible and of all things, worried about someone other than herself. Four years of patient guidance, long hours of supervised training and endless heart-felt speeches were finally paying off. Elizabetta was proud as punch, as if Susannah had been her biological daughter. She felt for the girl's bright mind and sent a mental message to her. *Do not fear, daughter. We have Plan A and B and C. Our bases are covered, and then some. This is not Afghanistan and the Taliban.*

I can't believe Metolius found our base. I was so careless. I left a perfect trail for him. Gawd, how stupid can I be? I promise, Elizabetta, I will never be that irresponsible again. Really.

Elizabetta flashed her small cell phone at Susannah. *Shush now. The situation has been handled quite efficiently. Though I must admit Fiona's intercession was a bit startling. It was probably more than a bit startling for our human cohorts at the base! I can't wait to hear the details. Imagine, the Council of Elders interfering in this affair and supporting a request from a human. My goodness! Doctor Anderson's part in this intrigues me to no end. However, now we must concentrate on what is at hand and things will work out just fine. You have your team and your backup plans. You have simply to, how do I say it? Git'er done!*

Susannah stifled a giggle at the comedic statement, but it was true. AVS1 touched down with a whisper and a soft thud.

It was time to *git'er done!*

Chapter 24

A Legacy Lost

From time immemorial, man hath sought to build,
Civilization, structure, a power he willed.
But 'oft in the building, doeth he go astray,
Forcing only one thought, as the true and correct way.

And when viewed beneath searching eyes
The true and correct way belies
What the world blesseth right,
And compels through might.

Thank the Gods that be
For a legacy lost by thee.

Sir Father Ignacias Trenchertt, Knights Templar
Personal Journal
Daytona Beach, Florida 2008

Monique and Susannah ran for the solar cell as Natalia and Yuri covered their backs. Fortunately there was nothing to cover. The estate was quiet, the lawn and decks empty.

MorningStar flew on ahead, preferring the air to the terra firma.

The first floor of the main house was lit up like a royal party was in full swing. Voices raised in revelry could be heard above the music. The out buildings and lawns were deserted. It was as if a silent calm descended around the chaotic frenzy within the mansion, wrapping it in a kind of equalizing tranquility.

"This is wrong… spooky." Susannah spoke the words that were transmitted to the entire team via her comm implant. "There should be noise, lights, people and…stuff out here! It's not dawn yet. When I was here before, the place was not so oddly quiet."

She and Monique reached the edge of the solar cell at the same time as Morningstar.

"Your man is here." Susannah looked at her levitating sister in surprised alarm. "There are others beneath, within the earth. They wait." MorningStar hovered above Jordan's cell like some delivering angel, without shoes or wings. The Native American vampire rarely wore shoes. She said it muted the connection between she and the spirits of nature.

Susannah pulled Monique back from the edge. "Shit! This isn't right. I don't know what is going on." She touched her implant and whispered, "VS5 to team, status report!"

"VS1 here. The humans we have found are unharmed and docile. There was no guard. V-force is with me. We shall remain here to protect these pathetic people." Something in Elizabetta's voice made Susannah shiver.

How pathetic were the culls?

She could only imagine.

"Maddox, here. VS1 and V-force in place. Situation under control. No hostiles. I'll search the out buildings. Blue Boy's with me." Susannah heard the crisp declaration, as did everyone else. "Rendezvous at Bravo later."

Susannah tapped her implant in anger. "Negative, Maddox, Blue Boy. Stick to the plan."

"Listen, Susannah, I will…"

As team leader, Susannah's transmission overrode her father's response. "Negative, Maddox. Hold position." She quickly motioned for MorningStar to alight by the side of the cell wall. "VS4 and Hubby, head for the house. Surveillance only. See what is up with the party inside. Something is really wrong. Be extra careful."

Yuri took Natalia's hand and disappeared. Susannah could just see them reappear near the house behind some bushes and patio furniture.

Susannah stood for a moment, more questions swimming in her mind than answers. "MorningStar, do you feel graves below us? Or is there another room or corridor down there beneath the ground? You have that thing going on with the earth, right?" She watched as MorningStar wiggled her toes in the grass then took small steps in a strange pattern.

Morningstar smiled at Susannah after a few seconds.

"There is a tunnel from the cell to the house. It is damp but well constructed. Mother Earth caresses, but it does not give in to her touch. I feel our kind within." The Native vampire sunk to her knees stroking the ground with a sensual touch. "She calls to me for help. Our mother's heart aches for the emptiness that burrows through her body like a cancer."

"Qui apelle? Who calls to you, ma soeur?" Monique bent to touch the earth and shrugged feeling nothing but damp grass.

266

Monique was as often puzzled by MorningStar's way of speech as the rest of the squad.

"Mother Earth cries to me. Shall I answer her call?" Mysterious as always, Susannah needed a little more in the way of comprehension.

"MorningStar, what do you mean, answer her call?" Susannah bent and whispered quietly.

"She wishes me to close the hole that eats within. I can help it be. Shall I?" MorningStar slid to her stomach laying a cheek against the wet grass. She spread her arms wide as if she could hold the entire lawn in her embrace.

"Tout qui est saint! Can you truly do this thing, ma soeur? Monique stood at once and tippy toed toward the cement sidewalk that connected the veranda and the solar cell.

"Wait, not yet MorningStar." Susannah touched her implant. "VS5 to VS4. Nat, can you tell who is below me in a tunnel?"

"Three vampires with really ugly taste in fashion, and a dead human. That's it. No one we know or care about. Why? There sure is a hell of a party going on inside. I'll bet the whole coven is here. I spotted the one you described as 'The Master'. He was feasting a minute ago but has just disappeared with, of all things, a priest?" The surprise in her voice was understandable considering Trenchertt's choice of dress. "I sense incredible power, Susannah. Be very careful if you go spelunking."

"VS5 out. You can close the tunnel?" Susannah squatted next to MorningStar as the native vampire continued to feel the ground. She lay spread-eagle probing for… a broken bone? The hurt ground?

"Of course. There is so much pain here. The earth cries for release from its torture. Brother water calls to appease the ache of his sister. He is willing to come." MorningStar took a deep shuddering breath, sat up. With her legs crossed Indian style, of course, she began to keen in some ancient language only her own ears and the powers of nature could interpret.

The earth vibrated as the strange song touched the wind and raced across the grounds. "Oh shit! Let's get Jordan out of there before the walls collapse." Susannah withdrew the bolt cutters and ran for the stairs."

"Fly, little sister, it is faster." Monique spoke from the bottom of the cell. She looked at the man chained at her feet. "You must be Susannah's Jordan."

"What's going on? Where is… oh my God, the ground is splitting. Get me-" Jordan strained against the silver chains to try to see what was happening.

"Hey, baby!" Susannah deftly slid the bolt cutters between Jordan's skin and the metal. Though she could not have broken the silver chains, the cutters did their job admirably. With a quick snip, the silver fell away.

"Monique, he's too weak to stand." Susannah freed his legs as fast as she could without causing more damage than necessary to his already bloody and swollen tissue.

As Monique hefted Jordan and leapt into the air, the earth beneath them opened, cracking the painted sun on the floor of the cell in half. "Follow me, little sister, before MorningStar's Mother Earth gobbles you up."

Amazing herself, Susannah accomplished her first independent levitation... with a little help. A geyser blew from the chasm where Jordan had, seconds before, been chained.

MorningStar sat serenely on the cool grass, her hands lifted to the sky. "I thank the Spirits for this gift of healing. I am humbled by your greatness and power." She closed her eyes and let her hands fall, then rose elegantly with a smile. "It is done."

Landing less than gracefully on the grass a few feet away, Susannah stumbled toward Monique and MorningStar, who now held Jordan on his feet. "No kidding. That was fantastic." Susannah heard several voices in her ear as the rumbling earth stilled. "Oh my God, MorningStar, I had no idea you could do anything like that. And apparently neither did anyone else. You rock! Literally."

"Susannah, you did it! You flew by yourself!" Her congratulations cut short, Monique released Jordan who promptly crumpled to the, now motionless, ground. In complete surprise Monique stood, staring at a three-foot deep trough leading from the house to what used to be the solar cell. The big round hole now filled with water. "Regardez cela! Look!"

Susannah tapped her ear. "Okay, okay! Depressing her implant to communicate with the squad, vampires and humans alike, she responded to the frantic questions. "VS5, slight earth mother quake. Explain later. Jordan is safe. Heading for the house. Out"

"Can you stand without help?" Dressed in black and armed to the hilt, Susannah extended a black leather-gloved hand toward the man she loved.

"I can do more than that, you tease, you." Jordan took her hand and pulled her to him on the grass. Their lips met and the world moved again, but only for the two of them this time.

The real world remained calm, the calm before the storm. Just waiting for the fight to come.

Sparks flew between the two young lovers just as they always had. Whether in the midst of a life-threatening situation, or on the floor of a steamy shower, neither could deny the other's lust or need to always be in each other's arms. The word *love* floated between them like a sweet aroma, dancing on the night air. Their lips met in an electrifying kiss that sizzled through the vampire members of the squad.

Monique winked at MorningStar. "I think our little sister has forgotten her head. Are we not on a mission? And is she not mission leader?"

MorningStar grasped Susannah's utility belt and unceremoniously pulled the young woman from her entanglement. "Mission, sister?"

Susannah giggled quietly wiping a gloved hand across her glistening mouth. "Right. Mr. Burke, are you up for this?"

Exposed to three sets of scrutinizing eyes, Jordan had to blush.

He was up all right!

Never one to let the moment for a sexual comment pass, Monique murmured, "Il est apparemment. "

"Where are we going?" Jordan was confused as they headed toward the house, instead of the opposite direction. "Metolius is on a roll. I could hear it from the cell. The entire coven is out of control in there. It's not a place I want to be, nor should you. Any of you. He wants you Susannah, and he'll get you if we go inside. I won't be able to stop him." Jordan was tugging on his two beautiful escorts to slow them down and get them to listen to reason.

"Holy shit! Who are they?" Jordan stopped in his tracks upon discovering Natalia and Yuri. Monique and MorningStar jerked to a stop, surprised at the young man's strength and his quick recovery. Natalia and Yuri crouched behind a huge potted bougainvillea, watching through the glass windows.

"Shhh, Jordan. This is my family. We're on a mission to save you and the humans here. The entire squad is with me. You don't have to worry about my safety, or yours for that matter. Those two are mine." At that point Susannah touched the implant in her neck and transmitted. "VS2, 3,4, and Hubby, rendezvous at Charlie."

"Come along, petit frère, we have work to do." Monique had seen the revelry and was raring to party.

"Did she just call me 'little brother' in French?" He looked at Susannah with a puzzled expression.

"Yep!" A brilliant smile glowed against the twilight of the imminent dawn. "It's a compliment. Come on. Just play it by ear."

As they ran, half dragging a recovered and confused Jordan between them, Susannah heard Elizabetta's voice in her ear. "VS1 to VS5, your father has left the stables."

"Shit!" The three heard the comment via their implants, but not Jordan.

"What?" He glanced around wildly looking for trouble.

"My Dad just can't follow orders." Anger flashed across Susannah's creamy complexion. "Men! You can't live with 'em and you just can't shoot 'em."

The three women giggled quietly as Jordan scanned the lawn for the father of the woman he loved...and had spent a day in bed with. The situation was no longer deadly, but becoming more and more precarious.

*****

Colonel Maddox and Blue Boy snuck silently across the wide expanse of lawn toward a small shed by the edge of the swamp. A flicker of movement could be seen. Someone was inside moving about, obviously looking for something.

Maddox motioned to Blue Boy to take the rear. Communicating through pre-established hand signals, the Colonel indicated he would take a quick look through the small dirty window in the door. Crouching in a run, Maddox covered the distance and knelt below the window. Popping up for a fast peek, he made a V with his fingers, moving them from his eyes to the shed. The Colonel raised one finger indicating there was only one person inside.

Blue Boy gave the go sign with five fingers up and snuck around to the back of the shed. It opened onto the swamp through barn-like doors that stood ajar. Apparently the shed was used as a boathouse at one point. At the end of five seconds, the V-Force soldier crashed through the barn doors at the same time Maddox burst through the front door.

A startled Sal stared at the two men dressed all in black for all of one second. Then he leapt into action.

Maddox realized immediately, his daughter was correct. Humans were no challenge for these old fashioned vampires. Before he could draw a last breath, Blue Boy lay dead on the floor, his head torn completely from his shoulders. Maddox managed to fire a single round before his gun disappeared and reappeared in Sal's hands across the shed. The side arm Maddox thought securely in its holster plopped into the swamp behind the smiling vampire.

Sal laughed and pointed the rifle directly at the Colonel's head.

"What is this? Some tiny game you humans play? Hunt the vampires?" Sal sniffed and his nose curled. "Paint ball with garlic. How inventive!" His finger moved just a hair on the trigger. "Maybe you would like a taste of your own spices."

Directly behind Sal a mammoth white body rose with a growl. Damien's pet had smelled Blue's blood and come for its dinner. Sal screamed, grabbed a box on the table next to him and disappeared in a flash. The gun clattered to the floor as the albino alligator snapped viciously at the empty air that was Sal.

A split-hair second faster and Bengie would have had dinner between his jaws.

"Candy ass vampire." Disgusted, the Colonel reached for the rifle just as Damien's pet realized another chance at a live dinner waited a few feet away. Lumbering across the weapon, it hissed and snarled at the Colonel. Bengie's huge body eliminated any retreat, through either door.

Maddox was pinned in the shed with a hungry gigantic albino alligator. Always one for strategic planning in a pinch, he hopped up on the counter, pressed himself against the wall and proceeded to remain as silent and inconspicuous as possible while the alligator tore into Blue Boy's remains with its huge maw.   The Colonel had witnessed horrendous loss of life on the battlefield, but this was almost more than his stomach could take. As the monster crunched bones and tore flesh, Maddox closed his eyes and concentrated on keeping the contents of his stomach in place. He perched precariously on the tiny ledge that kept him upright and above the monster's reach.

Colonel Maddox held on for dear life. His eyes were closed tight but it did nothing to dull the chomping sounds.

*****

Inside Metolius' bedroom, Marisella lay still and apprehensive in the Master's wide bed. She focused on looking as pathetic and dying as she possibly could. Consciously draining the blood from her features and sucking in her cheeks, she hoped against hope her ruse would work. If not she wouldn't have to pretend for long.

The door to the room slid open almost soundlessly. She could hear two distinct sets of footsteps cross the plush carpet.

This was it.

She whimpered as helplessly as she could.

"Trenchertt, I had no idea. I seemed to have inflicted so much damage on our poor Mari. I am disconsolate." Metolius approached the bed, wringing his pale hands in mock concern. But Metolius could not disguise the cold smile that played across his lips. A trickle of red saliva leaked from the side of his mouth, remnants of the vile orgy in progress downstairs.

"I am consoled by your concern, Metolius." Trenchertt had to swallow against the bile that rose in his throat and threatened his lying lips.

He and Metolius both knew the truth of it. Now, the question remained; did Metolius know Trenchertt's truth? Did he suspect the knight?

"Ah, such a waste of one so beautiful and talented. She did serve me well." Metolius stood at the foot of his bed, peering at the woman he wished would just die and be out of his hair.

He rested a light hand on the heavily embroidered silk comforter near Marisella's foot. It made an almost indistinguishable lump beneath the cover. She moaned pathetically and moved her head a fraction of an inch, clearly in tremendous pain and close to complete destruction.

"Ah my poor, sweet Mari. I am truly ashamed of my part in your discomfort." Metolius moved to stand by the side of the bed, scrutinizing the woman who lay there. She did seem helpless inches from his clenched fist. *If only she would hurry herself along*, he thought. *After all, there was a party downstairs he was missing.*

"Can you ever forgive me for such brutality? You, if anyone, understand that my needs and desires can sometimes run away with my better judgment. Ah, but we did have fun, didn't we? Well, I did, in any event." He just couldn't help the snicker that escaped his thin cold lips as he bent over Marisella.

She knew he would be congratulating himself on his handiwork. If Metolius enjoyed anything, he enjoyed watching pain.

The drop of saliva had made its way to Metolius' chin and dropped to land on the tip of her nose. Surprised, Marisella flinched and opened her eyes.

Immediately, Metolius realized the ruse. He spun on Trenchertt.

"A lie, Sir Knight. A betrayal! I shall..." His sentence never completed, Trenchertt swung with well-aimed precision.

Metolius' head landed in the middle of the silk comforter. Its mouth agape as the body it had been attached to, fell to the floor, hands stretched out clawing for the traitor who ended its long life.

Marisella screamed, kicking the head away as she jumped from the bed in horror. Though it was their plan all along, they actually accomplished the unthinkable; they had killed their Master.

Before she knew it, she was enveloped in the strong arms of the knight, as she shook with the fear and reality of their actions. Plans were one thing but execution? Of a Master?

"May the Gods forgive us." She pleaded as the ground began to shake and rumble. "Trenchertt? What is happening? What have we done?"

Shrieks from the coven members partying below, rose through the floor. Marisella hid her face against Trenchertt's chest, waiting for some unknown power to end their lives.

Killing a Master was a horrendous transgression.

The end did not come.

But silence did.

The earth stilled and so did the wailing of the coven. All of Metolius' line was instantly aware the life of their master had ended. Marisella knew those who Metolius sired would be unconscious for a time, until the terrible pain of his destruction was passed and faded. She remembered how the end of her maker debilitated her for days.

However, she did not recall the earth trembling back then! Was Metolius' power that incredibly strong?

Mari pulled from the knight's arms and looked at his quizzical expression. "Was that not interesting, my dear?"

He was loath to let her go, but stood embarrassed at the strength of his feelings holding a cowering Marisella in his arms. Their physical contact stirred desires long ago extinguished by the very cloth he wore, and the vows he had taken before God. "Shall we go below stairs and see, what perchance, has happened?"

Trenchertt placed her hand on his arm, as if escorting a queen through her castle. "Years of planning and now it hath come to pass. We shall face the consequences of our endeavors with a glad heart and a worthy hand. All that lies before us, is of our own making now, my dear." Trenchertt paused at the top of the stairs leading to the main ballroom. The conscious coven members gathered below. The question remained. "Was it not our desire?"

Marisella gave Trenchertt a tenuous look. Her quivering smile told him much. "'Tis what we planned, Sir Knight. Now, let us be about the business of cleaning it up."

Holding Marisella firmly, they descended the stairs together. Approaching the bottom, Marisella gasped and missed a step.

Metolius' coven members remaining upright, stood as if in a trance, simply staring off into space. Many bodies lay inert, scattered between the billiards room and the ballroom. A couple of Metolius' henchmen not of the Master's lineage, struggled to clear their heads, trying to understand what just happened. Obviously none knew the effects of the end of a Master.

"Now our work begins." Trenchertt spoke quietly as they moved toward the ballroom, stepping carefully over bodies.

"Yes, of course. Trenchertt? Jordan! Quickly." Marisella dropped all pretenses and flew across the room toward the veranda doors. Her Jordan was still chained in his cell and dawn was approaching.

Trenchertt understood immediately and was right behind her.

Stephano DuPrerre lay next to the doors, quickly recovering his wits. Drechell's planned replacement suspected something was up the minute Metolius had left the party. Not yet trusted completely by the Master, he could only watch as Trenchertt left with Metolius just before the earthquake struck. At the same time, a ferocious, all-encompassing pain knocked him to the floor. Now Marisella and Trenchertt were headed toward the patio at top speed.

Marisella?

Wasn't she supposed to be on her deathbed? DuPrerre shook his head to clear his thoughts. He was just close enough to overhear Trenchertt whisper the news to Metolius before all hell broke loose. Okay, so… now Trenchertt and Marisella looked to be walking, or running, just fine.

Stephano stretched out his arm and grasped Trenchertt's leg as the knight sped by. Half dragging DuPrerre with him, Trenchertt crashed out onto the veranda.

The last time Susannah had been on this particular veranda, she was preparing to meet Metolius. Just a little cocky girl detective meeting the big bad Master, and all that. Now she stood a lot less cocky and a lot more frightened, in fact, scared out of her mind. *Buck up girl, you are mission coordinator. This is your op, act like it*, she told herself! Still, what waited within terrified her to the bone.

Just about the time Susannah gathered her newfound determination and approached the top of the patio, she froze in mid step. Marisella came flying through the open doors at vamp speed only to screech to a halt, a hair's breadth away. Trenchertt, dragging a flailing vampire on his leg, was not as quick with the brakes and slammed into them all. At once a melee ensued as Trenchertt and the unidentified vampire struggled. Catapulted across the law, bodies flew in all directions while the huge knight pummeled the man who fought back with determination.

Alerted by the noise and commotion, three of Stephano's cohorts stumbled onto the patio. One dragged Marisella to her feet and the other shouted at the fighting men, as he held a sword to the First Female's throat.

Everyone froze, except for Stephano, who viciously kicked Trenchertt away. "Move and the Master's whore loses her head. Not that Metolius would care." He stood and moved behind his two friends. Pinning Marisella's arms behind her, he spit at the third, "Marcus, go find Metolius. Last I saw, he was headed for his quarters to witness the untimely passing of his First Female."

With everyone's eyes on Marisella and Stephano, no one noticed a silent Yuri position himself behind a huge potted palm, just a few feet away.

No one that was, except Susannah.

The plan came to her in a flash. Finally she had a good use for her long blonde hair and the reputation that accompanied it. Flipping her hair behind her shoulder she dissolved into feigned tears, begging piteously. "No, please don't hurt her. Mari was the only one who was nice to me here. Please, she doesn't deserve to be harmed. I…" on and on Susannah whined drawing a scowl from Stephano, but holding his attention none-the-less. Drawing attention was something Susannah was very good at. She made enough noise to keep everyone's eyes on her.

Trenchertt caught Yuri's signal communicating the intention to v-port just as Marcus called from the upstairs window.

"The Master is nowhere to be found. There's a lot of ashes on his bed. I think-"

Immediately, all hell broke lose one more time as Yuri appeared behind Stephano's soldier dispatching the vampire with a single stroke of his Spetsnaz long knife. He flung the decapitated body several feet from its rolling head. It turned to ashes in mid air.

Trenchertt pitched himself at the vampire who held the sword to Marisella's throat, tearing the man's sword arm completely away.

Susannah leveled her side arm at Marcus, who hung out of Metolius' window. She fired, emptying the magazine into the

275

vampire. He slid from the window and fell to the ground in a pile of ashes.

Stephano found himself on the business end of Monique's special FN 40g and chose not to move or speak. He was much smarter than Drechell.

It was over in seconds.

Somewhat planned, chaotic seconds, but over and done.

Trenchertt stood holding a disconnected arm with its dangling sword, looking slightly embarrassed but thoroughly relieved to see Jordan and Susannah. Dropping the bloody appendage in a hail of ash, Trenchertt took the distance in one giant leap, pulled the young couple into his arms and enveloped them in a bear hug to end all bear hugs. Overjoyed at finding Jordan free and healthy with pretty Susannah at his side, Trenchertt bounced up and down with the children in his arms.

It was a sight to see.

The reunion resembled a WWF match gone all wrong and funky!

Susannah looked like Secret Agent Man with the arsenal strapped to her body flopping about as she bounced in Trenchertt's arms.

Jordan was Mr. Yuppie incarnate.

Trenchertt wore the usual robes of his Order.

The vampire who had been connected to the hand and sword seconds before, huddled on the ground holding a profusely bleeding stump, the wound already beginning to close and heal.

A flustered Marisella sat on her backside in the dewy grass laughing uproariously. Having been released so quickly, she tripped, landing in a heap at Yuri's feet.

"Sir Knight, do let them go before someone is broken!"

Yuri, ever the gentleman, carefully lifted the coven's First Female to her feet, gingerly brushing the grass from her backside.

His action drew a slight scowl from Natalia who appeared from her hiding place behind the luscious vegetation, near the side of the windows.

The patio resembled a circus gone wrong.

Marisella was next in line to soundly embrace the couple. "I believe there is a story here of which we must all find the bottom, at some point. I am so glad that you are safe, Jordan. Ignacias and I were just on our way to free you." She turned to the gathering group and paused for a moment, cleared her throat and confidently pronounced, "Metolius is destroyed."

Several of the coven members smiled. Obvious sighs of relief were heard from many. Others looked confused, but few seemed angry or disappointed. Metolius was not loved by his coven. Their reaction to his demise was clear proof of that fact.

"May his soul finally rest in peace." Trenchertt crossed himself. "And may we welcome our new Mistress, Marisella Ferreira. I prayeth she lead with strength of mind and heart." He sank to one knee, took her hand and raised it, placing a kiss on the back. "I vow here and now, who so ever challengeth the Mistress, challenges me in battle." He roared, and then rose to stand behind Marisella, his hands clasped behind his back looking like the ominous guard he intended to be.

Behind the huge knight, warm light spilled from the room casting pooling shadows in the pre-dawn moments. The coven was recovering, gathering together, confused and wary. It would have resembled a large family gathering, if circumstances had been different.

Slowly but surely the conscious coven members in attendance began to clap. Soon a cheer rose and several followed Trenchertt in giving allegiance, each coming to kneel and kiss the hand of the new Mistress. Looks of relief passed between their leader and many of the coven members as they pledged their loyalty to the new guard, then and there. Several looked questioningly at the well-armed guests.

Despite the intimate little scene, Susannah still had a mission to complete and things were not wrapped yet. "Where?" She mumbled and stepped to the edge of the veranda, her azure eyes searching for the rest of her team. "I need to find the rest of my team."

"Susannah!" Jordan was not yet ready to be parted from his love. He flashed across the veranda at the same time Susannah turned to tell him she needed to find her father and Elizabetta. Unable to circumvent the laws of gravity, despite vampiric power, they collided at the top. Jordan tripped as Susannah grabbed for him in free-for-all attempt to catch the flailing man. Jordan fell backwards cracking his skull on the cement as Susannah came down on top, an unfortunately placed knee landing in the softest place possible.

Someone's elbow caught the leg of a bystander, casting the innocent vampire into the melee with the force of an explosive projectile. The unsuspecting projectile let loose of his glass of bloodwine, just in time to land flat atop a stunned Susannah cracking several ribs and pinning her leg to the ground between Jordan's aching testicles. The glass flew several feet splashing across Natalia and Yuri.

It could not have been better executed if the Three Stooges choreographed the entire prat-fall.

Natalia stood next to the fuming Yuri, biting her tongue and trying not to laugh, rather unsuccessfully. She trailed a finger down his shirt then licked it clean. "Um… O negative I believe. I have experience with this lovely beverage." In an overtly sensual act she licked a tiny drop from his chin. Ducking his half-hearted swing, she giggled at the whole mess, in a playful newlywed kind of way.

A muffled quasi-silence ensued as the team tried, unsuccessfully to hold their obvious merriment within.

Monique, both hands plastered across her mouth, actually snorted then just gave up and howled. Smiles played across the faces of many of the members of the new Ferreira Coven. Some looked away in confusion, not knowing the appropriate response in the wake of so many strangers.

The three tangled bodies on the veranda squirmed and wiggled attempting to extricate themselves from the entanglement with as little damage to Jordan's sensitive 'area' as possible. Marisella finally moved to assist. "Ignacias, help them!" she gasped through laughs and hugs.

Both Marisella and Trenchertt lifted the top flailing vampire from the heap and stood the victim on his feet with a pat for good measure. Trenchertt then pulled Susannah gently from Jordan, who immediately curled into a ball gasping in relief… or pain. It was a toss up as to which.

Holding her ribs, Susannah knelt next to a groaning Jordan. "Oh my God, I'm so sorry. I didn't mean to do that. Jordan? Jordan!"

"WHAT? Can't you see I need a moment here, Susannah? I'm in a little pain. It seems to be a habit around you." He rolled to his back and tried to sit up. Susannah reached to help and Jordan cringed. "No, no. I think I've got it."

Hurt and riding the emotional runaway train of the last few hours, tears welled up in the young woman's eyes. "You're alive. You should be grateful for that, at least."

"Just barely. In the future could we be a little more careful, please?" Jordan stood and took Susannah in his arms, cradling her frowning face against his chest.

A quick kiss from her man was all it took to wipe the frown away and replace it with the dreamy look of young love.

Trenchertt stood next to a dripping Natalia, shaking his head. "Your sister, huh? I shall sayeth many a prayer for that boy." Both chuckled together.

Susannah pushed away from Jordan and spun around with her arms open. "Ya know, I'm damned if I do, and damned if I don't. I just can't make it right." She snuffed half in jest, half in honesty.

Jordan stepped up to the plate, ready to block any unforeseen accidents. "It's okay, baby. The sun's not up yet. You're safe. I'm safe. And I am grateful. Stop worrying and let's go find the rest of your... what? Family? Team?" He smiled at the love of his life, and death. His was such a crazy existence, but hours in the solar cell had straightened out his mind.

She *was* the love of his life.

She came back to rescue him.

There was no doubt in his mind that she shared his feelings.

Just about the time an exasperated Susannah was about to assault Jordan with her lips, her ear bud transmitted a harried request from Elizabetta.

"VS1 to VS5. Status? Please! Your father and Blue Boy have not returned." Susannah caught Monique's raised eyebrow.

On to the mission at hand.

Susannah was still the leader and there was work to be done. Her new 'responsible' self was not allowed personal time when the job wasn't finished.

"VS1 maintain location. We're on the way." She released pressure on the neck implant. "We have to go, Jordan. The rest of our team is at the stables, and it seems I have a missing father." She shrugged in way of apology.

"Susannah, can we be of assistance?" Marisella had no idea that there was more of the Vamp Squad roaming the grounds.

"Marisella, my Mistress is with the humans in the stables. My father and his V-Force, human soldiers trained to fight vampires, were supposed to remain there. Dad doesn't like being told what to do, I guess. Can you keep your coven here at the house until we sort this out? That would be great. I don't want anyone else to get hurt." She looked at the cement steps of the veranda for a moment. "You know I can't leave humans here, right? I came for Jordan, but the squad came to liberate the culls." Susannah felt like she was apologizing for the gruesome habit that had been a way of life at the Proctor coven.

"I understand completely, Susannah." Marisella took the young girl's hands in hers. "Ignacias and I have never approved of Proctor's stables. That is only one of the things you will see come to an end here. I am sure this will all play out in some fascinating story at some point, but right now I should very much like to meet your father. Go and find him before he gets himself into some kind of trouble. Jordan will be safe with me." She smiled and waved Susannah on. "In fact, I am looking forward to meeting all of your curious family, vampire and human alike."

Jordan turned to the huge knight. "Now, will someone fill me in before I expire of curiosity? Please?"

Trenchertt laughed and pounded the young man on the back.

Marisella ushered her coven into the ballroom with an eye for the sunrise. The drapes were shut tight just as the first rays of the morning peeked over the horizon. "Well, Jordan, short story long; this coven would not have survived long if Metolius remained Master. It has been clear to both Ignacias and I, for several years now. We have been planning with," she used her fingers to show little quote marks around the next word, *friends* to solve the problem. The arrival of your little Susannah and the disappearance of Drechell stepped up our timetable. I just could not let you perish. You have been like a son to me. I care for you dreadfully much." She paused in her explanation to hug Jordan once again.

Several of the coven members sat close, listening to everything they missed in the mass unconscious period, after the destruction of Metolius.

"When Metolius flew into a rage and beat me so terribly, I feigned death hoping the Master would come to make sure I was finally out of his way. Our little ruse worked. Trenchertt took Metolius with his own sword. A fitting end to one who lived by the sword. Of course the official story will read much differently. We, Ignacias and I, have worked behind the scenes for years now, positioning certain people to take control of Proctor Pharmaceuticals, avoiding unnecessary questions and belaying suspicions. It has become crucial, in these last few months, that the leadership change. No one will be surprised at the demise of the elderly Proctor. Nor will they question the rise of his favorite niece to the vacant presidency. I have worked by his side for so long. I think we shall say, with appropriate sadness of course, that Metolius Proctor died quietly. At his estate. Surrounded by friends, family and his priest."

"A quiet and private end for a very private family man. No?" Trenchertt clapped Jordan on the back again, almost bringing the young man to his knees. "True story, son. He did not ushereth a shred of sound from his lips as I took his head. He is but ashes in the breeze of the coming dawn. Speaking of which, we should allow our family to retire after such a traumatic evening."

One by one, the vampires and humans disappeared, leaving only Jordan, Marisella and Trenchertt in the billiards room.

Jordan flopped down in an overstuffed chair "All the time I was chained down in that cell, all I could think of was Susannah. How dying was worth it. She was safe. That was all that mattered. I love her, you know." He sighed leaning back in the chair, exhausted, considering the latest events and a tense evening spent contemplating his own demise. Something like that had a way of bringing a man to his senses. "Susannah Helga Anderson Maddox, whoever you are, wherever you are, I love you."

Marisella patted him on the shoulder. "She will return shortly. All good things are worth waiting for. She is a lovely young girl and I believe she does love you as well, Jordan. Despite the danger, she returned to rescue you. She is a very lovely and *resourceful* young girl."

*****

In short order, Susannah reunited with her team members, aghast at what she found. The 'stalls' were cages more fit for vermin, than humans. A variety of young men and women, some still children, lay about in their own filth, groggy and incoherent. One pitiful thing sat in the corner of his cage, sucking his thumb and rocking back and forth, his eyes wide with terror.

The Colonel and Blue Boy were still on the MIA list.

Monique tossed a can of v-screen to Susannah after coating herself liberally. "It is time to find your papa, ma petite soeur. The big Bear will help, will you not?" Monique swagged a finger at the V-Force commando.

"Mon plaisir, Mademoiselle Monique." The soldier checked his gun and moved to stand as close to Monique as he could.

When had Bear learned French?

The why was apparent.

Elizabetta helped Susannah coat herself with the sunscreen and plopped a safari hat atop the girl's damp blonde hair. "Have a care, my daughters. It's bright out there. Last I saw, your father and Blue were headed for the shed by the swamp." She handed both women special wrap-around dark glasses and ushered them out the door with a motherly shove and a whispered warning for the mission leader. "Susannah, be nice to your father."

Monique and Susannah made the shade of the giant weeping willow before Bear was two steps out of the stables. He just shook his head and ran as fast as he could to catch up. Ducking around the side of the small building, all three could hear a great growl and sounds of tearing cloth. Bear was the first to peek through the open door. He turned and signaled to the women. With one finger in front of his head, he drew a big smiley face.

Why didn't he use his com unit instead of some weird human gesture? Susannah pressed the implant in her neck. "Bear, that's not a signal I remember learning." She looked at Monique who raised her shoulders in a shrug.

Me either, cheri. Monique mentally commented.

Bear stood up and sauntered over to the shady spot where the two girls crouched. "It means, my fair ladies - you're gonna love this." With a chuckle he took Monique's hand, tucked it under his arm and walked her to the shed door. He made sure to keep the French vampire in his shadow.

Susannah followed behind, just a little confused. Bear was a great soldier and he was strolling arm in arm with Monique in the middle of a tactical search.

What was that about?

This mission was turning out to have more surprises than the funhouse at the fair.

As Monique peered through the doorway, her hand flew to her mouth in an attempt to cover something.

A scream?

A giggle?

Susannah shoved Monique out of the way and looked into the dim shed. There, on the floor, lounging on top of one of the team's specially designed rifles, was an enormous white alligator. Curled into a tight ball on top of a workbench sat her father, brandishing a half eaten oar like the Sword of Damocles. With the addition of three more spectators the huge animal roared, then yawned and lay it's head atop a pile of guts and bone.

Damien's pet had pinned the Colonel in the shed!

"Colonel, what are you doing up there?" Bear just had to ask. He had to bite his tongue twice to keep from laughing out loud in the middle of the question.

"Sergeant, get that thing out of here." Disturbed by the Colonel's shouting, the alligator raised its ugly head and hissed, snapping at the end of the oar.

282

"'Scuz me, Sir. I believe VS5 here is in charge of this mission." He turned to a flabbergasted Susannah. "Your orders, Ma'am?"

For a second, Susannah held her breath to keep from laughing at her father, an insult she knew he would never forget. An insult she would pay for later. Composing herself, she spoke clearly and concisely, "Sergeant, assist the Colonel. Where's Blue Boy?"

The Colonel lifted a shredded glove with a partial hand still inside.

"Oh my God, get him out of there, Bear." The situation wasn't funny anymore. Monique moved toward the Colonel, but froze when the vicious animal growled and lunged forward. It seemed the alligator would let no one separate it from its meal.

Bear raised his gun but was stayed by a gentle hand from behind.

MorningStar slid between the soldier and the doorway, singing a soft melodious song as she approached the alligator. Surprisingly enough the animal seemed to perk up and listen to her song, tilting its huge head to one side in interest. Within seconds, its scaly lids slowly closed over creepy, Albino pink eyes. Continuing her song, MorningStar stepped over the sleeping animal, to its tail and hauled it back the way it had come. As the beast sunk beneath the inky black water of the swamp the native vampire smiled and walked towards the stables with a small nod.

"Holy shit! She's amazing." Susannah commented to herself, more than to any one in particular. "Note to self: spend more time with MorningStar."

Chapter 25

A Woman's Way

We women live our lives for a reason,
In birth, we are blessed with a season.
Childhood's freedom from woes and strife,
Before God's wonder, grows to life.
Then in change, unavoidable but true,
Love gives us strength and life anew.

Elizabetta Zoeltel
Coven Mistress
Olney Farm, Maine, 2008

"Jordan, I didn't want to leave you, but Ted dragged me off. All I could think of was you dying, and it was all my fault. I hated myself for deserting you. I had to come back. I don't want to live without you." She kissed him passionately and felt something near his groin jump. "Ou la la, I think you like that."

Jordan rumbled deep in his chest and returned the kiss just as passionately, shifting to accommodate the growing tightness in his slacks. "All the time I was chained up just waiting to die, all I could think was that at least you were safe. But you came back for me! I love you, Susannah Maddox. That is your real name, isn't it?"

"All right, enough with kissy-kissy face. You, cheri, have a mission to debrief. Tisk, tisk, business before pleasure." Monique sidled up to the chair in which the couple cuddled. She perched on the side and ruffled Jordan's hair. "And you must formally introduce your young man to your father. It is the way it should be done, little sister." Monique flounced across the room and dragged a resisting Colonel Maddox from the other room. "Utilisez vos façons, ma soeur."

Faced with a stalwart Army Colonel who just happened to be his lover's father, Jordan immediately stood. Susannah slid to the floor with a less than graceful plop.

"Jordan!"

"Sir." Flustered by the woman at his feet and her father staring them down, Jordan extended his hand. "A pleasure to meet you, Sir."

In all his years, in fact ever since his daughter's species transition, he had never been at a loss for what to say or how to act. Now he stood before a young man who obviously loved his little girl.

He was dumb struck.

Never before had one of Susannah's boyfriends treated him with respect. Most had avoided him like the plague. He remembered one fellow knew what a handshake was, but the kid was only ten years old or so, and an officer's son. Over the years and the school grades, one thing Susannah's male friends all had in common; a failure to look him in the eye. None lived up to his standards.

But here stood a well-dressed young man calling him sir with his hand extended looking him straight in the eye. It was all he could do to keep from fainting in abject fear. This man wanted his little girl, apparently loved his daughter… and *wanted* to shake hands with her father!

"Frank, shake his hand." He felt Elizabetta's cool breath next to his ear. "Take his hand and make it go up and down. It's called meeting the boyfriend."

A full minute passed, but Jordan remained standing with his hand out stretched, just waiting. Both men had no idea how to handle the pregnant silence.

Finally Maddox raised his hand an inch. It was all Jordan needed. With a giant smile displaying perfect teeth and pearly white fangs, he grasped the Colonel's hand in both of his and shook vigorously.

And continued to shake!

"Nice to meet you, Sir. You have a wonderful daughter and I love her, Sir. If it's all right with you I'd like to see her on a regular basis, Sir. And she loves me. Well, I think anyway. She said she did, Sir, so if it's okay with you, I'd sure like to…ah date her? Sir?" Jordan was running out of steam and Maddox was running out of undamaged skin on his shaking hand.

They resembled two wind-up toys running down slowly with only one action between them, so the shake continued.

"Okay, enough you two! Jordan, stop shaking my father like a rag doll. Dad, breathe and close your mouth. This is not the 1920s and I'm a big girl." Susannah stood and pulled the two men apart. "Jordan, you don't have to ask to date me. And Dad… you don't have to give your permission."

Both men answered at the same time. "Yes I do. It's proper." They turned and smiled at the mutual love of their lives.

Two crazy men who loved one woman in two very different ways.

It was almost comical.

No!

It was actually very comical.

Susannah scowled and stomped off in disgust. "I have a mission to debrief. Let's just git'er done. Team! Coven leaders! With me, NOW!" She ushered everyone who was listening without laughing, into the conference room that Metolius used to hold court. As mission leader, she took the seat at the head of the table. It was early morning and the sun shone just a little over the horizon; the tinted windows automatically darkened, filtering its UV light.

Vamp technology was a wonderful thing.

"Alright, let's get down to business." And that is exactly what Susannah did.

By noon, Marisella and Sir Ignacias had recounted their tale of the end of the mighty Metolius Proctor as well as plans for a new direction with the coven they now led together.

Unbeknown to everyone except Trenchertt, Marisella had groomed the company Board of Directors for the passing of an icon, ie. Metolius Proctor. Everything was in place for a smooth transition and an end to the production of CE itself, along with any research on the dangerous drug.

The two covens would forever be bound by the actions of the last few hours. Though vastly different in make-up, agreements as well as plans for mutual events were organized over a hastily installed satellite link. Susannah watched Miller over the vid-link and wondered at the way the Sergeant's continually scanned the corners of the command center.

Doctor Anderson was on her way to assist with the culls who had all been transferred to a local private medical facility for treatment. Natalia was tending to the minds of the humans who were so horribly used, as best she could while awaiting the arrival of Doctor Anderson. When they recovered, each would possess pleasant memories of very special treatment after a devastating accident or natural disaster of some sort.

Monique, ever the woman of fantasy, was crafting new lives for the humans with a very enthusiastic Almaund, former administrative assistant to Metolius. Incredibly intelligent and knowledgeable about coven affairs, as well as the identities of the culls, Monique found working with the French assistant invigorating, and just a touch melancholy. She missed her native country and thoroughly enjoyed speaking her primary language with someone who could hold a fast paced conversation, and understand her jokes, without lengthy interpretations.

Yuri was off in the swamp with Jordan, hunting the alligators that had become accustomed to eating human flesh. It was a nasty job but the two grinning men graciously accepted the dirty duty and virtually ran for the gun locker and v-screen. Amazingly enough, MorningStar trailed not far behind, speaking to the spirits in the dark waters, easing the animals' way into the next world.

Elizabetta sat proudly watching Susannah, efficiently conduct business. Colonel Maddox remained quiet for the most part, answering questions, filling in information and grinning like a cat that ate the rat. Every once in a while he would lean over and squeeze his daughter's shoulder or pat her hand.

As for Susannah, she handled her father's newfound respect like any teenager would, casually tolerating it, but bursting with pride inside. The business of the team kept her occupied, but her mind and eyes drifted at regular intervals toward the swamps.

By late afternoon the mission wrap-up and debrief were done. Monique was asleep on a couch somewhere, scattered files and miscellaneous papers strewn about the floor. Susannah's head drooped in her chair and Elizabetta sat with Maddox quietly talking about the mission and the last few days.

Marisella's new quarters were cleaned of any ash and she had retired to rest. Trenchertt was in the gym burning off the last of his built up tension from the past few days. He was swinging a broad sword at imaginary foes, to the tunes of The Grateful Dead.

Maddox peered at his dozing daughter slumped in the Master's wide leather chair. He grinned like a new father seeing his baby for the first time. He was still stupid in love with his sweet, helpless daughter. With stunning recognition, it finally dawned on him that she was no longer a baby nor was she helpless.

"I can't believe she pulled this off, Elizabetta. I just…every time I think of her running off like that, so irresponsible, knee deep in trouble… Then I watched her last night and today. It's like she is two different people. My wild little spirit is gone. In her place is a skilled and responsible young woman who takes her job seriously. And then there is this Jordan? He's a real man, not just a boy she wants to flaunt or manipulate. She said she loved him. She's never said that, not even to me. Not since her mother was alive anyway." He looked down quickly, starring at his big gnarled hands tightly clasped in his lap. "Geeze, Betta. I never thought I'd see anything like this, not in a million years. Part of me wants her to stay that cute little baby I used to rock on a pillow, but the rest of me wants her to grow up and be, well, what she obviously is now, an adult. And one hell of an operative I might add."

"Frank," Elizabetta patted his hands. "Every parent goes through this. Somewhere along the line your children grow up and become adults. Your daughter just took a bit of a side turn. Died. Became a vampire. Ran off. Found a vampire boyfriend. Started a war with a coven. Fixed it. Saved her man and finally, voila - she's all grown up. Well, sort of anyway. Don't think there won't be more challenges. Maturing doesn't exactly happen overnight. Especially not for our kind."

They sat there like two old folks talking about their children. Frank felt his age for the first time. It was an uncomfortable feeling.

"It's all normal parent stuff." Elizabetta smiled and patted his hands again. "Really. You'll see. And don't forget how far you've come as well. Five years ago, did you ever think you'd be sitting at a table negotiating with a coven of vampires? Surrounded by your own coven of the like? And feeling like it was just another normal operation?"

At that statement the Colonel had to chuckle and shake his head. "Normal has reached new heights in my playbook. It's hard to look back and not see vampires as an acceptable part of my life. It's like having your first kid. A month later, you can't remember what life was like without them."

Both sat in companionable silence for a few minutes, each considering the changes in their lives over the last four years. Frank's entire world was shaken upside down and he found a new view of life and death. That new view encompassed an entirely different way of thinking. Elizabetta found a family, after hundreds of years of dashed hopes and isolation. And they both had a daughter they loved with all their hearts.

Frank finally broke the silence with an issue heavy on his mind. "So this woman-faerie-vampire that showed up with the firepower, what's that all about? She sure has Miller spooked. He can't focus for more than a few minutes without looking around for this little gal to appear out of nowhere. Who is she anyway?" Elizabetta's lecture was way too close to the heart for his comfort. It was time to return to the safe ground of Vamp Squad business.

"Fiona? She's the wife of the Librarian for the Council of Elders. Over the centuries, vampires as a collective society, decided we needed some form of judicial hand, an objective force that would keep covens in order and deal with rogues. The Council of Elders evolved to satisfy that need. They have an organization of sorts that helps to ensure our existence remains a superstition and not a reality in the minds of humans. It was the Council who helped Natalia find me in the beginning." Elizabetta's forehead wrinkled. "They do not generally delve into human entanglements or interfere with human society. Which is why I was so surprised that Fiona would show up, and at the request of a human! Very strange indeed. I will have to chat with Helga about that." Elizabetta pondered the question as she watched Maddox slide a small couch pillow beneath the crooked head of his sleeping daughter. His tenderness impressed her. Father and daughter had come a long way since Susannah's turning. As a matter of fact, they'd come a long way since yesterday.

"Is this Council something we should worry about? If they can just pop in and waste six vampires, they could be a threat. Something the Joint Chiefs should know about."

"The Council has existed for more than twenty-five hundred years. In all that time has the United States been threatened or even affected by their actions? The Council takes extreme care to only involve themselves in vampire affairs. It is something, I believe, we should keep within our house, Frank. The Council is comprised of very old and powerful vampires who value their anonymity. I respect that. I hope you do too. It's safer that way." She cast the Colonel a knowing glance. "And, they do come in handy at times."

"So I've learned. I'm too tired to think anymore and everyone but you is asleep. I think I may join them. I was told I have a room on the third floor." He took Elizabetta's hand gently and pressed a kiss to her fingers. "Thank you, Mistress Elizabetta Zoeltel. For everything."

✶✶✶✶✶

Susannah cuddled next to Jordan in his expansive bed. The tangled and torn sheets, evidence of a day of pure bliss, lay in a pile at their feet.

"You didn't bite me! I really have to tell you, I sort of miss that part of our love making." Jordan tickled her stomach with a flower stem - all that was left of a dozen roses that had graced the side of his bed. "I get such a high from your blood, but it has a very strange effect on me. I am so weak afterwards. Why do you think that is?"

"Hmm, I don't know Jordan. Maybe we can get the Doc to check you out once we get home." Susannah drew a circle around his nipple with her index finger and giggled at the reaction of his chest muscles.

"Whoa, hang on there a minute. I am home. And stop that! I can't think when you do that." Jordan took Susannah's hand from his chest and kissed her fingers before capturing them against his stomach.

"Stop what? We're teenagers with raging hormones. You said that yourself!" Susannah was grinning like a wolf on the prowl. She licked her lips and nipped where her fingers had just played.

"Yes, and unfortunately we will be for several hundred more years." Jordan huffed.

"Unfortunately? What's so wrong with that? All the energy in the world, those lovely raging hormones, unbreakable bodies." She picked a sliver of wood from the splintered headboard. "Too bad we can't find an unbreakable bed." She continued with a clearly faked, but wistful sigh, "no wrinkles or broken nails. Tons of money and great toys. Then there's that never-ending libido of yours, not to mention the never-ending appetite of mine. Seems pretty perfect to me." She rolled atop Jordan and nipped at his chin. "And no whisker burn. How great is that?"

"Don't forget the bad judgment, lightning quick anger, compulsion to be completely invincible, barely controllable blood lust, oh, and last but not least, we're stuck in these bodies that won't mature for a couple centuries." Jordan dumped Susannah off of his chest and rolled to his side. Propping his head up with one hand, an elbow dug into the pillows. He frowned at the intoxicating beauty who lay next to him completely naked, except for a few rose petals plastered to her body in unique places. "Do you have any idea how hard teen years are on the male species? Girls have it easy compared to us."

"Oh, give it a break, Jordan. Are you going to start lecturing me about the Mars/Venus thing? Come on. You might be ninety years old but you certainly haven't figured much out in those ninety years." Susannah sat up and crossed her legs shaking her head. Now she too was frowning. "Life is what you make it. You can stay here in this fantastic mansion and whine about not being able to shave for five hundred years, or you can look at the bright side. Just think how much you'll save on razors! Now that our covens are working out a formal relationship and Marisella has entertained the idea of going techno-modern, we're almost family. You have a great career ahead of you with Proctor Pharmaceuticals and a fabulously gorgeous and incredibly talented girlfriend who also happens to be an undercover operative." She crawled to her hands and knees, stalking Jordan across the bed. "Da, da, da-da. Da, da, da-da." She began the famous movie theme.

He recognized the song at once. "You are an impossible mission, woman!" He slid over the end of the bed, taking cover beneath the pile of sheets. Jordan aimed his finger at Susannah and fired in rapid succession.

"Hey you, handsome-but-not-to-bright. I'm already dead!" She leapt off the end of the mattress and tackled Jordan pinning him to the floor. Her mouth covered his and all discussion ended for a length of time.

In that length of time, the legs of an antique Victorian chair were somehow smashed. A table containing the crystal vase, an alarm clock and Jordan's wallet flew across the room. A blanket got mixed up in the melee, ending up strips and fluff... and Jordan's raging hormones got the work out of their raging life.

Susannah, covered in sweat lay on a Persian rug on the floor, rubbing rapidly healing rug burns on both elbows and one knee. Jordan thought her quick little pants were quite endearing. For his part, well, he thought he might just let his gym membership expire in the future.

"I'm starving." Susannah tried to sit up. "We have to keep a bit of distance, Jordan. I don't know if I can keep my fangs in, I'm so hungry." She scooted away and tried to sit up again.

"Oh, now look who's whining." Jordan stood on wobbly legs. "I know I heal quickly, but I wonder if I can wear this thing off before it regenerates?" His soft member dangled red and inflamed from its previous over-activity.

Susannah dissolved into a fit of giggles lying on the rug as Jordan walked purposefully bow-legged across the room. "Stay where you're at and I'll fetch us a little something from the frig." Jordan stocked the refrigerator in his bar with synth-blood, anticipating an evening of fun and frolicking after the melee. He didn't particularly care for synth-blood, but like the coven's new direction, it was something he would just have to get used to.

"Here ya go, babe. Chilled and...ah, red. I guess." He tossed a bag to the prone Susannah. "Do you really like this stuff?" Jordan slapped a bag to his fangs and sucked.

"Actually, I have come to really like it. I equate it to drinking beer. I never really met anyone who liked the taste of beer at first. In high school we all drank it because of the alcohol and peer pressure. After a while you acquire a taste for it, and you begin to like it." Susannah lisped the words around her fangs buried in the little plastic tubes. A tiny red dribble slid down her chin. "Oopth!" She giggled again and wiped the trickle away with a finger. She used that same to give Jordan the come hither signal.

"No way. I won't have any furniture left, let alone something to regenerate, if I get within arms reach of you." Jordan made a face at the stuff he was drinking then continued to suck the bag dry. "I didn't realize how hungry I was until you mentioned it. The stuff isn't half bad, it just doesn't have the same kick as real blood. Like drinking light beer when you're used to Guinness."

"The team and your people are probably wondering where we are. Guess it's time to face the music and see what my dear old Dad, and your new coven leadership has decided." Susannah sighed.

"What's wrong? I thought you were all happy and excited about all this." Jordan sat on the floor next to Susannah, curious about her sigh and her thoughts.

"Well, for starters, have you considered what will happen to us? I love you, Jordan, and I want to be with you. If you go to work for Proctor and stay here to help out Marisella and Sir Ignacias, I'll have to give up my work and my coven in Maine. If you come to Maine and join my coven, you'll have to give up your family and a career with incredible potential. I love what I do. I'm just getting good at it." Susannah hung her chin on his shoulder. "Dad developed the Vamp Squad just because of me. I'd feel really guilty, like for life, if I left now. And your coven needs you with your level head right now, not to mention supporting Marisella at Proctor Pharmaceuticals." It seemed to be a no-win situation with no way out in Susannah's mind.

Jordan tapped her nose tenderly. "We'll figure it out. I think your Dad actually likes me. Well, anyway he didn't try to hit me or shoot me when I introduced myself. I think he was sort of stunned about the fangs and stuff, but he didn't say a word." Jordan smiled wide, his white fangs gleaming. "And I think I have a man crush on Yuri. We had a blast in the swamp."

"Jordan! Dad is used to the kind of guys I always hung around with. They were okay for high school parties, but not exactly serious material. I used to like terrorizing him with the idea I would run away and get pregnant with one of the tattooed football players, or a pot smoking Rasti with dreadlocks. It was the teenage terrorist in me." She kissed his cheek. "You, my love are educated, shook his hand and spoke in real English he could understand. He was probably shocked beyond reason."

Another loud kiss punctuated her last statement.

"Right! Let's see… should I let my daughter date a football player, a Rastafarian or a vampire? Gee, hard choice. I think I'll go with the blood-sucking vampire. Not funny." Jordan shook his head.

"But you are forgetting, I'm a vampire too. It would make clear sense to me, if I were a parent with a vampire daughter. At least he would know who I was sleeping with at night, or during the day I mean. And no chance of pregnancy." She finished her bag and got up, pulling Jordan after her. "Come on, let's get showered and worry about what my father thinks later. I'm curious what the old folks are arranging, aren't you?"

"Ah, Susannah, that may not be such a good…" Jordan trotted after the perfectly round ass disappearing around the bathroom divider.

"OH MY GOD! Look at that shower! Holy shit. Where in the world did you get that shower surround? Monique would die for something like this!" Susannah was fingering the etchings with interest. "She would never get out of the shower if she had this in her bath."

"…a good idea." Jordan watched Susannah's reaction with renewed interest. His previous inflammation had disappeared to be replaced with one of a different nature. "Why's that?" He drawled in a deep sexy voice as he joined her in the shower enclosure.

Susannah's fingers trailed across the artistic relief. "Oooooh baby, you have a treat in store for you. My sister is a complete sexual being from the word go. French roots, wanton fangs and a wiggle that sends men into orbit." Susannah turned to wrap her arms around Jordan's neck with a coquettish grin. "You think I have an uncontrollable appetite for encounters of the juicy kind, just wait till you get to know Monique!"

Jordan turned the shower on and lifted his love into his arms, settling her against his growing sex. "I'm not sure I could handle much more than you, my sweet love." His lips traced a trickle of water as it ran down her neck and shoulder. She smelled of love and vanilla.

Susannah wrapped her legs around Jordan's waist and pulled him into her. "Is it breakable?" She rasped as her body immediately ignited.

"The surround? God, I hope not." Jordan's mouth closed over Susannah's swollen, luscious lips.

*****

293

Marisella and Trenchertt sat at the table in the Proctor estate conference room. In front of the large flat-screen television, they spoke quietly with the Proctor Pharmaceutical's Board of Directors via tele-conference. Wearing only the top half of a black business suit perfectly concealing her lace negligee, Marisella affected the appropriate attitude of a somber woman in mourning after the loss of a family member and boss. Only visible from the waist up, she appeared to the Board as a serious professional, conducting sad business during a very difficult time. Amazingly enough, a petite woman in an emerald green suit sat serenely next to Marisella. Almaund sat at her side taking careful notes. With flaming hair piled neatly in a conservative bun, she spoke with a thick Gaelic accent.

"I'll surely be keepin' me eyes on the comins' and goins' eer. Me clan's a might touchy about that sort, deren't ya know. Cousin Mari, here, will be me eyes and ears." With that said, the fiery haired woman was quiet for the rest of the conversation, tiny hands clasped delicately on the polished oak conference table.

"Yes, Eric. Metolius has known for over a year that he didn't have a lot of time left. That is why we have been working toward this seamless transition. The Legal Department has provided a copy of his Last Will and Testament for the Board, as well as his wishes for his family here at the estate. I would have come to Miami, except the family has need of me here, for the next couple days." Marisella paused and looked down for a few seconds, composing herself in the wake of such sadness. "As was his wish, Metolius' body will be cremated and the ashes scattered in the swamp near the estate. The service will be very quiet, with family only, as were the last few years of his life. I know you all understand how sensitive Metolius was," Marisella looked down again, seeming to fight for control of her grief, "…was to publicity and the media. His family is just as covetous of their privacy and keeping their personal grief to themselves." She sniffled softly.

"Of course, Marisella. Please accept the Board's condolences and let the family know they are in our prayers." Eric Mendolla's tone sounded authentic despite the fact that he hated Marisella and most of the Proctor 'family.' He'd tried to sabotage Kellan at every turn and had more than once, attempted to stage a hostile take-over.

"Ms. Ferreira, please let young Mr. Burke know I will expect to see him assume his internship when he is ready to face company business. I suspect, after the tragic death of his father, Proctor's passing was a terrible blow to the boy." Martin Sanderson just could not pass up the opportunity to rub Mendolla's nose in company politics, even in the wake of the company's sad news. "It is more important now than ever to continue grooming our youth for the important job of running this business correctly, the older we get. Let this be a lesson to all of us," Sanderson pointed at each of the Board members one at a time, "no one lives forever."

Marisella smiled at the camera through what seemed to be the beginning of huge tears, human tears at that. Jordan's internship had been in the works for several weeks and Martin was a staunch supporter of Marisella.   It was part of the master plan she and Trenchertt worked hard to design and put into action. Jordan would be a huge asset and staunch ally.

Colonel Maddox and Elizabetta stood a few feet away, just off camera. Visibly, they tried to contain their enjoyment of the scene. No one lives forever, huh? Little did the Board truly know.

"Thank you Martin. I will be sure to pass the word on to Jordan. I am sure he will make a very good officer some day. Metolius would have heartily approved. Gentlemen and lady, if that is all, I will get back to assisting with the family arrangements. Billings in PR has a statement to issue to the media after Metolius' remains have been scattered. I am sure, you will all do your best to keep the sad news from the media in respect for the family's wishes." She looked directly at Eric Mendolla then Faith Morrison, the two worst schemers on the Board.

"You will have our utmost cooperation in this time of grief." Faith spoke sympathetically, but did not raise her eyes to look at the camera. Marisella thought she detected a slight smirk on the woman's lips. How careless of Faith to have let her expression slip. She was usually much more devious than that.

"Thank you all for your consideration and prayers. I should be in the office after Monday. I'll let you know if something changes between now and then."   Marisella smiled and reached to flip her camera off. The Board could no longer see her, but she could see and hear everything that continued on in the room in Miami.   She motioned to Maddox, Elizabetta and Trenchertt to watch the screen.

"Now we will see the wolves circle. Watch closely. I'll bet… yep! Eric and Faith can't wait to begin plotting. Look. They are already putting their heads together and have no idea I am watching. Guess I shall go to the office this weekend, Almaund. A preemptive strike is better than getting caught with your panties down."

"I shall arrange it, Madame." Almaund quietly rose and left with his notes.

"Augh, my dear, must you be so graphic?" Trenchertt closed his eyes and made the sign of a cross.

Maddox laughed. "Having known this woman for something less than twenty-four hours, I would venture to bet that graphic, is the least of what she can be. My hat is off to you, Madame. You are a strategist extraordinaire."

"You are so right to distrust this blonde human called Faith. She brings evil to this company. I can feel it here." Fiona touched her heart then her head, her Gaelic accent muted when off camera. The faerie vampire reached to Marisella with a clenched fist, knuckles first. "Mari, it is the newest way to say farewell. This very big man with an animal name showed me. See?" She curled Marisella's fingers down then touched their knuckles together.

"I think I like it." Then Fiona was gone in a blitz of twinkling faerie dust that slowly drifted to the floor.

"She's got that right!" Jordan chimed in from the doorway, dragging a fresh and smiling Susannah behind him. "Faith is a conspirator, and just plain nasty. Ah, but Marisella is the mastermind behind everything, the company, my freedom and – ow!" Susannah aimed a punch toward Jordan's belly, "despite the fact that I was never in any real danger. The Vamp Squad was on the way to save the day. Led by my own beautiful savior, of course." He planted a quick kiss on top of Susannah's head.

"Good try, but no cigar, buddy." Susannah mumbled as she took a chair at the conference table next to Ignacias. "And how does the world find my favorite knight on this lovely evening?"

Trenchertt planted a chaste kiss on the back of Susannah's hand. "Surrounded by beautiful women and light of heart, Mistress Susannah. Thanks beeth to God and yon father, here. On my mind layeth but one dark spot bearing the name of Salvatore. He seems destined to face certain changes somewhat less amicably than the others. Fact be told, he is nowhere to be found."

Jordan stood behind Susannah, his hands gently placed on her shoulders, his protective stance apparent to all. "Sal will come around. He has no choice." Jordan was confident.

Where would Sal go?

What coven would accept him after word gets out about Metolius' destruction?

Maddox took the chair across from his daughter. "That only leaves one more question now, doesn't it?" He watched his daughter closely. All eyes turned to Susannah as she placed her hands over Jordan's.

"I guess so." The words were soft and laced with a kind of desperate resignation.

Jordan slid his hands from beneath hers and took the chair next to her. He sat down quietly and folded his hands on the table. The silence stretched for what seemed like an eternity, then both Susannah and Jordan spoke at once.

Okay, I'll be the one to…" The young couple looked at each other in surprise. The rest of the adults in the room, human and vampire alike, broke out in laughter. The young vampires had obviously given great thought to which should sacrifice for the other.

"No, Jordan. I caused you more trouble than you ever deserved. I should be the one to make it right." Susannah spoke from her heart. "I love you. I don't want to be without you, even though you're not my bonded mate. After all, that's what started this whole thing and what I came here to find in the beginning. What I actually found was a truth I never even considered. Love is what is important, not some genetic fluke that makes us an incredibly compatible mated pair. It's what's in the heart, not the blood, Jordan. I know that now. Just as I know I love you more than anything in the world."

"I have no idea what a mated pair is but, what I do know, is we mated…as a pair, and it worked amazingly well." Jordan took her hand and raised it to his lips. "Sir, I would like to have your permission to court your daughter. If it's okay with you, of course. My intentions are strictly…" He was at a loss for words. He'd never officially asked a girl's dad for anything before. Especially a girl who everyone, including her father, knew he had already been 'familiar' with.

On several occasions.

Elizabetta let out the most precious sigh and Maddox grinned at the young vampire. "Male? Let's just leave it at strictly 'male intentions', young man. I'm not sure I can handle much else. Susannah?"

Susannah was completely taken by surprise! Her father was leaving the decision up to her? When did the Colonel lose his mind?

"Ah… I don't know, Daddy. We were talking about that earlier. Jordan belongs here with his coven. He needs to begin a career and help rebuild this place. I've got, or I mean, you've got so much invested in me, and my training. It seems a shame to leave Olney Farm and the squad. I mean, I really like what I do, when I'm not screwing up, ya know." She looked pleadingly at her father. It was the first time she really had to make a life decision… and she couldn't.

Colonel Maddox bit his tongue so hard he could taste blood but refrained from speaking. It was time his little girl faced the world as an independent adult and took the hard decisions by the horns. His heart was crumbling, but he remained silent, watching the turmoil on his daughter's face.

"Susannah, may I make a suggestion?" Elizabetta gently interjected.

Thank God someone had come to her rescue! "Of course. You're like a mother to me. Right now I could use some help." Susannah took a deep breath.

"Perhaps you and your Jordan can have both. He can remain here to do that which he needs to, as you so eloquently stated. You can return to Olney Farm. Like high school lovers going off to college, visiting each other often, testing your love with a little separation. There are only four hours between the two of you, by plane. This trial separation will be a good motivator to learn to fly or v-port, Susannah."

Elizabetta looked directly at the young man who held Susannah's hand so tightly, his knuckles turned white. "Jordan, with a little practice can most assuredly v-port your way to the farm. There are so many things you and Susannah have yet to learn. You both have time, a lot of time. Do not be in such a rush to be together that you both make sacrifices you may regret later."

She turned back to Susannah, "As for the Vamp Squad, you are an accomplished operative. It would be a shame to lose you. That is correct, isn't it, Colonel?"

Not trusting his own voice, Colonel Maddox nodded in the affirmative. His heart was in his throat.

"Wow! When you act like a mother, you really act like a mother! I don't want to be apart from Jordan. I love him so much."

Jordan didn't relish being separated either, but was beginning to accept the sense of Elizabetta's logic. "Susannah, she has a point. I don't want us to be apart, but Elizabetta is right. If our love isn't strong enough to face a little separation, then maybe it isn't strong enough to last, like what? A couple thousand years? We can do this. And just think of all those little vacations together in between. You know what they say? Absence makes the heart grow fonder." Jordan pulled Susannah closer and held her tightly pressing his lips to her temple in a tender, but chaste kiss. It was appropriate, considering their location and the people watching them closely.

"I guess we do have time, baby. I should learn that v-port thing. I can't be the only grounded vampire in the family. But we're gonna have to stock up on furniture." She kissed Jordan firmly on the lips with renewed enthusiasm. "We can make this work, Jordan. I know we can. In the mean time you can learn all about the company and make lots of money and learn to talk like Sir Ignacias. Did I ever mention that I find all that archaic stuff sexy?"

Father Sir Ignacias Trenchertt cleared his throat uncomfortably and rose to take his leave, about the same time Colonel Maddox stood. "You have an incredibly unique daughter, Sir."

The two men reached the door at the same time, Maddox murmured, "It's not my fault. You should have known her mother." He smiled and pushed through the doorway ahead of Trenchertt.

"I cannot imagine." Trenchertt coughed and followed the Colonel in his successful escape.

"I do believe you have embarrassed your father, however I think he is very proud, young lady." Elizabetta smiled in a motherly fashion, obviously proud as well.

Still sitting next to Jordan, Susannah was amazed, and it showed. "That is the first time he has ever *not* told me what to do. I can't believe it. I'm just... I don't even have a word for it."

Marisella rose gracefully. "If you will excuse me, I have a great deal of work to do if I am to ward off any subversive attempts on the company. Faith and Eric are already planning something. Jordan, Martin Sanderson has offered, much to Eric's dismay, an internship in the Vice President's Office. It is an opportunity you should consider carefully." She switched off the monitor showing the empty boardroom and motioned to Elizabetta. "May I interest you in some form of refreshment, Mistress?"

When Marisella and Elizabetta were safely down the hallway, Jordan pulled Susannah to his lap and crushed his lips to hers. His kiss ignited a sensual heat that left her gasping for air. "Your father is not the only one who is proud of you, my love." He traced kisses down her throat and across a shoulder, pulling at the fabric of her satiny blouse with his teeth. It slid nicely down across her arm displaying a sweet little strap of delicate black lace.

"Jordan, quit!" She pulled the fabric back up onto her shoulder. "We should figure out how this is all going to work. You here. Me there? We need to..." Jordan kicked the chair away behind him, lifted her onto the conference table and pulled her legs around him as he bent and slowly bit each button off the front of her blouse, one by one.

"Jordan, pay attention here." Susannah lifted his head with both her hands. "No really, Jordan…"

His eyes burned deep red with lust.

She just couldn't help it as her legs, with a mind of their own, tightened drawing him closer. Susannah patted the table testing its strength, unsure if it would hold.

"No… really, Jordan…

Jordan?

Jordan!"

Susannah's mind spun out of control as she pulled his mouth to hers.

*****

On a deserted landing strip deep in the swamp, Salvatore Pena-Sollare boarded a private jet. It was sent especially to fetch him and his precious cargo.

He smiled.

Faith Morrison waited inside, her luscious lips and smooth tanned neck ready and available. Tucked tightly beneath Sal's arm was a small box of twenty-four perfect glass vials. Each vial held four ounces of a dark purple liquid that could send a vampire to heaven…then to hell.

Connect with Miriam Matthews

Each of the first five books in this series are about the Squad's vampires and how they came to be part of Colonel Maddox's group of top-secret anti-terrorist operatives. Each book is also a romance! Book 1 has been out since 2015 and is all about Natalia and the first VS mission. Book 3 is in development. It is Monique's story of facing her fears of San Leyre and learning love is more than a great set of pecks wrapped in a thousand dollar suit. Elizabetta finally begins to trust a human man in Book 4 and the sparks fly! In Book 5, Morningstar leaves the Vamp Squad to return to her tribe in Kansas, only to find home is not always what she thought it was.

The Vamp Squad Series
Book 1: Strange Beginnings
Book 2: The Death of Innocence
Book 3: The Secrets of San Leyre
Book 4: The Roots of Betrayal
Book 5: A Dark Deception

You can always catch up with Miriam, or send your comments to:
miriamthewriter@gmail.com.

See what's new in Miriam's life on her website at:
www.miriammatthews.com

You can also follow Miriam on Facebook and keep up with her news, new books and trivia questions at:
www.facebook.com/miriam.matthews.773

Other Books by Miriam Matthews

The Good, the Bad and the Bet
The Most Probable, Practically Real, True Story of DB Cooper

Ex-Navy SEAL, and decorated hero, Dan drifted through life until he found an anchor named Della and a reason to live. He loved her from the moment they met but two things stood in the way of happily ever after - a dangerous bet and a drug lord willing to win at any cost.

Della was never prepared for the hand life dealt her. A young widow with a daughter to raise, her world spun completely out of control when Dan Cooper gambled his way into her heart.

Days before he became the infamous DB Cooper, Della became his wife. Would their love survive? Would they survive?

The Ghost of Port Chicago

It all ended on a hot July evening in 1944, but that was just the beginning for one sailor and the woman he loved...

Amee McGee's life was just beginning. The vivacious little blonde had her first job, a secret love and the world at her eighteen-year old fingertips. Now if those pesky Nazis would just quit causing trouble, her world would be perfect!

Seaman Grady O'Sullivan had eyes only for his Amee. He never had the chance to tell her how much he loved her before the gigantic explosion at Port Chicago took her life. Now she haunts his shattered existence... and the present day military base, MOTCO.

A man can't suffer forever and time is running out for Grady and Amee both. Will the new Provost Marshal be the one to hear Amee's pleas, or will she be doomed to spend eternity as THE GHOST OF PORT CHICAGO?

Strange Beginnings
Vamp Squad Series, Book 1

Natalia protected the Russian royal family for nearly a century, even before she became a vampire. Now she must join the new American Vamp Squad to rescue her Russian Captain, the last remaining Romanov male. As they get closer to where Yuri is held, strange new powers surface to complicate Natalia's plans.

Betrayed by those he trusted, Captain Milassoviech now lies in a Taliban cave awaiting certain death. In his fevered dreams, a beautiful Dark Angel searches for him. Is she Life, or Death, or something worse?

Join Miriam Matthews and her group of amazing, sexy vampires as they take on the Taliban, Al Qaeda and ISIS in this first book in the Vamp Squad Series; Strange Beginnings.

Coming Soon!   Coming Soon!   Coming Soon!   Coming Soon!

The Secrets of San Leyre
Vamp Squad Series, Book 3

Having been rescued from the Monastery of San Leyre and the torturous hands of the Monks there, it is the last place to which Monique wishes to return. Unfortunately, the State Department has asked the Vamp Squad to investigate an outbreak of drug related deaths at the Diplomatic School on the grounds of the Monastery.

On loan to the Vamp Squad, Percy Seizmore, a pharmacologist with the CDC, has no idea he will be working with the sensual Monique to research a mysterious drug. Nor does he know she is a vampire! When their work identifies the drug as a derivative of Crysillus Extract, no one is surprised to find Salvatore Pena-Sollare and Faith Morrison involved!

Join Miriam Matthews and her group of amazing, sexy vampires as they investigate a mysterious new drug war, face old foes and triumph over an evil power in the Vamp Squad Series; The Secrets of San Lyre.

2

www.ingramcontent.com/pod-product-compliance
Lightning Source LLC
Chambersburg PA
CBHW071257170626
46809CB00001B/246